# BLACK TIDE RISING

## THE BLACK TIDE RISING SERIES by JOHN RINGO

*Under a Graveyard Sky* • *To Sail a Darkling Sea*
*Islands of Rage and Hope* • *Strands of Sorrow*
*The Valley of Shadows* (with Mike Massa)
*Black Tide Rising* (edited with Gary Poole)
*Voices of the Fall* (edited with Gary Poole)
*River of Night* (with Mike Massa)
*At the End of the World* (by Charles E. Gannon)
*At the End of the Journey* (by Charles E. Gannon)
*We Shall Rise* (edited with Gary Poole)
*United We Stand* (edited with Gary Poole)
*Mountain of Fire* (by Jason Cordova) - forthcoming

## MORE BAEN BOOKS by JOHN RINGO

**TRANSDIMENSIONAL HUNTER** (with Lydia Sherrer)
*Into the Real* • *Through the Storm*

**TROY RISING**
*Live Free or Die* • *Citadel* • *The Hot Gate*

**LEGACY OF THE ALDENATA**
*A Hymn Before Battle* • *Gust Front* • *When the Devil Dances*
*Hell's Faire* • *The Hero* (with Michael Z. Williamson)
*Cally's War* (with Julie Cochrane) • *Watch on the Rhine* (with Tom Kratman)
*Sister Time* (with Julie Cochrane) • *Yellow Eyes* (with Tom Kratman)
*Honor of the Clan* (with Julie Cochrane) • *Eye of the Storm*

**COUNCIL WARS**
*There Will Be Dragons* • *Emerald Sea*
*Against the Tide* • *East of the Sun, West of the Moon*

**INTO THE LOOKING GLASS**
*Into the Looking Glass* • *Vorpal Blade* (with Travis S. Taylor)
*Manxome Foe* (with Travis S. Taylor)
*Claws that Catch* (with Travis S. Taylor)

**EMPIRE OF MAN** (with David Weber)
*March Upcountry* • *March to the Sea* • *March to the Stars* • *We Few*

**SPECIAL CIRCUMSTANCES**
*Princess of Wands* • *Queen of Wands*

**PALADIN OF SHADOWS**
*Ghost* • *Kildar* • *Choosers of the Slain* • *Unto the Breach*
*A Deeper Blue* • *Tiger by the Tail* (with Ryan Sear)

**STANDALONE TITLES**
*The Last Centurion* • *Citizens* (edited with Brian M. Thomsen)

# BLACK TIDE RISING

EDITED BY

JOHN RINGO & GARY POOLE

Black Tide Rising

This is a work of fiction. All the characters and events portrayed in this book are fictional, and any resemblance to real people or incidents is purely coincidental.



A Baen Books Original

Baen Publishing Enterprises
P.O. Box 1403
Riverdale, NY 10471
www.baen.com

ISBN: 978-1-9821-9340-9

Cover art by Kurt Miller

First printing, June 2016
First mass market, May 2017
First trade paperback printing, May 2024

Distributed by Simon & Schuster
1230 Avenue of the Americas
New York, NY 10020

Library of Congress Control Number: 2016010520

10 9 8 7 6 5 4 3 2 1

Printed in the United States of America

As always
For Captain Tamara Long, USAF
Born: May 12, 1979
Died: March 23, 2003, Afghanistan
You fly with the angels now.

Thanks to Star for believing
in me for two decades.
"A path traveled together
overcomes all obstacles."

# CONTENTS

# Foreword

## GARY POOLE

When I was first approached about coediting this anthology, after working with John through the first four books of the series, my initial thought was, "Well, this could be fun." Then again, some people consider running with the bulls in Pamplona fun, so there's no accounting for taste.

It's been said assembling an anthology is akin to herding cats, except not as easy. And as it turned out, it was indeed quite fun, all cat-herding aside.

I was able to not only work with a number of writers whose work I have long admired (and luckily can count many of them as friends), but I was also able to work with a fresh group of writers who are in the early, bright stages of their careers. To use a baseball analogy, I felt like the manager of a team made up of experienced all-stars and a crop of talented rookies, all ready to go win the World Series.

What was really an eye-opener to me was seeing the many different ways that writers can look at the same situations and come up with very different takes on the prevailing theme of the Black Tide universe. Which, basically, is "Okay, the zombie apocalypse has happened, most of the population is either dead or infected, civilization has fallen, the survivors are horribly outnumbered... so now what?"

The "what happens next" theme is what I find, both as an editor and a reader, the most interesting. Can civilization be rebuilt? And if so, what kind of civilization will it be, and could it even possibly be a better one? Or could it be even worse?

Post-apocalyptic themes are all the rage these days. There is something about the destruction of civilization that connects with the modern reader. But, at least to me, far too many of these stories are all about the fall and not about the rebirth.

Human beings are the most resilient species on the planet. You can wipe out ninety percent (or more) of the population, and the survivors will regroup, rebuild and emerge stronger than before. It has happened many times in history and look around... we're still here and better than ever.

At least on most days, that is.

So when John originally proposed the idea for the series, a "what happens after the apocalypse" concept, I was hooked. I was intrigued to read about what people, in many cases just regular people, would do to keep humanity not only alive, but figure out how to make the race prosper once again. If you, like me, greatly enjoyed what John created in the novels, I'll hope you'll be just as entertained with what John and the rest of the writers have come up with in these shorter works. These aren't superheroes and superhumans; these are regular people making the best (or the worst, in some cases) of the situation.

That said, as interesting as I find the Black Tide world, would I like to live in such a place? Of course not. Take away my smartphone, tablet and my broadband Internet connection and I am not a happy camper. But I do believe in humanity as a whole, and am certain that even if I and my neighbors would perish in such a world, the race itself would continue.

And maybe, just maybe, if the apocalypse does indeed come to pass in reality, these books might help to keep a few more people alive and headed on the right path.

One can always hope.

Just make sure you have plenty of ammunition and a good melee weapon.

# Never Been Kissed

## JOHN RINGO

"Skipper, got a question," Hocieniec said as they were stripping down their M4s for cleaning.

The Harper's Ferry-class Landing Ship Dock *Oak Hill* was returning to Mayport from successfully clearing the CVN-72 *Abraham Lincoln,* which had been spotted aground off the coast of Guyana. It had been a hairy bitch finding the two hundred survivors in the bowels of the listed Nimitz-class supercarrier. They were due for some downtime but First Lieutenant Faith Marie Smith had already gotten the word there was a priority clearance in Baltimore. And since they didn't have Trixie along that meant another fucking air assault like LRI. Joy. At least they'd already Subedeyed Baltimore so the infected levels should be down.

She was about to go off on Colonel Ramos. Her guys needed some shore leave and she wasn't going to have one of them go off the reservation like she had from battle fatigue.

"Go," Faith said, flicking out her bolt and giving it a dubious eyeball. She'd found that bolts only tended to last her a few months at the rate she put rounds downrange.

"Back at Parris," Hooch said. "Before, you know, the incident."

"Yep," Faith said. She was past that, in her opinion.

"I get naming the gator who nearly ate you," Hocieniec said. "I even sort of get letting it live."

"All it was doing was following the natural order," Faith said, shrugging as she set the bolt aside. "No reason to kill it. And gators keep the infected population in check."

"Why 'Reginald'?" Hocieniec asked. "I hate to ask but . . . boyfriend?"

"Not hardly," Faith said with a snort, starting to swab the M4's barrel with a rod and cloth.

"I know it's not . . . good to talk about old times," Hocieniec said, shrugging. "If you don't want to . . ."

"He was a bully," Faith said after a pause. "When I was in fourth grade, Reginald Abrams was in fifth. He was always sort of odd. Didn't really fit in real well. Was already starting to go through puberty and had some . . . issues with it. It's pretty weird for a kid in fifth grade to be growing a beard and he was always trying to kiss girls and do . . . inappropriate things with them. Cop a feel, things like that. Kids were scared of him in general, not just girls. When I was in fourth grade we were out at recess and he was bullying some of the first graders. Hit one kid and pushed him to the ground. Calling him names. I just got tired of it and walked over and kicked him in the fork."

"Ouch," Januscheitis said with a chuckle.

"He started to get up and got another kick for his troubles," Faith said, shrugging again. "He eventually decided to stay down. I was always sort of the more violent of the Smith Sisters."

"Really?" Hocieniec said, raising one eyebrow. "That comes as a complete surprise, ma'am."

"Sarcasm is the last refuge of the incompetent, Hooch," Faith said, dimpling. "Yeah. Call it a short fuse for injustice. Anyway, he really took to me after that. Kept following me around with puppy dog eyes and trying to kiss me. Which I didn't take to; he ended up pretty bruised. Nor did other girls. Not a popular guy. When we went to middle school he was at a different school, which was fine by me."

"School bully," Hocieniec said, nodding. "Curiosity satisfied. Thank you, ma'am."

"I sort of wish I had kissed him," Faith said. Cleaning complete, she was reassembling the M4 swiftly and unconsciously, her eyes distant.

"Ma'am?" Januscheitis said, frowning. "Why? Sounds like a clear case for future sexual predator."

"Oh, agree there," Faith said. "But . . . Girls were scared of him, like I said. He was just creepy. Even wherever he turned up, I'm pretty sure it was the same. And now?"

She gestured out with her chin outwards towards the distant shore.

"He's either dead or infected," she said, shrugging again. "Ninety-nine nines on that. And as a young adolescent infected, probably dead. Those first graders I protected? Dead. Even if they turned, what's the survival rate on infected kids? Fucking near zero. See many my age or younger left around, *period*?"

She finished assembling the weapon and cycled the bolt several times, eyes still distant in memory, in distance, in time.

"There's nobody I grew up with who's probably alive," she said. "All the kids I went to school with are scattered bones. Friends, enemies, bullies, and victims, it's all one with the snows.

"I just hate to think of all the kids in the world who died. Even Reginald.

*"And they'd never been kissed."*

# Up on the Roof

## ERIC FLINT

On the roof, it's peaceful as can be
And there, the world below can't bother me.

—The Drifters (lyrics by Gerry
Goffin and Carole King)

### 1

"Well, that plan just went up in smoke. We waited too long to leave. Now what do we do?" Andrea Kaminski ran fingers through her hair. At the age of sixty-eight, her hair was gray now and a lot shorter, but it was still as thick as it had been when she was a youngster.

Nobody in the living room said anything. As was true of Andy herself, they were all staring at the images on the big plasma TV screen.

Staring at the images—and listening to the sounds.

"You can easily hear the gunfire," said the TV announcer, a middle-aged man by the name of Bob Lubrano. He turned to the younger woman sitting next to him at the long announcers' desk, who was looking at something out of the view of the audience. "Can you see anything, Karen?"

Karen Wakefield shook her head, still not taking her eyes from whatever she was looking at. Another TV monitor, presumably. "Other than the traffic jam on I-80 which we're showing our audience, nothing. I'm not sure where that gunfire is coming from."

Andy thought calling the scene being shown on the screen a "traffic jam" was like referring to Lake Michigan as a "body of water." Every single lane on I-80—westbound or eastbound, it didn't matter—was a solid mass of cars and trucks, not a single one of which was moving at all. There were a few vehicles trying to make their way along the shoulders, but not even many of those—and none of them were moving any faster than a man could walk. On crutches.

The female announcer turned her head back to face the audience. "The scene is pretty much the same no matter which interstate you look at. Here's some footage that just came in from I-55 near Willow Springs."

The image on the screen changed in detail; but, generically, it was identical. None of the vehicles on the interstate that connected Chicago and St. Louis were moving any faster than the ones on I-80.

"And here's what I-90 looks like a little past O'Hare airport." Her face twisted into a grimace. "Or what used to be O'Hare airport, before the plane crashes."

One of the men in Andy Kaminski's living room finally provided an answer to her question. That was Federico Rodriguez, who went by the nickname of Freddy.

"Maybe we could hole up in the Carson Pirie Scott building at Woodmar Mall," he suggested. "The place is built like a fortress. There's no windows at all and only two entrances. Yeah, sure, they're pretty big—three or four glass doors, if I remember right." He waved a big hand toward the street outside. "But I've got welding equipment in my truck. We could probably seal the entrances."

His father Luis perked up a little. "We don't have to seal it well enough to keep real people out. Just... those things..." He pointed at the screen, which was now showing a scene from the intersection of Michigan Avenue and Congress Parkway in the Loop, Chicago's downtown area.

The image, like all the previous ones, was being transmitted from a helicopter. No reporters on the ground could have survived more than a minute or two. The whole area was overrun by hundreds—it might easily be thousands—of naked figures.

"Zombies," Luis concluded. "Whatever you want to call them."

Freddy's proposal was tempting. Andy had shopped in that Carson's building plenty of times and knew it quite well. It *was* built like a fortress, leaving aside the big entrances on the north and south sides of the store. And since they'd torn down the rest of the mall, the building stood by itself. But...

She shook her head. "Guys, we already chewed this over. We can't take the risk of being inside a building. Whatever this virus is, it's virulent as all hell. We need to stay outdoors and as far away from other people as we can."

Luis' neighbor Pedro Vargas spoke up. "Yeah, fine. That's why we were planning to drive down to Shawnee National Forest. But like you said—that plan went up in smoke. Wherever we're going to go, it's got to be within a few miles of here. We'll never get any farther than that."

His Puerto Rican accent was thicker than that of Luis Rodriguez, but his English was fluent. So was Flora Rodriguez's, when she chimed in.

"There's no open area worth talking about anywhere in northern Lake County," she said, standing in the doorway to the kitchen. "Not that I know of, anyway."

For the first time since they started watching the TV news, Andy's husband spoke up.

"Yeah, there is." Tom's heavy face twisted into a smile of sorts. "In a manner of speaking. You should head for one of the tank farms."

Flora frowned at him. "Tank—what? Farms? What are you talking about?"

Unlike Tom, neither of the Rodriguez men nor Pedro had ever worked in an oil refinery or chemical plant. But because of the jobs they'd held, they were all familiar with the facilities. Northwest Indiana was one of the nation's major industrial centers, concentrated especially in steel making and all types of chemical production.

"He's talking about those big storage tanks," said Lujis. "You know—those white cylinders you see all over the place. There's a huge tank farm not far from here, part of the BP refinery in Whiting."

"God, no!" said Tom forcefully. "The last place you want to be in a catastrophe is right next to an oil refinery." He leaned forward in his wheelchair and pointed at the TV screen.

"That's what our grandson Jack calls a zombie apocalypse. Give it a few days—hell, give it a few hours, for all I know—and that big refinery less than two miles from here is going to become a catastrophe of its own. I doubt if anybody's still in control over there and I'm sure and certain they didn't have time to shut down the refinery properly. Sooner or later, something's going to blow."

He swiveled his armchair and rolled to the side window, looking to the southeast. "Go for the tank farm down by Cline Avenue. It's even bigger—must be a mile long, half a mile wide—and it's not close to anything dangerous. Get on top of one of the tanks in the middle of the farm. You won't be visible from the roads and you'll have a clear line of fire for at least forty or fifty yards in any direction, and hundreds of yards if no other tank's in the way. For all practical purposes you'll be on top of a steel castle with sheer walls that no naked mindless zombie can climb. The only access to the roof is a narrow winding staircase. That's easily defensible anyway, but if it was me I'd cut off the bottom ten or fifteen feet of the staircase with a cutting torch and substitute ladders for that stretch that you can haul up when you're not using them."

He wheeled back around to face the room. "Make sure you pick a tank with a fixed roof, though. Some of 'em got floating roofs. You can stand on those, more or less, but there'll be vapor leakage."

As he'd talked, Andy's apprehension had steadily grown. "What's with this *you-you-you* bullshit, Tom?" she demanded. "You're coming with us."

Her husband shook his head. "Get serious, woman." He gestured with his hands toward what was left of his legs. "I didn't think I could make it even in the woods, although I was willing to try. How the hell do you think I'm going to get up on top of an oil storage tank? They're more than fifty feet high. My legs are useless and I weigh close to three hundred pounds. Just go, will you? Face it—I'm done."

Andy knew there was more at work here than stoic practicality on her husband's part. Thomas Kaminski had been an outdoorsman and hunter his whole life, until an industrial accident had taken both his legs off at the knees a decade earlier. He still maintained his shooting skills at a firing range and went fishing from time to time, but those activities were a pale shadow of what he'd been accustomed to. He'd been in a state of depression ever since—which now seemed to have become suicidal. There was no way he could survive on his own in the crisis that had engulfed the whole world, and he knew it as well as she did.

"I said, cut the bullshit!" she snapped at him. "We'll figure out something."

"Won't even be that hard," said Freddy Rodriguez. "You still got plenty of strength in your upper body, Tom—I've seen you lift weights so don't bother arguing about it—and those spiral staircases have solid handrails. I weigh about two hundred and fifty and I'm pretty damn strong, if I say so myself. Between you working your way up on the rail and me hoisting your fat butt, we'll get you there."

Pedro Vargas weighed in then—and did it just the right way. "You *got* to come with us, Tom. We need you. You're the only one of us was a hunter and really knows how to use a rifle. Me and Luis—Freddy, too—we all got guns, sure. But they're pistols and shotguns." He nodded his head toward the far wall. "I don't think Jerry's got a rifle, either. He's never gone hunting that I know of."

Jerry Haywood and his wife Latoya were neighbors who were also planning to come on what they'd all intended to be an expedition into the forested hills in southern Illinois. Jerry was a security guard for one of the nearby casinos and Latoya worked in a factory that manufactured cardboard containers. They were both around Freddy's age—forty or so—and had two teenage children, a boy and a girl.

As if on cue, the doorbell rang. When Andy's grandson Jack went to open the door, she could see the Haywood couple standing on the porch beyond, along with their daughter Jayden. All of them looked worried.

"Come on in," she said.

Jerry started talking before he even got through the door. "You see the news? There's no way we're going to get down to Shawnee."

Behind him, his wife said, "Hell, we ain't got no chance of getting out of Lake County, much less the whole state of Indiana."

"Yeah, we saw," said Freddy. He gestured toward Andy's husband. "Tom thinks we oughta set up on top of one of the oil storage tanks."

Jerry stopped abruptly, frowning. "That's . . . maybe not a bad idea."

Latoya was frowning too. "But can we all fit? There's what? Fifteen of us, right?"

"Probably be more than that," said her husband. "Assuming our son comes back with his girlfriend and her father. Which I figure he will if Ceyonne's dad don't decide to just shoot him instead."

Andy chuckled. Ceyonne Bennett's father Jerome was a cop for the city of East Chicago, and while he was generally an even-tempered man he had the same attitude on the subject of *daughter's boyfriend* that most fathers of seventeen-year-old girls did.

Luis looked at Tom. "So what's the answer? Can we all fit up there?"

"For Chrissake, there must be at least twenty tanks in that farm," Tom said. "Even the smaller ones are eighty feet in diameter—and I think most of them are a hundred and ten feet across. Figure out the math."

Freddy's business as a mechanical and electrical contractor made him at ease with basic mathematics. It didn't take him more than a few seconds to come up with the answer. "He's right. Even an eighty foot diameter tank gives us about five thousand square feet on the roof." He glanced around Andy and Tom's house. "This is what? A third of that?"

"We got fourteen hundred square feet on the main floor and another thousand or so in the basement," said Tom. He'd been a machinist most of his life and he was proficient with numbers himself. "So we'd have twice as much space even on one of the smaller tanks. If we pick one that's a hundred and ten feet across, we're looking at . . ." His eyes got a little unfocused.

Freddy came up with the answer before he did. "Damn near ten thousand square feet."

Latoya was still frowning. "Yeah, fine—but there's no *roof*."

Tom shrugged. "We were planning to live in tents and those two big vinyl tool sheds, weren't we? What's the difference if they're on top of a steel tank instead of dirt and pine needles in a forest?"

"Can't drive tent stakes into steel," Jerry pointed out.

"No, you can't. But we've got lots of tape and every kind of glue you can think of." Tom nodded toward Freddy. "Best thing, though, is just have Freddy weld the stakes to the roof of the tanks."

Luis Rodriguez looked alarmed. "You want to *weld* stuff to a giant tank full of *gasoline*?"

Freddy smiled. "Relax, Dad. I'll be using oxy-acetylene, not arc welding. And all I gotta do is tack weld the stakes. We'll get some strong winds up there in a storm but tornadoes hardly ever come this close to the lake."

He pursed his lips. "Now that I think about it, though . . . Tom, what happens in a thunderstorm? Does lightning ever strike those storage tanks?"

"You better believe it does," said Andy's husband. "Refinery workers stay the hell off of 'em in a thunderstorm. The tanks do have lightning energy distribution systems—basically, pointed steel rods connected to copper alloy cables running down the sides of the tanks into the ground. To be on the safe side, though, I think we'll want to also weld on some sort of lightning rod too—better attach it to the staircase—and figure out some sort of insulation to put all the tents on. Rubber matting, if we can scrounge some up—we've got some in the basement—and whatever else we can think of. And I'd strongly recommend that in a thunderstorm everybody crowds into the two vinyl sheds and stays out of the tents."

Pedro made a face. "They're not that big!" he protested. "Ten by eight feet, that's all." Being an electrician, he was just as handy with arithmetic as any of them. "That's one hundred and sixty square feet—for fifteen or sixteen people."

"Subtract me," said Tom. "No way me and the wheelchair will fit. I'll just have to take my chances in a tent."

His expression was simultaneously lugubrious and self-satisfied. *Imminent likely doom for the cripple, just as I foretold.*

But Andy let it go, for the time being. At least Tom was now agreeing to come with them. Thunderstorms were a problem for another day.

"Still a tight fit," said Pedro.

Jerry Haywood shrugged. His expression no longer seemed worried, just resigned to the inevitable. "Yeah, it'll be tight—sitting room only, and some of us will probably have to stand. But thunderstorms don't come around all that often and they don't last long when they do. It's better than being fried by a lightning bolt coming down a tent pole."

There was a sudden commotion that drew everyone's attention back to the TV screen. They'd been showing images of jammed-up highways from a helicopter, but now the scene was jumping around wildly.

"*Get them off of me! Get 'em—aaaah!*" The camera swung around and they got a glimpse of the pilot. He was writhing in his seat and was apparently trying to tear his clothes off. A hand appeared from the side, holding a pistol. There was a shot to the back of the pilot's head that splattered blood and brains all over the cockpit window.

An amazingly calm voice now spoke—presumably belonging to whoever had fired the shot. "*He turned. I hope one of you knows how to fly this thing.*"

"*You idiot!*" shouted another voice. The image on the TV screen now flittered every which way, for a few seconds, before it went blank.

A moment later, the image of the two announcers returned. Both of them were still sitting behind their desk.

"Apparently we lost the chopper," said Karen Wakefield shakily.

Her partner Bob Lubrano rose abruptly from his chair. It turned out he was wearing blue jeans beneath the suit jacket. "To hell with this," he said. "I'm out of here."

A moment later he was gone. Wakefield stared after him for a short time and then brought her eyes back to the camera. "What about you, Ken?" she asked.

A voice came from somewhere—presumably belonging to whoever was operating the video equipment. "Where else is there to go? I figure we may as well keep working. But it's your call, Karen. If you leave there's no point in me staying."

She took a deep breath and let it out. Then, nodded firmly.

"We'll stay, then. The show must go on and all that." She even managed to smile at the audience.

Andy picked up the remote and turned off the TV. "Let's get moving, people. Tom, we got everything we need? The U-Haul's already loaded and so's Freddy's truck. But we still got some room in the pickups and the van."

Her husband tugged at his beard. "Well . . . we outfitted for camping, not perching on top of a storage tank. So . . . yeah, I can think of some things we could use."

"Where are we going to get them?" asked Luis. "If it's anything from Cabela's or Home Depot or Lowe's, forget it. Those places were already madhouses a week ago when we did our shopping. Today..."

Tom shook his head. He'd come to the same conclusion. "Yeah, I know. The Wal-Mart and all the supermarkets will be impossible too. What we need are places that nobody'll be thinking to stock up from—or loot, by now, probably—so we can get in and out."

"What about cops?" asked Latoya. "Seeing as how—don't lie about it!—you're talking about us looting too."

Tom scowled at her. "Damn it, Latoya, I'd be happy to pay anyone who asks for money. But nobody's going to be tending any stores today, you know it as well as I do. What choice do we have except to break in? Speaking of which—" He eyed Freddy.

"Typical white guy," said Freddy, grinning. "Wants the Puerto Rican to do the breaking and entering." He pointed a thumb at Jerry Haywood. "Why not get the Negro to do it?"

Haywood grinned too. "Me? I've never been arrested once in my life. My cousin James says I'm a discredit to the race. Well, would say, except he's serving time himself. I'd feel sorry for him if he weren't such an asshole, because good luck surviving a zombie apocalypse in Miami Correctional Facility."

Latoya was scowling at all of them. She had a lighter complexion than her husband, but at the moment her expression made her seem very dark indeed. "My husband is *not* breaking into anyone else's private property."

Tom shrugged again. "He's going to have to help break into something, Latoya. The tank farm will be chained and locked up too, y'know. So take your pick."

Freddy stood up. "I got more room in my van than Jerry does in his SUV, so I'll go on the shopping spree. Unless it'll take a cutting torch to get into the tank farm?"

"It'll just be a chain and padlock," said Tom. "The bolt cutter should handle it fine. Who you going to take with you?"

"How much heavy lifting will be involved?"

Tom mused on the problem for a moment. "Might be... quite a bit, actually. You better take our grandson. And you'll need someone as a lookout—and he better have a gun, too. Zombies are starting—"

He broke off, hearing the sound of a motorcycle coming down the street. "Is that Eddie?"

Pedro was already looking out the window. "Yeah, it's Eddie—and Ceyonne's riding behind him."

Tom nodded. "Good. We can send both of them with Freddy."

Latoya now focused her scowl on Kaminski. "Why you want to send my son out to break the law?" she demanded.

"I don't want him so much as I do his girlfriend," said Tom. "I'm willing to bet she's carrying—and she knows how to use a gun. There are advantages to having a cop for a father even if"—he smiled up at her slyly—"it probably makes your little boy nervous now and then."

Latoya started to say something but her husband put a hand on her shoulder. "Let it go, hon. He's right and you know it. There won't be any way to get anything legally today—and so what? Ceyonne's dad is the only cop I know pigheaded enough to still be on duty. Which I'm willing to bet is why he sent her along with Eddie."

His son confirmed that guess less than a minute later, when he came into the house.

"Yeah, that's what happened. Ceyonne's dad—"

"The stupid fuck!" his girlfriend snarled.

"—says he's got to stay on the job. Now more than ever, he says."

"The stupid fuck!" she repeated.

Eddie Haywood shrugged. "That's what he's like. Anyway, he told me to bring Ceyonne over here. He figures she'll be safer with us than anywhere else."

"Stupid—stupid—stupid!"

Ceyonne Bennett was a big girl, five feet nine inches tall, with a rather heavy build. She was normally attractive, in a round cheery-faced sort of way, but right now she just looked furious.

"He's the only cop in East Chicago still on the job!" she said, half-wailing. "What the hell good does he think he can do on his own?"

Andy was inclined to agree with her. But there was no point in pursuing the matter so she got right down to business.

"We need you and Eddie to help Freddy and Jack go—ah—shopping. You got a gun on you?"

Ceyonne sniffed. "You mean go break into someplace and steal stuff. Yeah, I got a gun. Two of them, actually." She moved her jacket to the side showing a small pistol in a holster in her waistband. "This isn't exactly legal, since I'm not old enough for a concealed carry license. But my dad's not totally crazy about minding the law. He's the one got me the holster as well as the gun."

She jerked her head backward. "And I got my nine millimeter in the saddlebag on Eddie's bike. That's got seventeen rounds to go with the six"—she patted the gun at her waist—"in this little .380. Ought to be enough, no matter what we run into."

Jack Kaminski grinned at her. Andy's grandson liked Ceyonne a lot. Andy thought he probably had a crush on her, but given that Ceyonne already had a boyfriend and was a year and a half older than he was—a big deal for teenagers—he'd never acted on it.

"Zombie *apocalypse,* remember?" he said to her.

Ceyonne blew a raspberry at him. "Zombies, my ass. They ain't dead yet, I'll make 'em so. When are we leaving?"

"Right now," said Freddy.

"Better take one of the walkie-talkies," urged his father. "Cell phones are still working, but who knows how long that'll last?"

Freddy nodded. "I got one in the van already. You figured out where we're going yet, Tom?"

Kaminski nodded. "The Office Depot down on Indianapolis Boulevard. If things are too crazy there because it's pretty close to Meijer's, then try the OfficeMax across the street. I can't think of anything over there that'd be drawing much attention right now."

"*Office* supplies?" said their grandson, looking startled.

Tom chuckled. "Yeah, who'd ever think of looting *that* in a zombie apocalypse?"

"So what are we looking for there?" asked Freddy.

"First of all—these will be heavy and a bitch to load, but we need them—are cases of paper. Each one will hold ten reams and they're about eighteen by twelve by twelve inches. We want..."

Tom's eyes got unfocused again as he calculated. "At least forty cases. Fifty would be better."

Freddy's eyes were wide. "*That* many? What the hell for? You're talking about the better part of a ton."

"Sound proofing."

"*What?*"

"Think it through, Freddy. We're bringing two generators with us because whatever else, we need electricity and when the grid goes down—which it's bound to sooner or later—the only way to get it is with portable gas generators. They don't make a whole lot of noise but they do make some, and one thing that's been established about these zombies is that light and noise attracts them. So we need a way to deaden the sound."

Freddy scratched his jaw. "Okay. But . . . can't we use something like, I don't know . . ."

"The only way to really deaden noise is with mass, Freddy. The best thing would probably be sheets of dry wall with insulation between them, but we've already agreed there's no way we'll get into a Lowe's or Home Depot. The one thing that will do a good job in an office products store is cases of paper. We'll use them to build a hut for the generators. Then cover it with plastic sheets to keep the rain off. Which is one of the reasons you also need to grab as much bubble wrap as you can find. Big garbage bags, too."

Freddy sighed. "Fine. What else?"

"You know those clear plastic mats they sell to put under a chair so as to protect floors and carpets? Grab as many of those as they've got. They're vinyl and while they probably aren't as good as rubber mats—"

"Insulation, I got it. In case of lightning strikes. What else?"

"Bubble wrap, like I said, all you can find. And tape. We already got a lot of duct tape but we're going to need more. We weren't figuring on living on top of a steel floor fifty feet in the air. I don't know if they'll have duct tape but for sure they'll have shipping tape, which is pretty damn good stuff."

Jack piped up. "I saw an episode on *Mythbusters* where the two guys got out of being stranded in a desert just using duct tape and bubble wrap. They made insulated clothes out of it—even made a boat."

Tom nodded. "Duct tape is the best evidence there is that God really exists." He waved his hand. "But you need to get going, Freddy—and so do the rest of us. We'll meet you down at the tank farm. If the cell phones go out, switch to the walkie-talkies."

Freddy left, with her grandson Jack in tow along with Eddie Haywood and Ceyonne Bennett. Andy turned to the people still in the house.

"Okay, let's get moving. By now, I think most everything's already packed except the rubber matting we got downstairs in the exercise room. We'll need to pull all that up."

"On it," said Latoya, heading for the door to the basement.

"Give me a hand, Jayden." Her daughter followed her. So did Freddy's wife Victoria.

Andy looked around. "Is there anything else we're overlooking?" She waited a few seconds. "No? Okay, then, we'll leave as soon as we've got the mats loaded."

## 2

They hadn't gotten four blocks when Andy saw someone she recognized walking down the street ahead. It was one of the waitresses at a nearby diner. When the girl turned her head to look at them Andy saw she'd been crying.

Andy pulled the truck over. Tom, riding next to her, already had the window down.

"What's wrong, Sam?" he asked.

Samantha Crane was short, a bit stocky—and about as pretty as any nineteen-year-old girl Andy had ever met, in a cute streaky-blonde sort of way.

"My mother," Sam said. She wiped her runny nose with the back of her hand. "She ... she tried to *kill* me."

Andy hissed in a breath. She liked Sam—but if she'd been bitten by a zombie ...

"Did she bite you? Even get close to you?" asked Tom.

Sam shook her head. "No. I was coming home from work—Rochelle shut the restaurant down, since there wasn't any business anyway—when Mom came charging out of the house. She was *naked*. And screeching like you wouldn't believe. I took off running and she followed me for a couple of blocks before something distracted her."

The girl pointed down the street. "I'm heading for the diner. Rochelle's planning to just stay there even though it's closed because ... well, she's got nowhere else to go. I figured I'd join her. Don't know what else to do."

Sam and her mother lived alone. The truth is, the two of them didn't get along that well, which Andy thought was part of the reason the girl worked so many hours on her job. Rochelle Lewis, the restaurant's manager, had become something of a surrogate mother for her.

Andy glanced at Tom. He had that mulish look on his face

that she'd come to know very well, having been married to him for damn near half a century.

She sighed. She had her doubts, because the more people they added the greater the chances became that someone had been infected by the zombie virus. But...

She pointed with her thumb over her shoulder, indicating the short line of vehicles that had come to a stop behind her. "Come with us. Get in Pedro's truck. He's only got his mother with him so there's room. If need be, put her on your lap. Yarelis doesn't weigh more than ninety pounds."

Sam looked at the pickup. Then, shook her head. "Thanks, Andy. But I can't leave Rochelle alone. She's got nobody either since her mom died and she threw out that asshole husband of hers."

Tom cleared his throat. "Rochelle's good people," he said. "And we got too damn many old farts. Need some more young folks."

Rochelle Lewis wasn't exactly "young." Andy wasn't sure of her age but the restaurant manager looked to be somewhere in her late thirties or early forties. But given that their group did have a high percentage of older people—Pedro's mother was in her *eighties*—she could see Tom's point.

What the hell. She liked Rochelle herself and the idea of leaving the woman all alone in a shuttered restaurant was just...

Creepy.

"Okay," she said. "We'll swing by the diner and pick her up too. Now get in. We're in a hurry."

As if to add emphasis to her words, they heard a screech coming from somewhere nearby. Several screeches, in fact. Zombies weren't exactly pack hunters, but from what she'd seen on the television they did usually come in groups.

Sam hurried over to Pedro's truck and the caravan was on its way again.

Fortunately, the diner didn't take them very far out of their way. When they pulled up outside, Sam hopped out of the truck and went over to the door and started slapping it with her hand.

"Open up, Rochelle! Open up!"

A few seconds later, the door swung open. The African-American woman standing there was not much taller than Sam herself and just about as pretty, although her good looks were more on the elegant side than what you'd call "cute."

She seemed a little startled when Sam gave her a fierce hug.

Technically, the younger woman was Rochelle's employee, after all, not a close friend or relative. But within two seconds she was returning the hug.

Tom leaned out of the window. "Come on, girls! We gotta *move.* Rochelle, there's room in the Haywood's SUV since they just got their daughter with them."

Rochelle looked at the vehicle in question, then back at Tom and Andy. "Where y'all going?"

"Just . . . call it 'up on the roof.' Best place we can think of—and sure as hell a lot better than being holed up by yourself in there."

The manager still hesitated. Andy leaned over and shouted past her husband.

"Damn it, Rochelle—*come on!* That door you got on the restaurant's mostly glass. It won't take zombies more'n a few seconds to smash their way in."

After a moment, the woman nodded. "Okay." She gestured behind her. "Anything in here I should bring with me? The owner's off visiting his folks in Ohio and he's a shithead anyway."

Apparently, Tom had already been thinking along those lines because his answer came instantly. "Yeah, there is. Grab whatever big knives you got and toss 'em into the biggest pots you got. Then—you'll need help"—he gestured with a thumb to the vehicles behind them—"because we want all the tablecloths you can bring."

"Tablecloths?" Rochelle frowned, obviously puzzled.

"Yeah. They're some kind of plastic, right? We'll want them to collect rainwater. Ain't no Artesian wells where we're going."

Andy heard the sound of more screeching. It seemed to be coming from a distance—but no distance was great enough to suit her, in a zombie apocalypse.

"Do what he says, Rochelle! And please—*hurry.*"

It seemed to take forever, but it was probably less than five minutes before they were on their way again. They'd managed to stuff the Haywood's SUV with all the tablecloths in the restaurant and both Rochelle and Jayden now had big pots on their laps filled with cutting implements. Rochelle had added some ladles also, Andy was glad to see. Men could wax poetically about the wonders of duct tape but any sensible woman knew that a ladle was God's true gift to humanity.

Next stop—finally—was the tank farm. It wasn't more than a couple of miles away now.

Freddy had quickly figured out that trying to go straight down Indianapolis would be hopeless. The big boulevard had too many places on it where looters would be congregating—and where there were looters, there were bound to be zombies. The huge Cabela's store just south of I-80 had to be a lunatic bin by now.

So, he detoured down Kennedy. There were plenty of commercial strips on that street also, but none of the really big stores that would be drawing whole crowds.

Even then, driving was tricky, between reckless drivers and even more reckless pedestrians—not to mention a zombie here and there. They were the worst, in a way. Naked as they were and unarmed, Freddy wasn't worried that a zombie could smash into his big commercial van before he got away from them. But what he *was* worried about was simple contact between a zombie and his vehicle. God forbid he should run over one and have zombie blood splattered all over the underside of the van and its wheels. Freddy wasn't sure exactly how the zombie virus got transmitted, but he figured zombie bodily fluids were pretty much guaranteed to be a vector.

So, he had to weave around the zombies—three of them, north of the interstate; thankfully, they got sparse once he crossed I-80—which required some driving that you could either call "artful" or "crazy," take your pick. Ahead of him, on his motorcycle, Eddie Haywood had to do the same, of course. But dodging zombies on a motorcycle was a piece of cake compared to doing it with a van designed for industrial work.

They probably couldn't have avoided one of the zombies at all, except that Freddy had had the foresight to insist that Ceyonne ride with him and Jack instead of behind Eddie on his motorcycle. Neither Ceyonne nor Jack had been happy with the arrangement—Ceyonne because she'd rather have been with her boyfriend and Jack because no fifteen-year-old boy thinks it's proper for a man to be riding in the middle, dammit—but it put Ceyonne at the passenger's window.

With a gun and the temperament to match.

"Fuck you, asshole!" she'd yelled at the one zombie impossible to dodge. After Freddy brought the van to a screeching halt, Ceyonne hopped out of the vehicle, took a shooter's stance she'd clearly learned from her father, and brought the zombie down with four shots.

And then complained about it for the next mile.

"Dinky little .380," she groused, as she reloaded. "Took me *four rounds.* Coulda done it with one—okay, two; Dad trained me to always double-tap—with the nine millimeter. Which is stuck inside Eddie's saddlebag where it ain't doing any good at all."

Sitting next to her, Jack's face was even paler than usual. Truth be told, Freddy was a little shocked himself. The girl was only seventeen and he was sure this was the first time in her life she'd ever killed anyone. Yet she seemed no more rattled by what had happened than she would have been by shooing away flies.

Something in their expressions must have registered on her, because Ceyonne's expression became half-defensive and half-belligerent. "Look, guys, they ain't *people.* They got no brains left—hell, not even as much as a dog or a cat. My dad told me not to think of 'em as anything except targets."

"It's okay, Ceyonne," Freddy said, trying for as soothing a tone as he could manage. "I'm just glad you're along."

Which, he realized, was the plain and simple truth. *Focus, Freddy. Zombie apocalypse, remember?*

"Yeah, me too," said Jack.

Cutting the padlock on the gate leading into the tank farm took but a few seconds. Within a minute, the entire caravan was inside the grounds, as Andy looked for the best storage tank she could find.

She picked one right at the center of the facility, which was at least two hundred yards away from the nearest road. It was one of the bigger ones, too, which would give them the most space.

"Don't park right next to it," warned Tom. "Otherwise zombies might climb up on it trying to get to the roof. They won't manage anyway, but they might wreck the truck and we'll probably need it again."

That seemed good advice—for later. Right now, she wanted to be as close to the base of the staircase as possible. They had a twenty-foot moving truck to unload, along with two pickups and an SUV—and then had to haul everything more than fifty feet up a narrow steel staircase. With, as her husband had pointed out, way too high a percentage of old farts to do the work.

Not to mention that getting *him* up there was probably going to be the hardest work of all.

Tom knew it himself. "Don't worry about me until Freddy gets here," he said. "Just get me out of the truck and onto my wheelchair—and hand me the rifle in the case behind the seat. I'll keep guard while the rest of you do the scut work."

It would have been nice if he hadn't been smiling like a damn cherub when he said it.

Damn old fart. This was going to be *exhausting*.

First, they hauled the tents and tool sheds up to the top. When Andy got to the roof for the first time, she was a little stunned by how big it was. She'd never seen one of these storage tanks from up close before. *One hundred and ten feet in diameter* doesn't sound like much until you're standing on top of it. Whatever concerns she'd had that they might not have enough room vanished instantly. They had about as much in the way of square footage as a fricking *mansion*—a real one, too, not a McMansion.

Not so much in the way of furnishings, of course. Still, she was cheered up a lot.

Her good mood faded as the work progressed and she got more and more tired. The tank, as it turned out, had a functioning crane hoist that was capable of lifting more than a ton. But it couldn't work that fast and they needed to get everything up on the roof as soon as possible. So while the heaviest items got brought up with the hoist, that still left most of the stuff to be hauled up the old-fashioned way. All sixty-eight of her years were complaining loudly and bitterly, before too long.

Having a husband who spent his time providing advice—while *he* was perched on a wheelchair—didn't improve her mood. The fact that it was mostly good advice didn't make it any better.

"Don't bother setting up the tents and the tool sheds yet," Tom said. "No point in it until we've got insulation down. Speaking of which"—he pointed to the south—"on the way in, I spotted a big stack of wood pallets over by the asphalt plant. We oughta use them for our base flooring. They'll not only help insulate against electric currents but they'll keep us above water when it rains."

Andy might have snarled at him, but Luis and Pedro nodded and took off in the now-emptied pickups to get the pallets.

It *was* good advice. And so what? Andy knew she loved the

old bastard, even if sometimes—like right now—she couldn't remember why.

Trying not to curse out loud, she started up the staircase with another load. Maybe she'd get lucky and have a heart attack before she died of exhaustion.

Just as Tom had foreseen, the Office Depot was empty of people. There was a mob across the street looting the Meijer's store—hypermarket, they were sometimes called. Like a Wal-Mart, it combined a supermarket with a cut-rate department store. Filled with stuff that people would need to survive a zombie apocalypse.

Unlike an office goods store. Quiet as a church mouse.

Until an alarm went off when they smashed in the door. Freddy was a little concerned, then. Not because the alarm would draw cops—he doubted if any were still on duty besides Ceyonne's stubborn father—but because it might draw zombies.

"Ceyonne, you stand guard out here while the three of us gather up the stuff we need. Come on, guys. We may as well start with the cases of paper."

As he'd expected, that work was a genuine bitch—and hauling the cases up a fifty-five foot staircase later was going to be even worse. But he was a big, strong man and his two helpers were both good-sized boys and, best of all, *teenagers*. Use all that energy for something more useful than what teenage boys usually got into.

Loading fifty cases didn't really take that long. Tossing in the floor mats took even less. And while it was going to take a bit of time to gather up things such as tape and bubble wrap just because there was a lot of it, the stuff seemed lighter than feathers compared to the paper.

And even the time spent wasn't that much, once Eddie figured out they could use big plastic containers to hold all the tape.

The only problem came at the very end. Just as they were carrying out the last rolls of bubble wrap, they heard Ceyonne hollering outside. She had a very loud voice, as you might expect from a girl with her impressive chest.

"*Get the fuck away from here, you assholes! I'm not fooling wit' you! I will shoot you dead!*"

Freddy dropped his bundles of bubblewrap and raced outside, fumbling at the pistol he had holstered to his own hip.

When he passed through the door, he saw that Ceyonne was

confronting three zombies. Two females, one male—but with zombies, even naked like they were, gender distinctions didn't register much.

He finally managed to get the flap undone on the holster. But before he could draw the pistol, Ceyonne started firing.

She was using her big Smith & Wesson M&P now, not the little Ruger. The nine millimeter rounds packed a lot more punch than the .380, but the recoil wasn't as bad because the gun was more than twice as heavy as the Ruger. That probably didn't matter all that much, though, given that Ceyonne had big hands to go with her overall size.

*Bam—bam. Bam—bam. Bam—bam.* Three double-taps and all three zombies were down. Down, and either dead or dying. He thought she'd missed one of the shots but it hadn't mattered.

Ceyonne stepped forward a few paces, aimed carefully, and shot all three in the head.

"Gotta shoot zombies in the brain or they don't stay down," she explained.

By then, Jack was outside too. "Uh . . . they're not actually undead, you know. Just people infected by a virus that makes them insane. I don't think you really need to shoot 'em in the head."

"I seen it on *The Walking Dead,*" Ceyonne insisted. "Hell, watch any zombie movie."

"It's not worth arguing about," Freddy said forcefully. "Come on, let's finish loading and get the hell out of here."

"I'm riding with Eddie on the way back," Ceyonne said, even more forcefully.

Freddy didn't contest the issue. Ceyonne was looking more and more like Annie Oakley or Calamity Jane and who in their right mind is going to argue with women like that? Much less seventeen-year-old girls.

"I don't think I've ever been so tired in my life," said Sam. She was perched on a stack of goods with her elbows on her knees and her head hanging down.

Next to her, Rochelle Lewis was trying to bring her breathing under control. "Me, neither," she said, almost gasping.

But as exhausted as she was, Rochelle's spirits were higher than they'd been in days. No, *weeks*—maybe even months or years. After her divorce three years earlier, she'd buried herself in her job as manager of the diner. That had kept her busy, but she realized now that she'd done it at the expense of being very lonely. And then the zombie apocalypse—she still thought that was a ridiculous name because, first, the people infected by the virus weren't actually undead even if they were monsters, and second, she'd studied the Bible and knew damn well this wasn't really the apocalypse, just a man-made catastrophe—had come along and left her completely alone. She'd thought she'd die in the bowels of that restaurant within a day or two—or, worse, get turned into a naked mindless shrieking monster herself.

Now, she had a purpose again—and people to share it with. Impulsively, she put her arm around Sam's shoulders and hugged her. "I'm really glad you're here, sweetie."

Sam's arm slid around her waist. "Me too, boss." *Boss* carried a weight of affection in it that was not usually found in that particular term.

Down on the ground below, they could see Tom Kaminski trying to maneuver his wheelchair. The old man's expression was a cross between determined ferocity and exasperation. He had his rifle perched on his lap and was simultaneously trying to keep it from sliding off while he patrolled the area looking for any signs of approaching zombies. He was at least one hand short of what he needed.

It was kind of funny, actually. Both Rochelle and Sam started chuckling.

"I'd better go down and help him," Sam said. She rose and headed for the stairs.

"A guardian angel for a guardian angel," Rochelle murmured to herself. "Hell, who knows? Maybe this *is* the apocalypse and Saint John just got some of the details wrong."

They'd gotten about half of their goods along with all the pallets up onto the roof when Freddy Rodriguez arrived with his industrial van full of more stuff to haul up—including fifty cases of paper each of which seemed to weigh a ton. They didn't have the equipment to bring up a lot of cases at a time using the hoist, so most of the paper had to be hauled up by hand. Fortunately, Freddy was a big man and the three teenagers he brought with him were all fresh and rested.

The general unspoken consensus among the old folks was: *let them finish the job.*

"Yeah, take a rest," said Freddy. "But not until you get all those pallets into position. And see if you can glue them down. We'll have to attach the tent stakes to the pallets instead of welding them to the roof, so we don't want them sliding around."

"What sort of glue should we use?" asked his wife Victoria.

"I got no idea, honey. Try all of them and see what works best. But before you do, see if you can scrape the paint off the roof using the chisels and files we got. Glue will bond better to naked steel than it will to paint, especially if it's roughed up a little."

The look Victoria gave him was not exactly full of spousal fondness. "I thought we were getting a break?" she said. But she didn't complain any further before setting to the work. Jerry and Latoya Haywood joined her, along with their daughter Jayden. So did Andy, after she got a little more rest.

Since there was no way to find out which sort of glue would work best before they had to start piling stuff onto the pallets, they just made sure to use every kind they had on every pallet. Gorilla glue, epoxy glue, super glue, Elmer's glue, Loc-tite—if they had it, they used it. Fortunately, Tom Kaminski had been adamant on the need to bring lots of glue even though their original plan had been to camp out in the woods. "Nothing's handier than glue except duct tape," he'd insisted, "and you never know when and how you might need it."

The old fart turned out to be right. He had a habit of doing that, which Andy had found annoying for decades. Forty-eight years, eight months and two days, to be exact, if you counted from their wedding. Longer than that, if you counted from their first date—when he'd claimed he knew a better Italian restaurant than the one she proposed and . . . hadn't been wrong.

By the time they got all the pallets in position and glued down, Freddy and the youngsters had gotten everything from the vans and trucks onto the roof.

"The rubber mats next and then the plastic floor mats for whatever the rubber won't cover," Freddy ordered. "They all need to be glued down too, because we don't want any metal—not even nails or staples—connecting us to the roof, and the pallets are already full of nails."

A shout came from below. "I need to get up there!"

Freddy took a deep breath and ran fingers through his hair. "Okay, I guess it's time to haul up the gorilla."

"Don't call my husband a gorilla," said Andy. "He's not *that* damn big and he's mostly bald now. Who ever saw a bald gorilla?"

"He's big enough to break my poor back," muttered Freddy. But he was already going down the stairs.

It took them a while to get Tom Kaminski up onto the roof. They didn't want to take the risk of using the hoist since they had no suitable rigging. Even as strong as he was, Tom was seventy now, so he needed to take a lot of breaks. Sam tried to help at first, but she was too small to make much of a difference and just got in Freddy's way. In the end, she got assigned to bring up the wheelchair, the rifle, and the custom-made shooting bench that Tom had had designed for him after he recovered from the accident that took his legs.

But, finally, it was done. And Tom didn't take more than a ten minute rest before he started patrolling again—and this time he had a nice flat steel surface to roll around on, along with a helper.

"Come on, Sam," he said. "You can be my spotter and set up the bench whenever we need it."

"Only if you teach me how to shoot the rifle."

"It's a deal. But you got to carry the rifle too."

"What am I, a caddie?"

"Hell, no. Caddies get paid."

By sundown, what everyone was starting to call "tent city" had been erected and most of their goods stashed away somewhere. The two vinyl tool sheds were positioned in the center of the roof. By mutual agreement, one of them would be inhabited by Tom and Andy Kaminski and the other by Pedro Vargas and his eighty-one-year-old mother Yarelis, but they'd both serve as emergency shelters for everyone in case of a thunderstorm.

Surrounding the sheds were all the tents. Those ranged in size from a couple of eight by twelve foot dome-shaped tents that would hold all four of the Haywoods and Freddy and Victoria and their two kids, to a couple of eight by six tents—one for Luis and Flora Rodriguez and one that had been intended for Jack but got turned over to Rochelle Lewis, Sam Crane and Ceyonne Bennett.

Jack would have to settle for a two-person tent. They'd brought several of those, figuring they could use them to hold supplies.

Assuming that Ceyonne's father eventually showed up, he could have one of them also.

The two generators were positioned in the hut they'd constructed with the cases of paper. The roof for the hut was made out of metal shelving Freddy had found in the Office Depot with more cases stacked on top of them. They used the hollow steel tubes that were originally intended to provide the frame for the shelving as a lightning rod that Freddy welded onto the staircase.

There hadn't been time to cut off the lower part of the staircase before it got dark, so they'd put that off until the next day. Someone would have to stand watch at the top of the stairs all through the night. Ceyonne volunteered for the first shift, from sundown until midnight. Freddie would take the next four hours and then he'd wake up Jerry Haywood for the last stretch.

Eventually, once the lower staircase was removed, Andy figured they could rely on the teenagers to be lookouts at night. But that brought up another problem—which, happily, she'd already foreseen.

"You know what's going to happen soon enough," Latoya said to her, "we let teenagers stay up at night without supervision. It ain't just gonna be my son and Ceyonne, neither."

Andy chuckled. "No shit. My fifteen-year-old grandson—he'll be sixteen next month—is already eyeing both your daughter and Sam and you give it another month and he'll be panting after Lucinda Rodriguez too."

"Jayden's a good girl," Latoya said, a little stiffly.

"They're *all* good girls. So was I and so were you, at that age—and I don't know about you but I got my cherry popped when I was sixteen."

Latoya sniffed. "I was older. Seventeen."

"Right. There's not going to be much to do up here and when winter comes along in a few months there'll be even less to keep them busy."

They were standing near the edge of the roof—not right next it, though, since there was no railing—looking at the sun go down. Andy gestured with her head toward the tent she and Tom were sharing. "I got a big box in there full of rubbers. I cleaned out the whole condom section in Walgreens." She cawed like a crow. "You should've seen the look I got from the cashier. She might as well have said out loud, *what kinda old slut needs any rubbers at all, much less hundreds of 'em?*"

Latoya was by nature and upbringing a lot more straightlaced than Andy Kaminski, but she couldn't help bursting into laughter. After the laughter passed, she admitted quietly, "I bought some too, for Eddie. Me and Jerry don't need to worry about it because he got fixed after we had Jayden. 'Two kids is enough,' he said." Her expression got a little stiff again. "And I wouldn't be surprised at all if Ceyonne's already making him use rubbers, whether he likes it or not. That girl's . . . not exactly your best Christian."

Andy didn't say anything in response. She and Tom had both lapsed from Catholicism long ago, and she had her own opinion as to what constituted "proper Christian behavior."

Whether or not Ceyonne Bennett was the world's finest Christian young lady, Andy was glad she was with them. By now, they'd all heard about the shootings Ceyonne had done earlier that day.

And now, another shot rang out from behind them. Andy recognized the sound, having heard it before. That was no pistol firing. That was Tom's deer rifle, a Remington 700 .30-06.

Turning around, they saw Tom Kaminski near the opposite edge of the tank roof. He had his shooting bench in position and was taking aim at something in the distance past the fence surrounding the tank farm.

"You got 'im, Tom!" said Sam excitedly. She was bracing his wheelchair from behind and peering through a set of binoculars that Tom kept in a bag attached to it. "He's down. And now the other one's—"

Tom fired again. The recoil jarred him back a little, but between his own size and the wheelchair being both locked and braced by the girl with him, he wasn't thrown out of position. He worked the bolt and jacked another round into the chamber.

"Call it, Sam," he commanded. "Like I explained."

"That one's down too. The third one's still off a ways. I'd say two hundred and fifty yards, thereabouts, but it—well, she—is coming toward the fence. Uh . . . ten o'clock. Well, maybe nine-thirty."

"I see her. Wheel me around a bit." As Sam did so, Tom raised the bench with one hand while he kept the rifle high in the other. Within three seconds, he was back in position.

He didn't spend more than another three seconds aiming, and then—

"She's down, too!" Sam exclaimed. "Boy, you shoot good, Tom."

Andy's husband didn't say anything in response to the praise, but she knew what that expression on his face meant. She'd spent most of her life with the old fart and knew him better than she knew anyone, including maybe even herself.

After ten years of depression—no, more than eleven years now, since the accident—Tom Kaminski had found his life again.

A guardian angel in a wheelchair. Well, why not? Andy wasn't as familiar with the Bible as either Rochelle Lewis or Latoya Haywood, but she knew this apocalypse was a bastard version of the one in the Book of Revelations. You couldn't hardly expect archangels with flaming swords to show up for this sort of low-class brawl, after all.

# 3

Andy had been a little worried that Tom's shooting of the three zombies on the perimeter of the tank farm might have drawn attention to them. But the next morning, when she studied the scene of the killing through the binoculars, she saw that her fears had been groundless.

"I told you," said her husband. He nodded toward the knot of zombies in the distance who were still feeding on the corpses of the three zombies he'd shot the evening before. "That's somewhere between two hundred and fifty and three hundred yards from here. Even if they were still real people with brains, they wouldn't have been able to tell where the shots came from."

With the free hand that wasn't holding the rifle on his lap, he made a little circling motion. "We're in flat land, up high, with nothing to focus the sound. At that distance, the sound of the shot would have seemed to be coming from everywhere or nowhere, however you want to look at it."

He lowered the hand and shrugged. "Zombies? They wouldn't have even thought about it. A mysterious noise coming from somewhere—anywhere—in the distance? Could have been anything, if they had enough brains to think about it. But they don't."

"Okay," she said. "But I think you ought to avoid shooting any zombies except ones trying to climb over the fence."

"I haven't seen a single one try to do that," he said. "Why would they, unless they thought there was something on the other side they wanted? The chain link fence that surrounds the tank farm is at least six feet high and it's got three strands of barbed wire on top of that. Any naked-ass zombie tries to climb over it's going to get pretty badly cut—and the minute they start bleeding, you know other zombies are going to go after them."

"Yeah, but that's my biggest worry, Tom. From what I've seen on the TV, once zombies go into a feeding frenzy it gets out of control. Their own noise and the mayhem they're causing attracts other zombies and before you know it they're starting to swarm all over." She pointed at the distant fence. "Enough zombies pile up against that and it'll go down, barbed wire or no barbed wire. And then we've got zombies swarming into the tank farm. Maybe we can hold them off, as high up as we are on these steel tanks. But then we'll be surrounded by rotting bodies—dozens of 'em, maybe hundreds. D'you really want that?"

Her husband had a mulish expression on his face. Tom *really* wanted to shoot zombies. From long experience, Andy knew the best thing to do was not argue any further about it but just let Tom think it through himself.

After a while, he sighed and said, "I guess you're right. But that still leaves the problem of the gate we broke into. We could weld it shut again, I suppose—but we'll probably want to be able to get out ourselves at some point."

"Fine. You see any zombies heading toward the gate, go ahead and shoot 'em. Just try not to draw any attention. Our best defense is always going to be having zombies not even realizing we're here in the first place."

"Won't be a problem. The only thing any other zombies will know or care about is that there's some fresh meat lying on the ground."

She made a face. Andy still wasn't able to think of zombies as something other than . . . call it "very disturbed people." Tom's cold-bloodedness toward them was a little alienating.

You couldn't even ascribe it to the indifference of old age. His nineteen-year-old spotter and assistant Sam Crane was downright bloodthirsty on the subject of zombies. As she demonstrated again that moment by saying with great satisfaction:

"Especially 'cause there were only three shots. *Total.*" Proudly, almost possessively, she squeezed the big shoulder of the man sitting in the wheelchair in front of her. "Papa's really good, Mama. One shot, one kill."

So it was "Papa" now. That was okay with Andy. She wasn't

really surprised. In a catastrophe like this one, when people had their friends and families ripped into shreds right in front of them, it was only human nature for people to make new attachments wherever they could.

Truth be told, she was feeling pretty motherly toward the girl herself.

*Grand*-motherly, rather. Her days of dealing with the messy business of raising her own children were long behind her.

That memory brought a moment's anguish. Their son George didn't live anywhere nearby. George and his wife Janny weren't even in the country, since George's company had sent him off to Brazil for a couple of months to handle some sort of problem that had come up in their operations down there. That was the reason she and Tom had been taking care of their grandson Jack over the summer.

Their daughter Rita was long gone, killed in a car accident fifteen years earlier. She'd had no children of her own, and since her husband had never gotten along with Andy and Tom, they no longer had any contact with their daughter's step-children either.

She'd tried to reach George on her cell phone, even though Andy wasn't sophisticated in the use of cell phones for international calling. Eventually she'd asked Rochelle to help. But while the restaurant manager did know how to do it, she hadn't been able to make any connections either.

Which was not all that surprising, of course. As her grandson Jack liked to say, *zombie apocalypse, remember?*

About an hour later, Ceyonne Bennett's father Jerome showed up. He'd gotten in touch with Ceyonne via cell phone and she'd told them where they were.

Still in uniform—he'd probably *slept* in the damn thing—he slowly drove his police car into the tank farm until he came to a stop below them and perhaps twenty yards away from the tank they were on. By then, Ceyonne was halfway down the staircase, shouting "Dad! Dad!" For all the girl's grousing on the subject of her pigheaded and unreasonable father, she was obviously very attached to him.

Andy wasn't sure what had happened to the mother. Jack had told her that Ceyonne had told him that her mother had run off with a traveling salesman, but Andy was sure the girl had just been pulling his leg. That story had all the earmarks of a tall tale. Did traveling salesmen even exist anymore? She didn't think so—not the kind that went door-to-door and talked to people, anyway, as opposed to so-called "sales reps."

Before Ceyonne reached the bottom of the stairs, her father was backing up and waving her off. "Don't come near me, Ceyonne! Get back up on the tank." When the girl hesitated, he shouted, "Do it *now*. Don't fool with me, dammit!"

"What's the matter, Dad?"

He shook his head. "I'm sick. Feels like a flu—but I doubt if it is. I'm pretty sure I got infected with the zombie virus."

By then, Rochelle Lewis had started down the stairs. Seeing her come, Jerome Bennett said, "You're the manager of the Indiana Restaurant, aren't you? I've eaten there a few times."

"Yes, I am. Name's Rochelle Lewis."

He nodded. "Pleased to meet you. Do us both—do us all—a favor and keep my daughter up there with you. Do *not* let her come down here."

Exactly how Rochelle Lewis was supposed to restrain a teenage girl who was half a head taller than she was and outweighed her by at least thirty pounds, was not very clear.

But Ceyonne had stopped on her own, still a good fifteen feet off the ground. "Dad!" she cried out. The sound was a sheer wail.

He shook his head again. "There's nothing either of us can do about it, girl. It's the way it is. I just came by to say good-bye."

"*Dad!*"

Andy was at the top of the stairs, now. She cupped her hands around her mouth and shouted down to the police officer. "Where d'you plan to go, Jerome?"

He shrugged. "Home, I guess."

She shook her head. "Stay here. You may just have a normal flu, you know? And even if you got the zombie virus, some people survive it—I mean, don't get turned into . . . well, monsters."

Jerome made a face. "I've been briefed on the odds. We got a notification from the CDC in Atlanta. There's two stages to the disease. Stage One—that's what I think I got—just seems like a bad flu. Ninety-five percent of people survive it, but then they come down with Stage Two of the virus. That's the zombie stage. Twenty percent will die right off, and of the eighty percent who survive, almost all of them will turn into zombies. There's a few who don't, who survive both stages, but it's not more than ten percent."

Tom had wheeled himself to the top of the staircase. "Those are still better odds than pancreatic cancer, Jerome."

The policeman laughed humorlessly. "They measure cancer survival rates by a *five-year* standard. The zombie virus is all over, one way or another, within a few weeks. Three weeks, the CDC says, to run its whole course. Not even a month."

"Better still," said Andy. She pointed at one of the storage tanks next to their own, about forty yards away. "Get yourself up there and we'll see what happens. At least that way, if you do survive, you got people right here to keep an eye on you."

"And an eye out *for* you," added her husband. He pointed to a different storage tank, next to the one she'd indicated. "But go up on that one. I can see the whole staircase so even if you're out of commission 'cause of the disease I can take out any zombie tries to climb up and get you." He lifted the Remington off his lap and brandished the rifle. In its own way, the gesture was rather dramatic.

Jerome looked at him for a moment, then looked at the storage tank. "I don't have any supplies," he said. "Not even anything to sleep on."

"We'll bring what you need down to you," said Andy. "But get back in the car and drive off a ways, will you? We don't know how far that virus can travel, if you have it."

Fortunately, Bennett hadn't parked near the bottom of the staircase. So after they put together a couple of bundles for him—one holding enough food to keep him going, along with a walkie-talkie, and the other a sleeping bag and a small two-person tent—his daughter Ceyonne and Rochelle Lewis carried the bundles down the staircase and set them on the ground about halfway between their storage tank and the one that Bennett would be using. By then, the cop had moved the squad car still farther away and was waiting by it until they finished. He was now carrying a shotgun to go with the pistol at his hip. He had a bag holding something heavy, too. That was probably ammunition for the two weapons, Andy figured.

Soon enough, Rochelle and Ceyonne were back on their tank roof and Jerome was setting up his tent on the neighboring roof. He was close enough that, if need be, he and his daughter could communicate by shouting, but as long as the cell phones stayed operational they'd do far better. So would the walkie-talkies, when—nobody thought it was going to be "if"—the cell phones stopped working.

Unlike the tents on the first roof—which Jack Kaminski had taken to calling "Alpha Tower"—the one Jerome Bennett would occupy wasn't attached in any way to the storage tank. But although no one said it out loud, everyone thought that was a moot point. If he survived the virus, Jerome wouldn't be moving around much for at least a week. His own weight would keep the tent from being blown off the roof.

And if he didn't survive—or, worse, turned into a zombie—he made arrangements to handle that as well.

He'd had his daughter provide him with Tom Kaminski's cell phone number, which he called as soon as he got the tent set up.

"*You said you'd shoot any zombie who tried to climb up the staircase*," the policeman said.

"That's right," replied Kaminski. "Even if I'm asleep, we'll always have someone—two someones, in fact—on guard at all times. They'll keep an eye on your tower too."

"*I'm not worried about that. What I really need to know, Mr. Kaminski, is if you're up to the job of shooting a zombie who's trying to get* down *from this roof. That zombie would be me, you understand. Or what used to be me.*"

Tom hesitated. He hadn't given that problem any consideration at all. Stalling for time, he said, "Please. Call me Tom."

"*I come out of this alive and still human, I'll call you Tom. For the time being, though, I think 'Mr. Kaminski' works better. And you didn't answer my question.*"

Tom could see Ceyonne staring at him. The expression on her face was both anxious and fearful. The girl might have a brash personality, but she was plenty bright enough to have figured out why her father had wanted to talk to Tom Kaminski.

Tom sighed. "Yes, Mr. Bennett. If it becomes necessary, I'll . . . take care of it."

"*Thank you. If you can manage it, shoot me when my daughter's not looking. But don't take any real risks. I'd a lot rather she had PTSD from watching her dad get killed than become a zombie herself.*"

Tom would talk to Eddie Haywood about that. He'd make sure the kid understood that if the time came, his job was to make sure that Ceyonne *didn't* see it happen.

After Bennett got off the phone, it dawned on Tom that there was another problem—and one that would be a lot more intractable. If the cop did turn zombie and Tom had to shoot him, what in God's name would they do with the body? Whether Tom shot him on the roof or while he was coming down the stairs, the naked and slaughtered body of Ceyonne's father would be visible to the girl any time the sun was up.

*For weeks*—because they couldn't take the risk of sending someone over to bury the man, for fear of being contaminated with the virus.

"Hell's bells," he muttered.

Quietly, making sure Ceyonne wasn't around to hear, he raised the problem with his wife and Freddy Rodriguez.

Freddy came up with the best answer—not a good one; not even close, but the best they could manage. He'd weld together a jury-rigged grappling hook which they'd attach to one of their ropes. Then, if the time came, they'd toss it onto Bennett's corpse from a distance. Freddy figured he could manage the feat from at least ten or fifteen yards away. Once the grappling hook was embedded in the body, they'd attach the other end of the rope to one of the pickups and just haul the corpse out of sight.

"And what if the hook comes out?" Andy demanded. "You can't retrieve it and try again or you might get contaminated."

Freddy ran fingers through his hair. "We'll just have to make up another grappling hook."

"And hope we don't run out of rope," said Tom.

Around noon the following day, another caravan of vehicles came into the tank farm. It was a smaller group than their own, just two pickups and a minivan, and clearly not as well equipped.

The three vehicles drove up to Alpha Tower—by now, everyone was using Jack's name for the tank—and a man got out of the driver's side of the leading pickup. He was somewhere in early middle age, anywhere between his mid-thirties and mid-forties, and clearly Hispanic, but Andy couldn't tell if he was Puerto Rican or Mexican, either by birth or ancestry. In that part of Lake County, he could just as likely be either one. He might be from somewhere in Central America, too, but that was less common.

"Hello, up there!" he shouted. "I'm Bob Vasquez." He pointed a finger at the woman she could see sitting in the passenger seat.

"That's my wife Rosie." He now pointed with his thumb over his shoulder. "Behind us are our two daughters and their families."

He had no accent at all, beyond the clipped nasal one shared by millions of people in the Chicago area, which meant he was probably native-born rather than an immigrant. Not that Andy cared either way. She'd met some individual exceptions, of course, but by and large she got along fine with Hispanic folks, wherever they came from.

"Pleased to meet you," said Andy. "I'm Andrea Kaminski and this"—Tom had rolled up his wheelchair by then—"is my husband Tom. The rest of the people up here are our neighbors. Where you from?"

"Hessville, me and Rosie." That was a neighborhood in Hammond not far from the tank farm. "Our daughter Leticia and her husband Jim come from there too, and our other daughter Teresa and her kids live—well, used to—in Hegewisch."

Hegewisch was a neighborhood of south Chicago just across the state line, about a fifteen minute drive away. Not surprisingly, they were all local people.

"Our son-in-law saw you up here yesterday while he was driving by, and we talked it over and decided this was probably the safest place around. Is there any chance we can join you?"

Andy's decision came instantly, which meant that she must have been chewing on the problem somewhere on the back of her mind without realizing it.

"Yes and no. You're welcome to set yourselves up on one of the other storage tanks here, Mr. Vasquez. But—I'm sorry, it's just medical necessity—we can't let you come up onto ours. Nothing personal. It's just we got no way of knowing if any of you has been infected by the zombie virus. The symptoms don't show up right away."

Jerome Bennett joined the conversation from his own roof top. Apparently, he was still well enough to do so.

"She's right," he said, half-shouting. "I'm Jerome Bennett, with the East Chicago police department. We got a notification from the CDC—"

"What's that?" asked Rosie Vasquez. She'd come out of the pickup and joined her husband.

"Centers for Disease Control," explained Jerome. "They're based in Atlanta and they're more-or-less the national public health service. Anyway, one of the things they told us was that it takes three to seven days after you've been infected before the first symptoms show up. So one of you could already be sick and no one knows it yet including them."

He pointed to the people on Alpha Tower. "For that matter, one of *them* could be infected too. This is for your protection as well as theirs."

Bennett now pointed at himself with his thumb. "I'm almost sure I've gotten infected, which is the reason I'm up on this tank roof by myself even though my daughter's over there." He lowered his hand and shrugged. "It's cruddy, but there it is."

The Vasquez couple looked at each. Rosie said something too quietly for Andy to hear, and her husband nodded.

"Okay!" he said, looking back up at them. "Any suggestions as to which tank we should pick?"

Tom lifted his rifle and used it to point at a tank that was next to theirs but some distance away from Jerome's. It was also, Andy noted, a tank that had a spiral staircase that was within view of the people on Alpha Tower. She was quite sure that was one of the reasons Tom had selected it—just as she was quite sure he wasn't using the rifle as a pointer by accident. It wasn't subtle, no, but it was a way of making sure the Vasquezes knew they were armed without directly making any threats.

Partly to allay any antagonism that the sight of the rifle might have created but mostly just because she thought it was a good idea, Andy got one of the walkie-talkies and tossed it down to Bob Vasquez.

"You know how to use it?" she asked.

"Yeah, I'm familiar with them." He pulled a cell phone out of his pocket. "These are still working, though."

"Yeah—but for how long? But since they are for the moment, what's your phone number?"

After Vasquez gave it to her, she called him from her own cell phone just to get her number registered.

Which was a waste of time, because less than ten minutes later all the cell phones stopped working.

By mid-afternoon, the Vasquezes had gotten set up on the tank that Jack solemnly informed them was "Gamma Tower." (He'd already bestowed "Beta Tower" on Jerome Bennett's new domicile.)

"Why 'Gamma'?" asked one of Teresa's two boys. His name was Tony Ramirez and he looked to be about eleven years.

"We're naming 'em after the Greek alphabet," Jack explained, just as solemnly.

"Why?"

Jack spent the next several minutes in a long-winded and convoluted explanation that basically came down to "Because." Young Tony still seemed dubious of the logic but he didn't pursue it any further.

## 4

The big oil refinery in Whiting blew up just before daybreak the next morning. The initial blast was enough to wake everyone up, and even if it hadn't been the series of rolling explosions that followed over the next hour or so would probably have awakened the dead.

It certainly woke up all the zombies in the area—probably all the zombies within a fifteen-mile radius. Using the binoculars and the scope on Tom's rifle, they could see dozens of naked figures moving rapidly in the direction of the refinery.

By then, there was a huge column of smoke rising above the refinery as well. Between that and the ongoing explosions and the flames leaping high into the air, the zombies were drawn like moths to a lantern.

"How far away is that?" asked Rochelle Lewis nervously. "That smoke looks pretty toxic."

"About four miles," Tom answered. "And, yeah, it's nothing you want to be breathing." He pointed to the smoke plume. "But the way the winds usually blow around here, it'll go out over the lake. Might be pretty rough for anyone still alive in Miller, but I don't think we'll get hit with it."

"Unless the wind changes direction," Andy said.

Freddy Rodriguez spoke up. "You're all being way too gloomy, folks. The way I see it, we got one hell of an opportunity here." He pointed at the disaster in the distance. "That's going to last for a while, isn't it, Tom?"

"Oh, hell yes," said the former refinery worker. "Without a functioning fire department, it could burn for days—not even counting for the fact that it's almost sure to set other things on fire. Property values in Whiting are about to take a nose dive. Well, they *would*—if the zombies hadn't already trashed them."

That revived Rochelle's anxiety. "If houses start burning... That fire could work its way down here, couldn't it? And we're sitting on top of huge tanks of *gasoline*."

"Relax, Rochelle," said Tom. "There are a hell of a lot of fire breaks between here and there. The Indiana Harbor Canal, two huge steel mills, the high school and its grounds and the small golf course north of that, U.S. Route 12—not to mention that big vacant stretch of Cline Avenue that got condemned a few years ago which the damn politicians never bothered to rebuild."

As she pictured the area in her mind, Rochelle started nodding. "Well, yeah. But there are still likely to be... I don't know, cinders maybe?"

"Which brings me back to my point," said Freddy. "This is our chance to make a supplies run, folks. Every zombie in Lake County is going to be heading toward Whiting."

He turned and pointed to nearby Cline Avenue. "We can hop right onto Cline and head down to the shopping mall where it meets Ridge Road. That's not more than five miles away. Ten minutes there, ten minutes back."

It was tempting. Despite the "avenue" appellation, this stretch of Cline was a limited access elevated highway. Counting the wide shoulders, it was three or four lanes wide on either side. A vehicle could easily drive at seventy or eighty miles per hour. They could reach the shopping mall quickly and easily.

But...

Andy shook her head. "Even if you don't run into zombies—and they can't all be heading to the refinery—you're still running the risk of getting infected with the virus."

Freddy made a *so it goes* gesture. "Andy, there's no way to eliminate that risk, no matter what measures we take. All we can do is lower the odds against us. But zombies and the virus aren't the only risks we face, y'know. Just to name one other one that's getting really prominent, we don't have an outhouse and we're getting low on toilet paper. The longer we just keep shitting off the side of the tank—"

"Tower!" insisted Jack.

"For crapping, it's a tank. And as I was saying, there are other diseases we need to think about. I was talking to Rochelle—"

He turned to her. "Tell 'em what you said to me."

She grimaced. "Well, with open sewers—and we don't even have that—you're always at risk for cholera and typhoid fever. And we've got other problems that'll get worse as we head into the fall. We didn't bring enough bedding, for one thing. It'll get chilly up here at night and if—more like when—we start getting rained on . . ."

Andy raised her hands. "All right, all right! But wait until the afternoon. You want to give the zombies time to move out of the area on their way up to Whiting."

"Okay," said. Freddy. "I can use the morning for other things, anyway." He pointed to the staircase. "The ladder in my truck will extend to fifteen feet, so I'm going to remove the bottom twelve feet of the stairs with my cutting torch. Whenever we're all up here, we just raise the ladder. Unless there's a zombie out there who can break the world high jump record, we'll be untouchable."

"Can you do the same for the other two towers?" asked Jack.

Freddy hesitated. Andy shook her head.

"Too much risk of infection," she said. "Sorry, but there it is. I'm none too happy about making a supplies run. I'm putting my foot down on violating the tower quarantine rules."

She made a note to herself to write down Official Quarantine Rules and pass them around. The one thing they had plenty of was paper, after all.

"There's only the one tall ladder anyway," pointed out Luis. "The other one we got is a six-foot stepladder. What's the point of cutting away just five feet of a staircase?"

"I guess you're right," Jack said reluctantly. "I don't like it, though, us being so much better protected than the Vasquezes or Officer Bennett."

Andy didn't see any point in responding. The boy's sentiments spoke well for him as a person. He was a genuinely nice kid. But reality was what it was.

Ceyonne slapped Jack's shoulder playfully. "Hey! Aren't you the one keeps going around saying *zombie apocalypse, remember?*"

One other benefit of having the refinery exploding was that the noise was more than enough to cover the sound of the two generators running. Until then, they'd been careful only to run the generators very briefly and only one at a time. With both of them going they were able to recharge all their batteries—at least, the ones capable of being recharged—cook on all the electric appliances they had—there were four of those—and, best of all from Andy's viewpoint, she could use her laptop without having to worry about running down the battery.

Most of the Internet was down, as she'd expected—more precisely, the sites were still there but obviously hadn't been updated lately—and most of the active sites she could find were apparently military since they were encrypted. Oddly enough, a couple of weather sites were still current. She was relieved to discover that the ten-day predictions indicated rain on a couple of days but no severe thunderstorms. She really wasn't looking forward to experiencing a thunderstorm while perched on top of a huge steel storage tank.

Best of all, though, she was able to write up the Official Rules and Regulations she figured they needed by now, and run them off on her printer. Of course, the Official Rules and Regulations had no official authority backing them up whatsoever, but she figured her chances of getting people to accept them anyway would be improved if they weren't hand-scrawled.

There were two of the notices:

**QUARANTINE REGULATIONS**

*Anyone entering the White Towers compound must set themselves up on an uninhabited tower. NO EXCEPTIONS. Do not visit a neighboring tower and do not exchange items of any kind until a minimum of three weeks has gone by—for both parties—with no sign of illness. This is to ensure that the zombie virus is not spread around.*

*When you first arrive, please register with Alpha Tower. A tower will be assigned to you and you will be provided with a walkie-talkie so you can stay in touch with the other towers.*

She wondered if she should qualify that last part. They only had enough walkie-talkies to equip a total of eight towers with the devices, including their own. But she decided to leave the statement the way it was, since she had no idea how many more groups would show up at the tank farm. There might be none at all, or only one or two.

She consulted with Tom on the second notice.

**ZOMBIE RULES OF ENGAGEMENT**

*NO SHOTGUNS*

*NO PISTOLS OR REVOLVERS*

*NO RIFLES WITHOUT A SCOPE*

*Do not shoot at zombies beyond the fence except on two conditions: They are trying to climb the fence (or dig under it) or they are within 50 yards of the entrance.*

*Do not fire more than three shots at any one zombie. If you can't hit it with three shots, you shouldn't have been shooting at it in the first place.*

*Notify Alpha Tower via walkie-talkie whenever you spot a zombie and ESPECIALLY whenever you plan to take a shot at one.*

*Remember: DON'T BE STUPID. Our best defense against zombies isn't our weapons, it's that they don't notice us in the first place.*

"How much good do you think these'll do?" she asked Rochelle Lewis.

"Hard to say," replied the former restaurant manager. "But if nothing else it'll get everyone who reads it to at least think about what we're saying. All of those so-called 'rules and regulations' are just common sense. Of course, we live in a world where people think 'common sense' justifies the stupidest things you can imagine."

Andy chewed her lip. "What we're going to need, if a lot more people show up, is some sort of government. That way any rules we pass can actually be official instead of just me saying so."

Rochelle shrugged. "I guess. But right now, that'd be a little silly. It's just us and the Vasquezes and poor Jerome. If he survives."

Less than half an hour after that conversation, another caravan pulled into the tank farm. There were five vehicles in this one, including a small bus, and they were just about as well-equipped as the original party.

This new group consisted of four families and several other individuals, all of whom were African-American and all of whom belonged to one of the local African Methodist Episcopal churches. They'd made an attempt to get out of the Chicago area and find sanctuary somewhere in the countryside, but had turned back after a couple of days. The roads were just as hopeless as they'd looked on the TV.

The one place they'd found that initially looked promising turned out not to be. That area of rural Indiana was inhabited entirely by white people whose none-too-racially-tolerant attitudes had been put on steroids by the crisis. The AME group did have a number of guns with them and several of the men were experienced in their use, but they saw no point in getting into an armed confrontation with the local residents. So, they'd turned around and headed back to Lake County.

Their pastor, James Collins, explained that he was in charge of the group. Andy knew what that meant in the real world. While everyone in his congregation listened to him respectfully, the key for him to be able to get anything done was to convince the three very formidable-looking matriarchs with the party that he was right.

That was fine with Andy. She approved of matriarchy and thought the world would be a lot better run place if they'd just put the tough old biddies in charge.

Edith Jones, Yolanda Smith, and Estelle Dubose. She could see them, down there on the ground, looking up at her and obviously taking her measure.

After she got through tossing down a walkie-talkie and a few of the Official Rules and Regulations—and then going over the latter thoroughly, explaining all the reasoning involved—she pointed to a couple of the nearby tanks. "You can take those two, if you'd like."

Ever alert to maintain protocol, Jack piped up, "Those are Delta and Epsilon Towers."

The matriarchs looked at the two towers, then briefly conferred with each other, and then marched over to Pastor Collins and made their wishes known.

"We'll just need the one tower," Collins said firmly, as if he'd made the decision in splendid isolation. "It might be a little crowded, but we'd rather stick together."

They had a total of twenty-six people in their group, eight of whom were children—ten, if you counted the two teenagers. They could all fit on one tower, although depending on how many tents they had, they might be living very cheek-to-jowl.

"Wait a minute," Freddy said. "Let's not make the same mistake we did with the Vasquezes. I won't have time to cut away the bottom part of the staircase, but before you go up there let me weld a lightning rod for you onto the tank."

After the logic behind that was explained, the matriarchs and the pastor shooed their charges off to the side, allowing Freddy to move his welding equipment over to Delta Tower without getting close enough to them for either party to infect the other.

That took a little over two hours, which brought them late enough into the afternoon for Andy—grudgingly, reluctantly, but she did it—to let the expedition take off.

Freddy took Jack in the truck with him. As before, Ceyonne rode behind Eddie on his motorcycle, the two of them scouting ahead.

They were back before sundown, with the truck piled high with a truly weird assortment of goods. The strip mall they'd gone to leaned heavily toward discount stores and had already been picked over pretty thoroughly. So it was understandable that their foraging had been hit or miss.

Many of the items were certainly welcome, especially the toilet paper, blankets, sweaters, bleach and lots of jars of sauerkraut. For whatever reason, the people who'd looted the stores before them had passed up the sauerkraut. Fermented cabbage wasn't Andy's favorite food, by a long shot, but it was quite healthy and would make a welcome change from the steady diet of canned beans, canned corn, rice and processed dry sausage.

But some of the stuff had Andy scratching her head until Freddy or one of the others explained the logic.

Six mattresses, which made sense—but what was the point of all the plastic filing cabinets?

*Put the mattresses on the filing cabinets laid sidewise—and you don't have to worry about getting the mattresses soaked when it rains.*

What good were three big containers of Round-Up with spray wands? They were in the middle of a zombie apocalypse and they were worrying about *weeds*?

*Dump out the herbicide and replace it with water and a cup or so of bleach—and you've got a pretty handy all-purpose disinfectant spray.*

A bunch of folding metal chairs made sense—but why all the

plastic tubs and containers with lids? They wouldn't possibly need to collect *that* much rainwater.

And what in God's name had possessed them to load four big shopping carts on top of the pile?

*Specially designed rooftop toilets. And the shopping carts are for privacy screens, once they're cut up. We're tired of crapping out in the open.*

It was agreed by consultation over the walkie-talkies that the following day Freddy would cut away the bottom part of the staircases leading up to two other towers. Jack promptly labeled them Kappa and Omega, which wasn't maintaining proper alphabetical order but his knowledge of the Greek alphabet was hit-or-miss and it was the best he could manage. Freddy would also weld on lightning rods. After he was done, he'd spray bleach over everything he'd touched or walked on and the AME people and the Vasquezes could relocate from Delta and Gamma—which they'd also sanitize with bleach so that any newcomers could move onto them without too much risk of cross-infection.

At dusk, not long after the nearby street lights came on, the power grid finally went down. A few hours later, when the sun was well below the horizon, the people on the towers got their first experience of just how dark the world could be without electricity and with a new moon in the sky. The only light being provided was coming from the fires still burning in and around the refinery in Whiting. That was a fair amount, actually, but it was miles away.

They did use a few flashlights and lamps in the huts and tents, but Andy insisted that the people standing watch had to make sure that none of the light was leaking out. Any gleam of light was sure to draw zombies, in that darkness.

Andy herself spent a fair portion of the night using the walkie-talkies to consult with Pastor Collins and his three matriarchs, on the one hand, and the Vasquezes on the other. They all agreed that it would be wise to establish an official ruling body so that joint decisions could be made and any new arrivals could be presented with a formally established setup which they were welcome to join but had to obey the rules.

True, there was really no way to enforce those decisions, but they figured that as long as they were obviously common sense people would be willing to abide by them.

So, Andy's previously established "Quarantine Regulations" and "Zombie Rules of Engagement" got formally adopted. And they worked out the language for another set of regulations which Andy then keyed into her laptop and printed up.

**SANITATION RULES**

*Each tower will be provided with a toilet that can be used on a roof. The toilets will include portable sanitation tubs which must be kept covered except when in use. Once a sanitation tub starts getting full, it needs to be lowered off the roof with a hoist and taken to a trench which each tower is responsible for digging for its own use.*

Freddy and his fellow scavengers had brought back enough folding chairs and tubs to make eight toilets. They'd need three right off, for Alpha, Kappa and Omega Towers. Up on Delta, Jerome Bennett was still alive and unturned, although he said he was sick as a dog, but he'd just have to keep making do with a chamber pot until he got better. *If* he got better—but if he didn't, sanitation facilities for him would be a moot point.

If more than five more groups showed up...

Well, they'd deal with that when the time came.

*A shovel will be provided for any tower that needs one.*

Right now, they only had five suitable shovels. But shovels should be easy to find.

*Each sanitation trench has to be at least three feet deep. After you dump the contents of a tub into it, cover it up with dirt. Keep doing that until you need to dig a new trench.*

*Each trench should be at least twenty yards away from your tower and farther than that from anybody else's tower.*

*While someone is digging a trench or emptying a sanitation tub, at least two lookouts have to be maintained on your tower.*

*DO NOT DRAW THE ATTENTION OF ZOMBIES. IF IN DOUBT, LET IT GO UNTIL LATER.*

After she was done, Andy and Tom looked it over and then passed it around to everyone else on Alpha Tower for their input.

"Well, the prose isn't up to the standards of Thomas Jefferson and James Madison," said Rochelle, "but it serves the purpose."

"Fine for them to get all flowery and eloquacious," said Tom. "They were just dealing with redcoats, not zombies."

Jack thought the whole thing was hilarious. "They *never* talk about stuff like this in the movies and TV shows and adventure novels. People fight off alien invasions and extra-dimensional arch-villains and giant prehistoric monsters and nobody craps even *once*."

# 5

The next morning, not long after daybreak, they heard the unmistakable sound of a helicopter approaching. Everyone came out of their tents and shelters and stared up at the oncoming aircraft. The helicopter passed by not more than three hundred feet overhead and then circled back around. Painted on the fuselage was the logo of one of Chicago's news stations.

"Jesus, they're making a racket," said Tom. "Everybody keep an eye out! These idiots will draw every zombie within miles. And they won't all be at the refinery."

The helicopter was now hovering over the tank farm. Freddy was practically hopping up and down, he was so agitated. He kept making gestures at the ground and running his finger across his throat. The meaning of which should have been obvious to anyone: *Land the goddam thing and TURN IT OFF.*

It took a couple of minutes, but finally the helicopter set down on the open area between Alpha and Kappa towers. Unfortunately, the pilot kept the rotors turning while someone hopped down onto the ground.

It was a young woman, and as she approached the tower Andy recognized her.

"That's Karen . . . What's-her-name," said Tom. "You know, the TV news announcer on Channel . . . whatever-it-is."

"Karen Wakefield," Rochelle supplied. "What in God's name is she doing here?"

Remembering the last broadcast they'd watched, Andy said,

"I bet she stayed on the job until the power grid went down. Gutsy lady."

A man got out of the helicopter and came after her, carrying a big video camera. By then, Wakefield had gotten close enough to the base of the tower that Andy shouted down at her.

"Welcome to the White Towers, Ms. Wakefield! But please don't come any closer. We're maintaining strict quarantine measures."

Wakefield stopped and looked up at her. Then, cupping her hands around her mouth, shouted back up, "Can we join you? We don't know where else to go and we're running short of fuel."

Andy pointed to a nearby vacant tower. "You're welcome to use that one, but—"

"That's Phi Tower!" shouted Jack.

Andy waved at him to be silent. "But we haven't got much to offer you. We've got some extra blankets and food we can send down, and some water. We're using all of our tents and sheds, though. It's plenty warm at night, but it's supposed to rain in a couple of days. I don't know what you'll do for shelter."

By then, the AME people had gathered at the edge of their tower. "We can spare a tent," called down Pastor Collins. "It's just a two-person tent, though. How many of you are there?"

"Three," replied Wakefield. "Me and Ken"—she nodded toward the approaching cameraman—"and our pilot, Fred Vecchio. It'll be tight but we'll manage, and thank you all very much."

"Okay, then. Stand over by your tower," Andy instructed her. "We'll bring down the supplies and put them somewhere in the middle. We'll do our best to sanitize the stuff with disinfectant spray, but . . . I'm afraid you'll just have to take your chances."

Freddy now chimed in, very loudly, "*And tell the pilot to shut down the damn helicopter engine! You'll draw zombies!*"

"Too late," said Sam. The young woman pointed at something in the distance, coming down Chicago Avenue.

Andy looked. "Well, shit," she said. A small mob of zombies was approaching them from the east. As they emerged from below the Cline Avenue overpass, she saw that it wasn't that small a mob, either. There were at least fifty of them, with more appearing every second.

The crack of the rifle jarred her. Tom was already in position and starting to fire. But even if he didn't miss a single shot, the zombies would start swarming over the fence very soon—or, still worse, might head down the access road toward the open gate. Tom wouldn't be able to shoot at them for most of that stretch, because other storage tanks and part of the asphalt plant would be in the way.

This was exactly what Andy had always feared the most. Once a mob of zombies got attracted, the sound of gunfire would simply draw more zombies. Soon enough, they'd be buried under a swarm of the monsters.

"Dad!" shouted Ceyonne. "What are you *doing?*"

Turning, Andy saw that Jerome Bennett was coming down the staircase of the tower he'd been perched on. They hadn't seen anything of him for a day and a half, although he'd occasionally spoken to his daughter over the walkie-talkie. He was still very sick—he looked it, too—but at least so far he hadn't turned into a zombie.

Somewhat unsteadily but with obvious determination, Bennett made it to the bottom of the staircase and then started toward his patrol car, which was parked about thirty yards from the tower.

"Dad!" Ceyonne shouted again, now sounding a little hysterical. Her father looked back, waved his hand in a gesture making clear he *did not* want her coming after him, and kept going toward the patrol car.

Ceyonne ignored the gesture and headed toward the staircase of Alpha Tower. She was intercepted before she got there by her boyfriend Eddie, who tried to restrain her.

She wrestled with him for a moment and then started yelling incoherently and punching him. Ceyonne was a big girl and the punches were powerful, but Eddie just got a determined look on his face and kept clinching with her while ignoring the blows as best he could.

Andy looked back at Bennett. The policeman had reached his patrol car and started the engine. Slowly, he drove toward the open gate leading out onto Gary Avenue. By now, just as Andy had feared, the mob of zombies had come down the access road instead of trying to climb the face. They'd reach the gate within a minute.

But as soon as Bennett pulled out of the tank farm and onto Gary Avenue, he turned on his siren and lights. The racket that produced—not to mention the red-and-blue light show—completely distracted the zombies from the sound of the helicopter. Which,

Andy saw when she looked, had finally been shut down by the pilot so it wasn't making any more noise anyway.

Bennett waited until the nearest zombies were only a few yards away and then drove slowly under Cline Avenue, approaching the entrance to I-90.

The zombies went after him. Andy realized what he was planning to do. He'd lead them onto the interstate and then, moving slowly ahead of the mob, take them either toward Ohio or the Illinois state line. Once he got a few miles down the highway, he could speed up and escape them easily and come back to the tank farm after getting off on one of the exits.

Assuming he didn't collapse from being sick.

"Come here, Sam," said Tom.

He laid the Remington down on the shooting bench and backed his wheelchair away. "Pull up a chair," he said. "It's time for you to get some live target practice."

Sam stared at him. Tom pointed at the receding mob of zombies. "Hurry up, girl! They're getting away!"

Sam missed her first two shots, then took out a zombie's leg with the third. From then on, she didn't miss any more shots—seven, in all—until the last zombie was out of sight.

She hadn't killed all of them, of course. So now Tom had her shoot the ones she'd wounded until he was sure they were all dead.

It was a grim exercise. But the nineteen-year-old former waitress seemed to take a fierce satisfaction in the work, and, in any event, Andy knew what her husband was thinking. Between his age and health problems, Tom Kaminski had reached that point in life when a person could die on any given day. Maybe not for years to come, sure—but it could be tomorrow, too.

However short the rest of his life might be, though, he wouldn't be leaving his people unprotected. The guardian angel was training his replacement.

By nightfall, the TV news people were set up on Phi Tower—and were starting to film again.

"We're doing a documentary now," explained Karen Wakefield. "I figure we'll title it *How to Survive a Zombie Apocalypse.* Smile, everyone. Young man, if you carry through with that threat to moon us, just remember you'll be on video foreeeevvver."

Turning, Andy saw that her rambunctious grandson was hastily rebuckling his pants.

"Jack!" she chided him.

"I didn't do anything!"

By then, Jerome Bennett was back. It took him five minutes to climb back onto his tower after he parked the patrol car, but he made it. Without saying a word, he rolled into his tent and was out of sight.

Ceyonne had to be restrained again. By now, her boyfriend was starting to show bruises. He didn't seem to mind too much, though.

Andy wasn't surprised. Eddie was a happy camper, these days. Once Ceyonne's father had set himself up in splendid isolation on Beta Tower, she and Eddie started sharing a tent—after she came to Andy and got a supply of condoms. The girl might be headstrong but she wasn't foolish.

The next day, another caravan entered the tank farm. It was the largest one yet, at least in terms of people. There were only three vehicles, but one of them was a bus, whose distinctive red-white-blue paint stripes and *CTA* logo announced that it was—or had been, anyway—the property of the Chicago Transit Authority. It turned out that one of the members of the group was the bus driver and he'd seen no point in returning the vehicle to the compound once the catastrophe started getting completely out of hand. Instead, he picked up his family in the bus along with the supplies he and his wife had put together. Then, after adding two of the neighboring families, he'd driven to his church and more-or-less shanghaied the two priests who'd been there along with the dozen or so people who'd come for sanctuary. Those who couldn't fit into the bus after they loaded everything in the church that might be of use crammed into the priests' two cars.

Being an enthusiastic gambler, the bus driver—Harry O'Malley, he was called, and he looked the spitting image of a red-headed Irishman—led everyone out of Chicago, across the Skyway, and into the enormous parking structure of one of the big casinos by the lake. O'Malley figured the parking structure would be ignored by zombies since there was no food source in it, and it was so big that as long as they stayed in a far corner in one of the upper floors, they'd go unnoticed.

His plan worked for a few days. But then a car full of gangbangers showed up and tried to rob the bus. O'Malley was an ex-Marine as well as a hunter and three of the other men in their party were also well-armed. The gangbangers were too arrogant—or too desperate, after being on the run from zombies—to plan their assault. They just came swaggering up to the bus, brandishing their pistols, before two of them got cut down by the ensuing hail of gunfire and the other three ran off into the casino.

Which . . . turned out to be full of zombies. So, back they came into the parking lot—two of them; apparently the third had become a zombie snack—and exchanged more gunfire with the people in the bus.

The gangbangers got the worst of that exchange, as well. The one uninjured survivor raced off to parts unknown while his now-lamed companion got swarmed by the zombies who'd followed them out of the casino into the parking structure.

Got swarmed by *some* of the zombies. Most of them came toward the bus—which had to make its own hurried departure, trailed by the two priests' cars.

They'd then spent a day trying to get out of the area, which was made especially difficult by the refinery burning nearby. They'd just happened to be coming down Chicago Avenue when one of their number spotted the people perched on the oil storage tanks.

They set themselves up on Sigma and Pi Towers. Which put Jack's back against the wall because that exhausted his knowledge of the Greek alphabet and if anybody else showed up . . .

## 6

The following day, two more family groups showed up. Jack threw in the towel and announced that their towers would be Tango and Foxtrot.

"Since when do you know how to dance?" Ceyonne demanded. "And if we're gonna start naming towers after dances, why are you picking ones from the Stone Age?"

Jack spent the next several minutes in a long-winded and convoluted explanation that basically came down to "Because." But

Ceyonne let it go. Her dad was finally starting to move around and said he was feeling better—and still wasn't a zombie.

The next day, defying any and all to stop her, Ceyonne moved from Alpha Tower to join her father on Beta Tower. She insisted that by now he couldn't still be contagious and he obviously wasn't going to turn into a zombie, but he was still a sick man and needed help from his family—which meant her.

Eddie was not thrilled, to put it mildly. He offered to accompany her, but...

"Do I have this straight?" asked Ceyonne. "You want to keep sharing a tent with me right next to my cop dad? Well, you may be crazy but I'm not."

She patted her boyfriend on the cheek. "Don't sweat it. A week or two from now if I'm not sick either, I can come back over here for a visit, every other day or so."

She looked around. By now, the hodgepodge of tents and tool sheds that provided shelter for all the people on Alpha Tower had been melded together by a crazy-quilt of plastic sheeting and tablecloths from the diner held down by what looked to be a couple of tons of duct tape and designed to simultaneously shed rainfall and collect it in drinking containers. Ceyonne had seen a photograph once of slums in one of the big cities in Brazil—*favelas,* they were called, if she remembered right—and the housing on top of the storage tank sort of reminded her of that. Gamma, Sigma and Phi Towers were even more extreme.

"In this rabbit warren," she said cheerfully, "we can get laid without my dad being any the wiser. But not over on Beta. I'm not even sure where I'm going to sleep over there myself, since we've run out of tents."

Rochelle provided the solution to that problem. As did every adult in their group, she'd spent time looking out for zombies with the binoculars. In the course of doing so, she'd noticed a wooden shed on the grounds of the asphalt plant that formed much of the southern boundary of the tank farm.

"We'll use that," she announced. "Freddy, Jack, Eddie—get the truck and let's move the shed up on Beta Tower. If we have to, we'll dismantle it first."

"Ceyonne doesn't need anything that big," Jack protested. "That shed looks *heavy.* And it's probably full of tools."

"Good, we can use more tools," Rochelle said, in the same tone of voice which in times past had quelled incipient unrest on the part of waitresses, cooks and dishwashers alike. "And it won't just be Ceyonne because I'm going with her. She and I can share the shed."

"Why are *you* going?" asked Andy.

Rochelle spent the next several minutes in a long-winded and convoluted explanation that basically came down to "Because." But Andy was sure the real reason was that Rochelle was looking to the future—which they were all starting to do, at least a little. Now that it seemed fairly certain that Jerome Bennett was going to survive the flu and remain human, she'd figured out that he'd make a nice partner for a single woman about the same age. If she didn't dilly-dally.

Andy wasn't concerned. Rochelle Lewis was nothing if not sensible. Should something start to develop, she'd come to Andy for a supply of condoms before any problems arose.

And wasn't that something of a wonder? Here she was, Andrea Kaminski, sixty-eight years old and one of the tough old biddies who more or less ran the White Towers settlement. (Harry O'Malley had brought his mother, his aunt, and his grandmother in the bus and not one of them wasn't up to snuff.) And she was worrying about having to deliver babies before they were ready to handle the problem.

Things were looking up, sure enough. All they had to do now was last another three or four months until winter arrived.

That would be a *Chicago* winter, with temperatures regularly below freezing and sometimes dropping down to zero—even below it, on occasion—and the wind cutting like a saber. She didn't think the naked monsters would last very long under those conditions.

Zombie apocalypse, wimps and whiners called it. No wonder the archangels weren't bothering to show up. Let the junior varsity handle it.

# Staying Human

JODY LYNN NYE

Nora Fulton lay on the cold dirt and leaned over the sight of her rifle. *Turn, you bastard! Turn!*

She had spotted the gaunt naked man through the thick trees while he was hunting the squirrel he now gnawed. He was the right size and shape, and his pasty white ass and reddish hair fit the colors of the man she wanted to kill.

*Turn!*

She raised her head to glance around for her partner, Lou Hammond. She spotted his broad, dark forehead, and wide black eyes as dark as hers just peering over a fallen log. He caught her glance, and nodded. If she didn't take him with the first shot, he would finish the job.

A crack, as if of a branch that had broken off in the wind, made all of them jump. The zombie turned, squirrel guts hanging from his jaws, and stared wild-eyed in the direction of the noise. Nora moaned, but she squeezed her finger on the trigger. The man dropped.

Lou scrambled out from his hiding place and came to stand beside her and looked down at the corpse with its shattered skull leaking brilliant red blood and corrupted gray and purple brains.

"You got him?" he asked.

Nora shook her head. Her stomach felt like it had crept up her throat. It took her a minute to get her voice back.

"It's not him. It's just some other poor soul."

"Well, waste not, want not," Lou said. He unfolded a body bag from his backpack and laid it on the ground, then pulled on a bright yellow temporary hazmat suit. "C'mon. We don't have a bunch of time before other zombies hear the shot and come running."

"I know." Nora put her gun down and put on her own protective gear. She wound her long dark braid up into the cap before she brought the hood down and settled the clear panel in front of her face. They checked each other's fastenings to make sure there was no chance of exposure to the stinking body. Taking the time to yank the spine would leave them exposed too long in the woods without backup. Better let the team back at the lab dissect it out. She sent up an apology to the spirits for this man's soul, and thanked God that he would be able to help a lot of people with his earthly remains.

She passed by a tree whose upper branches were heavy with fruit just about ripe. It was September fifth. That had been her wedding anniversary, her and Troy's. Eight years. She had hoped she could give him a memorial that day by killing the bastard who had killed him. Not yet, though. Not yet.

They set out down the crest for the Foresight Genetics compound. Nora kept a dozen paces behind Lou's comforting yellow bulk, her shotgun cocked and leveled, scanning the woods as they went. With the coming of dusk, the zombies were moving around again, looking for food. Every so often they found a few unlucky people who thought by holding out in the hills above Nashville that they'd be safe. Most of the time, the zombies caught deer and rabbits. She'd seen the corpses of the ones that had taken on raccoons or coyotes. The claw marks and bites were deeper than anything that a human being could inflict on one another. Nora hated to think it served them right, but it did. Her Choctaw grandmother had told her that harboring feelings of revenge did more harm to her spirit than to her enemies, but Nora refused to let go. Not until that zombie was dead.

The arrival that morning of the government helicopter to pick up the weekly load of vaccine had brought the zombies out of hiding. A whole group of zombies had tried to batter their way in through the compound gate. The electric fence took care of a couple of them. The volunteers and Homeland Security people shot as many of the rest as they could and drove off the remainder. Management sent teams out to clean up survivors. When the cameras had picked up this man, with his red hair, Nora insisted that he would be their quarry.

Rustling in the bushes put her on higher alert. She and Lou had been vaccinated, once, but the immunologist on staff reminded them that they still needed another shot in a couple of days. Nora dreaded the effects of a bite, but she was determined to take down that red-headed zombie.

If it hadn't been for footage on their security system that Sid had insisted on installing in their house up in the hills, she would never have known what had happened to him and their son. Nora still cursed the day that she had had to stay overnight to monitor an experiment. It was common practice for any of the scientists, but her timing had been fateful. When she had called down to see how things were going, a neighbor had answered the phone, weeping. Nora had downloaded the contents of the security cameras off the web, before they went down for good. The zombie that had attacked Sid and Charlie on their own doorstep had been their longtime mailman. The bastard had even grinned up at the camera as if he knew she would see it.

The news reports were way behind the pace of the zombie epidemic. It had spread so fast that whole communities were wiped out in a matter of weeks. The police, what was left of them, advised her to stay where she was.

Foresight Genetics had always been a leader in research. They had several facilities in Tennessee, mostly centered in Nashville, but that had become a no-go area fairly early on. To her horror, Nora had watched an otherwise dignified corporate executive and scientist strip out of her clothes and go crazy while on an Internet conference call.

Luckily, Nora's facility had been situated on the edge of the city, not in the center of town, where everyone at the Grand Old Opry or any of the tourist sites became infected or died in a matter of days. The management of Foresight Genetics lived up to their name and moved their electron microscopes and centrifuges, along with the scientists and technicians to run them, and anyone else who had remained uninfected, out of the city, up to a small factory on the ridge northwest of Nashville that was powered by a dynamo in the river below. When the grid went down, they could still keep running. Foresight was one of the facilities tapped by the government from the Hole to stop every other project and work on a vaccine. Along with her fellow technicians, Nora had junked all her precious experiments and started to work on isolating and eradicating the bloodborne pathogen.

Lou had a similar horror story to tell. His wife and kids were returning from visiting her parents in Denver on a Greyhound bus. They came back infected. Lou had been lucky to escape a few days later with his life when all of them turned at once. He had set up a cot behind his desk in Receiving and refused to talk with anyone for days.

As a result, all of them had cringed when they got on the heavily guarded bus to take them up to the new facility, cleaned out and secured by grim-faced soldiers who wouldn't talk about their experiences, either. They collected as many family members and stragglers as they could who showed no signs of bites or symptoms. Only a couple disappeared in the first few days. No one talked about what had happened to them. Denesa Campbell, head of Human Services, took over organizing child care and housing. People who had lost loved ones paired off or created ad hoc family groups. Someone brought in a few chickens, five cats, nine dogs and a goat.

Using human spinal tissue for the vaccine weighed heavily on everyone's conscience. The management did their best to deal with the ethics, offering counseling and advice to the researchers and other staff. In the end, they established a parallel research track. Half the facility would keep on with vaccine manufacture, but Foresight would begin working to develop a treatment to give humans immunity against the microorganism that didn't require anyone to die for their manufacture. In the meantime, the zombies, unaware anyone cared that they used to be human, kept on hammering at the perimeter, trying to get at Foresight's employees to turn them or eat them.

Nora had been squeamish at first about the formula for the vaccine, but came to terms with it in short order. She thought it was hypocritical of the others to wail on and on about the source of tissue, when each of them going through high school and college biology, not to mention previous research programs, had sacrificed dozens, if not hundreds, of rats, guinea pigs, hamsters, even chimpanzees, in the name of science. This wasn't just science; it was survival. On a personal and spiritual level, she had been horrified beyond belief to have to kill people. An eye for an eye was a bad idea and bad practice. Wiping out a predator was not. When management had asked for volunteers to help defend the compound and bring in more "samples," Nora sucked it up and stepped forward. She had brought down her first buck at eleven. Mild-tempered Lou, from the middle of Indianapolis, turned out to have hunted rabbits with his granddaddy from the time he had been a tot. He couldn't kill the person who had caused his family's deaths, but he had volunteered to help wipe out the zombies around the compound.

They'd eyed each other askance when management teamed them up, the skinny little half-Choctaw woman and the big African-American man, but they turned out to be a good team. Her small, lithe figure allowed her to slip in between trees and rocks to take tricky shots. Lou never ran out of energy, and he was strong enough to haul a body on his shoulder for miles. They never talked about their mutual losses. It was just too painful. At least, they could do something to avenge them.

When they were a couple hundred yards out, they were in range for the radios to work. Nora clicked on her walkie-talkie and spoke against the hiss.

"Nora and Lou with a delivery."

"Gotcha."

The National Guardswoman on duty at the gate saw them coming and put out the call to the others. As soon as they got inside, two technicians with a gurney were waiting to take their kill. Gratefully, Lou and Nora stripped off their plastic suits and tossed them into the incinerator pit on top of a pile of yellow already there. That part of the lot was fenced off to keep the facility's flock of chickens from falling in or getting contaminated. Eggs and the occasional stewing hen were important sources of healthy protein for the inhabitants.

"Everyone else come back already?" Nora asked Brenda Hatton, one of her fellow lab rats, as they followed the wheeled table into the main building.

"Most of 'em are still out," the heavy-set young woman said. "Courtland Jones got bit. He's in isolation."

"How bad?"

"Dunno," Brenda said, her hazel eyes welling with tears. "He's only had the same one inoculation that the rest of us have. I hope he makes it." Nora squeezed the young woman's shoulder with sympathy. Brenda nodded. Everyone knew the risks.

She tossed her head in the direction of the side door, short blond braids swinging. "There's some chicken stew in the cafeteria, and fresh sweet tea. Y'all can go get some, but management wants to see you right after."

Nora exchanged a glance with Lou. "Anything wrong?"

"Not wrong," Brenda said. She grinned, an expression few of them saw those days. "Maybe right. Lincoln's got a breakthrough, he thinks. Go on and eat. Management will bring you up to speed soon's you finish."

"Hey, come and sit down!" Management, in the person of Lincoln Fairbrun, had held the whole group together for the last few months. He was a tall man, with weather-beaten, creased red skin, a high forehead and a little fringe of brown hair mixed with gray on top. For the first time, Nora saw how the strain all of them had been carrying was telling on their boss. His little sleeping room, the only real office he had anymore, smelled of stale tobacco. It was a polite fiction that nobody smoked anymore. Cigarettes from abandoned houses were almost as prized as untainted food. He played with a burned-out, crushed stub at the melamine table. A raft of folded metal chairs leaned against the wall. Only three were unfolded, including the one he sat in. He wasn't expecting anybody else.

"What's up, sir?" Lou asked, holding one of the chairs for Nora, then sliding into the last.

Management's gray eyes, swallowed up in nests of wrinkles, held a light. "Paul and Sarah are pretty sure they've got a working bacteriophage. It's one that normally goes after blood parasites. They've adapted some that seem to attack the microorganism. They're working to develop enough for ongoing therapy. If this works out, it could stop the zombie plague in its tracks."

Nora felt hope rising in her soul. "That's great news, sir! Do you need us to help them?"

Management waved his hand. "Not much you can do. I've got

volunteers already to staff every shift and watch its development. If this was happier times, we'd be waiting to get approval from the FDA for animal testing. But it isn't."

"No, sir," Nora said. She narrowed her eyes at Fairbrun. "What do you need from us?"

Management sighed. "These are desperate times, Nora. We've got a couple of hunters who have been bit, and we'll try the therapy on them. We need subjects for testing. Live subjects."

"Bullshit, man," Lou said, his eyes burning with fury. "You want us to bring zombies into the only place maybe in the state where there aren't any?"

Fairbrun threw up his hands. "We have to be able to observe them, Lou. If we treat and release, we can't track their progress. They could get eaten by other zombies. They could go into spontaneous remission that has nothing to do with the treatment. We need to know."

"These people are murderers," Nora said. "You know—" She stopped talking as tears filled her eyes and throat. Fairbrun reached over and took her hand.

"I know what I'm asking. We might be able to save a lot more people, reverse this plague. Six of the others have agreed to try to bring back live, er, specimens. You're the best team we've got out there. Will you help?"

Nora turned to look into Lou's eyes. He was torn. So was she. But to be able to go home, or to what was left of home, was something she ached for. She nodded. Her heart was full of anger and resentment, but it was a way forward.

"Good. Julian is leading the pack. Get some sleep. We'll start out at dawn, when the alphas are still out."

"Did you sleep?" she asked Lou the next morning, as they gathered in the predawn chill. The eight hunters and volunteers from among the nonemployees stood in the front lot near the gate, along with the six hunting hounds who had been among the dogs brought in. At least the dogs looked eager.

The big man's face looked slack with exhaustion. "No, but does it matter?"

"I guess not," Nora said. Julian Ferrar, a stocky man with silvering hair and tawny skin who ran the electron microscopy lab, handed out ammunition and stun guns.

"Shoot to kill only if you're threatened," he said. "We need survivors. Try not to get bit, okay? You're at your most vulnerable as the pathogen load dips in your bloodstream. Tomorrow everyone lines up for their second dose of vaccine. I don't want anyone to have to get stuck in isolation next to the specimens."

*Specimens.* No one was going to call them what they were: captive infected people to be used as laboratory experiments.

"How many of 'em do you want?" asked Patricia Strauss, belting her hazmat suit tight. The slim woman had been head receptionist and administrative assistant to Management, but she was a good shot.

"No more than twenty. No fewer than twelve. Truss 'em. We'll haul them back in the bus into Shipping. Daniel's got cages set up that ought to hold them. We ride the Jeeps."

"Can we shoot to wound?" Ricky Pirelli asked. He was a big man whose beard was usually confined in a hairnet. Like Nora, he worked as a senior lab technician.

Julian glanced around at his hunting party, and nodded sharply. "Let's go."

The situation called for the use of the company vehicles, and as much of the precious supply of diesel as it took. Nora and Lou boarded a jeep with Julian and Pat and two of the dogs. A big brown Basset hound flopped itself across her lap and demanded petting.

They drove down the ridge road as the sky started to turn deep blue. A waning moon was in the western sky over the treetops. The sky smelled fresh, with no bitter, sharp scent of decaying flesh or urine from the zombies.

All that changed as they descended into the river valley. The zombies needed water, a lot of it, and they made more mess than a million pigeons. Broken branches, scattered rocks and other debris blocked the main road into Nashville. Abandoned cars showed how effective the obstruction had been at trapping victims for the alphas to carry off. Nora and the others rarely came down this way. They would be too badly outnumbered. She shook with nerves.

"Now, remember, we don't have to get them all today," Julian cautioned them as they drove. "Get in, get out alive."

"Got it," Nora and Lou chorused.

"Here we go."

He had a boombox strapped to the front of the Jeep. As they hurtled down the hill, twangy country music rang out, echoing from point to point in the valley. Even as little as six months ago, the sound would have been swallowed up by the noise of traffic and a million other sounds of modern life. That day, that and the engine roars broke upon the ear like the last trump.

And it brought out the zombies, just as Management had said it would. Before they drove two miles, a group of filthy naked people broke out of the undergrowth and pelted after them. The second Jeep screeched around in a bootlegger's turn and drove straight for the trio. Mike and his squad leaped out, yelling. Several of the zombies continued to run for the uninfected humans, seeing a potential meal. Julian brought his car around, too, seeking to herd the zombies toward the approaching bus. He slowed down enough for Pat, Nora and Lou to leap out.

Zombies might not be strictly human anymore, but they weren't stupid. They saw that they were outnumbered. The smallest, a woman with a slack belly and pendulous breasts, one badly bitten and infected, tried to make a break for it. Pat went after her, brandishing the stun gun. The woman dodged away from her, hissing like a cat. Pat triggered the stun gun, sending a crackling blue tongue out like a whip. The woman shrieked as the electricity hit her. She leaped for Pat, jagged nails out. Pat dodged her until the stunner regenerated enough for a second charge. Another blast of lightning, and the woman dropped on the road. Troy Stokes and Brenda piled out of the bus and went to collect her, careful to bind up her hands with wire ties before she came to.

The three men, crusted with feces and scabs, looked like they had once been in good enough shape to be athletes or soldiers. Nora thought the latter was more likely, since they worked together like a pack of wolves. Once they figured out the humans weren't trying to kill them outright, they feinted here and there at the circle of hunters, looking for a way out. Mike had a stun gun in his left hand and a Luger in his right. He sent a tongue of lightning lashing out toward the biggest of the males. The stream missed, but it blinded all of the humans long enough for the zombies to rush at Julian, who was at their three o'clock. They brought him down on the pavement, tearing at his suit. Lou, Nora and the others rushed to try and drag them off.

The zombies might be naked, but they still had fingernails and teeth. The male sitting on Julian's chest gnawed at the neck of the hazmat suit and clawed at the yellow plastic, shrieking with hunger. Lou raised the butt of his rifle and brought it down on the creature's head. The zombie slid sideways at the last minute, so Lou's blow hit him in the shoulder. It lashed out at him. The big man jumped backward. The second zombie leaped off Julian and grabbed Lou around the legs. Lou fell sideways. His rifle hit the ground with a clatter, but he never let go of it. He and the zombie struggled. The dogs circled, snarling. The Basset hound closed its teeth on the zombie's arm and shook it. The zombie wailed. It bit at Lou's face, arms, chin, anything within reach. Nora moved around, looking for an opening to strike the man in the head. When he came up with a mouthful of yellow plastic, Nora swung the butt of her gun right in his face. CRUNCH! The zombie dropped backward, its eyes wide open, blood streaming out of its nose and mouth.

"I killed him!" Nora cried, disappointed in herself.

"Good for you," Lou grunted, pushing the body off. He stood up. "Thanks, little sister."

"Goddamn bastards!" Mike said. He rushed in and tased the third infected male. It quivered and fell over. Ricky kicked the body aside and heaved at the first zombie under its arms.

The male twisted in his hands like an eel, kicked him in the belly, and ran for the pine trees. Ricky looked at his empty hands in surprise. Nora, feeling that she had let the team down, dashed after the fleeing zombie. Lou and Pat pelted after her.

"Come back, Nora!" Lou shouted.

The sun was starting to rise above the ridge. She could see that the zombies' path was an old animal trail that led down to the river. The brush was thin enough to step over or plunge through. She didn't want the zombie to escape. He was yards ahead of them, taking the slope with insane leaps like his tail had been lit on fire. The shadows were tricky, though. She was a good woodswoman, but she had to slow down or break a leg.

"Let him go," Pat called out to her. "We got two! Come on, honey. Let's get back to the others."

"Dammit!" Nora said. But her mind was cooling off. They turned around and headed uphill toward the blaring music. Lou led the way, brushing aside branches with his big arms and holding them for Pat and Nora to pass. He was a good man. If this went on long enough to get lonely, she would ask if he wanted to be a couple with her.

The path thinned down and diverged into a half dozen gaps in the greenery about twenty yards from the road. Lou made for the loudest noise, beyond a bunch of bushes.

As he pushed past a massive red oak, a skinny arm looped down out of the branches and grabbed him around the neck. With amazing strength, it hauled Lou off his feet. He kicked, trying to free himself. The arm hauled upward. Lou's rifle dropped to the ground.

Pat screamed. They ran to take his legs and pull, but he disappeared up out of their reach. Through the leaves, Nora saw glinting eyes, one pair after another. At least three other alphas had been waiting there. They hauled Lou upward. He flailed and kicked at his captors.

"Help!" she screamed. "They've got Lou!"

"We're coming!" Julian bellowed.

Luckily, no other trees stood close enough that the zombies could escape. They had to come down, but what would they do to Lou in the meantime?

Nora slung her gun over her shoulder and climbed after them. The red oak was thick and broad. Its rippled gray bark had plenty of hand- and footholds, obviously why the zombies had chosen it as their lookout. If it had been a month later, she could have taken a shot at the zombies and been sure of missing Lou, but the foliage was so heavy she could only see movement through the gaps.

The branches were thicker than her arms as steady as the earth, so she might as well have been climbing up stairs. She had spent plenty of years clambering around in the trees on her family's property with her brother and sister.

"Do you see them?" Pat shouted.

"Yeah! Up about thirty feet," Nora called back. She felt for another handhold.

"Go back down there!" Lou yelled. The zombies had dragged him up to the highest branch that would support them and hung him over the branch on his belly. Nora counted four, all men, their filthy hides soiling the sunlight that touched them. One of them leered down at her, grinning. His red hair was caked with blood and dust, but she would never in her life forget that face.

"It's him!" she screamed. She braced herself on the branch under her feet and brought her gun up and around. The zombie mailman was no fool. As soon as he saw her rifle barrel, he moved up behind Lou. "The one who killed my family!"

"Damned fools for going up there where they can't get out," Mike said, moving around the oak's huge bole. The dogs quested back and forth, some of them leaping for the lower branches. The odor of zombie excited them into a frenzy.

"It'd be smart if there were only a couple of us," Julian said. "They could jump down on any side and run away before we could catch them."

"Help me!" Nora shouted. "We have to save Lou!"

"We're working on it, darlin'," Julian called. "Somebody go get Troy. He's got the beanbag gun."

The big man was fighting to free himself. He had to choose between keeping his hazmat suit or his balance, and decided on the latter. One of the zombies yanked the yellow hood off with a triumphant howl. Lou scooted away on the branch and set his back against the tree trunk. The zombies clambered around like monkeys, making the same kind of hoots and grunts they did in the zoo. They made grabs for his face and ears. He bellowed as one of them gashed his cheek with a handful of ragged fingernails.

Nora couldn't stand it any longer. She levered the gun to her shoulder and fired. The zombie that had scratched Lou gasped and dropped. He plummeted down through the branches, narrowly missing her. The body landed among the dogs, who swarmed over it.

The other zombies paid no attention to the fall of their neighbor. Lou took advantage of the distraction to swing down to the next branch and try to escape.

"Come on!" Nora shouted. "I'll cover you."

"I'm doing my best," he said. The gash ran with blood. The zombies followed him avidly, trying to bite him. When she cocked her gun, the naked males' heads perked up, and they scattered to hide behind branches. Nora tried to keep track of the trio, but they moved like squirrels. Lou gripped the trunk with both arms as he sought for a place to put his foot. Going up was a lot easier than coming down.

A shadow fell over his left shoulder.

"Look out!" she shouted, and raised the gun. One of the

zombies, hanging head down, tried to hook Lou around the neck. His skinny chest was exposed for a perfect shot. Nora went to pull the trigger.

The gun flew up out of her hands. She looked up. The mailman grinned down at her and swung the rifle at her like a bludgeon. Nora turned her head just in time not to take the stock full in the face. The blow to the side of her head made her ear ring.

Another ringing sound echoed through the narrow valley. A body hurtled downward past her. Nora shook her head to try and clear it.

"Got him!" Troy cried.

When Nora got her wits back, she peered down through the leaves. The mailman lay unconscious among the milling dogs. Troy lifted the beanbag gun and aimed through the leaves, tracking yet another zombie. He fired, and the zombie attacking Lou dropped like a rock. On the ground, Brenda strapped the zombies' arms and legs with the long plastic ties.

"Come on down here," Julian said, beckoning. "C'mon, I'll catch you."

Nora clutched the bark with hands running with sweat under her protective gloves. Mike caught her and swung her off the tree as if she was a child. When he set her down, Pat came to pull her into a comforting hug.

"You okay?" she asked.

Nora looked up. "Not yet." But as soon as Lou had dropped off the last branch and hit the ground, she ran to him and threw her arms around him. She felt his heart pounding hard in his chest. Then he put his arms around her, too. He dropped a kiss on top of her hood.

"It's okay, little girl. We both lived, this time."

The last zombie didn't give a damn about its fellows, but it understood that it was defenseless. It had no intention of being a target for the big gun. Screaming like a chimpanzee, it fled up into the crown of the tree and vanished among the foliage.

Julian shook his head. "We're not gonna get him. But we got four. That's a good start. Management'll have to be happy with that. Sun's up. Every other zombie is gonna be hiding out until dusk. Let's go back."

Mike shooed the dogs to one side and picked up their rifles. "Thought you'd like to have these back," he said.

Nora almost snatched hers out of his hands. "You had better believe I would," she said.

She marched over to the red-headed zombie. Brenda had rolled him onto his belly and hogtied him so he couldn't run away. When he saw Nora coming, he grinned up at her. Nora lowered the barrel of her gun until the mouth was touching the zombie's forehead.

Julian came over and touched her lightly on the arm.

"You don't want to do that, honey," he said.

"I sure do," she said. "I've been looking for this bastard for months."

"Step back a moment," he said. "This man's a human being."

"No, he's not!" Nora screamed. All the horror of the security footage from her home came bursting back in her memory. Her husband and son, torn to pieces. "He's a monster!"

Lou stepped up and crouched down beside the struggling zombie. The creature tried to bite him. Lou stayed out of reach.

"You could shoot him," he said, looking up at her with the blood still wet on his cheek. "But that's not you. You don't kill out of vengeance. You're sorry for every one of these zombies you've had to shoot. An eye for an eye's wrong, remember? This is how you know you're still a human being. Not like them."

Nora's eyes filled with tears. Charlie. Sid. She squeezed her eyes shut and let the hot drops spill down her cheeks. He was right. Badly as she wanted to take revenge, it wasn't decent, and it wasn't necessary. She was better than that.

"Let the scientists use him. If he dies, it won't be your fault. It'll be because the microorganism killed him. You'll get justice. One way or another."

"All right," Nora said. She lowered the gun and handed it to Lou. Then she brought her heavy boot back and kicked the zombie square in his face. Blood spurted from his nose. She kept on kicking him until the grin no longer looked like the grin in her memory. She turned away into the embrace of Lou's other arm. "Let them have him now."

# On the Wall

JOHN SCALZI & DAVE KLECHA

"Hi, Jim."

"Hi, Keith. What's up?"

"I'm here to take the watch with you tonight."

"... You."

"Yeah."

"Taking a watch."

"Yes."

"On the *wall*."

"I've done it before."

"Yeah, I remember."

"It wasn't *my* fault we had a breach."

"That's what the ruling was, yes."

"Then there's no problem."

"Where's Jenna? She's supposed to have watch with me tonight."

"She's in the infirmary."

"What happened to her?"

"She broke her foot."

"How did she do that?"

"*She* didn't do it. Brandon did. Accidentally dropped a big ol' pot of beans on her foot in the kitchen."

"How bad is it?"

"Doc Kumar wants to keep her in the infirmary overnight to make sure there are no complications. Should be up and hobbling about tomorrow. But in the meantime she can't take the watch."

"You don't have anything else you could be doing."

"I don't know how to break it to you, but it's not like we have much need of a communications watch these days."

"You could be monitoring the solar panels."

". . . It's *night*, Jim."

"They might need maintenance."

"Which is Brenda's job, actually. I'm just her helper monkey."

"She might need help."

"And if she does she'll let me know. Or she'll let Amy know, since Amy is also her helper monkey, when she's not otherwise busy."

"Fine."

"Is there an actual problem here, Jim?"

"No."

"Really?"

"The scavenger group that went out today saw a lot of active movement when they were out there."

"We know the town's got a lot of scurriers in it. That's not news."

"They said it wasn't just scurriers. Roxie says she thinks she saw some runners. And she thinks some of them might have followed them home."

"Have you seen anything yet?"

"No."

"So it might be nothing."

"It might be nothing. But that's not the smart way to think about it."

"So you're worried about some runners making a sprint for the compound."

"Yes."

"And you're worried about me because the last time we had a breach I was on the wall, even though what happened wasn't my fault."

"I didn't say that."

"No, you're just implying the *shit* out of it, Jim."

"You don't stand on the wall much, Keith. That's all."

"No, I don't. Some of us don't. But you know the rules. No one stands a watch alone."

"Yes."

"Well, there's no one else to stand the watch with you right now."

"Where's Corrine?"

"She's in the auto shop. The Wrangler is having issues again. She'll be there all night."

"Fred."

"Sleeping. He's got the next watch."

"Andre."

"Come on, Jim. Give it a rest. I'm here. You need someone on the wall with you. If you want to complain, then take it up with The Boss. But you know what she's going to say. She's going to tell you to tuck your balls back in and deal with it."

"She wouldn't say that."

"I heard her say that to Eric just the other day."

"Eric's a whiner."

"And what do you think The Boss would categorize complaining about a watch partner as?"

". . . Point taken."

"I thought so."

"When was the last time you slept?"

"I got enough sleep last night. I'll be good to the end of watch."

"You sure? Coffee's scarce."

"I don't drink coffee anyway. I'll be fine."

"You don't drink coffee?"

"No. Never have."

"Some sort of religious thing?"

"I just don't like coffee. So I don't drink it."

"That's kind of weird."

"It's not that weird."

"It's a little weird."

"Well, I have some bad news for you, Jim. Soon enough, no one's going to drink coffee anymore."

"Jim, I can't help but notice something."

"What's that."

"You have a gun and I don't."

"It's not a *gun*. It's a rifle."

"It's a gun. Technically it's a gun."

"It's a rifle."

"Which is a type of gun. If we still had Wikipedia I could look it up and prove it to you."

"You would be the sort of person who would say Wikipedia was authoritative about something."

"Pretty sure the 'Gun' entry wasn't contentiously edited. And you're missing my point. A rifle is a type of gun."

"That's like saying that technically, you're a mammal."

"There's no technically about it. I *am* a mammal."

"I mean that describing you only as a mammal would be sufficiently accurate."

"Depends on the conversation."

"Fine. In this conversation, 'gun,' is not *sufficiently accurate.* I have a rifle."

"And I don't, which is what I was getting at. I don't have a rifle. Or a handgun. Or a blunderbuss, for that matter. I don't have a gun."

"You don't need one."

"I'm on the wall."

"So?"

"So when I've been on the wall before, I had a gun."

"You didn't need it then, either."

"What if a bunch of runners come at the wall? That's happened before. We both know that."

"What did you do when the breach happened?"

"I yelled 'Breach!' and then other people took care of it, because I didn't leave my post."

"Right. One, you did the right thing by staying at your post, and two, you didn't need a rifle."

"But I *might* have."

"What would you have done with it?"

"Well, if I had seen the runner before it was up to the wall and inside it, I would have shot it."

"You would have shot it."

"Sure."

"You shoot much?"

"What do you mean?"

"Before all this. Did you shoot much? Go to the range? Go hunting?"

"I didn't hunt. I didn't see the point. Supermarkets existed for a reason."

"Did you go shoot at a range?"

"I went to one once for a friend's birthday party. Five or six years ago. Shot a Glock."

"How'd you do?"

"I hit the paper."

"How many times?"

". . . Once."

"Okay. What kind of rifle is this?"

"It's a military rifle."

"You might as well call it a gun."

"I *did* call it a gun, if you recall."

"What kind of military rifle is it? It an M4? An M14? An AK-47?"

"AK-47."

"Wrong. It's an M16."

"That was a trick question."

"It wasn't a trick question."

"It was a trick question. You didn't list 'M16' as an option."

"The point is if you knew which rifle it was, you would have known none of those options were correct."

"We need a judge's ruling on that."

"Since you don't know what kind of rifle this is, it's a pretty good guess you don't know anything about it."

"That's not necessarily true."

"What sort of ammunition does it shoot?"

"Bullets."

"It shoots 5.56 NATO rounds."

"I think you're making that up."

"I'm not making it up."

"You're doing that Star Trek thing where they give a bullshit name to a brand new subatomic particle."

"5.56 NATO round. Do you know anything about the 5.56 round?"

"It disrupts a tachyon field when you hit a deflector dish with it."

"The 5.56 NATO round is one of the most common rounds in the world. We used it in the M16, and the M4, and the M249. The British used it in the SA80. Germany used it in the G36. The French used it in the FAMAS. It means there was a lot of it out there."

"Okay. So?"

"The M16 can also fire a .223 round, which is nearly identical, and was also incredibly common. What does this mean?"

"It means there's a lot of ammo out there the M16 can shoot."

"No. It means that there was a lot of rounds that were *manufactured* that the M16 can shoot. Which meant our scavenger crews were able to find it more often than some other rounds. Right now we have about four thousand rounds that work with this M16."

"Which is a hell of a lot."

"It's really not. More to the point, it's not enough to train you on the rifle."

"It doesn't take much training to point a rifle at a runner."

"No. It takes training to hit one. And once those rounds are gone, they're gone. We don't have the capability to make more here. So you don't get a rifle. Or a shotgun, for which we have even fewer rounds."

"This is a 'macho former Marine' thing, isn't it?"

"No. This is a 'give the weapon to the person who has training on it' thing."

"So what do you want me to do if a runner makes for the wall?"

"I want you to do what you did before. I want you to call it out."

"And then you'll shoot it."

"If it makes sense to shoot it, yes. Otherwise, we have other options."

"I still think this is a macho bullshit thing."

"Fine. Here. Take the rifle."

"What do you want me to do with it?"

"I want you to hold it."

". . . Okay. I'm holding it."

"Aaaand you just shot off your foot."

"What do you mean?"

"When you took the rifle, you put your finger on the trigger and you pointed it at your left foot. You just shot off your foot."

"Except that I didn't. See? Left foot intact."

"That's because I'm not stupid enough to hand you a rifle with live ammunition in it with the selector switch in any position other than 'safe.'"

"I didn't shoot my foot off before when I was on watch."

"Was the selector switch in the 'safe' position?"

". . . Possibly."

"'Possibly.' Meaning that you didn't have the first clue as to whether you could fire your rifle at all."

"I think you're being unfair."

"I'll give you five seconds to find the selector switch on that rifle."

"And then what?"

"Then I punch you in the shoulder and take back the rifle."

"What if I find it?"

"Then I take the rifle back before you can shoot yourself in the foot because *you still have your fucking finger on the trigger.*"

"Look, just take it back."

"Thank you."

"I still want a weapon."

"We can start you on the bow."

"How are *you* on a bow?"

"Terrible."

"That makes me feel a little better."

"That's nice. Now shut up and look for runners."

"Do you ever wonder which famous people made it?"

"Made it?"

"*Made it*, Jim. Survived."

"Oh. No."

"Never once?"

"I've been kind of busy."

"We've all been kind of busy. Doesn't mean you don't think about these things."

"I haven't."

"Well, think about it now. Which famous people do you think survived?"

". . . I can't think of any famous people right off the top of my head."

"Do you live in a cave?"

"No, I live in an improvised fortress in the suburbs of Detroit, surrounded by goddamn zombies and a general apocalypse."

"If you don't have hobbies in a situation like that, you're gonna go a little crazy."

"Thinking about former celebrities is not a useful hobby."

"Hobbies aren't supposed to be useful. That's why they're *hobbies.* And why do you say 'former'?"

"It's the zombie apocalypse, in case you haven't noticed. No one's going to the movies anymore. No one's listening to Top 40 radio. No one's watching *Entertainment Tonight*."

"I don't think *Entertainment Tonight* still exists."

"*Nothing* still exists, entertainment-wise. That's what I'm *saying*."

"Indulge me here. We have six hours to go in the watch. There's nothing moving out there. I'm a little bored."

"The alternative is worse."

"If you mean things moving out there, then yes. Otherwise we disagree."

"Fine. Name a celebrity and I'll tell you if I think they made it."

"Justin Bieber."

"Jesus Christ, man. You can't just *lead* with Justin Bieber. You have to work up to that kind of shit."

"Deep end of the pool, Jim. Come on. You think Justin Bieber's survived?"

"Of course not."

"Are you sure? Fact: He had bodyguards. Fact: He had money to escape to an isolated area. Fact: He's owned a monkey."

"What the hell does a monkey have to do with anything?"

"Irrational crap-flinging primate. I suggest that's decent training for dealing with runners."

"One, no it's not. Two, he abandoned his monkey in Germany."

"The fact you know that and yet say you don't follow celebrities is something we need to revisit at a later time."

"Three, if you think those bodyguards stuck with him after everything started to fall apart, you're delusional. Four, money stopped doing anyone any good really fast. No. He's dead. Dead and probably eaten."

"Concur. George Clooney."

"I don't know. Maybe. He had that villa. Maybe it was defensible."

"Jay-Z and Beyonce."

"I have to think they made it to an island somewhere."

"Any of the Kardashians."

"Eaten. All of them. Every single one."

"Harrison Ford."

"He's a pilot. He may have gotten out."

"He crashed on that golf course, though."

"He walked away from it."

"The members of Metallica."

"You know what? Once I would have pegged them to survive. But then I saw that *Some Kind of Monster* documentary. I think the runners were feasting on Lars Ulrich's sweetmeats on, like, day two."

"Ted Nugent."

"Eaten."

"Come *on*. This is *Ted Nugent* we're talking about, here."

"Look. I don't want to say he didn't talk a good survivalist game. He did. But I think he's a prime candidate for being overconfident. I bet he thought he could just bowhunt the crap out of the runners, and they probably trapped him in a ravine or something."

"This is how I find out you're a liberal."

"This isn't a political position. I'm just saying overconfidence is a killer."

"Lady Gaga."

"You're talking about someone who once dressed herself in *meat*."

"So that's a 'no.'"

"I'm laying long odds. Who else?"

"Look who is actually enjoying himself."

"I'm both surprising and disgusting myself with how much I seem to know about all these people."

"Do you want to do any politicians?"

"Oh, let's not. We got dangerously close to politics with Ted Nugent."

"Fine. Writers?"

"Lunch meat. All of them."

"Wow. That's dark."

"They write fine. But it's sedentary work. I went to a couple of conventions in my time. I know what I saw."

"Back to real celebrities, then. Brad Pitt and Angelina Jolie."

"Brad, dead. Angelina survives."

"You would think that zombie film would have given him some training."

"No. He was Hollywood tough, not actual tough. But think of everything Angelina's been through. Double mastectomy. Turbulent early years. Billy Bob Thornton. That's one tough woman. I wouldn't bet against her."

"Batman."

"What?"

"Batman."

"Batman's not a celebrity."

"Batman's not famous? Batman's not known worldwide? Batman's not instantly recognizable?"

"Batman is all these things, yes."

"Then he's a celebrity. So: Batman."

"*However*, Batman is fictional."

"So?"

"What do you mean, 'so'? So, you can't go mixing up fictional and nonfictional celebrities."

"Why not?"

"It's against the rules."

"There are rules to this?"

"Yes, there are rules. I'm making the rules right now. Rule number one: No mixing the fictional and nonfictional."

"Fine. The rule takes effect *after* you answer the question. Batman."

"Of course Batman survives. He's *Batman*."

"Then George Clooney did survive. Because he was Batman."

"No. Not *that* Batman. Any Batman with nipples on his Batsuit was eaten first."

"First?"

"Yes. Even before Lars Ulrich."

"Hmmm. Tough but fair. I'll allow it."

"You better."

"I wonder if celebrities play this same game. If they're off on their islands going 'Huh, I wonder if George Clooney made it.'"

"No. They're all dead."

"But you were just saying which ones made it out alive."

"I was humoring you."

"...I don't think I want to play this game with you anymore."

"Then I win. Now keep looking."

"There."

"Where?"

"In the trees. By the road."

"There are a lot of trees by the road, Keith. Be more specific."

"In the trees, by the road, about a hundred yards out."

"Which *side* of the road."

"To our left."

". . . I don't see anything."

"There was movement there. I heard it and I saw it."

"You see that chest?"

"Yeah."

"Open it and take out the night vision binoculars."

"We've had night vision goggles this whole time?"

"Yes. We don't use them unless we have to because they don't exactly make batteries for them anymore, do they?"

"The next zombie apocalypse I attend, I want it to keep a manufacturing base."

"Cute. Take a look where you heard the sound. Tell me what you see."

"I don't know how to turn on these binoculars."

"And you were wondering why I wouldn't let you use the rifle."

"It's not the same thing."

"It's kind of the same thing. Give them here."

"I don't appreciate being made to feel incompetent."

"It's not a feeling. You actually are incompetent."

"Thanks."

"It's not meant to be an insult. There are lots of things I'm not competent in."

"Do any of those things have to do with surviving a post-collapse hellscape?"

"Not so far."

"This doesn't help me feel better, then."

"Sorry."

"Do you see anything?"

"No . . . yes."

"What?"

"Two deer."

"What are they doing?"

"They doing what deer do. They're standing around looking surprised that they exist in the world."

"I don't think it was just deer."

"I'm seeing deer."

"You were the one who said you were worried about runners."

"I am worried about runners. I'm not seeing any. I'm seeing deer."

"It's possible you made me a little paranoid by mentioning the runners earlier."

"It's not paranoia. It's a healthy reaction to the fact that runners exist."

"I remember the first time I saw one."

"Everyone does. What's your story?"

"A pack of them coming down my street."

"What did you do?"

"I hid in my kid's treehouse for two days."

". . . You had a kid."

"Yeah. Might still have. She was with her mom when this all went down. In Arizona. We'd been divorced for about a year and a half. She got custody. I get visits."

"Sorry."

"About the divorce and custody thing?"

"No, but that too."

"Don't be. It got bad at the end. She had family out west, she moved back there, and I didn't want to make a scene. She was living with her dentist fiancé the last I heard."

"Still rough."

"Yeah. Anyway, by that time the phones and Internet were already gone. I don't know how they're doing."

"I'm sure they made it."

"I'd like to think so. Well, except for the dentist. I hope that fucker got eaten."

"Huh."

"I know. Not very nice of me."

"No. I see something else."

"What?"

"Shhhhhh."

"Why do people always tell you 'shhhh' when they're trying to look at something?"

"Quiet!"

"Mmmmph."

"Well, shit."

"What is it?"

"Definitely not deer this time."

"You're killing me over here, Jim."

"It's human-shaped."

"You could be more specific."

"Too far away to be more specific."

"What's it doing?"

"At the moment it's standing there."

"It could be an actual person."

"Scavenging crews aren't seeing too many actual people anymore."

"A scurrier, then."

"Maybe. Maybe."

"What are you doing?"

"Remember when I told you that there were options other than shooting runners?"

"Yeah."

"I'm going to show you one of the options. Here, put these back in the chest and get me out the garage door opener."

"You're going to open a garage door?"

"No, you idiot. I'm going to use the garage door opener to activate something else."

"What?"

"You'll see. There's another pair of binoculars in the chest, too. A regular pair this time. Get those out."

"Here's a garage door opener. You want the binoculars, too?"

"No, you hold on to them."

"What do you want me to do with them?"

"I want you to watch and tell me what happens."

"What happens when?"

"When I press this garage door opener button."

"Holy shit!"

"Yeah."

"What is that?"

"It's a runner trap. We put it out there a couple of weeks ago. If one of them comes too close, we set it off. Activate it, the strobes go off and the music comes up. If it's a scurrier, it gets the hell out. If it's a runner, it attacks."

". . . What is that music?"

"Metallica. 'Creeping Death.'"

"I thought you were down on Metallica."

"The music is awesome. Individually they're a little soft. Tell me what you're seeing."

"It's definitely not running away. It's charging toward the trap."

"Tell me when the trap gets sprung."

"How will I know?"

"You'll know."

". . . Whoa."

"Disappeared?"

"Yeah. Like it fell into a hole."

"A moat."

"Is it going to be able to climb out?"

"Ten feet deep. Filled with spikes."

"So that's a no."

"That's an 'I'd be impressed.' Let me turn off the trap."

". . . Well, *those* screams are pleasant."

"Must not have punctured a lung."

"You were expecting a punctured lung."

"I wasn't expecting anything. This is the first time we've gotten to use it."

"But you were hoping for a punctured lung."

"Well, yeah. Or a severed windpipe. The screaming could become a problem."

"What does that mean?"

"It means maybe you should go back into the chest and bring out the night vision binoculars again."

"I'm not one hundred percent happy with the turn events have just taken here, Jim."

"It'll probably be fine."

"Which is why I'm getting out the night vision binoculars again."

"The screaming seems to be winding down. That's good."

"Here."

"Thank you."

"I don't think that qualifies as 'winding down,' by the way."

"Quiet."

"We're back to that again."

"Keith."

"Yeah."

"I want you to do a couple of things for me."

"All right."

"The first is to *quietly* go and tell The Boss it looks like we've got eight runners less than a hundred yards from our doorstep."

". . . *Fuck*."

"Yeah."

"This is on you with the 'Creeping Death' stunt."

"They were there already. The one in the pit was just ahead of the rest of the pack."

"I'm still blaming you."

"Fine. The second thing I need you to do is go over there to the weapons shack."

"This is where I get a gun?"

"No."

"What the hell?"

"I want you to get out the shovel."

"What the shit good is a shovel going to do?"

"When they start climbing up the wall, you can bash them in the head with it."

"You're joking."

"I'm totally serious."

"When I go talk to The Boss I'm going to ask for a shotgun."

"She's going to tell you 'no.'"

"I'm going to ask anyway."

"Whatever. Just go and tell her. And then get back here. Believe it or not, I need you back on this wall."

"That's a nice shovel."

"Shut up, Jim."

"What did The Boss have to say?"

"She said she's organizing a response and that until then we hold the wall."

"Okay."

"I told her about the 'Creeping Death' thing."

"What did she say?"

"She said she liked the choice of music."

"She would."

"I feel like there's some bias going on."

"What do you mean?"

"I mean that I was not at fault for the last breach we had and you still didn't want to stand a watch with me. And now you might be at fault for getting us overrun by a whole pack of runners, and the official response is, like, 'cool tunes, bro.'"

"I don't blame you for the breach."

"You still didn't want to stand a watch with me."

"Do we have to talk about this now?"

"Well, I might end the night having my fucking intestines being ripped out by a pack of things that used to be accountants and GM factory workers, so yeah, if you don't mind, let's talk about this now."

"Did you not hear what I said to you before you left to go talk to The Boss?"

"You told me to get the shovel."

"I also told you to come back here."

"I don't remember this part."

"I specifically said that I needed you back on this wall."

"I must have missed it."

"It doesn't mean I didn't say it."

"I only have your word for it."

"No you don't, because I just said it again. Not even thirty seconds ago."

"...You were referencing a previous alleged statement."

"Oh, for Christ's sake, Keith. I'm sorry, all right?"

"Are you saying that because you mean it, or because you think I'm whining right now?"

"You want the truth?"

"Of course I want the truth."

"Then it's a little of both."

"All right. That's fair."

"You have to admit you're whining."

"Maybe a little."

"You should *not* do that."

"It's one of my *competencies*, Jim."

"You're going to make me regret that comment, aren't you."

"I might. I mean, if we *live*."

"Quiet."

"You keep telling me that...oh. What's that?"

"Look over the backside."

"It's The Boss and about six others."

"What are they doing?"

"I don't know. They're all armed except for Clary. He's got a big ass boom box."

"Did you just say 'boom box'?"

"Yeah. So?"

"I just haven't heard anyone use that phrase this millennium."

"It's back. Like bell bottoms. All right. The Boss is going to the switchbox."

"She's going to turn on the flood lights."

"...Yup. There they go."

"Come back over here, please, Keith."

"She's going to draw them here, isn't she?"

"I'm guessing that's the plan, yeah."

"I'm not a fan of this plan."

"I don't think you get a vote."

"Apparently not. I'm just an asshole with a shovel."

"What . . . what the hell song is that?"

". . . It's 'Dancing Queen.'"

"By Abba."

"I think so."

"We're luring runners into attacking us with *Abba*."

"It appears so."

"I liked my choice better."

"Jim, if I die to Abba, I'm coming back to haunt the *shit* out of you."

"That's fair. Look, here they come."

"That looks like more than eight, Jim."

"I saw eight. That didn't mean there weren't more."

"I count at least fifteen."

"Tell The Boss."

"I'm guessing she already knows."

"Tell her anyway. Don't worry about being quiet about it."

"Too late. They're coming!"

"On it."

". . . Why aren't you firing?!?"

"Not until they're closer."

"You want them to hit the wall?"

"I need them close. We don't have enough rounds to miss."

"Jesus!"

"Shut up and let me aim."

". . . Oh shit."

"That's one."

"I've got a couple on the wall, Jim."

"Two."

"Here on the right, Jim."

"Three . . . uck! Three. Made me waste a round, runner."

"Jim!"

"What!"

"Fucking zombies on the wall!"

"Four! I'm busy!"

"You're the one with the rifle!"

"And you're the one with the goddamn shovel! Use it!"

"You can *dance*! You can *jive*! Having the *time* of your *life*! Holy shit!"

"Five! What?"

"'Dancing Queen' has the perfect beat for hitting runners with shovels! It's like The Boss knew!"

"That's why she's The Boss."

"Guess so!"

"Hold up. Firing's done."

"I think we got them."

"How many did you say you counted before?"

"I think fifteen."

". . . I'm seeing sixteen in front of the wall."

"I was close."

"Including two with their heads bashed in with a shovel."

"They deserved it."

"That's hardcore, my friend."

"I owe it all to you and your refusal to allow me firearms, Jim."

"Tell me I was wrong."

"I say you're wrong. My foot probably thanks you."

"I accept your foot's thanks."

"Now what?"

"What do you mean 'now what'?"

"We just fought off a runner pack. There's a pile of corpses at our door. Now what?"

"We stay on the wall, Keith. The Boss will assign a detail to deal with the corpses. We'll guard them while they do. You keep the lookout. I'll provide the firepower."

"Makes sense."

"It does. We make a pretty good team."

"I think you're right."

"Glad you think so."

"I still think I should have a gun."

"I know."

"You going to let me have one?"

"No."

# Do No Harm

SARAH A. HOYT

## THE STRING'S ALREADY BROKEN

Bethany realized she was watching the end of civilization when Dr. T zombed out on her COW.

Yeah, she knew she wasn't supposed to call the second stage of the H7D3 virus zombing out, but that's what all the Emergency Room scribes had been calling it, since it had overwhelmed all the ready beds at the hospital and got a designation and everything.

For that matter, she wasn't supposed to call the Computer on Wheels a COW. Administration was very clear that it should be called WOW for Workstation On Wheels, but it was black and white and had four legs, and it was best not to get too attached to it, because sooner or later it would die on you. So everyone in ER called it a COW and Dr. T—because everyone was always mispronouncing Tomboulian—was one of the cool docs. A little green-eyed china doll with an infectious smile, she had attached longhorns to the front of her COW and a bell beneath the screen, and she ran around with it every shift doing most of her own data entry, which was cool from where Beth sat because it was one less thing landing on the overworked scribes, most of them pre-med students.

The scribes were paid for by the doctors out of pocket, and in return were supposed to handle all the crazy paperwork the bureaucrats dumped on the docs. Some scribes were trained to deal with only one doctor, and that seemed relatively simple, but Beth hadn't been able to promise she'd stay more than one year, and therefore couldn't take that training. So she was supposed to handle other doctors, and most doctors weren't so easy to deal with or so nice, and Bethany was trying to take dictation on a patient disposition from Dr. Barfuss when Dr. T zombed.

Dr. Barfuss had a bad habit of whispering to something other than the poor scribe following him around, and had just mumbled something about giving the patient hot sitz baths which couldn't be true for a case of pink eye, and was now whispering confidentially about—Beth would swear it—playing tiddlywinks, when Dr. T yelled, "What is this? What is all over me?" and started ripping at her clothes.

Before Dr. T started biting there were two doctors and a patient on her, trying to hold her. The signs had become that well known. The bell around her COW's neck was tinkling like mad as they tried to hold her, and she fought them, and her teeth started snapping at them, and Dr. Hayden yelled as she got bit.

Dr. Nikhil Pillarisetti—whom no one called doctor P because he'd just say "psych, not urologist," must have been in ER for some psych eval because he yelled, "Hold on, now," in his Texas accent and plunged across groups of people, to hold Dr. T in a headlock. He yelled calm orders to bring him restraints, and the next thing, Dr. T was on a cart, her hands and feet bound to the railing and two people from transport were taking her away to be evaluated, not that anyone doubted what the diagnosis would be.

Beth tried not to look at Dr. T's face, as all personality and sense had gone from the doctor's eyes, and there was nothing there.

She had a strange sense something had broken, that something had left the doctor and it wasn't going to come back.

The world was coming to an end. Bethany couldn't say it had been wonderful before. Sure, life with Mom and Dad on the ranch had been pretty great, but the ranch being kind of far from civilization meant she'd never had that much of a social life.

And it turned out that if you wanted to be a doctor you needed glib social skills. She'd volunteered at hospitals since middle school and she really wanted to heal people. But the applications for med schools all wanted you to say how you'd overcome adversity, and how you had some story of hardship.

Just wanting to heal people and do no harm wasn't enough. Beth was starting to suspect she'd never get in when H7D3 hit. And now none of it would matter. She'd be a scribe until she caught it and then—

"Did you get the disposition for the patient?" Dr. Barfuss asked.

But Beth caught at the sleeve of Dr. Pillarisetti as he walked by. "Doctor?" She said. "Dr. T is not going to be all right, is she?" And as Dr. Pillarisetti looked back his lips tight, she realized he'd understood "she's going to be all right?" and hastened to correct, "She's not coming back, is she?"

He opened his mouth, and closed it, shook his head, and walked away, while Dr. Barfuss insisted, "Ms. Arden, did you get that dispo?"

"No, I'm sorry, Doctor, I couldn't hear through the noise," she said meekly, by habit avoiding mentioning that he dictated to the floor and his left sleeve, and sometimes his foot, but never to the poor scribe following him around.

He made a scathing sound at the back of his throat, and pushed his glasses up. He was a little, mostly bald man, who clearly thought he'd become a divinity the day he'd got his medical degree. There was a way he had of looking at people that gave them the impression he was looking down on them, even though for that he'd need a ladder. "The patient is to give his eye saline baths, or rinses, and put in the antibiotic drops, and observe proper hygiene in the future. And call us if anything changes for the worse."

She typed the notes quickly into her tablet, while an irreverent voice at the back of her head said, *Like it matters. He'll probably get his face eaten on the way home, pink eye and all. Why did Dr. T have to zomb out? Why couldn't it be Dr. Barfy?* Then she shuddered, because really she didn't want anyone to zomb out. One moment there was a person there, and then nothing. Just a feral critter with human shape. But the person was gone, as effectively as if they'd died. And it was worse that the body stayed around to bite and spread the virus.

She knew that the disease had been transmitted by fake air freshener units with an ecological slogan put in the bathrooms at international airports. She wondered if it was really the enviros who had done this. It seemed to her there was a branch of them who was sure that the Earth would be better without humans. Better for what she didn't know, but they seemed very sure.

Dr. Hayden was waiting to dictate a dispo, and Beth hurried to take it. She'd considered getting trained to be an individual scribe, but she'd been hoping against hope to be in med school next year, and if she'd taken the training then she would have had to work for the scribe service for a year to pay it back. Of course, she was very much afraid she'd fail in the application this year as she had last year and would be here forever.

And on that, she stopped, some inches from Dr. Hayden as her mind readjusted. With the emergency room and all available beds filled, with more and more people, like poor Dr. T, zombing out and becoming mindless killing apes, what prospects did she have in the future? What part of her carefully laid med school plans was still operative? Would there even be a medical school? Were any med schools still even interviewing?

"Beth?" Dr. Hayden asked. "You all right?"

"Uh. Oh, yes, Doctor. I was wondering when this will end, and what it will mean for me. I mean, I was hoping to go to med school—"

Dr. Hayden snorted. She looked hot, like a fever had come on her suddenly. Her cheeks were flushed, and she was trying to fumble a bandage on, one handed, where Dr. T had bitten her. "I'm supposed to tell you everything will be all right, right?" she said. "That if you work very hard everything will turn out all right. Only that's not true, if indeed it ever was except in rare cases. It wasn't ever just hard work, but hard work and aptitude, and contacts and confidence and all that. I don't believe in lying to the young. It might not have been all right even in the past. Oh, thank you," she said, as Beth slapped the bandage over her wound. "I disinfected. They say this will lessen the risk of transmission, but I'm not sure I believe it. Not from what we're seeing here." She frowned at her arm. "You know, Beth, I don't believe everything will be all right. I've studied epidemiology. I know this is exponential, and without an official vaccine or a cure, we're . . ." She paused and it was obvious she was moderating her language. "In trouble. At the very least there's going to be a serious . . ." And she just stopped.

"You were dictating a dispo?" Beth said, seeing tears sparkle in the older woman's eyes. Dr. Hayden, like Dr. T, was one of her favorite doctors to work for. She wasn't as tech competent as Dr. T and so wouldn't do her own data entry, but she was always kind to the scribes and didn't treat them like serfs or blame them for her mistakes. She had a daughter about Beth's age, who lived in Seattle and who had stopped answering her cell a few days ago. That Dr. Hayden hadn't mentioned her daughter since was part of why Beth knew she was worrying about her all the time. Before, she'd always had her cell in hand, texting back and forth.

Beth's parents... Beth's parents also weren't answering their phone, and she hadn't been able to, or had the courage to, drive all the way to the ranch near Goldport to check on them. She wished she were back at the ranch, as hard as she could, but her name wasn't Dorothy. Maybe she should never have left. "The patient you were seeing when Dr. T zombe—came down with phase two of the H7D3 virus."

"Oh, that," Dr. Hayden said, and blinked her water-shiny eyes. "Yeah, admitted and restrained for H7D3 virus, second phase. We're down to carts on the corridors, Beth, and I don't know where we'll put the next zombie." She smiled, a wry smile. "Even if it's me."

"Some people don't catch it. It happens."

"Yeah, but everyone I've attended for bites has caught it, and some caught it within hours," Dr. Hayden said, as Beth copy-pasted the normal dispo for H7D3, second phase, on her portable work screen. She no longer bothered to even try to type it individually. "The odds aren't good, and I never even won a cent on the lottery. I'm not the lucky type."

Beth opened her mouth but said nothing. What in hell could she say? The doctor was right of course. The chances of her still being herself in a few days were about none. And Beth didn't want to lie to her.

"If I zomb out," Dr. Hayden whispered, urgently. "Kill me?"

"Doctor—"

"Yeah, I know, do no harm and all, but Beth I've autopsied zombies who died. There's nothing there. All the parts of the brain that make us human are gone. I don't want to live like that and be a danger to others. Shira... Dr. Tomboulian, and I have been friends since med school, and it's harder to think of her as a zombie than to think of her dead. So—Just put an end to me."

"Doctor, I want to go into medicine," Bethany said. She didn't want to talk back, but it was important to make Dr. Hayden understand. "I don't—I don't want to kill people."

Dr. Hayden gurgled with laughter at that. "Sorry. If you get into medicine, I guarantee you will."

Beth felt herself go red. "No, I know," she said. She tried to explain. It was the same trouble as med school interviews. She could never explain properly and it came across like she didn't care. Last year an interviewer had actually asked her if she was only doing this because of prestige and told her to go back to the farm. She struggled for words. "No, I know you kill people accidentally and all. But I mean I never wanted to kill people on purpose."

Dr. Hayden looked intently at her and sighed. "Of course not. But with H7D3 . . . Don't you see that you have to kill to save? Look, I never believed in all that crap about *community medicine* they gave us. It seemed like an excuse not to do the best you could for the patient, with some nebulous social justification. But in this case, you can *do* nothing. Once the patient zombs out, he or she isn't coming back. There's nothing in there to come back to. All you can do is save other people from catching it. If we'd started killing them when we realized that, Dr. T would still be fine, and I . . . I wouldn't have been bitten." She took a deep breath. "I, too, never wanted to do harm, and I don't want my body to do harm after my mind is gone. I need to know someone will stop me before I spread it. You're a ranch girl. You're practical."

Beth wanted to say that it wasn't as easy as all that. She'd killed deer in season, but they needed culling or they'd destroy the crops, and she'd killed chickens. Of course, being made into nuggets probably raised a chicken's intelligence. Killing a *person* or what had once been a person was something else again.

But she met Dr. Hayden's eyes, and nodded.

Later, in the doctors' lounge, the people still on shift gathered around the TV.

The doctors' lounge was really just a small room, with a loveseat in a corner, a TV on the wall, and a table where people tended to throw whatever sweets they'd brought in from home. It was a dirty little secret that doctors and most medical personnel in the ER lived on sugar, like some form of bee. In what Beth was starting to think of as the good old days, before H7D3, there weren't many people in the lounge. Even in these days, there weren't as many people in the lounge as now. For one, the nurses had been failing to come in when scheduled and didn't answer their phones, so it was anyone's guess whether they'd zombed or hightailed it out of Denver. Which, Beth thought, was arguably the sane reaction.

The few nurses that were in just used the doctors' lounge. And the physician's assistants who kept coming in did the same, as did the scribes. The weird thing was that nearly every doctor dragged himself or herself in, by grim determination, as though their presence there could stem the tide of the infection. As Dr. Clithero, a beautiful Samoan woman with an inability to suffer stupidity gladly—or indeed at all—had said that night, in desperation at the seventh H7D3 patient, "I feel like I'm trying to empty the sea with a conch shell."

But that hadn't stopped her coming in, and now she was munching on a brownie and drinking coffee, while about ten doctors, half a dozen scribes, and a PA took a break from the mess in the emergency room.

From behind the break room came the low-grade growl-screams of the infected, housed in all the rooms of ER and in all the hallways. Since all their space for H7D3 was taken up, St. Thomas the Martyr hospital had started to divert to the other hospitals in the city. Which meant there was a lull that allowed doctors to gather and socialize for the first time in days. Weirdly, there weren't many patients otherwise. Not even frequent flyers or drug seekers. Then again, maybe it wasn't weird. After all, if you got eaten on the way to the hospital, it was not that easy to get in for that pain in your left foot that had bothered you for three years but was an emergency now that you were bored.

Since the crisis, the TV was set permanently on news and all the remaining anchors sounded on the verge of hysteria. Though seeing one go full zombie on camera before chasing the other anchors around trying to eat their faces had been completely worth it. And it was a sign of how jaded they'd got in the last few months that it warranted no more than snorts from a couple of the doctors and Lucas Fiacre, one of the physician's assistants, saying in his best camp voice, "Oh! That is nothing to brag about," when the news anchor tore all his clothes off.

"The thing is," Dr. Pillarisetti said when laughter died down.

"When does it all come crashing down?" He spoke without drama, in a grinding, flat voice, that made his words seem more scary than if he'd shouted.

Beth, leaning against the door frame of the room, was so startled she said "What?" aloud, even though normally she tried to stay quiet when doctors and other trained professionals discussed things. It was okay, because hers wasn't the only "what?" Just about everybody else said it too.

Dr. Pillarisetti swept the room with a concerned gaze. "Seriously? None of you has thought of that? An advanced technological society needs a certain number of personnel with knowledge and ability to keep it running."

And Beth spoke in a gathering of doctors for the second time, somewhat shocked to hear the words coming out of her mouth, "But wouldn't a small population be better for everyone? It seems like after the Black Plague in Europe—"

Dr. Pillarisetti's ancestors came from the Indian subcontinent. He had very dark eyes and an unnerving way of bringing his heavy eyebrows down over them that made it look like he was contemplating where to hide your body after he was done ripping off your head and beating you to death with it. Now he turned the full force of it on Beth and said a word that, if everything weren't falling apart, would certainly have got him a process open with Human Resources. "Is that what they teach you kids these days? Well, they're wrong. The Black Plague did not hit an advanced technological society. Remember your first year classes and how many people dropped out of bio or chem or engineering to take a humanities degree? And that was from the ones who got into college to begin with. The pool of people who can handle math and science is limited. Not even an intelligence thing as the type of intelligence they have. Not all smart people can handle science. Given the morbidity—or at least the zombidity—of this virus, leaving maybe one per cent of the population untouched, how do you think technological civilization can survive? The virus is not selecting for intelligence."

Beth bit her lip to make sure she didn't say anything more. The certainty that Dr. Pillarisetti was right sank in, even as the TV flickered, and then an announcer said, in an eerily calm voice, "Folks, we're getting reports that the lights went out in New York City." The TV flickered again. "And now our lights have gone off and we're working with backup generators." There were screams behind the man, and the sound of breaking glass, and someone yelled, "Turn the farging lights off and shut up! Zombies are attracted to light and sound!" And the man in the screen who couldn't be a regular announcer because he was wearing sweatpants and a stained T-shirt that read *You Can Have My Coffee When You Pry It From My Cold, Dead Hands* said "They're tearing into the station now. Folks, stop listening to me and save yourselves. It's the end of the world."

The TV picture went to snow. Doctors, nurses, physician's assistants and scribes had just the time to look around at each other with horror, when the lights in the hospital blinked. Then the backup generators hummed, and the lights came back on.

They looked at each other, each as pale as he or she could get.

St. Thomas the Martyr was not quite downtown, but was set right off Colfax. If the city was dark, and the uncountable population of zombies out there *was* attracted to light and sound the hospital had just become a magnet for a horde of zombies that would submerge them all.

Beth loved the hospital, wanted to be a doctor, and all she could think was, *How do I get out of here*? And read the same thought in everyone else's gaze. She heard glass break from down the hall, at the emergency room. Then there were very distinct human screams. Of course, the hospital was modern and the façade was mostly glass. Beth choked on a chuckle at the thought that if they'd known what was coming they'd have built like the middle ages, with narrow windows and small doors. She gave herself a mental shake. Hysteria was one thing she didn't need right now.

"We can't go out the door," Dr. Barfuss said.

"The roof," Lucas Fiacre shouted.

"Why the roof? What do we do after?" Cody, an older scribe yelled.

"How the hell do we get off the roof?" one of the other PAs asked.

"Helicopter-ambulances," Lucas said. "Bound to be some up there at the rate they've been bringing us patients."

It made sense. St. Thomas the Martyr serviced all the southern suburbs and all the outlying areas up to Aurora, whatever wasn't covered by the med school hospital there, so it had six helicopter ambulances, donated by a kind benefactor, which brought in the stroke cases, the heart attack cases, and the alcohol poisoning cases of a Saturday night.

"And who the hell is going to fly them?" Dr. Barfuss asked, in his annoying, superior manner.

"If the pilots aren't with their 'coptors, hell, I can fly one," Fiacre said, grinning over his shoulder. "Flew helos in 'stan."

"And what about the others? We can't all fit into one!"

Dr. Sarah Clithero, who had been looking out the door of the lounge said, "Oh, I can fly another. Learned to fly them when I was young." As though anticipating the question, she said, "Was bored."

"But the ambulance helicopters—"

"Are designed to be an easy to fly vehicle," Fiacre said. "How does it look out there, Sarah?"

"From the sounds, they broke the front glass panes, and anyone who wasn't a zombie in the waiting room is dead. We're going to have to fight our way up. Grab whatever you find that can be used as weapons," Dr. Clithero said.

It gave Bethany a little shock, and it was stupid. Of course they needed weapons, unless they just wanted to be zombie chow.

"It might surprise you," one of the other PAs, Albert Schoen, a tall, blond man, said, "but the emergency room and this lounge weren't designed to have a lot of impromptu weapons on hand."

"Grab what you can," Dr. Pillarisetti said, pulling a fire extinguisher from the wall. "Just try not to get bitten."

"Gait belts," a nurse said. "Attach something heavy to the end and you have a mace." She ran out of the room, then back in and started distributing seven rainbow colored belts around. "We had some in the nurses' lounge." Some of the men were taking their own belts off and attaching heavy objects to the end of them.

Beth didn't have a belt and she didn't get a gait. In despair she grabbed a standing lamp, by the lamp end, holding the weighted base in a defensive position. As a weapon it sort of sucked, but not as much as the others. It was fine. She wasn't sure she could look into a human face and smash it, anyway. She was afraid she wouldn't last long.

Just then, she heard, at the back of her mind, what her dad had said, when she failed the first round of med school interviews, *Of course, you'll try again. If you're sure that's what you want to do you try again. Life is trying and failing and trying again and sometimes succeeding. If you stop trying for something you really feel you should do, you might as well be dead, Beth.* And so she'd promised herself not to give up her dream of being a doctor.

"Come on," Lucas Fiacre said. He hadn't got one of the gaits or a belt either. He'd grabbed the curtain rod and tied a knife to the end of it with strips of curtain. He probably wasn't supposed to have that knife in the hospital, a weapon-free zone, but she was damn glad he did. His grin looked entirely feral. "We have to get higher. We'll go to the second floor and bar the stairs. Come on."

Beth wondered why Lucas seemed more alive than she'd ever seen him. She knew a lot of PAs, Lucas included, were war vets. She wondered if learning to survive under fire changed you, if it made you even like it.

She wondered, if she survived, would it change her the same way?

## AND IT WON'T LAST FOR LONG

It all turned surreal very fast. Beth had been going hunting with dad since she was about five, and, being a farm kid, she'd seen animals killed. In the hospital, too, she'd seen her share of bleeding and dying.

But all that was different. Now she was killing people, or at least hurting them very badly. No. Not people. She remembered what Dr. Hayden had said. Zombies. Vectors, who'd infect people. The back of her head screamed that this was a dangerous slippery slope, but damn it, they knew you couldn't come back from zombie. Not to kill them just meant they took over the whole world.

Her mind was torn between *do no harm* and *but it's self-defense.* All she knew was that as the zombies tried to come in, she and the others fought back.

The first time Bethany hit a zombie and heard the sick crunch of a breaking cranium and got splattered with blood and brains was bad, but she couldn't stop. She turned her head not to get splatter in her eyes or mouth, but there was so much gore flying, she had to just hope nothing got in. Her mind said *vector. Save people from the vector.* She argued with herself, *slippery slope.* But then she looked at the vacant eyes, the gnashing teeth. There was no human there. There was no coming back. They were vectors. *Just vectors.*

She swung the lamp. Somehow they cleared a space so they emerged into the hallway. She found herself in the front lines, swinging the lamp at zombies' heads, as they gnashed teeth and whined and tried to reach them. If you swung the base with sufficient force it stopped them. *Vector.* She was saving people.

Then a zombie grabbed for her. Dr. Pillarisetti's fire extinguisher broke its shoulder and then its face. The hand let go of Beth's arm, and she swung her lamp at a zombie trying to bite Lucas Fiacre.

She and Lucas—probably because they had longer-range weapons—moving back to back managed to clear the cluster around the lounge enough to get their group to the hallway that led to the service stairs up to the second floor.

They were stepping over zombies' still-twitching corpses and she was glad she was wearing her ankle boots, otherwise she would have been bit thirty times over. Fortunately, the zombies slowed long enough to eat other fallen zombies. As it was, as they reached the second floor, Lucas Fiacre looked over his shoulder and said, "Stop. How about the patients?"

"What patients?" Dr. Barfuss asked. "Good God man, you can't mean the zombies."

"No, the other patients," Fiacre said. "Second floor." He squinted. "Oncology?"

"Mostly," Dr. Clithero said. She was splattered in blood and gore, and held a blood-splattered reinforced computer case nonchalantly. "Right now. Usually anyone we need to do a lot of tests on, but right now mostly oncology. I don't know how many patients we have, or how many are ambulatory."

Fiacre looked at the door to the ward, then down at the door to the first floor they had locked in their wake.

Beth heard the glass on the door break and knew it was a matter of time before the zombies either squeezed through the door, or broke the handle. "I'll go in," she said. If they just let people be eaten, what was the point? "I'll see how many of the patients here are ambulatory and how many we can rescue." She didn't say *and how many have zombed out.* But she thought it. Just because you were a cancer patient, it didn't mean you couldn't catch the zombie plague. Until now that had been their biggest problem: people admitted for other things turning and wreaking havoc in their units.

That much was obvious as they stepped out of the elevator. Whoever had been on duty in the hallway nurse's station was dead. Even from a distance that was easy to tell because people are rarely alive with half their face missing. A trail of blood led deeper into the ward. As they got deeper in they checked the first room. A man tethered to the bed and to machines that were making a long, continuous beep was also very sincerely dead and partly eaten on the blood-soaked sheets. Then they heard from the end of the hallway the moaning growl of the zombies.

She and Lucas rushed forward, side by side, while Beth hoped that the people they'd left by the door would keep the zombies from attacking them from behind. The hospital smelled of blood and feces, overlaid on the normal disinfectant smell, and the polished tiles of the hallway were spattered in blood, which made it hard to run without falling on her face. Once she almost fell, but Lucas Fiacre grabbed her shoulder, without ever slowing down, and hauled her upright.

At the end of the hallway, they were faced with a knot of people, all wearing hospital gowns. It was clear a lot of them were zombies, covered in bite marks and groaning-moaning.

But the thing was, when formication—the sensation of something crawling all over their skin—hit, as people were zombing out, they ripped all their clothes off. With the hospital gown that was not easy—them being tied behind the back.

Which posed the problem.

"Shit," Lucas said as he came to a skidding halt. "Is it just zombies fighting?"

"Oh, hell no," a voice said from the middle of the melee. "About time you guys got here. I'm going to give this hospital a very bad review in my patient satisfaction form!"

## HE LEFT YESTERDAY BEHIND HIM . . .

Zachary Zodiac Smith had been having a bad day long before this. Actually if you really wanted to be specific, he'd had a bad decade. Maybe a bad life. But he balked at that idea. His life hadn't been bad. At least not until Mom had decided to off herself when Dad hadn't come back from 'Nam. But even then there had been intermittent good times. Hell, yeah, very good times. Like Rosie.

But he turned his mind away from his first wife, Rosamund. Damn good thing, all things considered, that Rosie and the baby had died. Otherwise now he'd have to worry about her, and about a twenty-year-old son. Okay, maybe it wasn't a good thing they'd died, but at least they hadn't zombed out. Thank God. Until now ZZ hadn't understood *a fate worse than death*. Now he did. Even if a part of him still longed to know that when he died he left something of him behind. But how many people would be able to do that now?

He stood with his back to the wall. He'd wrapped his arms in blankets, haphazardly because he hadn't exactly had a lot of time when the patient on the bed next to him had started screaming there was stuff crawling on him and throwing the bed clothes around. ZZ wasn't an idiot. Not him. He knew damn well what that shit meant, and he was out of his bed, wrapping his arms in sheet and blanket with a lot of it trailing, and grabbing the nearest defensive weapon. Which wasn't a very good weapon, being the tray on wheels that they'd put next to the bed.

Given he'd come in for throwing up all his food and catastrophic weight loss and the stomach cancer and all, he probably wouldn't have been able to lift a tray like that normally, but fear, like love, makes a man stronger. He was swinging the tray table around, and caught the guy getting up from the other bed, teeth gnashing and hands groping, on the side of the head and sent him flying.

Of course he came back. ZZ had seen zombie videos on YouTube. There was a reason people were calling this the zombie apocalypse. The damn things just. Wouldn't. Stay. Down.

He tried to forget the guy had been named Bill and that he had cancer of the bladder, and that he had a two-year-old grandson and a granddaughter in Arizona. There was no Bill now, only a zombie, chomping and clawing as it dragged itself upright, and lurched towards ZZ.

Who, this time, managed to catch him harder on the other side of the head, and, when Bill dropped, rush him and smash his head flat with the tray table.

Apparently Bill was not the only one to have turned, because there was the sound of chomping teeth in the hallway and someone rushed in, running like a gorilla, on feet and knuckles, and dragging a mess of tubes and an IV stand behind her. ZZ had smashed her against the wall, hitting out with the tray and catching her head between it and the wall. Her head went crunch and then splat, with a sound not unakin to a cabbage getting dropped from a great height, and he turned his head just in time to avoid being splatted with blood and brain matter.

But there was another zombie. Right about the third, he realized that they had to be coming from somewhere, which left him with the question *where in hell are all these zombies coming from?* It was impossible they'd all zombed out at the same time as Bill. Okay, not impossible, but not likely.

Before he could think to investigate, he was surrounded by zombies, and then it was crunch, smack, hit. And he realized after a while they were going to get him in the end. There was only one of him. Which meant that they'd kill him and—

And he heard two young people talking, a man and a woman.

He called out to them. Then he thought that even as they waded into the fray they might have trouble telling the zombies from the not-zombie, to wit, himself.

As the young lady—and she was a looker too, with that braid of red hair—deployed a floor lamp—it occurred to him she might select his head for crunching. And like that, unbidden, came to his lips the song his mother had sung when they went walking when he was a tot, and he found himself singing aloud. "Rocky Mountain High, Colorado!"

The young lady redirected the club, the young man stuck his lance in someone else, and ZZ made to help them with the table.

In a moment—seemed like—they were panting and covered in sweat and blood, the zombies were down, and ZZ said, "Thank you."

The man, a dark-haired guy, lean with a sort of sharp face, which made ZZ think of Caesar's line about lean men, said, "No prob. But stop singing hippie songs, okay? I can still change my mind and stab you."

"Hey, it was my momma's favorite song, youngster, and besides get off my lawn."

And then there was the sound of groaning and of teeth from the hallway, and zombies poured into the room.

"Where in Hell are they coming from?" ZZ asked.

"I don't know. We have the emergency stairs blocked and we—" the guy said, as he turned to stab zombies. Fortunately this set was easier, as they stopped to eat their fallen comrades. But not too easy as there were at least twenty of them.

"The other emergency stairs," the girl said.

"Shit. There's more than one of them?" the guy yelled, putting his lance into a zombie's eye and twisting.

"Fire regulations or something," the girl yelled, swinging her club and spraying out brains. "I can't believe we forgot."

"Why not? I always used the elevator."

To show he was willing, ZZ stepped up to stand with them and slam his table into zombies.

"But that means . . ." the girl said. It was weird that she looked even better like that, splattered in blood and fighting. She reminded him of Rosie is what it was, and he shouldn't be eyeing a girl half his age. Particularly not when he was dying. But ZZ had never felt less like dying. He had trouble concentrating on the rest of her words, as they all killed zombies. When they had taken care of that wave she said, "That means the people we left blocking the stairway from the zombies below—"

"Might be overtaken?" the lean man said.

"No, might be lapped," the girl said. "I mean, when we get to the other floors, there will be zombies there ahead of us."

"Shit," the lean man said. He turned to ZZ. "You—what's your name?"

"Zeezee."

"Right. I'm Lucas Fiacre, and that's Beth Arden. Is there anyone else alive on this floor? Not zombies?"

ZZ eyed the door. "If there were, they're probably eaten. Going to sue the fucking hospital for not issuing fucking guns to fucking patients when this fucking Pacific flu started."

"Tell me about it, man," the lean guy said. "I fucking hate that we have nothing designed to kill these sons of bitches on hand. I'm going to run down the hallway and check. Just to make sure."

"Don't," Beth said. "Just call out."

"It will attract zombies."

"We are anyway."

Fiacre stepped forward, while Beth and ZZ lent support, and as soon as they were through the door, Fiacre shouted, "So, anyone not a zombie in here? Scream or knock or something."

There was no answer but the gnash of teeth and the groaning. "Hey, you hoo!" Fiacre said and did his best attempt at the hundred meter dash towards the door to the stairwell while slaying zombies—now that would have been a game for the Olympics—stab zombie, run, stab zombie, run, trip over zombie that Beth killed, almost fall and get eaten except ZZ caught him and pulled him forward.

Then both of them tripped on a still-live zombie—stab, scream, smash head with table. Beth saved them from falling and pulled them along.

By the end of the hallway, they were all fighting with one hand and holding the other up with the other, while jumping, dodging, tripping over fallen zombies.

## I'VE SEEN IT RAINING FIRE IN THE SKY

When they got back to the landing there was pandemonium. Dr. Hayden was alternately opening and slamming the door, managing to catch some zombies in it each time, while Dr. Barfuss wanted to know precisely what this meant and why they were not going up as promised.

People recoiled from Beth and Lucas and ZZ as they came in. Dr. Barfy said something about contagion. Yeah, well, he should try killing zombies without getting it all over himself.

Lucas told them about the other staircase.

"Does that mean there will be zombies up ahead of us?" one of the nurses asked, dismayed.

"Yep. We'll have to fight all the way up."

"And where are we going once we get to the top?" Dr. Barfuss asked. "Bet you haven't thought of that young man. Even if we can fly the helicopters—"

*Do no harm*, Beth told herself. It was weird, because with adrenaline pumping through her, she could have smashed Dr. Barfy in the face, like a zombie. She realized she'd have to control it. *That's the slippery slope,* she thought. *Kill zombies because they can't come back and are just vectors, and then start thinking of people who annoy you as better off dead too.* And she was almost sure it wasn't true. Dr. Barfy might be an annoying paper-pusher, but what Dr. Pillarisetti had said about the collapse of civilization? *If there aren't enough people who can learn, who will be doctors?* They might need even Dr. Barfy.

Lucas was saying something, answering Dr. Barfuss "...can.

We'll go to Plynth. You know, the new hospital, which was supposed to open on Monday. They're fully stocked. They have generators. They're empty."

"They won't be empty once the generators start and they have light and sound," someone said.

The group was going forward, up the stairs. Beth looked back at where Dr. Jonna Hayden was still holding the door. "Doctor, do you see any way to secure that door? To delay them? This stairway seems to be free of zombies."

"Only because they're eating people in the wards," ZZ, the man they'd rescued said. He was tall, middle-aged, a bit gaunt, but tanned. Black and possibly native American and white and who knew what else, Beth thought, looking at him, so that tan might be built in. It wasn't displeasing. Whatever he was, he was a scrappy fighter, and he still had that table clutched in his hand.

Beth chose not to argue and Lucas inclined his head. "Probably. But all the same. If we can get to the top with a minimum of fuss."

"Okay," Dr. Hayden said. She'd taken something off her white coat and seemed to be jamming it under the door.

"What was that?" Lucas asked, as she started up.

"My cell phone," the doctor said. "Figured end of the world, didn't need it."

They started running up the stairs, but Lucas stopped at the door to the third floor.

"What are you doing?" a woman asked.

"Going to see if anyone can be saved."

"That's insane. The zombies will just get ahead of us," Dr. Barfuss said.

"Fine. You go ahead, then, run on up. You and whoever wants to go with you. I'll go see if anyone needs saving," Fiacre said.

"I'll come with you, son," ZZ said.

"Me, too," Beth said, surprised to hear her own voice as she said it. But after all, she was here to save people, right?

Third floor yielded three people, all women, one coughing violently with the early stages of H7D3. For a moment Beth thought it would be faster to kill her now and easier on everyone, but after all you couldn't. Maybe there was a chance she wouldn't turn. At least the woman was wearing a mask. And all three survivors had been blooded in combat with the zombies. The coughing woman was holding an IV stand as a mace. People who really did fight as cornered cats were probably as valuable as normal doctors and twice as valuable as Dr. Barfuss.

Fourth floor, Maternity, yielded a desperate woman clutching a baby in one arm, and a jagged, broken flower vase in the other. The vase had blood on it, and there was blood sprayed up her arm and on her hospital gown. The problem hadn't so much been rescuing her, as stopping her from stabbing them as they approached. But in the end, she'd staggered and sobbed, lowering the arm that held the vase, and sobbed, "My husband. He was visiting. He—"

"Turned?" Beth said.

"I had to kill him, I had to."

"Of course," Beth said. "You had to." She said it because she needed to comfort the woman, but her brain told it was right too. "Can you run?"

And they ran.

By the seventh and top floor, as they emerged onto the terrace that held three helicopters, they'd gathered fifteen people in addition to their starting-out two dozen.

Beth almost expected to hear Dr. Barfuss greet them with "That's too many people, you idiot. You'll never take off."

But he didn't because Dr. Barfuss was dead. And Ron, the helicopter pilot, was happily tearing pieces of flesh off Dr. Barfuss and eating them.

"Oh, hell," Beth said, and brought her lamp down hard on the head of the helicopter pilot, again and again and again, beating head and face, and neck to pulp long after he'd stopped twitching.

"Stop!" Dr. Pillarisetti yelled, and grabbed her arm. He was covered in blood and unidentifiable fragments and had just come from the stairway. "Stop, Beth. Stop. He's dead."

And then Beth had started crying. ZZ, the patient, had kind of gathered her in and said, "It's all right. It's better than freezing up, kid."

He only let go of her as they were apportioning people between helicopters. He patted her shoulder as he called out, "Oh, hell, yeah, I can fly one of these. Better than the crap I flew in Desert Storm. At least no one will be shooting at us. Probably."

When they were trying to cram more people than should be possible into each of the rescue helicopters, Beth found herself next to Dr. Pillarisetti and asked, "How did you get so bloody? You weren't on the stairs."

"No," Nikhil Pillarisetti said. "I doubled back, to go . . . to euthanize those people we left behind strapped in carts. Some of them were our friends. And at any rate, leaving even a zombie strapped down and helpless to be eaten by other zombies felt wrong. So I cut their throats. Well, those I could reach. Definitely Dr. Tomboulian. I couldn't leave her. Don't look at me like that."

"No. Thank you," Dr. Hayden said quietly.

"Yeah, it was hell managing to get back here, though. Someone had jammed a cell phone under the bottom floor door," he said, and grinned as he handed it to Dr. Hayden. The doctor just looked sad as she took it back.

When Dr. Hayden zombed out, as they rose high over the city—which was burning, flames licking up to the sky—it was Beth who strangled her, quickly, efficiently, and before Dr. Hayden could bite anyone in the press of terrified people. *She would have preferred it*, Beth thought, as she held her friend and felt her spasm and fight and finally go limp. There was no Dr. Hayden left, not really. This was stopping a vector. And doing no harm.

"I'm sorry, Beth," ZZ told her as he got to her, just too late to help.

"It was a promise," was all she said. To Dr. Hayden, and to herself.

# Not in Vain

## KACEY EZELL

Once upon a time a very good friend had described a cheerleading competition as the seventh circle of hell. It was probably sacrilege for a cheerleading coach to feel that way, but Mia Swanson had to admit that her old flying buddy had a point. After eight hours of squealing, chanting, hyper high-schoolers throwing each other up in the air, tumbling down open hallways and quite literally bouncing off the walls . . . Mia had a headache. And there was still most of an hour left on their seven-hour drive back to Albuquerque from Colorado Springs.

*Two hours*, Mia promised herself. *Two hours and I'll be home, in a bathtub, waiting for Max and the girls to get home. We'll have dinner. It will be great.*

One of the most irritating things about this particular competition was that it had fallen on a Shooting Weekend. Once every other month or so, Mia and some friends and their families got together and went shooting out on White Mesa, just outside of Albuquerque. It was all BLM land out there, and as long as they took precautions not to hit anyone or any animals, there were no restrictions. It had started before she retired from the Air Force a year ago, and it had rapidly become one of her favorite traditions.

Alas, retirement meant a new career, and a new career meant new commitments. Mia glanced over her shoulder at the teenagers sprawled in various seats in the fifteen-passenger van and smiled. Seventh circle of hell aside, this really was her dream job. These were good kids, and Mia was proud to coach them.

"What's that?" Jessa asked, sitting up and pulling her iPhone earbuds out of her ears, as if that would help her see better. Mia looked up and cursed lightly under her breath. Blue and red flashing lights stained the sky up over the next slight hill, and she'd been doing closer to eighty than seventy mph. She eased off the gas and began to brake, just as they crested the hill.

"A roadblock?" Mia could hear the incredulity in her own voice as she continued to slow the van. "Jessa, have you got signal? See if you can pull up the news." The senior immediately set to work as Mia pulled to a stop, rolling down her window as a uniformed officer approached her window.

"Officer. Good evening," Mia started. "What's going on? I..." She'd been about to disclose that she was armed, even though she hadn't exactly told the team that, and she was certain that she'd hear from some irate parents. It might even cost her the job, new as she was, but there had been no way Mia was going to be taking a three-day competition trip, with a fourteen-hour total drive time with twelve teenagers and no weapon. No fucking thank you.

"I-25 is closed," the officer said, cutting her off abruptly. He appeared to be sweating, and his expression looked agitated.

"Just the road? Is there an accident?" Mia asked. Maybe they could cut over to Bernalillo and take one of the state highways down through Rio Rancho.

"City's under quarantine. Governor declared a state of emergency—" The officer abruptly stopped talking and started scratching vigorously at his throat, where his collar met his neck.

"Coach?" Jessa called. She and another of the seniors were huddled over her iPhone, the glow from the screen throwing a white, eerie light on their faces in the growing dusk.

"Not now, Jessa," Mia replied, trying to keep the patience in her voice. "Sir? Officer, are you all right?"

"No, what is on me? Oh God, they're all over me!" the man screamed, and then, to Mia's complete astonishment, he began to strip off all of his clothing.

"Officer, stop! There are children in this car!" Mia said, aghast. She glanced out the front window of the car, only to see two more half-naked officers coming toward them, shedding clothing and gear as they went. "What the fuck is this?"

"Coach!" Jessa screamed. Mia turned in time to see a fourth naked man reaching in through the half-open window at them. She and two other girls flinched away from the window and his grasping, reaching hand. For no reason whatsoever, Mia noticed that his arm was covered in coarse, dark hair.

In her past life as a combat helicopter pilot, Mia had often faced situations where she had to make a decision quickly, and it had to be right or she and her crew could die. She'd thought that being a high school cheerleading coach would have been different. Apparently she was wrong.

The officer at her window had stopped cursing and began screaming. Keening, more like. When she was a kid, Mia had devoured Anne McCaffrey's dragonriders series. In that series, when a dragon died, its fellows were said to raise a keen that damn near shattered eardrums with its sound. Mia could only imagine that sound was much like this one. That was the thought that flitted past her consciousness as she made her decision and acted. She thought of dragons crying out in mourning.

In one smooth, mechanical move, Mia removed her Ruger .45 from her concealed carry purse and put the gun against the head of the officer now reaching for her through her open window. The back of his head exploded outward, and Jessa and some of the other girls screamed, Mia supposed. She couldn't really hear, thanks to the fact that she'd just fired a gun in a mostly enclosed car. Then she turned and shot the man on the passenger side, still reaching for the girls through the window.

Then she turned and gunned the engine. The van leapt forward and slammed into the naked bodies of the two remaining officers. They went down and she felt the sickening crunch as her wheels went over one of them. Then she threw the van in reverse and backed up far enough to shoot the one whose skull she hadn't crushed.

Sound suddenly came back all in a rush. Behind her, cheerleaders where whimpering in shocked tones, while Jessa continued to call for her. Incongruously, the opening chords of Ellie Goulding's "Anything Could Happen" came out through the speakers, thanks to her iPhone plugged in to the van's radio. Mia couldn't help it. She started laughing.

"Coach?" Jessa asked again, her voice scared.

"It's all right, Jessa," Mia said. "Just give me a minute. I won't let them hurt you guys."

"N-no, we know that," Jessa said, though her voice trembled. "But I think you need to see this." She held out her phone. On it, on one of the mobile news websites, were the words Mia had been refusing to think.

"ZOMBIE OUTBREAK HITS LA, NY! Major cities under quarantine. States of emergency declared all over the nation..."

There was more, but Mia had seen what she needed to see. Anything could happen, indeed, Ellie, she thought as she handed the phone back to Jessa. "All right. Jessa, read the rest of the article and get anything useful out of it and any other news pages. Anything about cures, vaccines, instructions, whatever."

Mia put the van back into drive and rolled forward until she could pull off next to the roadblock. They'd just passed the exit to NM 550. They'd go back and take that exit, she supposed. "You guys stay here and keep a look out for any other cars. If someone comes over the hill, lay on the horn. I've got to get some stuff."

The team was too shocked to argue as Mia took her gun and hopped out. First up were the downed officers' weapons: standard issue 9mm pistols. Mia grabbed the officers' gear belts as well. Might as well have somewhere to holster the 9s, she supposed. One of the officers' car keys had half spilled out of his pants pocket during his striptease, and Mia took the opportunity to look in the trunk of the APD car.

"Jackpot," she said lowly. The article had mentioned quarantine, so Mia hadn't wanted to take the officers' body armor, in case it had gotten blood on it when she'd killed them. Here, however, were spare tactical vests and two twelve gauge pump shotguns. She quickly took the items and headed back to the van. While her cheerleading team watched with wide, disbelieving eyes, she threw this loot, plus all the ammo she could find in the cars into the empty passenger seat of the van. Then she went back and took the mini-igloo cooler that she'd found on the floorboard of the car. Inside were several bottles of water and glory of glories: a twelve-ounce can of Sugar Free Red Bull. She brought this back and started the van back up.

"Looks like we're taking a different route," she said as she wheeled her way back around. Luckily, there was no one else approaching as they took the exit off of I-25 onto NM 550.

It took a full ten minutes of driving in silence before one of the cheerleaders spoke up. As Mia might have suspected, it was Jessa.

"Coach?" Jessa asked, her tone steadier, but still uncertain. "Um . . . ?"

"What happened?" Mia asked, humor in her tone, despite everything. "Was that what you were trying to ask?"

Jessa tittered nervously, and a few of the others laughed in the growing darkness. The sun was sinking behind the desert mesas directly in front of them, and Mia had dug her dark Oakleys out of her purse.

"Well, yeah. I mean, that was pretty . . . um . . ."

"Weird?"

"Yeah, weird."

"Yeah," Mia agreed. "It was. I'll explain it here in a second, okay? I need to do a few things first. Actually, I need you all to do something for me. You all have your phones, right?"

A chorus of *yes's* filled the back seat.

"Okay," Mia said. "Of course you all do. I need you all to text your parents. Tell them that we didn't make it in to Albuquerque before the quarantine. Tell them that I'm taking you to a safe place to wait out the plague. Tell them that they can meet us at the following coordinates. Are you all ready?"

Another chorus of *yes's*.

Mia checked the note on her phone and read off: "North 38 degrees, 18 minutes, 6 seconds. West 111 degrees, 25 minutes, 12 seconds. Sam," she said, calling out her one senior male cheerleader. Sam, she knew, was an Eagle Scout. "Check everyone's phone and make sure they got it right before they hit send."

She heard a few sniffles, some more whimpers, but eventually, everyone did it. "Now, I need to make a phone call. I need you guys to be quiet."

Normally, Mia wouldn't dream of driving and talking on the phone in front of her team. It was setting a horrible example. However, she was not about to stop again before she had to in order to get gas. Luckily, they'd filled up in Santa Fe, so her tank was mostly full. She pulled out her phone and dialed her husband.

"Baby?" Max Swanson asked, picking up on the first ring. His voice was filled with anxiety and worry, and it damn near brought tears to Mia's eyes. She blinked furiously.

"I'm all right," she said quickly. "We didn't make it in to Albuquerque before they closed the Interstate."

"Oh, thank God," he said. "Neither did we. We just got the news on the radio and got packed up. We're bugging out to your mom's. We can wait here for you . . . wait . . . Hashim wants to talk to you," Max said, his voice strained.

Mia blinked. Hashim Noori was a very good friend. She'd met him in Iraq almost seven years ago. He'd been her interpreter then, but he'd since gotten a visa and moved to the U.S. He was a microbiology professor at UNM. Mia couldn't imagine what on Earth could have made Hashim interrupt her husband on the phone, but then, this morning she couldn't have imagined that she'd be bugging out in a zombie apocalypse scenario with her cheerleading team, either.

"Hashumi," Mia said into the phone. "*Salaam wa alaykum.*"

"*Walaykum salaam,*" Hashim said, his lightly accented English impatient. "Mia. I must ask you. You were in a city?"

"Yes, we were in Colorado Springs, at a cheerleading competition."

"There were many people there?"

"Yes, Hashim, why?"

Her former terp was silent for a long moment. "Mia. You have all been exposed. I have been reading messages on the Internet. This virus is unlike anything else. It is airborne like a cold, but it is also passed through the blood, or a bite or cut. Body fluids from an infected person."

Mia pursed her lips. "Infected person. Hashumi, do they strip down? Go crazy, like?"

"Yes, Mia. You have seen one?"

"Four. The cops at the roadblock. They attacked us."

"Mia!"

"They are dead," Mia said, her voice blank. She still wasn't thinking about the fact that she'd just killed four cops. "No one got bit or scratched."

"That is good, but Mia, this is very bad news. You must not join up with us."

"No, I think you're right. We'll follow along behind until we know if any of us have got it. How long?"

"The incubation period is approximately a week, but if the police are turning now...we should know in a day or two."

"Got it. May I speak to my husband again, please?"

"Of course. *Fe aman Allah.*"

"And you, my friend."

"Baby? How long till you can be here?" Max asked.

"I'll be there in about thirty minutes, but you have to go on ahead without me."

"What? No!"

"Baby, listen," Mia said, blinking quickly to keep the tears at bay and remain focused on the road in front of her. "I have twelve cheerleaders with me. We were just at a fucking cheer competition! You know what those things are like! Hashim said this thing is like a cold. We could all be infected, and I'm not bringing that around you or the girls. You go to Mom's. Hole up. Stay alive. I'll join you as soon as I know it's safe. I love you."

Max was silent. Mia could hear him breathing deeply, quickly. She heard the distant giggle of her youngest daughter through the phone. Finally, Max sighed.

"All right," he said, softly. "But you stay alive too, you hear me?"

"I will," she promised, knowing it wasn't in her control at all. Knowing it could already be a lie, she promised. "I'll see you soon."

They'd gone on ahead to White Mesa anyway. It was slightly out of the way, but Mia didn't want to take the chance of catching up to Max's group. After she'd finished talking to Max, her friend Allison had gotten on the phone and told her that they'd leave a cache of supplies at their normal shooting site. Mia had very nearly cried again, but she'd managed to hold it together. Mostly because the sun was fully down now, and she needed to concentrate in order to see the road and the unmarked turn-off to their shooting spot.

Though the sun had just gone down, the half moon was already riding high. The dust from their slow rumble up the dirt road filled the air, as Mia stepped out of the van. The moon turned the dust a silvery color and she was abruptly reminded of another night, in another desert, under the same moon, but a world away.

*"Salaam wa alaykum,"* a voice called out of the shadows. Without thinking, Mia had the .45 up, pointing at the voice and the figure that emerged from the shadows. *"Qaf!"* she shouted.

"Mia, my friend, it is me," Hashim said, his hands up as he walked closer. Mia lowered her weapon and let out an explosive breath.

"Hashumi!" she said, walking forward to hug the wiry microbiologist. He might have hesitated for just a moment, but he'd been in the U.S. long enough that he hugged her back. "You idiot, I could have shot you!"

"That is why I called out," he said reasonably. She gave him a Look.

"Hashim, you called out in Arabic. This has been a very weird day. I like Arabic, but it doesn't exactly calm me down."

Hashim laughed. Mia shook her head, but eventually she gave up and chuckled with him. "What are you doing here, anyway?" she asked. "I told you guys to go on ahead."

Hashim abruptly sobered. "I came to help you. You are one adult with twelve teenagers. It will be hard for you to keep them all safe alone. And if any are infected... well. I may be able to make a vaccine."

"Vaccine?" she asked, her voice rising, her eyes widening. "You can cure this?"

"Not cure, vaccinate," Hashim said. "We were working on something at the lab this week, when the first rumors started. UCLA sent us some samples and some protocols... it isn't hard, and it works. I have been vaccinated. But... this will be hard for you, I am afraid."

Mia took a long look at her old friend. On the surface, Hashim looked like any other professor of vaguely middle-eastern descent. He wasn't particularly big, and his wiry frame sometimes looked as if a stiff wind would blow him over. However, Mia knew him, she knew his history. She knew that he'd been hunted by Al Qaida since he was younger than her cheerleaders. She knew that he'd been shot, that his brother had died in his arms. She knew that he'd killed in his own defense before. He'd stood shoulder to shoulder with her brothers in arms, and that had earned him a ticket here, to the so-called promised land.

Hashim was hard. He would do whatever it took. He loved her like a sister, but she had no doubts that he'd shoot her between the eyes if she turned, in order to keep himself and others safe. And that was just what she wanted.

"Tell me," she said, her eyes going flat as they hadn't been for years since she got back from Iraq.

"The vaccine must be made from infected spinal tissue," he said softly.

Mia closed her eyes momentarily while she absorbed this bit of information. Then she nodded, shoved the moral implications away in the back with the picture of the four dead cops and opened her eyes.

"All right," she said. "Let's take you to meet my team."

"Coyotes," Mia called in to the van. "Come out here. Time for a team meeting."

One by one, the cheerleaders filed out of the van. True to New Mexico form, the temperature had dropped rapidly as the sun went down and a few of the freshmen were shivering in their warm-ups. Mia hefted the duffel bag that Hashim had carried and opened it up. Inside were several sweatshirts and jackets. It looked like Allison had raided their camping gear and left it for them.

Mia let a smile cross her lips as she passed out the warmer clothing. Allison and Evan Dwyer were good friends. Evan had been a flight engineer in Mia's last squadron. The families had bonded over camping and shooting excursions, and Allison was one of the kindest people Mia'd ever met.

She was also a damn good shot with rifle, pistol and compound bow. And Evan had an arsenal that a gun dealer would envy. They were exactly who Mia would have picked for her zombie survival team. If she would have had time to pick a team, that is. She could think of no one better to help Max protect her girls, as well as their own baby girl, Kimber.

"All right, Coyotes," Mia said, bringing herself forcibly back to the present. The cheerleaders had distributed the warmer clothing and stood in a rough circle in front of her and Hashim.

"I promised I'd tell you what was going on, and I thank you for being patient while I figured it all out. Basically, here's the deal: the shit has well and truly hit the fan. Jessa, you want to brief us on what you found from the news sites?"

Jessa looked a bit startled, but she stepped right up. There was a reason she was the team captain. "Um, there's been an outbreak.

Most people think it's a biological terror attack. People get sick, like the flu, and then they go crazy and strip, like those cops back on the highway. And then they act like zombies. They'll try to bite people . . . and if they do, then those people turn into zombies, too. That's about all I've got. The news sites are talking about a vaccine and a government response, but everyone's saying something different."

Mia nodded. That had been about what she expected. "Thank you, Jessa. I had you all text your parents and give them the coordinates of a town in Utah near a safe place. My family is headed to that place now. We've got supplies there. We can wait this out and survive there . . . but there's a problem.

"I won't lie to you guys. There's a good chance we've all been exposed. If we have, then we'll turn, like those cops."

The shocked looks travelled around the circle. Elia, a sophomore, stumbled and sat down, hard, on the ground. Tears began to stream down her face, and she wasn't the only one. Danny, a junior and her only other male cheerleader bent down and put his arms around her, whispering in her ear.

"Listen to me," Mia said. "Listen!" When she had their attention, she took a deep breath and went on. "I can't promise you won't get sick. But I promise you this. If you do get sick, I can promise you that I won't let you become like those things back at the highway. I won't let you hurt anyone."

She looked over at Hashim. He nodded slightly.

"This is Dr. Noori. He is a very good friend of mine. Dr. Noori has been vaccinated. He knows how to make more vaccine. But in order to do that, we have to use spinal tissue from infected people. I know that's horrible. I know it is, but that's the reality we have to deal with." Mia kept going, relentlessly driving the point home. They are adults now, she reminded herself. Their childhood ended two hours ago.

Elia raised her tear-wet eyes. "Coach?" she asked tremulously.

"Yes, Elia?"

"If I . . . if I get sick, can I . . . can Dr. Noori use me? Because I don't want to die for nothing."

The tears came hard and fast to Mia's eyes. She swiped savagely at her face and nodded, not trusting herself to speak as each of the cheerleaders, her cheerleaders, murmured their agreement with Elia. Even her two freshmen, Sonia and Dawn. Even at fourteen fucking years old, they were nodding vehemently. Mia waved them all in, and she subsequently found herself mobbed by twelve cheerleaders all trying to hug her and each other, all at once.

"I promise you," Mia said, her voice ragged and tear-soaked. "No one dies for nothing."

They stayed there for another hour or so while Mia handed out weapons and explained the basics of shooting to those who hadn't done so before. Both of the boys had been hunting, so they got the rifles that Allison had packed. Jessa got a shotgun, as did Cassidy, another senior. Yolanda and Bella, both seniors, got two of the cops' 9mm pistols, as did Gina and Mackayla, juniors. The younger girls were instructed to partner up with the seniors and stay with them. Mia distributed the body armor as best she could, but she kept most of it for herself and Sam. It was too big for pretty much everyone else.

When she was at least confident that no one would shoot themselves by accident, they piled back in the van and continued on down the road. Mia broke into the cops' Sugar Free Red Bull and savored the kick of the caffeine.

"Going to need to stop for fuel and supplies before too long," she said. They were still at over half a tank, but it didn't hurt to start making plans.

"How do you want to do that?" Hashim asked.

Mia pursed her lips. "I don't know yet," she confessed. "I suppose something will come to me. Ideally, we'd just walk in and pay for it as usual, but I don't know how ideal this situation's going to be."

"Coach?" Danny, the junior asked. Mia looked up and looked at him in the rear view mirror. He sat, his face illuminated by a phone, Elia resting on his shoulder, eyes closed.

"What, Danny?"

"I used to work at the Circle K on Alameda. Last summer. I know how to turn the pumps on from behind the counter. If it's not ideal, I mean."

Mia exchanged Looks with Hashim in the passenger seat. Taking one of her cheerleaders in to a potential deathtrap like a gas station was pretty high on her list of things she really didn't want to do . . . but no other option seemed to present itself.

"Okay," Mia said as they drove. "Here's what we'll do. Hashumi,

I'll give you my card. You hop out and start pumping. If that doesn't work, Danny and I will go in and authorize the pumps. We'll need to find a gas station that still has its lights on, though."

"Kill the lights!" Allison screamed, pulling the trigger of her 20-gauge and pumping another round into the chamber. "Kill the fucking headlights, Evan! They're attracted to the lights!"

Evan, on the other side of the camper, would have loved to have killed the headlights. Unfortunately, he was a little busy holding off a naked adolescent girl who was doing her ever-loving best to get her teeth into his neck. He got his feet planted under him and spun, smashing her head into the steel I-beam that flanked the gas pumps at the Circle K in Farmington, NM. The infected girl's skull caved in, and blood and other fluids leaked out of her ears and eyes. Evan threw her body away from himself as quickly as he could, and then reached for his Kimber 1911 as the sound of Allison's shotgun came around from the other side.

Suddenly, tires squealed, and a gunmetal gray Nissan plowed through the wall of naked bodies that streamed toward the beleaguered camper. Just as quickly as he'd arrived, Max threw the truck into reverse and backed back the way he'd come, running back over bursting rib cages, tires slipping on the blood and entrails in his wake. Several of the infected turned away from the camper, toward this new source of food and noise, and Allison, at least, was able to get her door open, throw in the bag of groceries she'd gotten, and climb into the passenger seat. Another blast from her 20-gauge rang out as she shot through the open door, severing the arm of the closest infected. She kicked the severed arm out of the car and slammed the door shut. "EVAN!" she screamed as she leaned over and turned the key, starting the camper's powerful engine.

Evan shot one, then another as they came at him. He fumbled at the door handle, his hand slick with sweat. Eventually, he got it open, but not before one of the infected managed to squeeze between the gas pump and the supporting I-beam and sink his teeth into Evan's calf. Evan howled and shot the attacker in the head, but the sting in his calf said that he was already too late. He'd broken the skin. He was infected.

"Allison," he said.

"Evan, no," Allison said. "Get in. Please."

"No. I'm hit. Slide over and drive. Stay with Max. Get Kimber to safety. I love you."

"Evan!"

"I love you, Allison," he said again, as he reached across the seat for the shiny red plastic two-way radio he'd been using to talk to Max in the gray truck. Allison, sobbing, did as he bid, sliding over the center console into the driver's seat while he turned and shot at another infected reaching for them. Evan Dwyer kissed his wife, one last hard, long kiss on the mouth, and then slammed the door.

Allison could barely see through her tears, but she slammed the camper into reverse and gunned the engine, her tires squealing on the concrete as she backed out rather than attempt to plow through the crowd that never seemed to end.

"Max, Evan."

"Evan, buddy, you guys out?"

"Negative. Allison's out. I'm hit."

Long pause. "Shit."

"Yeah. Got an idea," Evan said as he shot another one off of him. He had three bullets left in this eight-round mag. He'd left his spare mags in the camper. Good thing, too. Allison or Max could use the .45 ammo.

"Go with idea." Max said. He could see the camper approaching now. He could see Allison's face. Shit.

Evan lifted the hose of the gas pump and began spraying fuel. He wasn't sure if this would work as well as it always seemed to do in the movies, but he did know that gasoline atomized fairly well, especially when you held your finger over the hose in order to make it spray into the air. He mentally thanked Allison for jamming the shutoff mechanism when she'd gone inside. That had been a bit of genius.

The infected seemed to be thrown off by the smell of the gasoline filling the air. Evan found that incredibly funny as the first shiver of fever started to race through him.

"Evan?"

"Yeah. So. I've soaked this place down well with gas. You still got those .762 tracers that I don't have and neither of us knows where I got?"

Despite himself, Max smiled. "Yeah."

"What say I draw a big crowd into my little gasoline shower and you light this fucking place up?"

"You got it, buddy," Max said as he wheeled the truck around. He had Evan's AK-47 in his lap.

"Max."

"Yeah."

"Take care of my girls."

"Like they were my own, man. I give you my word."

"Ha! A gunner's word," Evan said, jokingly. Before he'd qualified as a flight engineer, he'd been an aerial gunner once, just like Max. "The fuck's that worth?"

Max laughed, blinking the tears aside as he pulled up to within the AK's range. He could see Evan there, on the radio, standing in the midst of a puddle of gas, spraying the shit out of the place.

"Evan," Max said over the radio, his voice little more than a whisper.

"Yeah."

"In place."

"Roger. Here's to gunpowder and pussy, man." Evan said, shooting one of the slowly approaching infected. The rest of the infected turned toward him and began to gather faster, lunging at him. He fired another bullet. "Live by one . . ."

"Die by the other," Max whispered. He braced the AK on the door frame and took aim at the puddle at Evan's feet.

"Love the smell of both," Evan finished with satisfaction. Then he put the 1911 in his mouth and pulled the trigger, just as the horde of infected surged toward him, entering the cloud of atomized gasoline.

Max pulled the trigger, sending a single red tracer winging through the night.

The crowd of infected enveloped Evan's body as a tiny blue flame flickered on the surface of the gas-soaked concrete. Then the air itself ignited in a blinding flash that had Max diving for the floorboard of his truck and had the truck itself rocking on its shocks, even at this distance. In the back seat, his girls woke up crying, both of them, for their mother. Max could barely hear them through the ringing in his ears. He shook his head and forced himself back up into his seat, where he wheeled the truck around and headed back to the sheltered spot where he'd left Allison and the camper.

The clock on the dash read 8:23. Not terribly late, but the events of the day were taking their toll. Most of the cheerleaders were sleeping, heads leaning on one another or the windows. Hashim was awake, but he was deeply involved in the message boards he'd pulled up on his tablet. Mia was sick of listening to emergency messages that never changed and was saving the charge on her phone in case Max called. So it was kind of ironically funny that she jumped a mile high in her seat when the phone buzzed against the plastic of the van's center console.

"Hello?"

"Baby?"

"Max? Yeah, I'm here. You guys okay?"

"Yeah." Long pause. "We lost Evan."

"Oh shit." Hashim looked up at that one, his eyes worried. Mia mouthed "Evan" to him, and the microbiologist closed his eyes briefly.

"Allison okay?" Even as she asked, Mia knew it was a stupid thing to say. Of course Allison wasn't okay. She'd just lost her husband. Mia knew she'd be pretty fucking far from okay if it had been Max. But she didn't know how else to ask about her friend.

"No," Max said. "But she's holding. For now. She and Kimber weren't hit. Evan got bit. Listen. We figured out that they're attracted to light and motion. We got mobbed when we stopped for gas in Farmington. So be careful going through there."

Mia looked up as they passed a sign. Farmington, 25 miles. "Roger," she said. "Where'd you stop?"

"At the Circle K we usually use. It'll probably still be burning when you go past. Evan went out with a bang. Took a lot of those fuckers with him."

Despite everything, Mia smiled. That was exactly how Evan would have wanted it. "Good for him," she said. "Right, so we'll watch out for Farmington."

Another long pause. "How are the kids?" Max asked. "Anyone sick?"

Mia glanced over her shoulder at the team. "Not yet," she said. "Hashim says it's early yet, but I'm hopeful."

"Me too. I love you, baby. Stay safe."

"You too. I love you too."

As she hung up the phone, a soft, almost apologetic cough sounded from the far back seat.

"Coach?" It was Sonia's voice, one of their tiny freshman "flyers." She was good, always stuck her stunts at the top of their pyramid.

"What is it, Sonia?"

"I don't feel so good."

Thanks to the van's auxiliary fuel tank, they were able to avoid stopping for gas in Farmington. As they rolled past the remains of the Circle K (which was, in fact, still burning) Mia could see what Max had been talking about. Not only was there a crater where the parking lot had once been, but the entire front half of the building was gone and the rest was in flames. Still, though, the light and sound of the burning wreckage seemed to draw the infected out. Mia was surprised. She didn't think that Farmington had had that many people in it, let alone that many who'd been infected already. When she mentioned this to Hashim, though, he just shrugged.

"The bloodborne virus is much faster to spread than the airborne version," he said. "If you have one infected who attacks a living human, and then that one turns, who turns another . . . it would not take long, especially not in such a small community."

Mia felt herself pale, and then shoved that thought away in the back with the thought of vaccine production and four dead cops. She'd deal with all of that later. "I see," she said.

Hashim nodded. "It is a shame that we cannot harvest some of them for vaccine, but it is not worth the risk at this point."

"No," Mia said, "I agree." Her eyes flicked up to the rear view mirror, where Sonia lay in the back seat, loosely bound by bungee cords so that she could be restrained when the time came. As of right now, she still just had a fever, but from what Hashim was saying, it wouldn't be long.

"What will you need to produce the vaccine?" Mia asked, determined to think of something else. "Besides infected tissue?"

"It is really very simple," he said. "A small X-ray machine, some minor lab equipment. That is all."

Mia frowned. Torrey, UT, the town where her mother lived, wasn't large by any stretch of the imagination. It had fewer people than Farmington and nothing resembling a hospital . . . except . . .

"The community clinic!" Mia said, snapping her fingers. "We had to take Micaela there when she was little and broke her arm. They've got an X-ray machine, and I'd imagine most of the lab supplies you'll need."

"Where is this clinic?" Hashim asked.

"It's in downtown Torrey, or what passes for a downtown in a town as small as Torrey. It's right on the main road . . . oh." Mia felt her enthusiasm drain away as she thought her plan through. "That's exactly where they'd go if they were getting sick."

"Probably," Hashim agreed. "But, it is small, yes? Perhaps we can fight our way in and barricade ourselves inside?"

Mia snorted. "Yeah, that sounds like a lot of fun," she said softly, but then sighed. "But, as I don't have a better idea, I guess your plan is it. But first," she said, slowing and flipping off her headlights as they started approaching a lit section of the highway. "We need gas, and Shiprock is about our last resort for a long ways."

Hashim looked up, focusing on the buildings coming in to view. "Big town?"

"Smaller than Farmington, but not by much. They're almost linked. There's a place we usually stop near the outskirts, after we make our turn. I think that might be our bet."

"What is your plan? Do you still intend to act as normal?"

Mia pursed her lips, then shook her head. "I think it's too dangerous. Max said that the lights attracted a horde of infected. I think we'll just have to go in and out as fast as we can."

"I will pump the gas, then," Hashim said, as though asking for confirmation, "while you take Danny inside?"

"I think so. Do you think you can keep them off the van?"

"Perhaps, if your team can shoot from the windows, that would also be good."

Mia nodded, then looked up in the rearview mirror to see eleven pairs of eyes open, listening to their conversation. She met Danny's gaze, and the junior nodded.

"Give Jessa your rifle, and take her shotgun," Mia said. "When we go in, you follow close behind me. I'll clear the store itself, you just worry about getting behind the counter and getting the gas turned on, you got it?"

"Yes, coach," he said. In the seat in front of him, Sam pulled off the body armor he'd been wearing and handed it to Danny. It was too big, but better than nothing, Mia supposed. Especially if they got mobbed. It might keep Danny alive long enough for Hashim to come get them.

"All of you, when we come to a stop, take aim out the windows. Don't shoot until you have to do so. One, we don't have ammo to waste and two, we don't want the noise to draw more of a crowd than we have to." Mia turned the wheel as she spoke, not stopping for the red light, turning on to U.S. 491, the highway that would take them north into Colorado and then Utah.

A few more blocks, and Mia slowed. The gas station looked good. Parking lot was empty, lights were off. Nothing moving. Yet. She turned in to the driveway and cut the engine, coasting to a stop next to one of the pumps in a move that impressed even herself. She glanced back over her shoulder at Danny, who was poised next to the door. At her nod, he opened it, slowly, trying not to make too much noise. She followed suit and dropped softly out of her seat onto the concrete. She left her door open and began to jog toward the building. Naturally, it was locked, but Mia solved that problem neatly by shoving a sweatshirt up against the glass and having Danny hit it with a rock. Not a perfect solution, she mused, grimacing at the muffled crash and tinkle of glass hitting the ground, but it was what she had on short notice. She reached inside, flipped the deadbolt open and opened the door to the convenience store.

It was dark inside, and Mia blinked quickly, trying to force her eyes to adjust. Not for the first time on this adventure, she wished she had a pair of night vision goggles. She'd probably look pretty damn ridiculous, rolling around in her old flight helmet with a pair of goggles on the front, but it would be super useful to be able to see in the dark.

Goggles or not, she had a job to do here. Danny was already moving for the front counter, doing a passable job of being quiet and careful. He didn't really know how to professionally clear a room, but neither, for that matter, did she. All either of them had was good sense and self preservation. It would have to be enough.

She moved quietly through the store, methodically checking each of the four small aisles. She quickly looked in the restrooms and the back storeroom. All appeared to be clear. She went back out to the front to see Danny smiling at her, giving her a thumb's up. Apparently, he'd gotten the pumps turned on. A quick glance outside told her that Hashim was fueling the van, and all looked quiet for the moment. Time to get some supplies.

She motioned Danny over to the snack aisle, and pointed out the things she wanted. Mostly beef jerky and bottles of water, though she did throw in another four pack of Sugar Free Red

Bull. It was still five hours from here to Torrey, and with Sonia sick and others to follow, Mia had the feeling it was going to be a long night.

Speaking of which, she thought, turning to the small stash of automotive and hardware supplies the little store carried. She grabbed every roll of duct tape they had, plus some more bungee cords and a couple of multitools.

"Coach!" Danny called out in a harsh whisper. "I think we'd better go!"

Mia looked up right as the first infected came crashing through the hole they'd made in the front door.

"Shit!" she yelled. "Danny, get around the other side, get back to the van!" She drew her .45 and kicked the metal shelf, knocking several items to the floor with a resounding crash. "Hey!" she yelled, using her best "gotta be heard over turning rotors and screaming cheerleaders" voice. "Hey asshole! I'm over here! Come get me!"

Sure enough, the infected turned for her voice, as did the one following him through the door. The third one, however, turned for Danny as he tried to make it back toward the door. With presence of mind she wouldn't have expected from one so young, Danny cooly pointed the 12-gauge at the infected's head and pulled the trigger.

Mia's ears rang from the report, and blood and brain matter sprayed everywhere. Praying that Danny didn't have a cut on him somewhere, Mia shot the infected closest to her and dodged around the metal shelf as the second one lunged at her.

"Why," she said out loud, "Why the fuck did we have to get the fast zombies?" She said this last as she grabbed a tire iron off the shelf and swung it, hard, against the head of the second one. The infected's head deformed, almost as if it were made of putty, and the body slumped to the floor.

"Coach! We've got more coming!" Danny called. Mia scrubbed her sleeve across her face and looked up to see that he was right. There were easily twenty infected between them and the van, and the number looked like it was growing.

"C'mon," she said. "I think I saw a back door." Her tennis shoes slipped a bit in the zombie's blood as she took off toward Danny, but she kept her feet, barely. Mia turned down the hallway she'd checked earlier, finding the door marked "Emergency Exit Only" and half blocked by a hand truck. For no good reason at all, Mia grabbed the hand truck. It seemed like a useful thing to have, if nothing else, it could be used to bludgeon attacking infected.

More glass crashed in the store, and so Mia waved Danny through the door, her .45 still in her hand. She followed quickly, pausing just long enough to pull the door closed behind them. Hopefully, the infected in the store would cause enough of a ruckus to draw any others that way and keep them off the van.

They moved quickly, staying low, crouched next to the building in order to try to hide in the shadows as much as possible. When they rounded the corner, they could see the gas pumps, but no van. For one heart-stopping moment, Mia couldn't decide between being grateful to Hashim for getting her kids out and to safety, or being furious that he'd left her and Danny behind.

Fortunately, she didn't have long to waffle. Before they could blink, the van came out from the alley that ran along the back of the building and pulled alongside them. The door opened and arms reached out from inside to pull them both in. Mia felt a bit like a kidnap victim as she was tossed to the floorboards, hand truck and all, and the van took off, tearing across the parking lot, lights off, headed back to the highway and freedom.

"Mia?" Hashim asked as Jessa and Yolanda pulled the door closed behind her and Danny. "Mia, were you bit?"

"No," Mia said, pulling herself up and into the passenger seat. "No, I wasn't. Danny?"

"Nope!" he said. "Didn't even get any blood on me!" He sounded so ridiculously pleased by this that Mia laughed, despite herself. After a moment, Jessa giggled too, followed by Elia. Before long, they were all laughing, even poor Sonia, tied in the back, flushed with fever.

"We got some supplies, too," Mia said, as soon as the laughter died down. "But how'd you know where to find us?"

"We didn't," Hashim said. "We just saw the horde at the front door, and knew you would not make it out that way. Jessa suggested the alley around the back."

"You should have just left," Mia said, looking down to reload her magazine.

Hashim looked over at her wryly. "Mia. I am only one man. You gave weapons to nine of your twelve cheerleaders. Do you think they would have let me leave you?"

Mia looked up, startled, then back in the back. Jessa met her eyes, a hardness in them that Mia had never seen before.

"We're a team, coach," Jessa said.

Mia felt a lump rise in her throat. She nodded. "So we are," she said. "So we are."

By eleven, Sonia had turned. Dawn, Yolanda, and Gina were also showing signs of infection. They'd all been restrained in the back couple of rows, making liberal use of both bungee cords and duct tape.

Mia and Hashim had traded off driving duties. Both of them subtly bearing down on the gas, and the van, surprisingly, would do ninety on a straight stretch with very little issues. Max had called once more, to tell them that he'd stopped for gas in Aneth. Aneth was a tiny little town in the middle of an oil field on the Ute Mountain reservation in southern Utah. Mia knew the gas station Max mentioned. They stopped there sometimes when they travelled during the day. Mia wouldn't have stopped at night if she could help it. It had always looked sketchy. According to Max, though, the old guy who ran it was uninfected, and he appeared more than happy to help. Mia was keeping it in mind, just in case. Since Hashim had been able to fill up both tanks back at Shiprock, she didn't think it would be an issue, but it was nice to have a backup plan.

Or any kind of plan, for that matter.

Mia scrubbed her hands over her face and lifted her Red Bull to take the last swallow in the can. She made a face as it went down. Sugar Free Red Bull was meant to be drunk over ice, in her opinion. It was never the same out of the can, and its flavor deteriorated rapidly if it wasn't icy cold.

She had the sensation of diving through the darkness, as the van carved its way down the apparently deserted highway. While, given the circumstances, Mia was more than happy to be in such a sparsely populated part of the country, it was, to say the least, a little eerie as they drove.

Particularly with more than half of her team dying in the van behind her.

"Hashim," she said softly, not wanting to wake him if he were asleep. The microbiologist stirred and opened his eyes, looking at her. "If they haven't turned yet, can you use the vaccine on them?"

He shook his head sadly. "I could try, but Mia, if they are already sick, then the virus has begun to attack their tissues. The vaccine will only be more viruses. It would only make the problem worse."

Mia nodded. That was about what she'd expected. She drove on, accelerating just a little faster, as Sam and Bella, both seniors, started to join in the coughing behind her.

The eastern sky was starting to lighten when they had to slow down. They'd made it in to Utah, but the road to Torrey took them through Capitol Reef National Park. The Park, as it was known locally, was a geographic wonder, and one of the best kept secrets of the American southwest. Towering red stone formations thrust up into the sky, creating near-vertical canyons and labyrinthine twists and turns. Butch Cassidy and the Hole in the Wall Gang were known to have had hideouts up in the Park back in their day. Legend had it that there was still stolen railroad gold cached up there somewhere.

Mia slowed the van as they wound down the scenic highway, in part because it was necessary, thanks to the lingering darkness and the windiness of the road. Also, there was also the threat of hitting one of the huge herds of deer that lived in the area. But the real reason she slowed was because she knew that Max was somewhere up here. Somewhere in the Park, there was a cache of weapons and supplies that her mother and stepfather had prepared for an "End of the World" type scenario. She had the coordinates for it on her phone, even. That was where Max would be.

But she couldn't go there, not yet. Not with Sonia, Dawn and Yolanda already turned, and from the looks of things, Gina, Sam and Bella not far behind. They had to get to the clinic. They had to get Hashim to the vaccine. She had to keep her promise. Her kids would not die in vain.

Torrey was only about six miles past the park, and the gray light of false dawn lined the eastern horizon by the time they came to the town limits. The sign claimed a population of 180 people, which Mia thought was a good sign. Especially since many of those would, theoretically, be living out on their land away from the town center. Torrey was as rural as it got.

"The community clinic is up here on the left," Mia said as she drove, slowing to turn in to the parking lot of the small, nondescript building with the sign that proclaimed it to be their goal. She pulled up next to the door, killed the engine and set the parking brake. There was no movement in the parking lot.

"Now, how do we get these guys inside?" she asked.

"Let me go in first," Hashim said, hefting a bag he'd stashed under the passenger seat. "I must find the lab and the X-ray machine, and we may need to clear it out. We can leave the kids here with the weapons."

Mia looked over her shoulder at Jessa. The team captain nodded and hefted the rifle she hadn't given back to Danny. He'd taken Sam's instead. "We'll be fine," she said. "We'll get them ready to take in for you," she said.

"Don't take any chances," Mia said, wishing she had some better advice to give. "Don't get bit."

Jessa smiled grimly. "Don't worry," she said. "I have a plan."

Mia raised her eyebrows, "I'm glad someone does," she said under her breath. When Jessa's only answer was a widening grin, she shook her head and refused to comment further. Instead, Mia took one of the shotguns and her .45 and slid out of her seat, after tossing the keys to Jessa. Just in case.

"Do you know where the lab is?" Hashim asked her as they approached the front door of the clinic.

"Not a clue," Mia said.

Hashim laughed. "Fair enough," he said. "Let's go."

He pushed open the door which, surprisingly or not, was not locked. The metal squealed against the linoleum floor, letting out a sound which raised the hackles on the back of Mia's neck, and made her curse softly in response. So much for stealth.

From somewhere down the darkened hall in front of them, an answering keen rose. Then another. Hashim grabbed her arm and hauled her quickly behind a counter that had once served as the receptionist's station. He reached in his bag and pulled out a road flare. "Cover your eyes," he warned, then popped the flare.

Red light hissed to life as Mia belatedly turned her head and covered her eyes. She looked back just in time to see Hashim toss the light into a room opposite, that looked like a bathroom or something of that kind. Sure enough, three infected came running, stumbling down the hallway toward the light and the noise. As they came, Mia stood and began firing the 12-gauge. Three rounds, three dead infected. Five more followed after, drawn by the light and the noise. Mia dropped behind the corner as Hashim took her place, firing his pistol economically, dropping them with the headshots he'd perfected a lifetime ago in another desert a world away.

The 12-gauge could hold six rounds, and Mia took the time to reload three more while she had a moment. As she was doing so, another infected, this one a child of about five came around the corner of the counter from a back room.

"Aw, shit," Mia said as the little zombie rushed toward her. "You're gone already," she told the little boy as she kicked a rolling chair over to intercept his path. He stumbled, which gave her time to get her weapon up and fire into his face that had been framed with soft golden curls. Still cursing, Mia got to her feet and went over to check the room that had produced the infected little boy. The smell about knocked her over. There was another child in there, a girl, about three or so. This one was still clothed, and her middle was one bloody mass where it had been eaten away. From the resemblance, Mia guessed that they'd been brother and sister. She closed her eyes briefly, then turned and emptied the contents of her stomach into a corner.

"Mia," Hashim called softly. She straightened up, wiped her mouth with her sleeve and went back out to the reception area. An impressive pile of bodies lay in front of the desk, but there was no more movement toward the back. "I think we must move on," he said, his eyes sympathetic. Mia nodded, and forced one foot in front of the other.

Despite all the odds, the building appeared to be clear. Mia and Hashim checked every closet, every compartment they could see, but there was no one else. Either no one else had made it to the clinic, or all the survivors had already evacuated. They did find the remains of several others that had been partially eaten, and Mia threw up one more time.

In the last room they checked, Hashim found what he was looking for. He immediately went over to the X-ray machine and began pushing buttons and dials. It must have had an integrated generator of some kind, because it fired right up, though the lights in the room stayed off. Mia watched him for a second, feeling lost, before backing up a step. "I'll, ah, go get the kids," she said. Hashim was already absorbed in his work and didn't appear to hear her. So she shrugged and went back the way they'd come.

Outside, seven or eight more headless bodies bore mute testimony of the amount of noise she and Hashim had made, but her kids were all okay. Elia opened the van doors as she approached, and Danny and the two sisters, Mackayla and Mackenzie, started moving their turned teammates out. Mia nearly laughed when she saw them. The kids had emptied their cheer bags out and were using them as hoods to cover the faces of the infected. With the cheer bags duct taped over their heads, and their hands and feet tied, the infected cheerleaders were effectively helpless. All of a sudden, Mia was extremely glad she'd grabbed the hand truck back in Shiprock, as it came in very handy for transporting their lost teammates as gently as possible.

One by one, they transported them inside. Sam, the senior, and Jessa's cocaptain. Sonia and Dawn, their two freshman flyers who'd been good enough to make the varsity team. Yolanda, another senior, who had earned a cheerleading scholarship to the University of Texas, Gina, a junior who had been earmarked for captain next year, and Bella, another senior, who had had plans to get married next spring. They rolled them in and strapped them down to the rolling gurneys that Hashim had assembled in the lab area.

"I don't want to hurt them, if you can help it," Mia said, her voice rough as they finished securing Bella in place.

"They do not feel pain at this stage," Hashim said, "But I understand. I will give them morphine to kill them, and then we will harvest the spines. We must hurry, though, I can do nothing with the tissue if it's too long dead."

"We'll help," Mackayla said, and her sister nodded.

Elia nodded too. "We'll all help," the little sophomore said. "Just tell us what to do."

Hashim nodded. He walked over to Sonia with a syringe, which he inserted into her arm. The infected girl thrashed against her bonds, letting out that high, keening wail before falling silent. Without a word, Hashim grabbed a very large bone saw from a drawer and began cutting around her neck. While her teammates looked on, Sonia was decapitated and her spine removed and placed into what looked like an emesis basin.

"Can you do this?" Hashim asked. Mia nodded, and though their faces were white as sheets, the surviving cheerleaders followed suit. Hashim handed out the syringes and bone saws, and they went to work.

It was the buzzing of her phone that woke her. Despite everything, Mia had drifted off to sleep, leaning against the wall of Hashim's lab beside the sheet-covered gurneys that held the remains of half her team. Her surviving cheerleaders lay curled together on the floor next to her, Danny and Jessa holding Elia between them, Mackayla and Mackenzie holding each other. Mia stretched the crick in her neck and pulled the iPhone from her pocket. It was a text, from Max.

*Found cache. All good. You? Max.*

Mia looked up at Hashim, only to see the microbiologist standing over her with tired eyes, a triumphant smile on his face, a syringe in his hand. "Mia," he said. "If I could have your arm, please? Your vaccine is ready." Mia smiled back at him as tears of relief and reaction filled her eyes.

"Do the kids first," she said, blinking furiously as she fumbled with her phone.

*Vaccine done. Hold tight, baby. See you in a bit.*

# How Do You Solve a Problem Like Grandpa?

MICHAEL Z. WILLIAMSON

Andy Thompson was tense. Going to see his grandpa shouldn't be a meeting. It should be a visit.

This was a meeting.

The house was a nice brick split, well-maintained. The grass and trees were trimmed and pruned, but there was no other landscaping. It was plain, and clean.

Grandpa Thompson had always liked guns, hunting, the outdoors. His collection of knives and guns had been amazing. Now it was full-on hoarder. The man had crates of MREs, racks of cans, drums of water, god knows how many military rifles. He'd blown through most of his income and savings, keeping just enough to pay the bills.

The man did pay his bills, and his food, and his taxes, but there wasn't much left over, and the next progression in behavior would be past that point.

If they could resolve it now, he wouldn't have to try to put Grandpa in a home. Although, with Grandma gone, that still might be something to discuss later.

James C. Merritt, his attorney, was graciously coming along on a very modest fee, and Dr. Gleeson was along to gently advise. Grandpa was as areligious as Andy, so there was no point to a clergyman.

Grandpa met them at the door.

"What's wrong, Andy? A lawyer?" Grandpa said after a glance. He was still sharp. "And who's this other gentleman? Come in, sit, please."

"Grandpa, Dr. Gleeson's been mine and Lisa's marriage counselor. Good man. He's along for support."

"I hope no one's died. Is Andy Junior in the hospital?"

"No, everyone's fine, Grandpa. This..." he looked at Gleeson, who nodded. "This is about your spending, and the guns."

The cabinet here in the living room contained high-end hunting rifles, behind armored glass to protect them while showing them. That case had cost a couple of thousand dollars. It was also the wrong background for this discussion, because those were valuable and personal.

"What's the issue? Everything that needs to be papered is. I have a lot of them in trust for you and the great grandkids. I don't spend more than I have. I'm pretty sure my debt's less than yours."

The old man didn't seem to be angry, but he was certainly alert.

"Grandpa, it was fine when you had a dozen, or even a couple of dozen, but you've got what now, a hundred?"

Grandpa leaned back in mock relaxation. He was tense.

"Since you ask that way, none of your goddam business. Andy, I don't want trouble with you or anyone, but how I spend my pension and my wealth is really not your concern. You've seen the trust and the will, and even if I was cutting into those, which I'm not, that would be my choice while alive. But I'm not. You don't have some notion of trying to declare me incompetent, do you? I have lawyers, too, and probably better ones, with no disrespect intended to you, sir," he added to Merritt.

This was not going well. Andy nodded to Merritt.

Merritt said, "Sir, my client is concerned about your assets, and has asked that I act in an advisory capacity. While I assume you are completely within the law, your collection has been mentioned at the city council and elsewhere. They've got concerns."

"Mentioned by whom? I don't generally advertise." Grandpa's gaze wasn't getting any more relaxed.

It had been Andy's younger brother Sam, who meant well, but wasn't very good at these things. He'd gotten a bug up his ass, decided the government would know what to do, and gone to see the mayor. It was a small town. Word got around. They all knew the old man needed to stop "collecting," but that hadn't helped. Although, that had gotten the action they had here, if it worked.

Merritt was good. He answered the old man's inquiry with, "You've been seen at various gun shows, stores, swap meets. Someone took an interest and started following you."

"Stalking me, you mean."

"Legally it has not reached that level. They are free to observe, as you are free to buy."

"And everything I have is legal. If the cops show up with a warrant, they'll find exactly that."

Merritt said, "I'm quite sure, sir. But if the police do show up, they'll confiscate everything on at least a temporary basis, and then there will be articles in the news. You know how they paint gun owners."

He followed with, "Sir, I'm on your side. I've got a safe full of ARs, an early Russian SKS, an FAL—"

"Metric or Inch?"

"Metric. Imbel. Imported back before you had to chop barrels and sub parts."

"Nice. Do you know the Empire ones can take metric mags as well as their own?"

Merritt nodded. "I'd heard that."

Grandpa twisted his mouth and shook his head. "So you're saying some asshole is pitching a fit about me being a collector, and if I don't want my collection ruined, I need to divest."

"There's more nuance than that, but that is the rough summary, yes, sir."

"Goddamit."

Grandpa sat staring from man to man for about three minutes. Andy said nothing.

"And what will convince the concerned idiots I'm not some sort of deranged Nazi or whatever?"

"I don't think there's any specific number on it. But some of the racks of MREs and such, and ammo, and the scarier guns.

One AR is not an issue. Five different ones, I can make the case that they're for different target shooting, or collectible. Once you get to a dozen, people start to freak out."

It was another three minutes before Grandpa said, "I'll think about it."

Andy felt like crap. Grandpa had taught him to shoot, and he'd enjoyed it. He just never got into it the way the old man did, almost an obsession. If Grandpa had fifty cars, it would have been the same, or if he'd been binge buying collectibles on eBay. Even if he wanted to be safe against disaster, four or five guns was enough. He had taken that one trip to Africa, and a couple of the hunting rifles were really gorgeous.

But adding in all that food... it was hoarding, and it had to stop.

Dr. Gleeson was soothing, and feigned interest in the details, or maybe he was interested, but he kept the discussion moving about liquid assets that could be accessed in case of illness. That tack seemed to help.

While everyone was busy in the living room, Andy took a surreptitious look in the garage, at the rafters above it. MREs, canned goods, toilet paper, plywood, pallets of something. Down in what had been bedrooms were a couple of racks of rifles, three gun vaults, another pallet with boxes stacked on it, and some footlockers. The closets had various camouflage clothing and a lot of things like parkas. They were mostly different, but there were dozens of them.

Maybe they should try to coax the old man into a retirement home. Otherwise, he could open his own surplus store.

The other bedroom contained more varieties of knives, machetes, axes and clubs than he'd ever known existed. Some were on racks and stands for display, which was either awesome or creepy, depending on the presentation.

At least the front room was a perfectly normal office, with computer, filing cabinet and bookshelves, until he realized the books were all about gunsmithing, emergency medicine, and survival, with military manuals and a bunch of woodworking and craft books. At least the latter was normal.

He knew that a lot of people raised in the Depression hoarded stuff out of habit. Grandpa had been born after WWII, though, and had a middle class upbringing, then had worked as an engineer after Vietnam.

It could be something war related, or maybe he was just old and obsessive.

Andy wanted to help the man live to a healthy, normal old age.

Reggie Thompson looked around his living room and sighed.

He'd reached a deal with these pansies that involved selling his collection slowly. As long as his numbers were going down, the limpwristed little shits felt better.

He really didn't care how they felt, but the world being the world, they'd make life hell on him. If he had a choice, he'd just move fifty miles out and tell them to go piss up a rope. He needed to be near the hospital, though, in case of another problem with his lungs. No good to live in the boonies and die from something treatable. He also suspected as soon as he was in hospital, stuff would start disappearing. Even if he had a spreadsheet for reference, he'd be told he was crazy and steered toward a home.

This was how his grandkids repaid him for all those hikes, fishing weekends and range trips.

He thought about calling John and his wife but his son was out in Oregon, and they'd had some words over that idiotic election. That was partly Reggie's fault. He was a blunt, unrelenting son of a bitch, and he knew it.

He looked around. It really was a collection, not just prep. He'd had one of every pattern of AR, from the original Armalite AR15, to the first USAF issue, first Army issue Model 602, that he'd carried in 'Nam in '65. Then he had the A1 he didn't care much for, the A2 that was better, A3 and A4, several M4gery variants including the Air Force's. He'd paid to have the proper markings on them, even if they were semi-only civilian guns.

One of the buyers had about gone apeshit at the "BURST" markings. The next had taken a quick look at the internals, saw they were all legal, and grinned. He'd paid a decent price.

So now he had five. The old school, the functional civilian modern one, and three carbines.

Those didn't hurt so much. They could be bought anywhere. He'd been willing to take a few hundred dollar loss overall. He'd probably have to. Which one did he really need? One of the carbines would have to do.

But they wanted to thin out his Mausers and Lee Enfields. Those things were appreciating in value, fast, and were both pension and his grandkids' inheritance, though he got the idea that little bastard Sam was the whiner about it, or at least one of the whiners.

Those would have to wait a while, as would the H&Ks. He didn't care for them much, but their fan club sure did. Okay, so those before the classics.

He really hadn't made a big deal about them, but he did sometimes load a dozen gun cases into the van to go to the range. This area was increasingly young liberals moving into older homes for the atmosphere. What were they called? Hipsters, that was it. He thought about the irony that these days there was no one *under* thirty you could trust.

He had a month's worth of food now, the rest donated to charity, sold cheap to the Scouts for camping, and most of the MREs sold on Craigslist.

He'd sold the suppressors, but still had the M60. That was worth a damned fortune, and more all the time unless they reopened the Registry. With .308 running what it did, the Pig cost two hundred dollars a minute to shoot, but that really wasn't a bad price for an orgasm.

Fuckers.

That would be near the end. He could milk out this sale for a year or more. Hell, he might be dead by then.

When the last of the AR rack sold on Gunbroker, he had some AKs to start listing. And then all the mags.

He'd still have the tents and winter gear.

He was almost certain Sammy had been the problem. The boy had never really got into guns. He'd been a video gamer from the '80s on. Not shooting games, either. Then there was his wife, who'd constantly talked about, "Endangering the children."

"I'd hoped to leave some of the antiques to you and the great grandkids," he hinted.

Sammy seemed to be choosing words very carefully when he said, "That's a kind gesture, but we wouldn't really know what to do with them."

Andy didn't have kids, and his interest in guns stopped with a Remington 870 he'd last used, as far as Reggie knew, a decade before.

Dammit, there was culture here, and craftsmanship, and collectible value, and they just didn't care. They were the same kind of people as Maxwell's kids, who had no interest in his classic '64 1/2 Mustang and '69 Cuda. He'd watched his friend sell them at auction. He got good money, but they were gone and he'd never see them again. The man had slumped as he handed over the keys.

This was his estate, his life, his heritage, and they just didn't care.

That was the unkindest thing he could imagine.

What always pissed him off in these arguments, first online, now here, was that the hunting rifles in that case packed two to three times the power of the so-called "assault rifles." Hell, if they knew what the Merkel .375 double rifle put out, they'd need Depends. You could use that on a charging rhino. 5.56mm wouldn't even puncture the skin on one.

But the lawyer and the counselor had been correct. If he tried to fight this, the little bastards would just dial up the press, the soccer mommies, and the panty-wetters until someone came along and took everything for "examination" and tossed him into a don't-care facility.

His plans didn't allow for that. They did, very reluctantly, allow for this.

But he still hated the ungrateful, nosy little bastards.

Andy sat with Sam in Chili's, drinking margaritas and waiting for fajitas.

"That spreadsheet was impressive," he said.

"It was creepy," Sam replied.

"Yeah, but it listed everything."

"That's what's creepy about it," Sam said as he licked salt and took a drink. "Guns, magazines, cases, slings, cleaning tools, every goddam screw that might go on a rifle. And hell, he had more stuff than the local police."

Sam probably didn't know what the police actually had, but there had been a lot.

"Well, I got him into a good mutual fund. It's near a hundred thousand now."

"It's obscene. A hundred thousand dollars on guns. How rich would he be if he'd put it into something useful?"

"It wasn't all guns."

"Right. I forgot. Enough food for a year, like he's a Mormon or something. Even they don't do that anymore."

"Well, he's smart enough. I think it's partly our fault."

"Huh? How?"

"Dad lives in Oregon now. We should have been visiting a lot more often, especially after Grams died. He needs company. I doubt there's much of a dating scene for seventy-five-year-old widowers."

Sam frowned. "Oh, there probably is, but I doubt he cares. He did love her a lot, and he does miss her I'm sure. But you're probably right. We should visit at least once a month, maybe even swap off."

"And take the kids."

Sam said, "Monica isn't comfortable around him. You know how she voted. Grandpa is loud about it, even online. She feels he's angry enough to be scary."

"I hate being critical of your wife, Sam, but she needs to remember she joined this family. We visit hers, she needs to return it."

"It's not that easy."

It probably wasn't. Sam had never been the strong one. He read a lot of books, sat in the corner, and even now, he sat in an office writing corporate reports. Andy actually traveled and looked at the sites he was insuring, ladders, hoists, the works.

He hated to think his little brother was a wuss, but in many ways, he was.

The screen showed a dozen people, naked and vacant-eyed, suddenly turning angry and charging toward the camera. Then there were rubber bullets, then tasers, and cops wrestling with angry, snarling, biting people.

Reggie wasn't sure what to make of the video. It could be drugs, like Krokodil or bath salts, but it was a lot of people. It had to be some sort of disease. So he'd need to start quarantine protocols. He'd also need to make sure he had plenty of diesel for the generator.

He pinged his friend Kevin in the State Department, for any info he might have, and Ted, who was a neuroscientist. Both had private emails that didn't go through official servers.

Ted didn't reply. Kevin's response was very short. "It's real. Global. Duck and cover."

He stared at the screen for a few moments, then composed a new message.

"My place is available. Ping if you're inbound." He addressed it to six people and pressed send.

He felt bad that none of them were family.

He slammed the locks into the doorframes, and he was glad the kids had never seen those. Steel doors with internal crossbars were proof against a lot of things, and they were Kevlar lined with light ceramic backing.

The windows, though, on the ground floor especially, were going to be tough. He had the sandbags. He needed to fill them. There were a lot of them, and the fill pile was at the bottom of the yard, nicknamed "goat mountain."

The video from the cities got worse over the summer. There were rampaging mobs of naked, insane people, and someone used the "Z" word. Zombies. Whatever it was was communicable and nasty. He was going to have to secure things as best he could.

The food, more than the guns, would be useful now. He had a well out back, and there was a seep from the cornfield that he could filter. It might contain a few fertilizers he couldn't neutralize, but that was less important than not going near anyone communicable.

He took to ordering all his food online, and having it delivered to the garage. It was all packaged, and he ran them under the UV light, spritzed them with bleach, then rinsed them off with the hose. Then he put on his paint respirator and used tongs and gloves to shelve stuff. After several days, he dated each item with a Sharpie, then placed them into regular storage. They'd still need to be rinsed again, though. He'd need to be rinsed, actually, and it was hot enough a shower was a pleasure.

At his computer, he ordered a lot more bleach, soap and respirator filters.

He also realized that he might have to triage his own grandkids, if there was a risk they were contaminated.

As he was thinking that, he heard a car out front. He stretched to look out the window. It was Andy, pulling into the driveway, still doing about thirty. His wife was with him.

He sprinted and strained up the stairs to the door, before they were out of the car.

Andy called, "Grandpa! I called in sick at work. Do you have room?"

"For what?"

"Have you seen the news?"

Yup. That was it. "Yes. Why did you come here?"

Andy spread his hands and said, "Because you have all that food and gear."

Oh, he was going to make them sweat.

"I see. So now that you actually need help, you want me to take care of you. After you already told me I didn't know what I was doing and made me get rid of most of it."

Andy looked ashamed and embarrassed. "Dammit, I'm sorry, Grandpa. We couldn't know."

"And what are you bringing?"

"Uh?"

"What do you have that's useful? Skills? Food? Ammo?"

"Uh . . ."

"Did you even bring your shotgun?"

"No."

Reggie gave the young man The Look. It was the look all old timers kept on hand for these occasions. Tommy Lee Jones did it perfectly. Reggie had practiced while watching him.

"Grandpa . . . please."

He tilted his head. "Go out back. I'll send out a tent, and it even has a heater. Park it down the street and walk back slowly so you don't scare people."

"Tent?"

"Quarantine, for a week. Then you can come in."

Andy gaped. "Are you serious?"

Reggie was serious, and had to make them believe it. Besides, he owed payback on Andy helping Sammy cut back his preps.

With The Look, he said, "Don't make me shoot you. Park, then 'round back."

The man did so.

So, was Sammy going to come running up with his brats? Reggie had been gentle with John; John had been downright wimpy with Andy and Sammy. And once it got to Sammy's boys . . .

Andy parked, but he walked back awful briskly. It was obvious he was tense. Reggie noticed he didn't bring anything from the car. Not even sunglasses.

Meanwhile he called his neighbor Wendell.

"Hello?"

"Hey, old man, seen the news?"

"Only a bit. Some drug gang or something?"

"That's what I thought, but it's worse. Quarantine is in effect."

"Crap. You're serious?"

"Yeah, my friends in State and elsewhere say it's depopulating large chunks of Africa and Asia already."

"I ain't got more than a couple of weeks of groceries."

"I still have you covered."

"Thanks."

"Any time, brother. But when did you last go out?"

"Two days ago."

"So you stay there five days, and don't answer the door or get close to anyone. Then you come here on Saturday."

"Will do."

Wendell had far less preps, but the man had skills. He'd volunteered for a second tour before Reggie was drafted, and had real decorations from it. He still knew how to shoot, too.

Andy squealed and sprinted as he reached the driveway.

"I saw one!" he said.

Reggie looked up the street. Yeah, that was a naked old man, soggy and flabby, who seemed aware enough to track Andy and follow him.

Reggie reached inside the door, grabbed the rifle he had there, and took two shots. The second one dropped the man.

"It's started," he said.

There were eyes at curtains and windows around the neighborhood, and he saw Davis across the street in his front porch, holding a rifle. Davis had been Navy during the Cold War, but he knew how to shoot.

Andy set up the tent with difficulty, but managed. They had an airbed, blankets, an electric heater for night, extension cord for laptop, and his wireless. He put food outside the French window every meal, and they took it. He handed out a box of bleach wipes, and they dug a slit behind the hedges. Reggie wished he'd stocked lime. If they were contaminated...

Sammy arrived the next day, with Monica and kids. He pulled into the driveway and parked, fussed around, then got out.

"Move it down the street," Reggie said.

"That's not safe."

"It's in the way there."

"Why? You're in the garage."

He sighed.

"Anyone getting close can hide behind it. It needs to be moved away from the house."

"But the—"

Reggie sighed because he already was responding to what the boy was starting to say.

"Leave the others here, and *move it*."

Monica tried to run for the house.

He pointed his M4 at her.

She just stared, then started screaming at him.

"I knew you were an all-out right-wing gun nut! You—"

"Shut it, woman."

She gawped and stared.

"Now listen closely, because your life depends on it. I've got a second tent. You will take it to the bottom of the back, a hundred yards from Andy. You will camp there for a week. You will not touch, get close, or even move near Andy and his wife, or they have to wait as long as you do. I'll put food out. You'll have heat and Internet. Or, I lock this door right now, and shoot you if you try to go near them. Whatever this disease is, it's a killer, and I'm not taking chances. Otherwise, I wish you luck, you can have a shotgun, a box of shells and a crate of MREs, and you go elsewhere."

Sammy didn't argue. They stared each other down for several minutes, in silence, and the boy said, "Okay." He turned and let the kids out of the car, spoke carefully, and pointed around back.

Reggie said, "I'll do dinner in an hour."

"Ya got macaroni 'n' cheese?" Jaden asked. He was five. He looked scared because the adults were arguing.

"Sure do." He looked at Monica. "I can make that for them? And just soup and sandwiches for the rest of you."

Sammy barely parked past the property line, and sprinted across the yard. Reggie sighed. It would have to do.

Up the street were several more wandering naked bodies. They went to the first house and started breaking in the front windows. The widow Mrs. Lee's house.

To Sammy, he said, "I took you shooting when you were young. Did you ever stay with it?"

"Uh, no."

Reggie stood another rifle outside the door.

"Then you learn again now, and fast. Keep that in your tent. Wait until I'm inside to pick it up."

He looked back to Mrs. Lee's house, where the three might-as-well-be-zombies were still breaking in the glass. He raised the rifle, aimed carefully, and squeezed off a shot. He hit, but not solidly. Again. Torso, and the man started to slump. The second one took three bullets.

Because he couldn't leave Mrs. Lee like that, he dropped the last of the three, but knew he couldn't waste ammo like that again. The distance wasn't impossible, but moving targets made things a lot tougher, and he didn't have enough ammo.

He pointed at the rifle for Sammy, then went inside and latched the door bolts.

He didn't have her number in his phone. He called Wendell.

"Wendell, can we get Mrs. Lee?"

Wendell said, "I dunno. Maybe Davis can help. Anyone else coming?"

"Yeah, my friends, but I don't know when. I'll check."

"Okay. I'll tell Davis to check on her. Anything else?"

He thought for a moment and replied, "Yeah, if they can move out to the country, they should. Much as I'd like to form a neighborhood watch, people want to vote on things, then they vote for what they want, not what they need. Imagine that in 'Nam."

"No thanks. I'll tell them. I'm not sure they'll do it."

"No, but we have to try."

During the days, he fastened barricades inside the windows, and bars outside, drilling into the masonry. He ducked inside when the mailman came past, and waved off some salesman or other. They got lots of them around here.

Wendell came over after six days. On day seven Reggie let Andy and Lisa in. He was going to make Sammy's family wait an extra day plus, just to make sure. He thought the car had moved slightly and the boy had made a late night burger run or something. He couldn't entirely blame him. The five-year-old and three-year-old were bored and angry.

Every major city was now reporting outbreaks. Once the infection took, people got violent and vicious within a few hours.

Things started falling apart.

Lots of people were trying to quarantine, few had enough supplies.

Andy and Lisa came in, and he pointed to the bathrooms.

"You should shower. We have hot water for now. The food won't hold out for long with all of us here," he said. "It would have, but...and you know what I'm going to say, right?"

Andy felt a burn and said, "You told us so. But how the fuck could we predict zombies?"

"Zombies, commies, Nazis, angry native tribes, aliens, mutant bikers, something, sometime, will require the use of guns and food. Remember that, you little shit." He wanted to smack the boy.

"Yes, Grandpa. I'm sorry."

Grandpa turned and said, "Wendell, I think it's time we started stacking stuff."

Wendell said "Roger that," as he walked into the room.

Andy blurted out, "You're black."

"And?" the man replied. He was about Grandpa's age, carrying that civilian variant of the M14 with a scope on top. He looked pretty damned fit and lean for someone near seventy.

"Nothing." He had no idea why that had come out. Inadvertent racism? This was a bad time to even discuss that.

Wendell jogged upstairs and went into the garage.

Grandpa said, "I have friends coming. They're bringing more stuff. Then we're going to see about moving farther out, where there's less people and more food."

"Farming?"

"Maybe. Farming takes fuel and effort. Depends on how many people die. If it's enough, we just hunt and plant a truck garden."

That was a frightening thought.

From upstairs, Wendell shouted, "And we have another bunch, up the street."

"Okay, after this, we get out the backup supply. Andy, Sammy, grab the rifles." Grandpa snapped his fingers and pointed. Andy did so. Sam hesitated, but he did as well.

"Outside, on the porch."

Andy asked, "Shouldn't we fight from in here?"

Wendell said, "No, we fight where we can see and maneuver, and lock up later. Those gooks aren't even visible from the house."

It was scary to be outside, but Grandpa made sense, and there were four of them with rifles.

He stood on the porch, which now had a couple of planters and some sandbags around it. The old men had been busy. Up the street was a nightmare.

Four filthy, naked, raging men were beating on a car, trying to break into it, and the passengers inside.

They were people, and they were sick, but they'd kill him if they could. He lined up sights and shot, and missed. Sammy went through five shots before he hit one, a creepy-looking guy with a beer belly, who drooled. The shot was into the leg and tore a hole that just seemed to make him madder.

Behind him, Grandpa said, "It's always tough the first time you shoot a man, but you need to get over it fast, because we're not getting any resupply."

"Sorry," he said. He took two more shots to hit one, who clutched and screamed and thrashed around on the ground before stopping. Dying.

He shot at another shambling body. There were a lot of fat people around here, it seemed.

Then Grandpa and Wendell started shooting, and that hurt his ears.

As he winced and cringed, Grandpa said, "Yeah, hurts, doesn't it? You little fuckers made me sell the two cans for the rifles. I guess you get to deal with the noise. It's not like my ears matter anymore."

The rifles cracked, and bodies fell.

*Come on*, he thought. *What were the odds?*

He shot. Another went down. Then he froze, because the next was a pretty young girl, under the stains of blood, dirt and waste. But he couldn't do anything to save her, and she was trying to kill the people in the car, who seemed to be young girls, too.

Behind him, Grandpa said, "Better reload and save the partial mag."

"Yeah. Thanks."

He swapped out for a full clip, fumbling with it.

Honking sounded down the street, and a black Toyota Land Cruiser with bars and racks raced through the moving obstacles. It stopped on the pavement, the doors flew open, and two thirty-ish men rolled out, followed by a red-headed woman. They had black web gear, pouches, handguns, and were holding AR carbines. The woman wore stockings and a miniskirt with combat boots under a tailored web vest. It would have been hot under other circumstances. That, and when she got closer, she appeared to be a well-kept fifty.

"Reggie, sorry we're late!"

"Glad you could make it."

The two men charged up the steps onto the porch, pivoted, and took positions at each corner. The woman dragged a bag behind her. Once she was up, the men took turns grabbing more gear.

"Where's the heavy stuff?" one asked. "Yes, we've been in Q all week."

Grandpa said, "Yeah, there was a personal issue that got in the way. This is it until I can fix things." He fixed Andy with another gaze. The old man wasn't going to let him forget it.

"Crap. Well, there's a shit ton of zeds moving this way. We left ahead of them, so you've got a while, but they're probably closing."

"I was afraid of that. But it's looking light for now."

There were perhaps a dozen wandering bodies, though one suddenly started jogging and sloshing toward them.

One of the newcomers put a bullet right through the figure's head.

"Nice shot, Trebor."

"Thanks. Is it okay to be excited?" The man smiled faintly. He had a very high-end looking AR15, and an Uzi slung behind his gear. It had Israeli markings.

"Sure. Trebor, Kyle, Kristan, this is my grandson Andy, and that's Sammy. You know Wendell."

"Hey, Andy, Sammy." "Hi." "Sup."

"Boys, these gentlemen and lady are card-carrying members of Zombie Squad."

Kyle pointed to the ID badge on his web gear. "We are America's elite ambulatory cadaver suppression task force." He faced back around with his rifle, a perfectly respectable bolt action with muzzle brake and folding bipod.

Andy said, "You're kidding, right?"

Trebor said, "We were kidding. It was all metaphor for disaster prep and fundraising. But here we are."

"Yeah." He kept twitching over that. Zombies. Guns. But Grandpa really had been overdoing it. Except...

Grandpa said, "Wendell, you got it?"

"I do, Reg."

"Good. Boys, Wendell's in charge. He'll tell you when to shoot, what to shoot at, and where to place yourselves. Got it?"

"Uh, yes."

"Uh huh."

"Kristan, Andy," he said, with a jerk of his thumb. "Come with me."

Andy followed Grandpa inside the house, and felt a ripple as the old man locked the door and twisted a second lever. Something clanked like a vault.

"Just in case," he said. "We are going to come back."

Kristan was smoking a cigarette. Grandpa didn't like smoking, but he didn't say anything so Andy didn't. Monica, in the kitchen, looked like she was going to, but stopped. The kids were watching TV and looked very agitated. Lisa was upstairs cleaning. He couldn't see her.

They went down the stairs and into the office in the front. Those windows were exposed at ground level outside, even if they were high up here. They had bars now, but...

"Once we get upstairs, there's sandbags out back. But for now, I've got plywood. The back windows have to be done."

Grandpa pulled the closest door, reached in, and grabbed a tool chest. He dragged that out, popped the top and fumbled with both hands.

"Screw gun," he said, handing it over. He grabbed three pre-cut sheets of three quarter inch marine grade plywood.

"Now we do the back windows and the garage. You know what to do?"

The boards had holes for the screws, which were more like small bolts.

Andy said, "I see. Smart." Damn, the crazy old man really had thought everything through.

"First, help with this stuff."

He started grabbing boxes while Grandpa unpacked the closet. He handed stuff to Kristan, Kristan carried everything through.

Clothing came out, some of it old fashions. Winter clothing came out. Boxes came out. Another tool chest.

"C'mere," the old man said with a wave.

He stepped closer to the closet.

Outside, there were bangs of gunfire, some of them very loud. That must be Wendell's rifle.

Grandpa said, "Christ, we need to hurry."

But he continued moving methodically.

One side of the closet had an inset door. With the shelves and clothes out, that opened. The closet continued under the stairs.

There were more boxes, some of them ammo crates.

"Oh, good." Andy sighed in relief.

"Yeah, it would be, if it wasn't two hundred and sixty troy ounces of silver each. Ammo crates are the only thing strong enough."

Jesus. What did the old man have stuffed down here? He'd unloaded an easy hundred grand in weapons, and still had bullion?

He took the crate and lugged it through to the rear room.

When he came back, Grandpa was down like a ferret, pulling more stuff. He took that, too, and came back.

*What the hell is under here?* he wondered as the closet kept going.

There was a hole.

So, into the office, into the closet under the stairs, to the left and under the landing, then a short door to the left. He shimmied into it behind the old man.

*We're under the porch*, he thought. Gunfire directly above, muffled through the slab, proved it. It was a concrete block vault with LED lighting and a dehumidifier, under the porch.

More guns. Under here, where no one would ever have seen, Grandpa had more guns.

"I never told you goddamn punks how much I really had," the old man said. "You'd have shit yourselves. There are two spreadsheets."

There was another entire rack of AR15s. Next to that, some old military rifles in red lacquered wood stocks. A rack of those. There was a shelf of Glock pistols. There were crates of ammo. Four sets of body armor and helmet hung on a rail.

"Well, grab stuff and start passing it out."

In short order, Grandpa, the two brothers and Lisa were in armor, though they all felt very uncomfortable. It was like wearing a fridge. Wendell and the zombie hunters were already armored up.

He was really glad of that, because there were a lot of running bodies out there now.

Back out on the porch, there was a low wall of sandbags. In between surges, the men stacked more while Kristan and Sam kept eyes out. She really was in good shape, and a pretty damned good shot.

"More!" she called, leaned across the railing, and shot.

Kyle leapt back up, squinted through his scope and fired. Wendell stood alongside and fired, his rounds ejecting and tinging off the house.

The defense was layered. They had big bore rifles, smaller rifles and carbines, and if it got close enough, Trebor's Uzi and the shotgun leaned against the doorframe.

Andy hoped it wouldn't come to that.

This was nothing like the movies, either. With all the firing he'd done, he thought he'd hit three. Moving targets weren't easy, he didn't like shooting at people, and they didn't want to let them get close.

Not at all. Several of them bashed through the bay window of a house down the street, then poured into it, scrambling over the frame and each other.

Reggie watched them swarm into the Erdmans' house, and knew there was nothing he could do. If he had some kind of artillery, or could set it on fire, he would. But the poor couple and their baby were either dead, or soon to be worse than dead.

A dozen more followed the first gaggle, and he started shooting into the mass. He winged one, caught a leg, blew chunks of flesh from another, and put one down with two torso hits. They ran on even when shot, like a combination of PCP user and meth head.

That just stirred up several others, who rumbled their way, limbs and skin flapping.

"I count twenty," Kristan said, sounding remarkably calm.

Trebor said, "I'm getting low here."

Andy stuttered, "Oh, y-yeah. Last clip."

"We need more mags!" Reggie shouted and banged on the door.

The mail slot, that hadn't been used in years, opened, and a single mag slid out. It bounced off the ground and a round popped loose.

"Open the goddamn door!" he shouted to Monica.

There was a loud clack of the bolts latching.

Oh, shit.

He sprinted off the porch, around the garage, and went in the back. The plan for that was a two by four into metal slots, and she hadn't got to that yet.

But she had locked the door to the garage. He had his keys, quietly unlatched the knob first, turned it with one hand, then unlocked the deadbolt fast and threw his shoulder into it.

She was standing at the bottom of the stairs shrieking, screaming and flapping her arms.

He slapped her hard enough to stagger her off the wall.

"You are an adult woman, get a hold of yourself and act like one."

She stared at him in complete shock.

"Domestic violence!" she whimpered.

"There is no domestic relationship between us and never will be. Now, you can either do as you are told, or I will throw you the fuck outside with the zombies. And Sammy? That goes for you, too. I realize being a man is alien to you, but you need to learn right now. Your sons need the example."

He turned, took the stairs in three steps, panting in exertion. Dammit, he was old. He unlocked the door and stepped back out. He left the front door open, jammed a bolt into the lockplate, and got ready to shoot. Things had quieted down again.

Over his shoulder he said, "Fill the goddamn mags."

Yeah, it was ugly out here. There had to be a finite number of them, but they could get very numerous very quickly before that slowed down. There were near a million people in the city, most of them either unaware or useless.

Sammy joined them, hiding just inside the door. It wasn't as if they wouldn't have warning, but his grandson was a pussy.

Andy, at least, was shooting like a man who was protecting his family. Maybe Sammy would come around.

"How do I use the clip loader thingy?"

The boy didn't know the difference between a charger clip and a magazine.

Reggie reached over and showed him. "This is a clip." He held up the ten round stripper. "This is a loading spoon. This is a magazine. Clip goes here, and press." He showed, and ten rounds slid into the magazine. He pulled the clip loose, dropped it and grabbed another.

"Work on that stack."

"Hey, these clips jam at five rounds."

He glanced over, and saw Sammy trying to press the rounds down.

Shit, those mags.

"Crap! Bring 'em back in!"

He ran for the garage. Bench, where was the drill index? There. Eighth-inch. Downstairs, swap driver bit for twist drill.

"See this rivet? It blocks them at five rounds. Drill that out on each. Bring 'em up."

"What happened?"

"Got 'em cheap out of New York. All you have to do to make them work is drill out a stud. Worthless gun control law, but now we're stuck with goddamn zombies because of some . . . never mind, just drill."

He'd erased chunks of the spreadsheet as they went through his collection. He had a backup copy in the vault, under a false name, but he'd completely forgotten about these. They'd been bought online through a gift card, and delivered to a friend in Ohio who'd reshipped them as "used tools."

Drilling each rivet took about ten seconds. Stuffing in ten rounds took another five, and those mags went right up to Wendell and crew. Once there was a small stack, they could start putting two clips in each magazine, then three.

He looked around.

They had the windows reinforced, and wire set. The boys had completely missed the loops of concertina he'd stowed in the garage rafters during their intervention. Sandbags, plywood, those he'd called "Storm supplies."

He'd never understand the mindset that being prepared was somehow immoral or dangerous. He hoped, going forward, to not have to do that again.

He stood on the landing where he could give instructions up, down, and out.

"Okay, tomorrow we toughen things up. More wire and traps, barricades around the property. We have to worry about people who didn't prep who'll be hungry."

"We're not turning away starving people," Monica said.

He gave her The Look.

"We don't have enough for everyone. We'll be charitable, within reason, and these are my supplies. You're welcome to leave if you don't agree."

She wrung her hands and went back to the kitchen.

He figured she'd come around. She wasn't stupid, she was compassionate, she'd just had a very easy life. She was learning.

"Okay, we're secure enough unless they start using prybars, which might happen. We have bars and plywood on all the lower windows, nothing they can climb on, and not much they can hide behind. It's heading toward dark. We need to move inside and bed down. Wendell, can you take the office?"

"Sure."

"Z Squad, how are you splitting?"

Kristan said, "I trust the boys. Will the room with the gun vaults work?"

"Just what I was thinking."

Trebor said, "Yeah, I don't think my wife is gonna make it. I hope so, but she was on business on the West Coast."

"Sorry, man. Good luck."

"Thanks. We can hope."

"Yeah. Kyle, you're a bachelor, right?"

"Since two years ago, yes."

"Then we all bunker down for now. We'll take turns on watch and be ready to respond. Keep a loaded gun with you. Sammy, your boys need to learn the Four Rules of Firearm Safety right now. Bring 'em over."

"Okay."

"Oh, and Sam?"

"Yes, Grandpa?"

"Go make us some coffee. It could be a long night."

He figured the boy was at least good for that.

He looked over their new, small stronghold and started thinking about long-term supplies. Water wasn't a problem, but food and waste would be. They'd need to get on those fast.

Once there was an opportunity, they needed to move out to Russell's farm. He'd take Andy and Wendell. The ZS people were in, he was sure. As for the others, he'd have to make sure they were up for the task. Regardless of anything, they were family. He couldn't leave them. He figured they needed to leave in about a week.

He was going to miss this place. He'd had it set up just how he liked, and Russell's place was a converted corn crib. They'd be tight in there. It was a lot more secluded and defensible, though, and this might go on for a long time.

Andy sat behind his rifle, twitchy and nervous. They were going to need to have someone on watch around the clock. He hoped he wasn't going to get the middle of the night alone in the dark with animal noises shift.

Grandpa said, "We're going to take turns packing stuff, and it'll be a lot of food and ammo. As soon as this wave of idiots dies down, we'll move out to the country where we can hold them off better."

He said, "I guess that means I'm quitting my job."

Grandpa looked very serious and calm as he said, "If they're going to miss you, yes. Unless you want to hang around in a large city waiting to get infected. The outbreaks are getting bigger, and I expect they're going to get worse. When this current panic is over, I'm going to have to restock. Delivery is going to be a pain. You're paying for any shortages in the market. I expect prices are going to be high."

"Yes. Yes, sir." He flushed again. Really, the whole idea was ridiculous, but it had happened. They were still alive because Grandpa was a devious son of a bitch.

"So you need to close any accounts you've got, cash in stocks while you can, and figure on taking the tax penalty on your IRAs, if there's even an IRS to worry about them by year's end. But right now, lay those last ten sandbags. Then you can have an MRE. Do a good job and I won't make you eat the Tuna with Noodles."

Grandpa was still a crazy old coot.

He was very glad of that.

# Battle of the BERTs

MIKE MASSA

"Chomp!"

Colleen's brother-in-law bred Presa Canario mastiffs just outside Austin. On her last trip to visit her sister's family, she had fed the dogs and noted that when they snapped a thrown treat out of the air they made a distinct *chompf!* sound. The suspected H7D3 victim that she and Larry were struggling to control was making the exactly same chomping noise as it fought to close the distance imposed by their field expedient lasso and stick arrangement.

The electrically insulated capture stick allowed them to control the likely zombie at a safe interval while the third member of the team disabled it with a taser. That was the theory at least, and it had worked so far. The captured man slumped to the ground as the repeated current overloaded his nervous system.

A banker, she judged from the tailored suit, and a recent turn. His shoes were still polished and his clothing clean. Usually, the detainees were naked, or mostly so. Her bank's team of lab types explained that an early symptom was profound skin sensitivity. However, some infecteds turned so fast that this step seemed to be skipped occasionally.

Once the potential infected was on the ground, the team was

ready for phase two—getting a photo of the detainee and then bagging his head with a Kevlar snake sack order to prevent bites. She spied a human bite mark on one scrabbling hand—the probable infection site.

"Hold onto the stick, Lare," she instructed. "Let me run a patch test."

"Why bother? He is infected, plainer than shit. You're wasting a kit."

"One, that's the procedure we agreed to when we started harvesting these poor fuckers. Two, there is a tiny chance that he is a vanilla EDP who is hopped up on bath salts or something and three, I am the team lead and I fucking well said so."

Larry was a few years older than her twenty-eight, and like many in the corporate security world, had spent time in the military and later as a contractor. His second guessing wouldn't be acceptable in the long term under normal circumstances. In the *current* circumstances of a slow moving zombie apocalypse, it was potentially lethal, *right now*.

Larry levered the capture stick down and put his weight on it, pinning the suspected infected if he should try to rise and placing the captured man in easy reach for administering the test kit. He didn't otherwise reply.

Colleen prompted, "Larry, I need a clear affirm before I get within grabbing distance of this guy, or you are going to be kneeling on that stick for a long time."

"Clear," he replied curtly.

"Crystal, boss." That was Solly, unbidden. Solly was a comfort. An Army lifer who'd retired to Long Island, he ended up driving for MetBank executives during the days of Occupy Wallstreet. He was a professional driver, easy going and the primary operator of their snatch truck—a panel-sided six-pack dually, complete with light bar and Biological Emergency Response Team labels on the front, side and rear. Solly was a huge add to her snatch team, the second one that MetBank had put together in order to accelerate the collection of the raw material needed to make a vaccine that would protect the critical staff who, in turn, kept the bank running. Each BERT member was promised a vaccination, another for the person of their choice, a seat on the bank's extract craft and a cool half million in specie and/or bullion, their choice. Most of the marrieds had already bailed out of the detail so her teammates were the bitter divorce survivors, the adrenaline junkies, and the unmarrieds. Solly seemed to be a mix of the first two, but his calm, cheerful manner under extreme stress over the last two weeks had reassured her as much as Larry's pushback was pissing her off now.

The BERT detail could sense the increasing apprehension in the city. Pedestrians were getting scarcer. Infecteds were easier to find. They had gotten both of their confirmed "donors" half-way into an eight hour shift. Her boss didn't ask any questions about the captured "stock" and the cops—the cops weren't even checking the test results anymore when the BERT truck cleared checkpoints on the way back to the bank. In the early days they carefully matched IDs to the capture picture to the test kits in order to maintain a paper trail and verify that the detainees were actually infected. The corporate BERT teams were careful to follow the protocol that had evolved out of the Bank of the Americas initiative, and eventually had been blessed and copied by the NYPD. Now, there was a palpable change to the feel on the detail. Sooner or later the rules of engagement on infected was going to change, or evacuations would start. Maybe both.

She glanced at the test strip after completing the jab through the potential infected's suit jacket. Red. Make that confirmed.

"Okay, this guy is infected. That's makes four and we are now full up. Bag the head, zip-tie the feet and hands and let's load him up."

They were closing up the back of the truck when Colleen glanced up at the sound of brakes squealing.

"Boss, company," called Solly.

The truck that stopped was a converted moving van and was accompanied by a chase car. She recognized the driver.

Ramon Gutierez had left MetBank for a bigger and better deal from a new competitor. That wasn't unusual on Wall Street. That the new outfit was the largest importer of recreational pharmaceuticals in the tristate area was a bit... unexpected. Based across the East River in Queens, their leadership had first struck an informal deal with the local PD in that borough. The unis had been taking the casualties in higher numbers and some cops were deciding to stay home. As the Blue Flu spread, the 125-odd precincts that policed the city were forced to consolidate, and entrepreneurs like Ramon's boss filled the vacuum. In exchange for "policing" their areas and suppressing any incipient panic, they were allowed to "harvest" their own raw materials.

Colleen's duties included vetting the deliveries that kept the bank running late into the night as the various desks reconciled their trades. Like their competitors, MetBank paid for whatever it took to broaden their profit margins, and that meant keeping staff onsite and working: dinner if you worked past eight pm, a black car home if past nine pm, and access to pharma based "help" if you were there all night. Therefore, she knew Ramon's organization at retail level. One large entity that followed the rules was much easier to manage than dozens of small time hustlers. Certainly the PD had thought so during normal business times and tolerated the limited distribution of stimulants in the financial district—after all the business of New York City was money, and like everyone else, the PD wanted business to be good. Now however, the tolerated "entrepreneur" was a potential competitor and an even more necessary evil.

Colleen had heard that Ramon's boss had expanded into the Bronx. She didn't know that they were this close to Manhattan.

"Hey chico, we got this," she called to the familiar face.

"Yeah, I see that. You a little far from midtown, aren't you?"

Three men had exited the car and truck. All were armed with holstered pistols and tasers and had the bright orange BERT creds issued by the PD hanging from neck straps. Two were wearing their hair with the signature tightly braided mini-dreadlock that so many in Big Mac Overture's gang affected, but otherwise, their appearance was anything but uniform. Big Mac wasn't big on a dress code, just results.

"Just leaving. Plenty more where these came from," Colleen replied, hooking a thumb towards her truck. Her glance took in Solly, now with a shorty AR hanging on a friction strap, calmly backing her up, and Larry, ostentatiously repacking a large gear bag, with both hands out of sight.

Ramon followed her glance.

"Sure, plenty more. Still, maybe we should cooperate. We can watch this bit around the Queen's Tunnel and you stay over on the island? We have plenty of manpower and you guys at MetBank, you have just the one truck, no?"

"More all the time Ramon, more all the time."

In fact, MetBank had exactly two trucks. The two teams each

averaged four infecteds per day. Eight "donors" meant two hundred or so doses of vaccine, under perfect conditions. MetBank had thousands of critical personnel and family to cover. Colleen wasn't sure of the math, but she guessed that they weren't more than halfway to the number needed to protect everyone while maintaining operations at either the main bank location or the primary Disaster Recovery, or DR, site.

"Ramon, let's talk about this later. We can talk during a break at the meeting at Goldbloom's, okay? If you need help, just come up on the BERT channel and we can roll a truck, like when your boys got stuck last time." She laughed easily, deliberately. "Next time, maybe don't try for so many infecteds at once, right?"

Colleen wanted to remind him that she had saved his boys recently. It is harder to force a confrontation with someone to whom you owed a favor.

Ramon grimaced. Colleen's team *had* helped one of his. The dumbshits had elected to leave their siren on while making a snatch. In the middle of bagging and tagging, another infected had appeared, and then another, and his assholes didn't hear them over the sound of their newly purchased cop siren. Colleen's team had arrived just as Ramon's crew had exhausted their taser cartridges and were preparing to start shooting. Even now, the police would have an issue with openly shooting infecteds. No shooting meant no cops. No cops meant that they could keep collecting infecteds, unpoliced. Good business.

"Sure, sure, chica." Ramon gestured to his team, who mounted back up.

She watched for a moment and then moved her hand in a circle over her head, still watching Big Mac's team get situated.

Turning around, Colleen glanced at Solly. Still perfectly composed, he slid behind the wheel and slipped the weapon into the rifle sock that had been bolted to the interior door panel. Larry was in the rear of the cab, visibly tense.

"Home, James," she said to Solly. "Let's dump these four at the lab. Then, I need to get ready for the pow-wow." She waved good-bye out the window to the other team.

Solly got the BERT unit rolling, turning south.

Larry asked, "Are we gonna jump soon?"

"Nope. We still need more vaccine," Colleen replied.

"Chill out, Larry. No need to be nervous yet."

"Fuck you, Solly, I don't have a death wish. I don't want to get infected and I don't want to square off against a big shot narco like Big Mac Overture. I just want my vaccine, my money and I'm good."

"I'll tell you guys when it is time to jump. You know that," Colleen tried to reassure her two teammates.

"All good." Solly's hands were steady on the wheel, and Colleen saw him smiling.

"Sure," replied Larry. "But who's going to tell you?"

They drove down Second Avenue in an uncomfortable silence.

Most New Yorkers never gained access to the fancy buildings that dominated the Manhattan skyline and didn't really know what went on in the various luxury skyscrapers, let alone appreciate just how amazing the view was from some of them. At this point, luxury views weren't the first thing on the famously insouciant New Yorkers' agenda. Pretending that they weren't fighting a deadly plague was.

Since she had to stand behind her boss at what promised to be a long meeting to divide up the management of the five boroughs of New York, Colleen appreciated the distraction of the view beyond the boardroom window, only slightly marred by the occasional plume of smoke from a car fire. The first gathering of its kind since Boss Tweed met with union representatives in the aftermath of the Draft Riots of 1863, this get-together had been organized in order to carve up the policing of the city, and the management of certain "assets."

The boardroom the meeting was held in was carpeted so deeply that it swallowed all sounds of footsteps as well as the bottom half of the soles of Colleen's tactical boots. The rest of her attire also clashed with the framed original art and wood paneling. The usual Herman Miller synthetic chic was not in view; rather, the room had honest-to-god wooden antique chairs with actual gilt, complementing the long bookmatch walnut conference table. She enjoyed the view north across the Hudson into Jersey from the top floor of the Goldbloom building. The newest headquarters among the major banks, it had been built after 9/11, and no practical expense had been spared to make it as secure as possible against infrastructure failure and kinetic attacks. Colleen suspected that "hardened against zombie attack" was not on the official specs, however. The city paranoia about weapons persisted too. All the non law enforcement attendees had obvious holes in their various rigs. Batons, tasers and firearms were all checked downstairs in what was ostensibly a city meeting.

She was covering her principal, the Chief Security Officer or CSO, of MetBank, despite the hosting bank's security assurances. Colleen was dressed to impress downtown, zombie apocalypse style. Her bank's executives were concerned about staff security looking too much like the military contractors made famous during the late Middle East war and had sprung for what they considered to be tactical attire. Both the rugged but stylish trousers which looked like dress pants and her matching business jacket were by Elite Sterling, incorporating Kevlar throughout and plenty of hidden pockets. Those were topped by a tailored blouse and a functional but insanely expensive Jaeger LaCoultre watch (thank you annual MetBank bonus!) which matched the richness, if not the tone of her surroundings. The effect was spoiled by the newly mandatory plate carrier, and Danner boots, added since the bank went to high security protocols following the May breakout of H7D3—the zombie virus.

Colleen thought she looked faintly ridiculous. Whatever, it was still more comfortable than perching upright on her four inch Laboutins for four hours while waiting for Mrs. Managing Director (fourth of her line) to spend her husband's money at Bergdorf-Goodman. Having suffered through several details where she was both expected to "blend" as well as be able to accompany either the one female member of the Regional Board or more likely the spouses of the male cohort, Colleen knew well the agony of designer heels matched with long hours on her feet. She kept the smile off her face. The new daily wear wasn't just more comfortable, it was also a lot easier to get the stains out of after a long shift performing her newest duties.

Topping off her rig were her security credentials issued by NYPD, clipped to a MOLLE loop under which the legend NYSI was printed in four inch tall white letters. The New York Security Initiative had grown out of the original Lower Manhattan Security Initiative post 9/11. Banks, DHS and the NYPD began sharing the video take from their various systems, as well as the local intelligence from an informal network ranging from building guards and street cart vendors to the local field office of the biggest "Other Governmental Agency" or OGA, of all. LMSI had successfully maintained a high level of situational awareness through lower Manhattan at first, and gradually expanded that northward across the island and then the other burroughs. That success was the genesis of this meeting. Some of the bigger banks and re-insurance corporations as well as the Police Commissioner, the NYC detachment commander for the New York National Guard and now some . . . irregular forces were meeting. The unofficial goal was to share intel on the number and location of recent H7D3 outbreaks. In reality, this meeting would formally establish the boundaries of territories, within which each group would harvest infecteds in order to manufacture the vaccine.

It had been several weeks since the initial reports of H7D3 appearing on the West Coast were officially acknowledged. Business in the City was proceeding, if not quite as usual, then at least it was lurching along.

The initial lack of information from higher authority gave way to reports that teams CDC and WHO were working on a vaccine and presumably a cure. Three weeks into the growing crisis however, the precinct system that was the NYPD had started to visibly fray due to attrition—between the increasing number of cops who were not showing up to work and their casualty rates, the NYPD had been taking it on the chin. So in addition to the large banks and insurance houses, some of the larger entrepreneurs, for values of the word "entrepreneur," that could afford to maintain a security infrastructure were increasingly policing their own "neighborhoods." These internal turf teams initially responded by capturing the infected and isolating or killing them. However, once the CDC bright boys had figured out how to make a vaccine and distributed the instructions, that changed. That vaccine depended on access to a supply of raw material—the spinal tissue from infected victims. Lab monkeys being in short supply and the banks being possessed of a proven ability to relabel their liabilities as assets, they had decided that infecteds were assets—just so many vaccine doses running around in precursor form. The "entrepreneurs" simply followed suit.

One of those entrepreneurs was making his entrance to the board room at that moment. The flashiest attendee yet merited a double take. Big Mac Overture was a figure best known for beating a racketeering rap six months earlier, only a few months before the world began to end. He was routinely cast in the role of Public Enemy Number One, New York style, in every free paper that littered the subway. Everyone just knew that he ran the Dominican mob that was competing with the Chinese and the Mexicans for the drug trade that came up from the border, across the Gulf and into Port Elizabeth just across the river in Jersey. Apparently, "everybody" was right, because here he was at the meeting that was going to formalize the participants as a sort of city council for addressing the increasing number of infected New Yorkers. And sharing them. His detail actually looked about the same as Colleen, gear wise, right down to the NYSI badges. Big Mac flourished his walking stick and swaggered over to a group of bank representatives to say hello while his security man greeted Colleen.

"Hey chica, how they hanging?"

"One higher than the other, Ramon, same as always," Colleen knew that the gangs from the DR operated on a level of machismo that wasn't exactly Wall Street style. Or maybe it was, come to think of it.

"Look, I'm sorry about rolling up on you earlier—I see that it could look a little aggressive. But there is something else."

"No worries about today. No blood, no foul, right?" Colleen waited for the other shoe to drop.

"Thing is, some of our boys saw your truck out the other night, well past Tunnel. You know that we take care of Midtown East and Murray Hill, right?"

"Maybe. So?"

"You know that those 'zombis' are ours, right?" Ramon finally got to the point. "You are over the line."

"I know that we're not gonna wait for you to get around to responding to some EDP call when they could start making new zeds in the meantime. You know the deal that the cops set. The closest Biological Emergency Response Team responds to any call. If you can bag it and tag it, your BERT keeps the asset. Speed of response first, everything else second."

Colleen wasn't the CSO, but she knew the ROEs and the policy. If anything, the fact that it wasn't yet "shoot on sight" was crazy, but the Commissioner wasn't ready to go that far yet, and her boss was still making nice with the cops. It was an open question if her boss would make the final evacuation call off the island to the DR site before or after such an order was promulgated by the PD. Colleen had been told that she was on the evacuation list, but she knew that when the wheels came off there would be little warning and the first casualty would be their careful plans. Until then, vaccine manufacture was the priority. Keeping the rate of infection as low as possible in order to buy time was the utmost priority.

Ramon laid a little "street" on her, "Hey, I like you, chica, you did good work when we needed help a couple calls ago. But you got to stay out of nuestro barrio—my boss ain't gonna sit for you taking what we need to make our own medicine."

"Ramon, you know and I know that the only reason that you are hot to get more infected is because the street price for a unit of vaccine is actually twenty times higher than the price of street cut heroin, or a hundred times as much as grass. At least we aren't selling it to the highest bidder."

"Sure, sure, and maybe we are making money off the people now. We like, have something in common with you banks, no?" Ramon was unflustered that she knew of their own processing for profit operation. "I'm am giving you a, what you say, professional courtesy. But listen, chica, you roll up in that fancy BERT truck in our neighborhoods again, and you might come across something special, like we used to find in Najuf."

Colleen frowned. The threat was no joke. Plenty of the demobbed soldiers that had been riffed from the Army during the current president's "peace dividend" knew enough to cobble together an IED like the ones that they had dodged in Fallujah or Helmund. Or Najuf. Plenty of those vets had returned to their neighborhoods to find legitimate work scarce, and "entrepreneurs" interested in adding their experience to the portfolio.

"Look—" she began, only to be cut off as the meeting was called to order. "Look, we can talk later, right?"

Ramon looked at her steadily. "We can always talk as long as you stay out of our turf."

"If we could all take seats now, please ladies and gentlemen," called the Goldbloom managing director. "We have a quorum of interested parties and can start."

"Later, chica," Ramon waved over his shoulder. He wasn't making a threat, she knew. He was just relaying his truth to her. "Come into 'my' areas and there is going to be a problem." Colleen was a first-generation, American-born Chinese—she understood tribes and community obligation. She also understood fair warnings.

There were many new faces at the table, most of the city and police representatives appeared to be deputies, or newly promoted. The meeting proceeded along the usual lines. Introductions between the various groups were standard at first, but the police delegation visibly grimaced when Big Mac genially waggled his skull-topped walking stick as his name and organization was called out. They didn't change expression when the Triad representative, predictably impassive, was named. Their scowls deepened for the Italians. Previously shrinking in relevance, Franky Matricardi's network, affectionately named the New Thing, or Cosa Nova, had been bolstered by recent infusions of cash from a desperate but well heeled group of re-insurance firms. Recognizing that covering the data centers and vaults that were underground in Piscataway was beyond their capabilities, the company had funded Cosa Nova's newly established effective control of much of Newark, Red Bank and Jersey City. Matricardi pulled it off by resurrecting a combination of ferocity and a reality based willingness to work with some of the existing gangs, including the ones in uniform. It also helped that the Jersey police and state troopers were, if anything, catching the Blu Flu at rates exceeding NYPD's problems. Newark was nearly empty of cops, creating what the Cosa Nova cadre laughingly called, "white space."

The first documented instance of a disease response independent of the NYPD had been the Biological Response Teams or BERTs that the Aussie head of security over at Bank of the Americas had pulled together. This, in short order, turned into broader recognition of the need to discreetly harvest "assets."

Thus the current get-together.

Anyone who had lived through Katrina, or Sandy, or Irene knew that waiting for FEMA and the CDC to start shipping a vaccine was a forlorn hope. Anyone with a tearing need had either prepared for the worst by maintaining a large investment in security and awareness, like Colleen's employer or the German investment bank, or had enough funds to improvise a solution as they went along, absorbing the higher cost of buying what they needed at the last minute. That meant keeping "their people" safe, their businesses running and now, making their own zombie vaccine. The truly prepared were balancing the opportunity to really pad their profit margin with the belief that a cure would surely be found and if not, their preparations would get them out of the City if needed.

Even on the precipice of a world-ending disaster, bureaucracy proceeded in an orderly way. The meeting agenda points quickly devolved into why certain groups should have a greater amount of territory to patrol for infected. The banks were determined to have enough donor volume to reach their minimum safe dose levels. The police seemed torn between a relief that they didn't have to do it alone and a deep resentment that anyone else could do what they did and baldly asserted so. The deputy mayor, filling in for his increasingly absent boss, sparred with the leadership of various city special interest groups. Their political leaders sensed opportunity to assert more independence as the city services suffered from the disease. The commercial entrepreneurs, such as Big Mac and the Jersey crowd, were united in insistence that they could take on more than anyone else, if only others stayed out of their way.

Colleen tuned back into the previously droning remarks as someone raised their voice. Big Mac's deputy was losing his patience for this kind of protracted talk-talk.

"I don't care that you are cops and we aren't. I don't care that 'the public' isn't comfortable with my teams coming into their brownstone neighborhoods. What I care about is that we have the most trucks, that we can handle the most volume and we are. Getting. It. Done. Unlike your precious police who are quitting because it's too dangerous."

The precinct captain from the 10th stood up, red faced. "You already got all of the Bronx, most of Queens east of the 678 and now you want to take everything north of 116th? Fuck you!"

Big Mac's belly laugh was more shocking than more yelling. It quickly overcame the angry responses that were starting from half a dozen mouths. He motioned casually to his deputy, shutting him up.

"Mon, I don't have to ask you for ev'ting above hunned and sixteenth. I already got it. You can just smile and make it official. Sho, Big Mac is already protec'in da Bronx, and let's face it, most of Queens too. Why? Because no one else is."

"That's absurd! We have patrols all over Queens, keepi—" another city official tried to inject.

The Dominican kingpin shut that down.

"No, no. Your 'patrols' look good. Hell, Big Mac like your patrols. Keeps the civilians calm, makes them feel safe. My boys, we really be keeping dem safe. You know how many trucks I running? Fifty."

Gasps from around the table revealed that most had no idea of the scale of the operations that Big Mac ran. Colleen kept her mouth shut, even though she was as surprised as everyone else. Ramon looked a little smug.

"We taking more dan hunderd fifty zombis off the street every day. More dan I can, heh heh, process into da special medicine. We are holding back monsters, see? Maybe you think we are bad, maybe we are too dangerous, right? Well, sometimes little monsters that you know are better than big monster dat ends world. I running de trucks wherever I have to, keeping zombi from getting too big, too fast."

He paused to let the others absorb the size of his "take."

"You doan unnerstand. Big Mac's grandmere, she come from old school DR. She unnerstands about zombi—zombi is old news in Carribean, mon."

Big Mac looked around the group at the conference table.

"We comfortable with a little zombi. You all done made da big mistake, inventing way to make even more zombi. Now old school from the DR is gonna help put da zombi back in box, maybe find a cure, see? So know you know what Big Mac really want? Really need?"

The deputy major was getting over being gobsmacked, even if the police chief was still visibly stewing next to him.

"Okay. I give. What do you really want?"

"Big Mac want a hospital. An doctors. An techs. An equipment. I make all da medicine that everyone needs. You doan worry about how I get the zombis, or where I get the zombis. Big Mac do a better job than Eli Lilly, or J and J, eh? Do it quicker, quieter, that for sho'. Docs I try to hire, dey a little nervous about working with da Big Mac, maybe get dirty, maybe worried about how it looks be turning 'patients' into medicine."

He looked over at the groups of bank representatives.

"My friends from da banks, they unnerstand, they make their

own medicine, a little bit. So. Maybe I help. Maybe after, we talk about a little IPO for da best newest, biggest pharma company, da one that saves world."

Colleen wasn't surprised that some of the bankers actually looked like they were taking it seriously.

The cops were having none of it. The acting police chief stood up, and his immediate staff with him.

"No. Hell, no. We'll get more cops. We will process the infected humanely. We will keep order, we—"

His strong voice was drowned out by a very high pitched, piercing scream.

"No, no, no, no get it off, off. Get it off meeee!"

Colleen as well as everyone in the room snapped their heads around to look at a younger admin, part of the bank contingent's support. It appeared that she had been trying to make it to the bathroom as the first sensations of the disease manifested. Consequently, she was between most of the meeting attendees and the door.

There were two immediate surges of movement in the room. Most of the principals at the table jumped away from the woman, some pulled by their details, some moving with an alacrity belied by rich suits and doughy bodies. A few circles of relative calm remained, including the detail covering Tom Smith from Bank of the Americas and guards for Big Mac, headed by Ramon. Colleen's principal was already standing and she moved forward between the still-screaming admin and her group.

"No shooting!" Colleen wasn't sure if the police chief was talking to his men who had already unholstered, or to the group at large. "Don't just stand there, just immobilize her, quick!" No one moved forward. There didn't seem to be a lot of enthusiasm in the room to wrestle with a zombie.

As far as she knew, none of the contractors had been allowed to carry firearms or tasers into the room with the mayor's staff and the police chief present. Everyone had accepted the pre-gathering blood test screening as the primary protection mechanism. So much for that.

She cast about for some way to keep the zombie at a distance, or chivvy it away from the anteroom doors. The chairs looked likely…

The infected was starting to snarl and was tearing off the

remainder of its clothes. Colleen noted the La Bruna bra. Nice taste, bit overpriced. Who has six hundred dollars for lingerie?

"Solly, do you have a holdout?"

He pulled out a large folding knife. "Just this." He seemed as relaxed as ever.

"Well, fuck me."

Colleen made a double plus promise to never, never ever not carry again, and damn the rules. If that zombie started getting bitey, it was going to be a combination PD shooting gallery and aerosolized blood spatter zone. Not good. She also didn't particularly trust that the only armed people were nervous cops who (a) weren't known for their shooting accuracy and (b) already didn't like that the bank security contractors and "entrepreneurs" were doing their job for them.

A loud crash across the table got her attention. Ramon had just smashed a priceless antique chair across the table, producing some serviceable lengths of wood. The cops had formed a cordon across the back of the room and screened most of the attendees, but otherwise were holding in place.

"Okay, Solly. Smash me this chair and then we can go help Ramon move this zombie along, while the boys in blue admire our style, okay?"

"Sure thing, boss," he replied, hoisting the chair overhead.

"Hey, Ramon!" she called across the table, where Big Mac's crew was cautiously spreading out between the infected and their principal. Ramon glanced over.

Colleen added, over the sound of another antique being literally smashed to kindling, "Wait a sec, and we will come give you a hand."

She reached back for a sturdy if gilded chunk of chair leg and added with a smile, "Again."

Colleen walked west to Rector Street and hopped the 1 subway line to Christopher. Even on her salary, she couldn't afford the rent in the Village. Sarah could. She ran the agriculture commodity desk at JP Morgan. They had met earlier in the year while Colleen had been on a detail covering a meeting at the midtown offices of JPM. As a rule, she never rubbernecked the attractive people at the meetings. A short, pert blonde had caught her eye and discreetly slipped her a business card. A month later, Colleen moved in, and a year later they were still together. Amazing.

She had tried to convince Sarah to leave the city, without success. Her parents had a place in the Finger Lakes—not too many people, good defensible terrain. Sooner or later, it was going to be time to boogie, and Colleen was terrified that she would have to choose between her duty and trying to find Sarah if panic really took hold in the city. There really wasn't a choice, Colleen knew. She wasn't going to protect the suits if it meant leaving Sarah alone.

However, Sarah had just as much steel in her as Colleen, damn it. And she was still working.

The apartment was a fourth-floor walk-up and needed a remodel. The street noise was clearly audible inside, though it usually wasn't too bad. There was also an amazing bakery not even two doors down. Everything is better when you can enjoy a fresh palmiere over your paper. Sarah liked coffee.

And cooking. The smell of the pasta sauce bloomed across Colleen's face as she swung the door open, reminding Colleen that her last meal had been a late breakfast. The adrenaline from the way the meeting dissolved had masked lesser things, like fatigue and hunger.

Sarah looked up from the large pot that she was stirring. She wore a bright neon green strapless sundress. The thing practically glowed, but set off her tan.

"My favorite eighties dress!"

"Hope that you are hungry! I made the traditional amount!" Sarah replied.

Immediately Colleen's edgy feeling came back.

"What are we going to do with two gallons of pasta sauce? It takes us weeks to eat that!"

Sarah's face fell. "Are we going to fight about this straight away? Can't we eat first?"

Colleen closed the door and struggled to stay calm, the frustration of the day just below the surface. "Look, I love you, I worry about you, and I don't understand why you don't just go now. If things get bad, I can get out alone and come up to your folks' place. If it gets bad there won't be time to find each other and then . . ."

"I know you care. I know that you worry about me. But one, I am not leaving here without you and two, my job is actually more important than you think."

Colleen tried to hold her. Sarah moved a little, her face set.

"I am not a doll. I am not leaving alone. Are you ready to leave now, right now? I'll leave if you go, if you think that this is the right time. Right now." She looked steadily at Colleen.

"What? No. No, I need to stay longer in order to get the vaccine for us. Things are still pretty steady, we are staying ahead of the number of infected. I mean, there are more than there used to be, but nothing we can't handle, so far."

"Where are the clothes you left with this morning?"

"Um, in decontam. I got a little splatter at the meeting."

"Splatter? What the actual fuck, Colleen! You didn't say anything about zombies at Goldbloom!"

Colleen tried again to hold Sarah, who was even more upset. "I'm okay, it worked out. The entire crew is fine, none of our people were hurt. There was a leaker at the meeting. Somehow she bypassed the patch test and then turned during the actual meeting. Some of the suits panicked, and it was exciting for a moment, but nothing happened. I'm fine."

Sarah let herself be held, and put her face against Colleen's breast.

"You know my job is actually more important than you think, right?"

Colleen was a little whiplashed.

"Huh? I mean, what?"

"Do you know why there is no panic in the streets right now?"

"Well, sure. We are a visible presence. The civilians see us catching the infecteds. The National Guard has flooded the subways with troops to catch any infected down—"

"Gas," said Sarah.

"Huh? I mean, what, again?"

"Gas. And taxicabs. Fresh food and flowers. Using your credit card and the ATM. Hitting the invite-only sample sale at Chanel. Keeping your plans to hit the Met. Climbing the Cat's Eye in Central Park." Sarah liked to boulder on the weekends.

"No idea what you are on about."

Sarah, pulled back a little in Colleen's arms and looked up. "I'm serious. The reason that there is no panic is because except for the stupid zombies, everything is mostly normal."

"Well, sure, but..."

"No. The reason things are normal is money. Lots and lots of money, flowing through all the usual places, in the usual ways, to the usual people, in all of the expected amounts. That liquid money, literally spending cash, it what keeps everything mostly normal."

"Okay."

"No money, means no normal life. That leads to fear. That leads to panic in less than a week. Are your scientists going to have enough vaccine for the bank in a week?"

Colleen thought for a moment. "No. Depending how many we decide we want to vaccinate, we still have only the first three thousand units of the vaccine ready. Also, it is a multi-part course of injections. Our spoilage is off the charts. You have to get the radiation just so in order to damage the virus enough to make it harmless and yet keep it sufficiently intact to instigate the immune response."

She added, "I get it, I do. We need the banks to keep running in order to keep all the businesses open long enough to let us finish the vaccine."

Sarah waited.

"Dear heart, it is more than that. The banks don't just have to keep running, everything has to look so normal that it stifles any panic. The biggest enemy we have now isn't the disease per se. The biggest danger is that some event, some unexpected unknown which we could otherwise adjust to creates an irreversible erosion in the huge distributed consensual and shared hallucination that 'This Is All Going To Be All Right.' Do you see?"

Colleen replied, "I think that we are saying the same thing, actually."

"Not entirely..." Sarah tried again. "When things are going well, there is a sort of shared inertia—we all participate and keep working and playing as though things are normal. This is a strong societal defense against shocks. The more normal things are, the harder it is to 'break' a society. You know, the whole 'Keep Calm and Carry On' thing."

Colleen nodded, so Sarah continued.

"Our country, and this city in particular, have endured a serious shock. We are starting to consider that maybe, just maybe, this time is different, that things aren't going to snap back to normal. We are trying like hell, but collective determination is wavering. The government, the CDC, all the usual actors are working to reinforce our determination, but I can see that the money patterns are shifting. The biggest players that buy and sell government paper are shifting their spend. This is spooking the rest of the market because it is unexpected. We are getting really large, ahistorical intraday swings and rumors—each sparks a short run, and then gets reversed. Today was fucking crazy like that. The Fed had to suspend the rules about slowing trading when volatility is too high. Hell, some bond desks are doing it on purpose to make the market move up and down like a seismograph. They trade what are normally outrageous puts and calls on every jiggle. It isn't new, but the levels we see now are self-destructive—and everyone can see it building. They are doing it because if there is no long run to worry about, being destructive doesn't matter."

She was getting visibly agitated. Colleen tried to hold her closer, but Sarah moved back to the stove and reached for a spoon.

"So that is why my job is actually important. There is no more room for shocks. If the system breaks, even a little bit, the underlying infrastructure that we need to sustain the tech and talent to fight the disease will fall apart, and fast. Have you noticed that the Internet is a little slower than usual? That cell calls are dropping a little more often?"

"Not really, no," Colleen replied.

"Well, they are—we see all the data on major infrastructure providers because we need that to keep trading—it is a big circular cycle and it is coming apart. If people like me leave, even a little, it will come apart faster, maybe forever."

Sarah was crying quietly now.

"Baby, I am sorry for—"

Sarah interrupted Colleen. "No. I am not fragile. I am scared and that is okay. But I need you. I need to be with you. If I leave, you are coming with me. So no, I am not going to my parents' house up north, not unless you come with me. So, do we jump together, now, tonight?"

Colleen looked at her.

"Or do we make a shit ton of delicious pasta that we can't possibly finish in just one sitting and keep pressing on?"

Colleen wanted to reassure her, wanted things to be "normal" too. "You know, when we eat pasta we drink wine, right?"

Sarah smiled a little.

Colleen walked over to the wine rack and selected an Argentine red. "And you know how you get after we split a bottle of wine..."

"Why, Colleen Chang, are you hitting on me?"

Sarah was starting to smile even wider when there was scream from outside the window.

Colleen lunged for the kitchen light switch and looked outside.

There was a BERT she didn't recognize, bagging a man who was lunging about and snapping. Another man was continuing to scream hysterically and was edging closer to the two BERT techs who were starting to muscle the potential infected into the truck.

"No, he's fine, you don't have to do this. It's fine, don't take him, no!"

One of the techs hit him with a taser, and while Colleen watched from the window, bagged the second man's head as well.

Sarah started to open the window. "What the hell, that's Joey from the bakery, what are those men doing! Call the cops, Colleen."

Colleen snatched Sarah back from the window. "Don't open that, just leave it alone, we can't do anything." She saw that one of the techs was sporting the dreds that were popular in Big Mac's outfit.

"But Joey isn't a zombie, he was just trying to help..."

"Doesn't matter, babe. We don't know what the call is, and the first guy was definitely showing symptoms. If we go down there, we become part of the problem. We could even become part of the 'solution.'"

They watched quietly as the second man was loaded, twitching, into the back of truck. No cops, no one else came out on the street to intervene or ask questions.

Sarah was staring. "But they loaded Joey in the truck. Where are they taking him?"

Colleen hugged her.

"Better not to overthink it. Let me hold you."

"But..."

Colleen stroked Sarah's hair. "It's okay. Things are pretty normal."

A few weeks after the bakery on her street closed, Colleen was leading her snatch team on a routine patrol on the Upper East side. MetBank's regional board had elected to add a third BERT. Each of the existing teams had to give up one person in order to ensure some continuity of experience for the new group. Colleen had not been sorry to second Larry to the new team—he had a shot at the lead role there, and wouldn't be aggravating her. She had been training up Erich, the newbie, a transfer from the executive protection detail. Many of the executives had decided that working remotely from their estates on Long Island a few days a week beat driving in, freeing up trained drivers. Erich was competent behind the wheel, though the inertia of the big truck still tended to surprise the driver who had spent the last year in an S600.

Around the City, conditions had become even more tense, though Colleen couldn't put her finger on it. Sarah kept her up to date on the financial markets situation. After some spectacular gyrations, the markets had steadied a bit. Money continued to flow into, around and out of the city. If Colleen squinted her eyes some, and kidded herself just a little bit, she could pretend that the City was reaching an equilibrium. The subway was running without drivers now, and although there were fewer trains on the tracks in order to provide a safety margin for the automated systems, there were fewer riders too.

All that aside, the city felt somehow different to Colleen.

The number of infected that they found hadn't gone up materially. Overture's crew continued to spread across the city. They were policing nearly all of the Bronx and Queens now. They had also ruthlessly absorbed all of the Triad's area. There were whispers that many of the Triad's gunmen simply went missing. Matricardi's crew owned everything south and west of the City, which they had effectively ceded to Overture. The PD continued to roll units, but the conditions in the "Afflicted Temporary Holding Facilities" were so bad that the cops were ceding nearly all the infected detentions to the nearest BERT. Since numbers weren't up, there was increasing competition for the raw vaccine "ingredients."

Colleen yanked herself back to alertness when Solly called out a possible infected.

"Heads up, left side, looks like a runner."

Sure enough, there was a single person running from a possible zombie, right down the west side of Second Avenue. Joggers had become increasingly scarce as the summer wore on, but this person wasn't jogging, he was sprinting ahead of another man. This one was naked, visibly bloody and slowly closing.

"Erich, get turned around and get us in front of those guys, Solly, get ready to unass the truck as soon as we stop."

"Got it, boss."

Colleen released her seat belt and checked her rig. Sidearm, capture stick, taser, bite bag—all good. Her new tactical jacket and gloves were bite resistant and she had gotten N95 respirators and face shields for her teams. After the close call in the boardroom where the infected secretary sprayed her with blood, she decided that more protection was in order.

Erich reefed the big truck around at the next intersection, foiled by the large concrete planter than ran the length of the median on every block. Colleen saw the infected sprint around the corner on East 96th. Despite being in a vehicle, they were actually well behind in the chase now.

"They're heading towards the park. Hook right and gun it."

Colleen didn't think that you could drift a ride as large as their BERT truck. Erich proved her wrong, buffering their turn by using a parked limo to stop their lateral movement. Knuckles white on the dash chicken bar, she looked in the mirror to see Solly grinning, imperturbable as ever.

"Are we making this too boring, Solly?"

"Hell, Colleen, this ain't nothing. I'll let you know when it gets exciting."

On the straightaway, the BERT closed the gap to the runners rapidly and Erich braked to stop on Lexington, just ahead of the pair.

Out of the car, Colleen already had her taser in hand when the runner blew past her and she shot the infected. He stumbled, clipping Colleen and driving her to the ground. She kept the power on and was levering herself to her feet when Solly yelled.

"Boss, another one!"

She locked the taser on and dropped it, hoping that would keep the first infected down.

The second was a truly large man. Wearing the ragged remains of a Yankees sweatershirt, he was lunging at Solly, who was trying to get the capture stick cinched down on his neck and arm.

"Erich, a little help," she yelled, as she drew the second taser from her belt.

"Erich..." Her second shout was drowned out by a very loud siren as two Suburbans squealed to a halt. Members of Big Mac's crew starting piling out.

"No, we got this," Colleen started to yell over the siren, which was still going, when an Overture tech casually shot her first zombie in the head.

Solly and Erich spun around at the sound of the shot, never seeing the movement of a third zombie emerging from the subway entrance on the corner of Lex and 96th. It was rapidly followed by two more, then three after that.

"Behind you!" she yelled as loudly as she could, trying to be heard over the sounds of the other BERTs. Her manner caused an Overture tech to turn around just as the first infected to reach him got its teeth well into his neck. His screams were actually audible over the ringing in her ears from the shot and the sound of the sirens. Nonlethal ROE was now officially out the door.

"Solly, go hot!"

He didn't bother to answer as he drew his sidearm and dropped the infected on the capture stick and then spun to engage the mass of infected lunging from the subway.

Colleen had never seen so many infected at once. There were at least ten now. The Overture techs were all shooting, mostly with pistols but at least one carbine barked as the infected dropped, one at a time. Body shots accomplished nothing unless they hit a spine.

More screaming, this time Erich was down, clutching his side. There wasn't a zombie anywhere near him. Colleen guessed that he caught a ricochet from the Overture guys. Two of theirs were down, covered in infected and the rest were slowly retreating the short distance to their trucks.

Solly started dragging Erich by his plate carrier while Colleen tried to make head shots. Except for the few on the two strange techs, the only surviving zombies were the ones still emerging one or two at a time from the subway entrance. She nailed her mag change, her hands steadying out, and started to heel and toe backwards to where her own truck sat idling.

The rate of fire picked up from the Overture people as the survivors pulled more carbines from their trucks. The zombies in the subway entrance were not gaining any ground and the growing pile of corpses was impressive and horrifying.

Erich was moaning in the rear of the vehicle.

"Solly, are you seeing this!"

"No likey boss! This one gets all my nopes," he replied cheerfully.

He attended Erich in the back, and was cutting his plate carrier side straps with a set of trauma shears.

"Hold still and stop freaking out, man!" he said without sounding more than a little excited. "Let me look at this scratch and get a dressing on it. Okay, now give me your hand and push on this."

He guided Erich's hand against the dressing to keep pressure on the gunshot wound. Someone mercifully turned off the siren in the other trucks.

Colleen was trying to line up a shot on the last zombie who was still mounted on the form of a prone Overture tech, but hesitated, worried about hitting the downed man.

The fire was slackening as fewer zombies appeared at the top of the subway stairs. Then the prone Overture man stirred, and got to his knees.

Overture's men started yelling at him to come back to the safety of the trucks. Colleen could see the bite marks on his face and hands. His wide open eyes and jerky motions were a plain diagnosis. He turned and started moving more rapidly, straight for the MetBank team.

"He is infected, don't get close!" She couldn't tell if anyone could hear her, especially if their ears were ringing from the gunfire as much as hers were.

Solly had their carbine out and was right on target. She distantly heard the yelling from the other teams.

"Boss?"

"Do it."

Solly dropped the new zombie with a single round.

"Motherfucking bitch! That was Manuel!"

She turned to see one of the Overture techs, a team leader judging from the radio and the jewelry. He was stalking towards them with a pistol in hand.

"He was infected, you saw it as well as me," Colleen answered. "Who was the genius who decided to try to take our assets? You! Who shot my guy first? Your assholes! Step off!"

The other two surviving Overture team members were tense, covering their boss from their trucks.

She heard police sirens approaching. This amount of shooting was a first, as far as she knew, so it wasn't too surprising that someone had called it in.

"You hear that, jackass? That is the cops. You might want to holster that before they get here unless you want to see them really excited. You know the ROE, and you shot first."

"Stupid puta, I don't care if Ramon likes you. He tell us you are competition now. I don't care about the fucking cops either. Overture is gonna end up running this city. After that happens, I will get back to you for shooting Manuel, bitch!" He holstered his pistol and spun on his heel.

"Load these guys in the trucks. We can still get some spinal tissue and make quota!" he yelled at one others.

Colleen slowly relaxed her white knuckle grip on her pistol, just becoming aware of how hard she was squeezing the grip.

"Erich, how are you doing?" she called.

"Been better," he coughed. "Can we get to a hospital sometime? Today is good."

The police sirens grew closer.

"First we deal with the cops, and we call another truck to come get you."

She turned to Solly. He had let the carbine hang from the friction strap and was calmly checking Erich's dressing. "I'll call it in. Then we can see if any of the dead zombies that those assholes are leaving are worth bringing in."

The first black and white pulled up and killed the siren. The cops got out, guns drawn and looked at the bodies piled up at the subway and all the spent brass.

"That is a fucking lot of zombies."

One yelled at the BERT techs from both companies.

"Who is in charge here?"

Without breaking a beat, Colleen and her opposite number yelled back, "They are!"

This time the conference wasn't held at Goldbloom. No one particularly trusted them despite the reality that the safety procedures anywhere are usually followed with exquisite perfection right after an "incident." The Chief Security Officer at Bank of the Americas had suggested that they meet outdoors in the gardens of the Elevated Acre located well below midtown. It had the virtue of taking advantage of both the warm August weather and the large number of exits from the conference dais area. The setting was less luxurious, but after the shock of seeing so many zombies in one place, Colleen really appreciated the longer sight lines and multiple exits.

The evening after the mass zombie attack and confrontation with Overture's BERT, Colleen's MetBank CSO had shared the information about their experience using NYSI. Reactions ranged from disbelief to near panic. The after-action pictures, as well as the eighteen dead zombies that their BERT, reinforced by the other two teams, returned for processing, forestalled most of the disbelief though not the fear. Larry's team had been first to respond after the cops, and Colleen had to tell him to snap out of it—his palpable fear had plainly affected the other two in his truck. It took several minutes of reassurance before they would approach the pileup at the top and along the steps leading down into the Green line.

Sarah had been ready to leave town that night, and Colleen almost agreed. She was torn, feeling a compulsive need after she led them one more time, and give them her own jump order. The exaltation she felt following the fight, when she realized that she *and* her team were alive and victorious, was headier than wine. She understood a little better about what her dad had tried to tell her about his experiences fighting in the Army. The profound sense of duty to her little team was amplified beyond reason when the doctors pronounced Erich's bloody wound mostly superficial—staples, a dressing and some T4 and he said that he felt good as new. There wasn't another driver available, so she planned to keep him in the truck for future calls.

The fallout from Overture's group was scarier, in a way. Ramon didn't respond to any calls. She saw him in Big Mac's group as the different BERT teams, law enforcement and the city government mingled prior to the meeting. The portable tables and A/V system delineated the meeting space, but multiple layers of security faced outwards from the group. Once her CSO's check-in was complete she started to head towards the Big Mac group for a quick word but was forestalled by Ramon's look and headshake.

"All right everyone, take your seats," called Smith, the BotA CSO. He had a no-nonsense look about him. "I have talked to His Honor the Deputy Assistant Mayor Sphalos, and he has graciously allowed me to expedite this meeting. There will be only two agenda items, a summary of the MetBank and Overture BERT response on 96th and Lex and a discussion on what we are going to do differently to ensure further safe operations."

Yelling threatened to drown out the end of his remarks, when Smith moved a microphone near a speaker to produce ear splitting feedback long enough for the yells to die down. "There will be a complete discussion of the tactical situation, the Rules of Engagement and discussion on asset territory. There will *not* be a general yelling match."

He looked around the open table. "As the largest BERT operator here, I will confirm that this agenda suits Mr. Overture. Sir?"

"Sure, sure. As long as you get clear on why da fuck there so many zombi and why my boys got shot!" Big Mac's statement had the flavor of prepared outrage.

More yelling yielded to the requisite audio feedback. "Fuck, stop yelling already!" Overture commanded once Smith stopped the feedback. Instantly his large group quieted.

Colleen swallowed. She knew that a lot of the hostility was directed towards MetBank. Okay, nearly all of the hostility. And most of it was aimed squarely at her, easily recognizable as the only woman attending in a security role.

"First item," Smith continued. "Between MetBank and Overture, a total of thirty-seven infected were recovered. This represents the largest group of zombies, by a factor of ten, recorded anywhere."

"In the U.S.?" asked the Cities Bank rep.

"Anywhere," Smith replied. "Anywhere that we have access to data that we trust. Second, a thorough reconnaissance of the immediate subway platform at the scene showed evidence consistent with the number of dead infected recovered."

"What the hell?" came from down the table.

"What he means is that the amount of crap and trash at the station matches the number of zombies we killed, shithead!" This from the team lead that confronted Colleen.

"Thank you," Smith injected. "This number is not by itself the total issue. That we didn't know that infected could gather, and in effect, coordinate a response however automatic is as significant as the number present. It appears that loud noises in certain frequency ranges serve to strongly attract infected. There is general agreement that the sirens on the BERTs, left running, served to stimulate the emergence of the infected group. We have tested this in a limited way by testing sirens and other loud noises near subways. In most cases, no infected appeared, but in two cases since yesterday's incident, a single infected has appeared if the sirens were left running for more than one minute. More complete testing is precluded by the limited number of assets available to respond.

"I have asked MetBank's CSO to present some additional details." Smith gestured at Colleen's boss, who stood and started talking.

"My team brought back some more useful information. You need to make head and spine shots in order to instantly incapacitate an infected. In this urban environment, you have to be certain of your backstop in order to prevent ricochets from striking friendly personnel. This is especially true for carbines and rifles. One of my drivers caught a bouncer from the only carbine in use at that time in the engagement, operated by Overture's BERT."

"BULLSHIT! I call Bull. Shit. We didn't shoot nobody but fucking zombies! It was this puta bi—"

Overture's BERT lead stood up, drowning out the MetBank CSO. This time Overture didn't intervene, but Ramon stood and put his hand on the shouter's shoulder.

"Easy, Emmanuel. Let me." He gently pushed the man back from the table.

"We are sure sorry that one of MetBank's people got shot. I used to work there, I know those guys. But you know, I am even sorrier that I lost *two* good men because the MetBank BERT couldn't and wouldn't coordinate their operations, although I tried to talk to their lead several times." Ramon's English was precise, perfectly suited to his audience.

"I am sorry that their team lead, standing right there, had one of her boys, also standing right there, put a bullet in the head of one of mine, without checking the diagnosis of infection. I am sorry that their lack of capacity placed everyone at risk. The good news is that we are ready to completely coordinate and deconflict the city-wide BERT management."

Colleen had flicked her eyes around the key players near her as Ramon spoke. Smith was listening intently, and seemed to be making small hand motions behind the podium. Solly had a slight grin, but his light windbreaker was unzipped and his right hand empty. Her boss was openly pissed and getting ready to jump in. Looking over her shoulder, she could see multiple pairs of Big Mac's people with clear sight lines to the conference group. Counting under her breath, she realized that there were as many of Big Mac's "security" as the rest of the PD and BERT tactical personnel combined.

Several people, including the MetBank CSO, stood and tried to talk.

Smith held his hand up. "No, please let him finish. Everyone just hold on for the moment. Mr. Gutierez, please continue."

Ramon looked startled for a moment, expecting more argument from Smith. Colleen blinked. How the hell did Smith know the name of a mid-level guy like Ramon?

"Like I was saying, we are a family. Any of us could have lost these people today. If we work together, it is avoidable. We don't have to have poor communications and competition. This tragic loss of personnel doesn't have to be repeated. Our organization will oversee and coordinate all the BERT efforts. We can embed NYPD observers from the NYSI into our operation center to provide top oversight."

The acting Deputy Police Chief appeared to perk up.

*There is a shot*... Colleen thought.

"We recognize that we have been harvesting more, heh, raw materials for the critically needed medicines that all of our organizations and indeed the entire city must have. We propose to sell your companies up to thirty percent of our total production at cost if we can directly manage *all* of the BERTs and are given access to the facilities *and* staff at Mt. Sinai Hospital."

...*and that is the chaser*, she finished silently.

Murmurs, then louder conversations spread throughout the meeting. Colleen met Ramon's eyes. He looked directly at her without expression. The BERT team lead, Emmanuel, smirked greasily over Ramon's shoulder. Overture still sat, lighting a cigar and looking supremely at ease.

Smith spoke again. "That is a very interesting offer, and provides a lot of things for us all to think about. However, speaking for the financial services groups now present and for those whose proxies we hold, I think we need a day to confer with our regional officers and respond authoritatively."

Overture waved his cigar expansively, while keeping a grip on his walking stick. "Sure, mon. Tomorrow is good."

"Wait a minute, I want to respond!" Another bank rep stood up angrily.

Smith easily deflected the comment. "Joe, not a problem but can you table this just for now? Let me talk to you right afterwards. We can get a sense of how all the banks are feeling. Bear with me, okay?"

The plainly aggravated speaker looked less than sure, but subsided.

Overture turned to the small group of city officials. "Mr. Assis' Mayor, would you like to be talking after this? I can tell you more details. 'Course, your police are welcome to join."

Colleen saw Smith gathering up his opposite numbers by eye, so she was ready when her CSO waved her towards the entrance. Solly coolly brought up the rear.

Smith and CSOs from half a dozen banks, all of them running their independent collection teams, were gathered on the landing.

"Gentlemen, I don't know how far you have made it towards your minimum required dose stock for the critical staff that you need to run operations outside the City. Bank of the Americas has not completed its topline requirements. Nonetheless, I very much doubt that maintaining operations while being under the city-approved oversight of Big Mac will yield much further progress," he said.

"First things first! Why the hell did you close debate up there? You don't speak for all of us!" Colleen's boss replied.

"Item the first: I hope that you all got a good look at the number of men that Overture brought along. I have been looking into the spread and martial capabilities of his group since he told us how many trucks he was running," Smith started. "Item the second: do any of you really think that the city staff and PD are hearing this proposal for the first time today, at this meeting? I don't, and I think that it is nearly all wrapped up. Pushing back now could lead to a . . . less advantageous negotiating position. If you are certain that you want to work for Overture, your best chance is to get clear of this meeting now, consult with your boards and then decide."

"What about you?" asked Cities Bank.

"We're still twenty percent short on primary personnel and fifty percent short on likely dependents. We need a few more days of collection, and we may take them up on the offer to buy the balance, if quality is high. I don't see us working for them under any circumstances. If we jump, we have to move our processing area to a jurisdiction that might not be as . . . flexible. So we collect as long as we can. Gangs I understand. Zombies are the larger unknown."

A few other banks' representatives nodded.

"We're similarly situated at Goldbloom," the CSO there stated. A thirty-year gold shield from the NYPD, he looked stunned at the turn of events. "But we already shifted half of our key personnel from the West Street trading floor across the river to the Jersey City secondary. I am not confident that we can predict when the bridges and tunnels will become . . . a problem."

Colleen looked across to Brooklyn. She saw the Staten Island ferry still plying its route, outbound from Manhattan. There were no tour boats to Ellis or Liberty Island visible, or much other river traffic for that matter.

Her boss spoke again. "I can't see our management ceding control of our BERTs to a known criminal. How long before the Overture gang has some sort of quasi police status?"

"It's worse than that," Colleen spoke up in front of the assembled leaders of the New York City BERTs. "I think that I saw one of their teams snatching a possibly uninfected person. We have all heard rumors about what happened to the Triad BERT. Big Mac has many more teams than we do. If the police give them legitimacy, there isn't much margin for our teams' safety. Problems could find themselves becoming . . . vaccine."

Grim looks answered her statement.

Colleen readied her crew for the night patrol. Officially, ROE was unchanged.

"Okay, guys, I know that you know official ROE. Here is the No Shit ROE. No sirens. No subways. No Central Park. No parking garages. If we get stuck in, and we see more than two infected, we go hot. We avoid any confrontation with other BERTs. If Big Mac wants our infected, we give them up. We will respond to direct threats defensively."

She looked at Erich. "Erich stays *in* the truck with one of the rifles. Clear?"

"Clear."

She was relieved that he didn't try to argue.

"Solly, you and I move as a team. We stay close to the truck. If we have to relocate, the truck comes with us. No chances, minimize risk. Do you guys have any questions or comments? No? Good. Mount up."

Their radios were tuned to the PD and Guard channels. The Army had pulled most of their people out of subways after the shoot. They had positioned several eight-wheeled armored trucks at key points, to what purpose Colleen couldn't say.

As they drove north along Broad, poking into the side streets that meandered unpredictably, south of Canal, Colleen tracked her surroundings while Solly scanned his side.

Was it time to jump tonight? Bring back a load. Tell her guys, and then demand her vaccine and money from the CSO? Would he accept her departure? Could she convince him? Was it worth it to risk staying too long?

Outwardly she was calm, like her rock, Solly. Inside, she was starting to squirm.

The radio started to chatter about the crowd at Sheep Meadow in Central Park being larger than usual, some band or other. Solly called out a possible infected a few blocks later. Female, black, stripping her clothes off haphazardly and screaming. By now the signs of infection were familiar. In a minute or less she was going to start getting bitey.

A screech of brakes and Erich neatly stopped right next to her.

Like a machine, Colleen and Solly dismounted.

"Ma'am?" Solly called. The infected looked up, eyes wide and bright. A low growl replaced the earlier screams.

"Tase her," Colleen said.

They shot the infected simultaneously, and smoothly bagged and zip-tied her. As they maneuvered the infected to the truck's rear gate, the bank's BERT radio relay on Colleen's shoulder sounded.

"Any units, this is MetBank Zero Three. We are at Union Square with three infected in the back. We have three Overture trucks boxing us in, and lighting us with spots. Need immediate support!"

Larry's voice was clear. Colleen's guts churned as she heard the fear in his radio call.

"Zero Three, Zero One enroute. Four minutes. Lock the doors, don't get out. If you can ram clear do it. If they ask for the infected, say yes and kick them out the back and leave. How copy?"

There was no reply. Colleen repeated her call, struggling to modulate her voice.

"Zero Three, Zero Three, acknowledge!"

She switched to the all bank shared channel.

"Any BERT, this is MetBank Zero One. We are responding to a help call at Union Park. Reports that contractor BERTs are confronting one of our units. Request support."

A moment later two radio calls stepped on each other. All she could make out was, "... Golf Actual..."

She broke in. "Break, break—station Golf you are go, all other stations wait one, please."

"MetBank, this is Two Golf, Golf Actual with you."

Colleen checked the call sign chart. She was talking to the CSO from Goldbloom.

"Golf, Zero One, can you support our unit at Union Square? They are not answering calls at this time. We are several minutes out. Ouch!"

Erich had driven over a tall curb to bypass a light and Colleen smacked her head against the passenger window. She missed the next couple calls.

Then she heard: "Zero One—yeah, we are about to turn into the square. We see three, four, five trucks. Looks like they are loading... fuck! They are loading BERT personnel in the back of their truck!"

"Golf, can you engage?"

"Shit, shit—taking fire! Joe turn le—" The Goldbloom transmission stopped.

Solly didn't need to check the GPS. "Two minutes, maybe less. Are we doing this alone?"

Colleen though furiously. If her guys were alive, they weren't going to stay that way. But they were her guys. Five to one odds were bad—but if she shot first? She couldn't just leave them, could she? A little voice in the back of her head started whispering "I told you so"s.

"Okay, here is the deal. If we just drive in, we are toast. We stop at the edge of the square, no lights, no siren. We see what we see. If we spot the container truck with our guys, we disable it, buying time for more help to arrive. The cops gotta be enroute with all the shooting. Got it?"

Silence answered her. Solly looked at her, his hands tight on a chicken bar, braced against the movement of the truck. Erich kept his eyes on the road, but didn't respond either.

"Hey! Got it?" Colleen yelled.

Erich said, "Yeah. Edge of the square. No lights, no siren."

Solly slipped the M4 from the door sock and checked the mag, then looked back at her silently. His eyes were calm, but his fingers were white against the black rifle.

*What the fuck?* thought Colleen.

There was no time; she could see the landmark Washington statue and the open MetBank truck nose first into its pediment, doors open and lights on. Steps away she could see a trademark Overture Suburban and in its headlights, the open back end of a Hyundai lowboy trailer. Bodies were stacked neatly, bare feet and boots both clearly visible.

"Oh, this is not on. Erich, stop where you can hit them with the highbeams when I say. Solly, priority to anyone you see with a long gun, then everyone else. If I shoot, or they shoot, don't wait for my call to light them up."

Erich eased to a stop, engine running. Solly opened his door, aiming towards the scene. Colleen did the same on the front passenger side. She spotted Emmanuel, that prick, talking into a cell phone and waving his arm. She'd ask him nicely. Once.

Aiming carefully, she said, "Erich, lights, now!"

As the headlights and cab-mounted spots blindly lit up the Overture crew, Colleen used her weak hand to key the bullhorn.

"Hey, Emmanuel. Don't move. You really don't want to even fucking twitch. Tell all your men to stop moving, and we can have a little talk."

He couldn't see her, Colleen knew. He knew the voice apparently.

"Hey, puta, that you? You want some zombies. Come help yourself! Plenty here!"

Colleen saw his men dodge behind their trucks, leaving their lead pinned in the light.

"Next man moving gets shot, Emmanuel. No warning." Colleen wasn't feeling calm. She unkeyed the bullhorn. "Solly, be ready."

"C'mon, MetBank. Come get your zombies. You might recognize some!"

Colleen knew at that moment that she wasn't getting her team back. She knew that cocksucker was waiting for any opening to add her, Erich and Solly to his take.

Aiming with exquisite care, she shot him in the mouth, snapping his head back and crumpling his body to the ground. She heard Solly shoot, and then a heavy, persistent chugging and muzzle flash appeared from behind the Suburban.

Solly yelled, "That's a fucking machine gun, we can't fight that! Move!"

Colleen yelled, "Get in, get in, Erich go gogogogo!"

The truck lurched backwards, gathering speed and Colleen heard bullets striking her vehicle. The windshield fractured. She gave up trying to close her door and held on, looking over her shoulder.

Erich tried to pull a Rockford, banging the front of the truck across parked cars, but getting the vehicle turned around.

"Head south, keep going," Colleen yelled. "Solly, you okay?"

She looked in the rear. Solly was belted in and bleeding from small cuts on his face, changing his mag, and looking at her evenly. "I'm good."

"Erich?" Colleen asked.

He didn't answer, but drove with one hand and held his head with the other. Blood streamed down his arms.

"Erich!"

"He might not be able to hear you," Solly said.

The truck lurched as they turned right and then left again, throwing them around the cab. She tapped Erich's shoulder to get his attention and pointed south. He nodded.

*Cops, call the cops!* she thought.

She transmitted on the bank channel.

"Any station, this is MetBank Zero One. Our Three unit is gone. The other guys have machine guns and shot us up. We're hurt and running south. Recommend that all BERTs disengage. Request call to law enforcement."

A few responses, including one "Holy fuck!" from someone holding the transmit button down inadvertently, were plain.

"MetBank BERT, this is the NYPD, pull over and stop." A loud speaker sounded behind them. Erich looked in his rear view at the same time and spotted a blue and white with its flashers running, but no siren. He took his foot off the gas.

*No siren. Huh, smarter cops than average,* Colleen thought. She looked closer. The driver wore his hair in braided dreds.

"Erich, punch it, that isn't a cop. Go!"

He didn't respond. She punched hard in the shoulder and pointed forward screaming in to his ear, "Go!"

The truck accelerated again.

Solly was looking left and right behind them.

"Two cop cars. Three. I don't think we can outrun them."

The BERT was blowing down Broadway, coming up on Houston, when more cop lights showed in front of them. Colleen punched Erich again and pointed right. He reefed the truck towards the Hudson at the next block.

Solly yelled over the windroar, "Where are we going? Bank is the other way?"

"Overture has the cops in his pocket. They aren't gonna arrest us, you understand!?" she yelled. "We have to go around, we can pick up West Street, or the Greenway and get past them. If you haven't figured it out, it is time to jump!"

Solly nodded, but the fingers on his right hand, holding onto the bar between the front and rear, started tapping.

The truck started lurching more, and side swiped a parked car, nearly spinning them. She looked at Erich. He was starting to sway.

"Solly, shoot the cop cars up, get us some room. I gotta drive!" Colleen yelled.

As soon as the fire started, the blue and whites fell back more than a block. Colleen recognized the neighborhood; this was the West Village. She was only blocks from home.

She started tugging on the wheel to get Erich's attention. Solly's rifle popped consistently as he peppered the cop cars, pushing them further back.

She pointed left towards Seventh. The truck slowed as Erich turned. He looked more ghastly than the yellow street light glare warranted, Colleen recognized. She had to switch places. She looked back after the turn.

"Do you see them?"

"Naw. They dropped back too far. Maybe they're giving up?"

Colleen wasn't feeling that lucky. She motioned to Erich to stop and hopped out to get in his door and push him over. The front of the truck was heavily damaged from gun fire and the reverse turn. The sides of the truck were scratched too. She had good tires, it appeared, and the engine roared when she goosed the accelerator. Erich sort of slumped against her now closed door.

Could they make it all the way to Tribeca on 7th? The streets were empty of all traffic. She spotted runners—pedestrians maybe, but infected probably.

*Sarah—I have to get to the bank, then get Sarah and go!* Her gut burned with regret and fear as she remembered her decision to make it one more night. *Stupid stupid stupi—*

She never saw the blue and white that perfectly crashed into her truck, punching them diagonally across Seventh. The blue and white took the brunt of the collision, and swerved crazily, hitting a building wall, the driver buried face first in an airbag.

She shook her head, seeing more lights behind her again. No headlights. The brake pedal felt weird, spongy. Her door was slightly dished in.

She tested the gas and the engine responded as she aimed back onto 7th. A loud scratching and rubbing sound accompanied her efforts to push the truck past thirty-five or so. She wasn't going to outdrive the blue and whites.

She spotted a narrow loading alley next to a street side restaurant and turned into it at speed. The truck ground into the alley, striking sparks and making even more noise.

She turned to get Solly and Erich. Her driver's head was laying past a right angle on his back. His neck was clearly supported only by muscle.

Solly looked back at her, his jaw muscle jumping.

She keyed the radio mic. Dead.

"C'mon, get out through the windshield!" Colleen said. "We can try to find another car while they work to get around the truck."

He pointed silently ahead of them. There was nothing but a blank wall, not even fifty feet away.

"Well, fuck. Fuck fuck fuck and more fuck. With little fuck sprinkles." Colleen wasn't thinking too straight. Her left arm was really starting to hurt too.

She could see the flashing cop lights reflecting in the alley.

"Hey, Colleen, that you?" a loudspeaker sounded behind her.

*Ramon. Perfect.*

"Fuck you, Ramon."

"What?"

She screamed, "Fuck! You! Ramon!"

"Colleen, let me help you; we got an ambulance. We can get you out. All you have to do is chill out. We just want to talk."

"Fuck you, Ramon," she whispered.

Solly limped back from checking the walls of the alley. He shook his head.

"Solly, you there man?!"

Solly jerked his head up, eyes wide.

Colleen shook her head.

"Solly, don't be stupid, man." Ramon went on, "You can live through this. I remember you from before, I know you and Colleen roll together, big man. Tell her that she has to chill out!"

Solly looked at her, his eyes still wide. "We are out of rounds for my rifle. I don't see yours in the truck, must have lost it somewhere. We got two mags of pistol each. This is not going to end well. Maybe..."

Colleen shook her head again. "Do you want to be vaccine?" She leaned back through the windshield. The engine was still idling but was suddenly drowned out by the BERT truck siren.

"What do you think you are doing?" Solly demanded.

"Siren. We're a couple hundred meters from the Canal Street Station." Colleen was feeling even more dizzy and her entire left side throbbed. "All we gotta do is keep that asshole Ramon from comin' over the top of the truck long enough for the fucking infected to show up."

Solly looked at her. "You are fucking crazy, you know that? Give me your pistol; you aren't in shape to shoot. I'll watch the top, because those Big Mac assholes are going to figure this out quick."

She could hear the loudspeaker over the siren, barely.

"Nice play, Colleen, but it's no good. We got enough firepower for a few zombies!" Ramon's voice was faint, but clear.

She heard some shots strike the back of the van. *Much good that will do them, with a locked armored panel between the cargo and the cab.* She laughed to herself. She must be getting really loopy and felt even dizzier.

The siren kept wailing. She could hear steady gunfire now, but nothing striking the truck. It sounded like a machine gun was shooting without stopping. *Good way to get a jam*, she thought. The firing went on for minutes it seemed, then tapered.

She could hear screams over the siren, faintly, but the firing stuttered and ended. A little while went by. The siren suddenly shut off and she looked up.

Solly sat down heavily next to her, with an angle to see under the front of the truck.

"I want to hear what is happening before I poke my head over or under," he explained.

Her ears rang. Her vision seemed bright but blurry. It was too bright. She tried to marshal her thoughts. The bank. Vaccine. Sarah.

Solly fired a few rounds at a scrabbling form under the truck. Then he fired a few more. "I think that was your friend Ramon."

"Did he say anything?"

"Well, if growling is saying something, sure."

*Huh. Near instant karma. Nice...* thought Colleen.

Solly stood quietly, but jerkily. "I'm going to listen at the panel."

He came back some time later.

"It's quiet. I peeked through the spy hole. No movement, no infecteds in view. No cops. No one. If we move quietly, we can try to get to a car."

Solly sounded a little jittery. "That's weird—if the bad guys are gone..." Colleen tried to focus. "You think?"

"Sure. Let me help you."

Slowly, with Solly helping, they crouched through the armored divider, then slowly eased the rear door open. Colleen noted that their sole infected capture of the night had been shot.

The street was clear of any living thing. The yellow streetlights didn't show blood well, but dark puddles collected near scores of corpses. Most were naked, or nearly so—infected that had attacked from the subway. A few bodies wearing uniforms were visible, but were hard to make out, being mostly disassembled.

They stumbled south a few blocks along the Greenway, dodging the ever present NYC construction debris, traffic cones and orange plastic fencing. The West Expressway, normally busy with traffic, was empty. They turned east towards the 9/11 memorial pools.

Solly stopped in his tracks. Colleen looked up. For at least a block in every direction, there were groups of infected. They were congregating around the edge of the memorial.

She jerked reflexively. Solly's grip on her arm tightened.

"C'mon, turn around!" she whispered urgently.

Too late. Loud growls rose from the groups nearest them, not even a hundred meters away.

Solly turned to her. "Sorry, boss. One of us is going to make it." He shot her leg, making her drop into a shallow hole at the edge of the Greenway construction. Colleen could see him as Solly turned and half jogged away as the growling grew in volume.

*Motherfucker...* thought Colleen.

A bright neon green shape drove Solly to his side. The pistol sounded, futilely. Solly screamed briefly.

The growling was closer and Colleen looked up.

She did like that green dress.

# The Road to Good Intentions

## TEDD ROBERTS

"TURN THAT OFF." Sally Metzger reached over and turned off the radio before the preacher got fully warmed up in his warnings about the apocalypse and end times.

Leonard Morris barely managed to keep from slapping her hand away from the dial. The mood in the house was tense enough as it was, with the reports coming in about folks going nuts and biting people. The President had made some announcement about a new viral disease, but none of that made sense.

"Sweetie, we should keep it on for the news. I don't want to listen to that stuff either. I can turn it to another station."

Len turned the radio back on, volume low at first, then louder as he started hunting for other stations.

The emergency radio could bring in multiple bands, and could even be operated by a hand crank in the event of electrical failure. He had deliberately stocked the "mountain retreat" with low-technology items—both to compensate for being up in the mountains, and as a deliberate respite from their usual habits. There were still stations that didn't carry constant news reports, so he selected one playing classical music in hopes that it would calm the tension.

"I still don't understand. Why can't we just go online? At least I could Skype with my friends," his wife Sally pouted.

She hadn't been too pleased about their sudden departure from the city, nor the prospect of an extended stay in their "weekend getaway cabin." Len knew that he would lose the argument, no matter what his justification, and frankly, he didn't want to argue with her. She started warming to her usual litany of complaints: "When you said you wanted a mountain home, I figured you meant one like you see on cable—sweeping vistas, hardwood floors, and a hot tub on the deck! I am so bored of seeing nothing but trees and cooking on a wood stove!"

That wasn't entirely fair, he thought. He'd bought the house to get away from the city, and had selected a lot with a decent slope and elevation. It was just that Sally had been set on one of the much more expensive homes and vistas up on the Blue Ridge. In truth, the house had central heating and a satellite dish for TV and computer—it was just that Len liked getting away from the electronic intrusions that ruined his normal working day. A log fire and lanterns were much more relaxing. Speaking of which, this would be a good time to go chop more wood; it would give him something to do that would get him out of the house and he could just take the radio outside with him. Sally had her phone and could text all her friends about what an idiot he was. She'd be happy and he'd be able to stop thinking and just lose himself in the exertion.

After an hour of chopping and stacking cordwood, he heard sounds of a vehicle on the road beyond his driveway. There was a gate at the end of the drive, but it was downhill and around a bend so that it was out of view from the house. Unfortunately, that also meant that he couldn't see the road from his current location.

Now he heard the sound of breaking glass and bending metal. That could not be good. Hmm, he needed a better view. He hurried down the drive and around the slight bend. Right, there it was, opposite side of the road, bumper crunched against a tree.

*Is that... the driver, slumped over the wheel? There's blood... is he dead?*

Len still had the axe in hand, his subconscious thinking that he might need it to break a window or pry open a door. There was a locked metal bar across the driveway, but a smaller gate was located to one side. He opened the gate and went across to the car to check on the driver. The window was down, but he hesitated to touch the driver, even to see if he was alive. There was a lot of blood, and many cuts around his face and neck. *That doesn't make sense,* he thought, *there's not that much broken glass or metal.* The man wasn't moving, so Len finally steeled himself to check him for a pulse—there was none.

The passenger door was open, and Len started around to check beside the car for another injured person when he heard rustling in the trees to his right; he spun, axe in hand to confront a woman struggling through the brush. She was naked, scratched and bloody; there was a large gash on her forehead. Len's first thought was that she had also been hurt in the accident—that is, until she snarled and lunged at him.

For a moment, Len froze.

*This isn't real. She's dazed, injured, and maybe amnesiac.*

He'd heard the news reports, seen the videos, but it was all far away. After news of the airplane crash in Pennsylvania last week, he'd packed up and brought Sally to the cabin, but that still didn't quite make it real.

*She's . . . she's one of the INFECTED,* finally registered in his brain.

He was numb, his brain sluggish, despite the self-defense training when he was younger and bi-monthly trips to the gun range the past few years. Time slowed, and he felt like he was moving in slow motion as he raised the axe, gripping it with a hand at each end of the wooden handle—it was all that he could think to do in his sluggish state.

The woman came at him, growling, and working her jaw as if to bite him. One arm was torn and bloody, the other hung at an odd angle, so she didn't try to grab him, just lunge and bite. He managed to keep the axe handle in her face, practically in her jaws, but she kept pushing, and he could feel himself losing his balance. The world was still in slow motion, and he saw her finally raise the bloody arm to reach for him at the same time he felt an obstruction behind his left foot. He was going down, and she would be on him immediately.

As he lost his balance and began to fall backward, there was a shot from behind him and to the side. The woman was knocked back, and turned to look at the shooter, but quickly turned back to Len despite the new hole and spurt of blood from her chest.

The first shot hadn't stopped her, but the next shot took her in the forehead and knocked her back and away from Len. He lay on the ground a moment, feeling dirt, gravel and rocks around and under him, but nothing appeared to be broken or lacerated. He looked up as the approaching man slung a shotgun across his back.

"You get any blood on you?"

Len looked down at his hands, arms, and torso. "No . . . no, I don't think so."

He looked up at Donald Collingsworth, his next door neighbor—"next door" being a relative term in an area where the houses were a half mile apart.

Don reached out a hand to help him up. "Good, I won't have to shoot you, too."

He wasn't joking, Len realized. Suspicions were high in this small community; there had already been rumors of folks shooting strangers.

"Don," Len said, "Thanks, I don't know what I'd . . . well . . . I don't know." He looked down at the axe he'd dropped in the brief encounter; picked it up, swung it a few times. "I never even thought to use this, just didn't seem like enough time."

"'Ya train and train, but ya never kin train for surprise.' It's like huntin', when a big ol' buck jumps out of the brush smack dab at you and you just sit there." Don's hill country accent was usually pretty thick when he tried not to show his own nerves. He pointed to Len's belt, then to the holster on his own. "You need to carry, Len. Open carry is legal up here, and 'tween the bears, snakes and the Zees, you need t'be able to react fast and pump out lead."

"I know, but Sally hates it." He stopped and worked his jaw a few times. "Damn, now I've got drymouth something fierce. Come up to the house for some iced tea?" He cocked his head in the direction of the driveway, and Don nodded agreement.

The two passed through the small gate, and Len swung it closed without latching it. "Best lock that, and you might want to add some fencing to the driveway instead of that bar, too." Len looked quizzically at Don's remark, and Don answered. "You and me kin climb fences; I hear tell Zees can't."

"You coming from the 'city'?" Len asked as they walked up the driveway. The small town of Lowgap was about two miles away in straight distance, but double that following the mountain lanes. Don grinned in return, it was a common joke between them—the recently incorporated "City of Lowgap" claimed a bare ten thousand residents, mostly due to extending the city limits five miles out from town to include the Cumberland Knob area of the Blue Ridge Parkway and the Boy Scout camp just south of town. They'd met at the university where they both worked, and Don was one of the reasons he'd bought this land and built the cabin. Don had lived up here most of his life, while Len was a relative newcomer, despite spending many summers at the camp, and spring-fall weekends at the hunting club to the west.

Don looked grim in response. "It's getting bad in town. Refugees from the cities. I guess we're lucky that few of them know we're here. Oh, and Pastor Garber has been asking for you."

Len made a face at that. Pastor Dwight Garber of the New Covenant Church of Lowgap, had somehow gotten it stuck in his head that Len was an electrical engineer. It was well known in town that the pastor wanted to extend the reach of his radio program.

"Aw, come on, I don't have time for his nonsense. Can't someone convince him I'm not that kind of engineer?" He shook his head. "You know Sally doesn't care for him, so I've tried to avoid him as much as I can."

Len was most comfortable with religion at arm's length. The… zeal of the local preacher was just a bit too much for him. "Changing the subject, what else is going on?"

"Well, word is, Mount Airy's had some trouble with gangs," Don continued. "Chief Griffith has instituted a curfew there and put up roadblocks. Folks in town are talking about blasting State Road 89 and putting our own roadblock on Hidden Valley." The state highway was the main road into town; with State Road 1338—Hidden Valley Road—it was the only way into town that didn't involve the mountain lanes.

"Oh, crap." They'd reached the house by now. "Come on in and sit, we need to talk about this. Where are they planning on putting the roadblock?" It was a question that was quite relevant to both Len and Don, since Hidden Valley was also their own route into town. If there was going to be a roadblock, it would affect them and their immediate neighbors.

They went into the house and Len waved Don over to sit at

the kitchen table while he grabbed a couple of glasses, a few ice cubes, and poured them both some iced tea, the standard drink for this part of North Carolina. The glasses had been another argument with Sally and their sons when they visited. Len had insisted that they use—and wash—dishes and glasses, instead of plastic cups and paper plates. There was no sign of Sally, so that probably meant she had gone back to the bedroom with a "headache." Len knew there was a big argument coming, but he'd deal with that when he had to. Right now, he and Don needed to discuss the roadblock.

Sitting down at his own chair, Len returned to the previous conversation.

"So, just where are they planning to block the roads? Clearly if they want a roadblock on Hidden Valley, they're not blocking 89 that close to town."

"Jesse Branch was talking about dropping trees and bulldozing the embankment at the Buck Mountain trail and dropping the bridge at Camp Branch Creek with a roadblock across the road between Mt. Vernon Baptist Church and Skull Camp Fire Station."

Don pulled a map out of his backpack and pointed to a spot about a mile from a point where the road cut a pass through the hills surrounding the town. He took a sip of the sweet beverage. "They both figure that anyone caught on the other side will know the mountain trails."

"Like the camp road?" Len asked. He and hundreds, even thousands, of youth had spent one or more weeks of their summer each year at the Scout camp. It was a well-known and marked road, although it would still be a fair distance to town via that round-about routing.

"There was talk of a roadblock on Old Lowgap Road and another at the Hidden Valley crossroads, just below the camp entrance. Clay Davis says we can use granite blocks from the quarry over in Mount Airy and block 'em good and solid."

Those two roads were the only other paved roads into town. Aside from the camp access, there would be no reason for anyone to travel those roads if they didn't live in the area. Even refugees would be unlikely to find their way to the narrow, hilly roads by accident. "For the crossroads, they're talking about setting up right at that hairpin turn on Eagle Point Camp Road. The corner is pretty blind, and they can set up a roadblock with clear line of sight from there to the camp entrance. With control of the bridge and crossroads, they can shunt people into the camp or turn them away back to the Interstate."

Actually, that wasn't a bad plan . . . except for one detail.

"What about the kids? Aren't the Scouts supposed to start arriving on Sunday?" With the end of the school year across most of the state last week, the summer camp should be starting up soon.

"There's a few boys here already, but Dave says the camp is considering sending them home." David Wright was one of the year-round camp staffers, and lived on the other side of Don's property from Len. Don would have gotten his information from Dave, who got it directly from the camp administration.

"With the news and the tone of the President's weekly radio speech, I hear tell the staff's mighty nervous about having an incident in a camp full of teenage boys. You heard about that airliner crash—where was that, Beaufort?"

"Bellefonte. Little town in Pennsylvania, practically a suburb of State College and Penn State." Len made a face.

"You know the place?" Don was surprised.

"Yeah, my grandparents used to live there. Nice town, but small and pretty bad economy for a while. I still have an aunt there."

"Any word from her?"

"No, I talked to Mom a couple of days ago. No word, and she's pretty worried. She's been calling the town hall, county seat, state police, and even tried to get my cousin to drive there from Philly." Len got rather quiet, and looked down at his tea for several minutes before standing up.

"Y'know, I think I need something stronger."

He went to the cabinet for another glass as Don continued.

"Well, anyway, Dave says they're still going to enforce a strict 'no firearms' policy in the camp proper, but the camp staff and adults in town are expected to carry at all times." Don caught Len's eye and made a stern face. "That means you too. If you don't have a good holster, I'm taking some guys on a run into Mount Airy for supplies, and I can get you one. Also, you need something with a substantial magazine, not that six-shot hand cannon you favor."

Len turned away and was reaching under the counter for a bottle. "It has stopping power and is accurate."

"It's a hundred-year-old design that only gives you six shots, seven if you carry it loaded—which you should, anyway. But if you hadn't noticed earlier, center of mass shots don't stop Zees. Head shots only... and under stress, you tend to miss... a lot. So get something you can shoot a lot, and keep shooting. Oh, and you don't want to be fumbling with safeties or clothing. Get a belt holster, not one of those tucked-in ones."

"Yes, Mother." Don laughed in response to his comment, but now Len was starting to remember the woman at the road. His hands started to shake as he poured whiskey into a glass. He gulped the first drink as they stared to hear thumping sounds from the back of the house. "Oh great, now Sally's packing. That means she's planning to head back home. I don't need this argument right now."

He started to pour another drink as a howl and scream sounded from the bedroom. He dropped the bottle and glass in the sink, and barely noticed the sounds of breaking glass and the pain in his hand as he heard Sally's scream "No, get it off, get them off of me! Ahhh!"

Len barely registered that Don was reaching for his pistol as Sally ran out of the bedroom, eyes wild, clothes ripped and falling off. With a scream that sounded more like an animal than a human, she lunged toward Len, mouth open, teeth bared. Don raised his pistol as Len put his hands up defensively. "No! Stop! Sally! Don, no! Don't do it!"

The pistol shot was loud inside the house. Len's ears were ringing as Sally crashed into his outstretched hands. He couldn't hear Don shout "No, don't touch her!" All he could see was Sally falling toward him, and Don shoving him out of the way such that she crashed into the floor.

Len whirled on Don. "Why did you do that? You didn't have to!" He put out his fists to pound some sense into his friend, but Don backed away, now pointing the gun at Len.

"Step back, Len, you've got blood on you." The cold voice shocked Len, and he looked down at his left hand, cut by the broken glass, and covered with blood... his own and Sally's.

"Oh, shit."

*He dreamed of light and noise. There was a struggle, shouting and loud arguments. Sally was there, so were Garrett and Sean even though they should have both been away. He was in pain and his hand was burning. Fire, he needed fire. Fire would burn it all away.*

*He dreamed of fire—felt the heat and the smell of sulfur. In the fire was the face of a preacher he'd seen as a child, laughing at him and telling him that he was one of the damned. Now it was Sally's face and she blamed him for taking her to the mountains and away from their home where it was safe. Now his sons stood accusing, pointing at him, telling him that he would burn.*

*Burning. He was burning up. Cleansing fire.*

It was dark and damp. Len felt like he hurt all over. The darkness was because his eyes felt glued shut. He tried to raise his left hand to wipe his eyes and felt some sort of resistance. Aside from that, he couldn't feel his hand at all. He tried to raise his right hand—after all, he could feel that one—but it seemed to be tied down.

"Easy there, Brother Leonard."

The voice came from the side of the bed. A hand reached out with a damp cloth and wiped his face. Opening his eyes, he could see a low ceiling of the type of tiles often seen in classrooms and public buildings. Turning his head, he saw that the room was rather large and filled with cots. Only about half the cots were occupied, but all appeared to be equipped with ropes to tie down the patients. He started to protest, but his mouth was dry and easily as stuck as his eyelids had been.

"Be calm, my son."

There still wasn't a face to go with the voice, but someone held up a cup and straw. They first dribbled some water on his lips, then put the straw in his mouth.

"Moderation, Brother Leonard. Just a few sips at first."

Len recognized the voice now, and turned his head—wincing at a tender spot on his scalp. Nevertheless, it was enough to see a smooth, round face with twinkling blue eyes. From what he knew, the man had to be over seventy, but you would never know it to look at his face.

"Pastor..." Len paused and coughed. "Pastor Garber." More coughing, and he was in danger of either spitting up the water, or choking on it. "Sir," he managed, "May I sit up?"

The cleric nodded and motioned to someone out of sight. Someone Len couldn't quite see came over and untied the straps holding his arms. Pastor Garber helped him sit up and placed some pillows behind his back for support. Len tried to reach for the water cup, but the motion made him dizzy, and he almost knocked it out of the pastor's hand.

The slight motion made his head spin, and the older man gently pushed the hand away and held the cup up for Len to drink, all while supporting his back with the other hand.

"How? How long?" Len managed without coughing this time, although his voice was low and hoarse.

"You've been very sick, my son. You have had a fever and convulsions for almost a week. There were fears that you would be Lost and go to the Other Side."

The pastor's gentle tone and manner surprised him. He didn't know Garber well, being only a part-time resident despite the years he'd been coming to the area. Once or twice he had tuned past the low-power radio program for the outlying mountain communities. For Len, that all added up to the type of hellfire-and-brimstone radio preacher that Sally had been complaining about. This aspect of the man didn't seem to fit the image.

*Sally.* Tears came to Len's eyes, and he started to cough again.

"Easy, my son, you had the fever, but you came through. The doctor says perhaps one in one hundred survive the fever. You are the first, here in town, although he has had two patients over at the camp. I call that a miracle."

Garber helped Len into a better sitting position and allowed him to hold the cup. As Len continued to sip . . . and think . . . the pastor retrieved the damp cloth and went back to wiping Len's face, neck and arms.

Len looked down at the mass of bandages on his left arm. It didn't hurt, but he couldn't feel anything, either. *That son-of-a-bitch shot my wife then cut my hand off. Probably used my own axe to do it!* It didn't matter that the action might have saved his life, all Len could remember was seeing the hole in Sally's head and her blood on his hands.

Garber must have noticed the grimace. He certainly couldn't have missed Len staring at the bandages. It didn't take much to figure out the direction of his thoughts.

"No, it wasn't amputated. You still have your hand, but it was badly cut. Brother Donald says you poured most of a bottle of whisky over it right away. He had to stop you from trying to cut it off or burn it."

*Huh. I don't remember any of that. Why don't I remember? People aren't supposed to get sick that fast.* Len turned to Garber and finally asked the question. "What happened?"

"You broke a glass and cut your hand. Your wife was Lost, and Brother Donald had to deliver the Final Grace. Her blood got on your hand and you panicked, started trying to clean the blood off, then insisted that you needed to amputate your hand. You were making the cuts worse, so Brother Donald hit you over the head with the flat of your axe."

Ouch. Perhaps that explained the tender spot on his head.

"He wanted to take you to the hospital, but the sheriff has been blocking roads into Mount Airy. There was a large disturbance that day, and they were overloaded from an explosion south of town. He took you to the camp instead. Fortunately, the doctor had already come in for the summer. This is the New Covenant Fellowship Hall, by the way. You were treated at the camp, stitched and bandaged. Since you are a resident, we moved you back here when the fever took hold."

"So." Len coughed again, but his throat was beginning to feel the effects of the water. "So, you tie people up in case they . . . turn?"

"Regrettably, yes. Most die when the fever peaks. A few become . . . something else. Lost. But you are a miracle, young man, A Rainbow After The Flood. God has not forgotten us . . . or you." The conversation made Len uncomfortable.

"I'd like to go home." Len put the cup aside and tried to rise, discovering that his legs were still secured to the cot.

"Alas, my son, that is unwise. Here, I'll untie those." Garber reached down and quickly released the bonds. It was a simple slip knot, but Len supposed it was more skill than an . . . infected would have. "You are still weak, and your house is a bit of a mess. You were quite—adamant—about injuring yourself, and fought with Brother Donald. He would be pleased to see you, by the way, now that you are awake."

"No. I . . . can't. I can't see him. He shot . . . no, I realize he had to, but I just can't."

"You must forgive him, my son. He administered Grace, nothing more. Your wife was already Lost. At any rate, because he brought you for medical care and you have been at the camp or here, no one went back to your house for several days. It is not pleasant." Len started to protest, but Garber held firm. "We will have someone fetch what you need, but you should not go back there, at least until you are much better recovered. There is a guest room in the parsonage and you should stay there. Now rest, my son, we will all need our strength in the days to come."

Len was moved out of the "ward" and into one of the parsonage guest rooms the evening after his fever broke. The doctor had come by and changed the bandages and checked his temperature, heart, lungs and reflexes. Len was the third patient in the small community that had survived the disease so far, although the other two were still coming out of the fever and their long-term survival was not guaranteed.

New Covenant was typical of small country churches, with a sanctuary upstairs, large hall downstairs and a two-story parsonage next door. Built to serve the needs of the Church as well as the pastor, in the parsonage the family rooms were upstairs, with two guest rooms downstairs to serve visiting clergy, church administrators or persons in need of temporary shelter. Len had one of those rooms and shared a bathroom with the other guest—Tracey Harris, a local woman who had grown up in the town before leaving to become a missionary to Indonesia. She had surprised the townsfolk when she arrived inquiring about friends and family after having walked all the way from Charlotte.

It took several days to regain his strength, but once Len was able to move around on his own, Pastor Garber insisted that he come visit the patients in the makeshift ward in the church basement. Just seeing a survivor seemed to give some hope, but Len noticed that he was still eyed with some suspicion by the large men with rifles and pistols that stood guard around the room. Each afternoon, the pastor and Tracey would travel out to the other homes, farms, checkpoints and roadblocks. Len would accompany them for as long as he had the stamina, and the more he saw, the more he realized that Garber played an important role in encouraging and uniting the community.

In the evening, the three residents would sit in the parsonage and listen to the radio news. The minister had insisted that Len call him Dwight, or even Brother Dwight, but Len could not bring himself to do so. He still struggled with the reality of the kind, concerned clergyman compared to the mental image of the Bible-thumper that Len could still not quite shake.

There was no longer any coherent programing on the television. Some satellite stations still had prerecorded broadcasts, but gradually they were all being replaced by static. The pastor had a ham radio that had belonged to his son, but it hadn't been used since before that young man had failed to return from Afghanistan. Tracey had tinkered with it, but the base station's aerial had been damaged several winters ago. One of the locals had brought Len's multiband radio from his house—along with clothes, toiletries and other personal items—so the three sat at the kitchen table each evening to listen to reports from the outside world:

A science fiction convention in Charlotte had dissolved in chaos when locals shot and killed several attendees who'd dressed in "zombie" costumes.

A nuclear power plant in South Carolina had to shut down when one of the operators "turned" on her shift in the control room. Protesters at the gates had been severely injured when several of the infected fell upon the crowd.

A free concert in New York had ended in hundreds of deaths when they were attacked by infected drawn to the light and sound.

All airline flights were grounded, passenger trains were cancelled, and countless thousands were dying in the ongoing panic to evacuate the larger cities.

Cellular and wired telephone services were failing as the ground stations and control centers no longer had anyone to service and maintain the systems.

Every night, Len tried to reach three phone numbers: his sons, Garrett and Sean, and his mother. His parents lived in Ohio, and there had been no word from them since before Sally . . . turned. Garrett lived near Washington, D.C. and worked for a federal agency as an analyst. He seldom spoke of his work, but in their last phone call he confided that he was working with a team trying to trace the source of the "Z-disease." Sean was a student in Wilmington, and was supposed to have come up to the mountain cabin, but after hearing about his mother, had announced intentions to get on a boat and head offshore. The last contact with any of his family had been early June, but he tried nonetheless.

One week later, the lights went out.

The town had been prepared for the loss of power. Most households had candles, lanterns, and wood stoves as well as emergency generators. There was water from wells, but also from spring-fed cisterns up in the mountains. Lowgap received its power from a fuel-oil-fired power plant near Dobson, but in recent years, the county electric co-op had been encouraging the installation of windmills and solar panels. As families fell sick and homes were abandoned, the townspeople, under Pastor Garber's encouragement, began to salvage individual installations and move or connect them to key buildings in town. A several-acre solar-cell test facility had been installed at a state agricultural facility between Lowgap and Mount Airy. It, too, was salvaged and installed on a south-facing hillside near the Scout camp. The power had to be severely rationed and at times it was barely enough to keep the lights on at the church. More severe shortages were certain to come.

The night was dark and cloudy. Len considered the fact that in the past, such low clouds would have reflected light from Mount Airy to the north, and more distant Winston-Salem to the south. Now the dark night was lit only by the lanterns the small group had brought with them.

It was a risk coming so close to the highway, but one of the Lowgap residents had driven for the company for several years and convinced Pastor Garber that it would be worth it if they could salvage some of the tanks and one or more of the propane-fueled company vehicles. Having fuel to cook and run the occasional generator meant that they could save gasoline and diesel for the vehicles. Preserving the ability to transport food and supplies could be the difference between life and death for Lowgap.

Len sat behind the wheel of a pickup truck that had carried men and women to the job, frustrated that lingering weakness and stiffness in his left arm consigned him to be driver and lookout. Should the Zees appear, it would be his job to draw them away from the site with lights and noise—and hopefully get away himself. Blackened trucks and buildings told the tale of an explosion some weeks ago. Fear of leakage and damaged propane tanks scattered over the fifty-acre facility had kept scavengers away, but he could see the dim red lights of his fellows over next to a building that looked mostly intact.

The CB radio crackled with static. "Pete, we got something here. Three tanker trucks, doesn't look like the fire got here."

More voices joined the conversation.

"Pete, I've got a truck of them little tanks you see at the gas stations."

"There's lots of the big tanks, but they're all empty."

"There's a few cars and a pickup over here. How do I tell if they run on propane?"

"This tanker's almost empty, that one's better than half full, the other is full."

"Listen up, every one." That was Pete Long, the person responsible for this salvage party. "The little tanks are good, we can use them for cooking if they are full. Pick them up, it they weigh more than five pounds, they're probably fresh—shine a light on the tank, if it looks freshly painted, it should be full. Take only full tanks, we can refill what we've got but don't need any empties.

"Forget the empty tanker, same reason. We'll take what we've got, it's not worth turning on the transfer compressors and attracting the Zees. As for the vehicles—look at the gas filler cap—if it looks funny, it's for propane, not gasoline. Take the pickup, but we're only interested in a car if it has high clearance or four-wheel drive."

"How about a station wagon?" asked the voice that had inquired about the vehicles.

"Sure, good. We can use it to haul stuff."

Len waited for the click that meant Pete had released his microphone. "Pete, it's Len. What if you pumped propane until any Zees show up, then you shut down, I draw them off, and y'all go the other way back to town?"

"Too risky, we have no idea how many will show up and there's no guarantee you can draw enough off."

Len was preparing a retort when Pastor Garber opened the passenger door and slid into the pickup. "No, he's right. I know you want to contribute, but your time will come. You are our miracle, and just being here gives us hope." The dome lights had been switched off so that they didn't turn on when a door was opened, and attract... unwanted visitors. Len could see the pastor's face, and it was obvious from his words that the pastor could see Len's. "I know you don't believe in miracles, but these people need to believe. It may be the only thing that keeps them together."

The two waited in silence, until they heard low engine sounds and six vehicles approached out of the dark—two propane tankers, a stake-bed truck filled with cylinders, a pickup and a car that looked like a cross between an SUV and a station wagon.

The sixth vehicle, Len would later learn, was a half-full fuel truck that had been delivering diesel and gasoline for operating the compressors and delivery fleet.

The drive back to Lowgap was harrowing. The direct way back would have been I-74 to NC 89, then the detour through the Hidden Valley checkpoint. Unfortunately, the interstate was blocked by wrecked and abandoned cars, and it ran too close to Mount Airy for comfort. The back roads would take them through Ararat and around Dobson, turning a thirty minute trip into nearly three hours at night with no lights. The older boys that had come early and been stuck at the Scout camp had been put to work hiking around the small towns and back roads throughout the region to gather information on the neighboring communities. Dobson was large enough to have a sizeable population of Infected, but the Scout reports said that the old Prison Camp Road would skirt the city and avoid most of the Zees.

The convoy mostly encountered isolated Zees on the road, easily outrun, or dispatched by men armed with hunting rifles that rode in the back of the pickups. Maneuvering trucks along the twisting country roads was a constant worry, but the only incident occurred around the half-way point near Dobson. The back road joined Old US-601 at an acute angle, and the fuel truck nearly jack-knifed on the turn. The lights and noise necessary to get the truck unstuck attracted a mob of Zees out of the town of White Plains. Len had to drive his truck—with most of the shooters—closer to the mob to keep them away from the men struggling with the tanker. By the time the word came over the radio that the convoy was ready to move, Zees were grabbing onto the tailgate. Fortunately, they had about three miles of good road on 601 to get up to speed and lose the Zees before turning on the Prison Camp Road toward home.

The sky was beginning to lighten as the convoy returned to Lowgap. The propane, like the food supplies that had been obtained in other "salvaging" expeditions (Pastor Garber refused to allow them to be called "raids") was delivered to the Lowgap Grocery where they had a tank that could be filled from the trucks and a compressor for refilling the small cylinders. Last night's haul should suffice until winter, and surely the disease would run its course and allow recovery efforts by then.

*He dreamed that night that he was back on the road. Len was driving the truck and being chased by Zees. He tried to step on the gas, but the truck just wouldn't go any faster. The Zees were gaining on them while Pastor Garber and Don Collingsworth stood in the bed of the pickup throwing things at the approaching mob.*

*The pastor was throwing some sort of liquid that burned the Zees when it touched. Garber turned and grinned at him. "Holy water," he said, "They need to be cleansed..."*

*"... with fire," said Don, throwing propane canisters at the crowd and shooting them with a rifle to make them explode.*

*The truck was still moving, slowly, but now Len was standing in the back holding a flame thrower. The approaching mob was engulfed in flames. He could see Sally, Garret, and Sean in the mob, mouths red with blood, eyes dead, festering sores all over their bodies. They were zombies and needed to be cleansed.*

*Cleansed with fire.*

Running out of ammunition was an unknown concept to a mountain community. Unfortunately, few of the residents had thought to stock enough ammo for a Zombie Apocalypse. The "salvage runs" had become even more risky since the trip to the propane facility. There were ammunition stores in Mount Airy, Elkin to the south, and Galax to the north up over the Blue Ridge. For that matter, there were National Guard Armories in Winston-Salem and Charlotte, but they might as well have been across the ocean for all the good it did the increasingly isolated community.

The church now served double duty as a de facto Town Hall, with the basement converted to storage of essential supplies now that the initial spread of the disease had run its course. Len sat quietly as Don and Pete Long argued the pros and cons of sending a salvage team to the gun shops in Elkin and Rural Hall.

"It's too far, and too risky!" argued Don.

"What of it?" countered Pete, "Compared to the risk of running out of ammo and having the Zees overrun us?"

"The camp has ammo, right, Dave?" Don looked over at his neighbor Dave Wright, who was one of the year-round staff members at Eagle Point Camp.

"Well sure, we've got a conex full—" Dave began before being cut off by Pete.

"It's bird shot, Dave, Don. You know that won't do a damn bit of good against the Zees!"

*Who would have ever thought that a Boy Scout camp would have a shipping container's worth of ammo?* Len thought to himself. *Well, maybe the same folks who think that it's still not enough.*

He continued to listen with only half of his attention as Don started to argue with Pete about converting the shells by recasting the lead shot and reloading the shotgun ammo; meanwhile Pete argued for the need to gather additional powder, bullets and brass casings.

"Damned risky!" both Don and Pete yelled at each other until Pastor Garber finally stepped in to calm the men down before the argument got worse.

"Brother Leonard, you have been awfully quiet," the pastor said, sitting down next to him as the two former combatants retreated to opposite sides of the sanctuary, each surrounded by friends trying to either reinforce or dissuade them from their stated positions.

Len sighed.

"I don't know. I just don't understand how we're going to make it at all, Pastor. If we're not fighting Infected, we're fighting each other."

"Yes, my son, I know. That's why I wanted to talk to you about the radio. I know you don't want to hear it, but the people in the surrounding areas need to know that we're alive, we're surviving, and there is Hope. God has a plan, for you, for me, for all of Mankind. We are here to be His Witness—"

"That's it! Witness Hill!"

Len's sudden outburst silenced the room. He realized belatedly that he'd jumped up and much to his chagrin, had hit the pastor in the jaw at the same time. By the time he'd sat back down, apologized and checked Pastor Garber for injury, the rest of the men had gathered around.

"Witness Hill is a myth. An urban legend," said an unidentified person in the room.

"No, it's real," said Don. Pete and Dave both nodded agreement. He continued, "My cousin did some home renovation work up there. One of the houses even had an elevator down to a cave outfitted as a safe room."

Witness Hill was the local nickname for an unnamed gated

neighborhood high up on Fisher's Peak, northeast of town. The town rumor mill had decided that the antisocial residents of those homes were either in the Witness Protection program or retired spies—or even crime lords. The fact that the residents were never seen in town coupled to the fact that it was a gated community in an area where the mountains and sparse roads made gates unnecessary, served to further the rumors. Whatever the truth of these mysterious neighbors, the few facts that were known suggested that they had very good security. In the mountains of North Carolina, security meant guns, and guns meant stocks of ammunition.

As the conversation turned to plans to "search for survivors and supplies" on Witness Hill, Len became aware that Pastor Garber was still waiting attentively at his side. With a sigh, he turned back to the minister. "Pastor, I've told you repeatedly, I'm not that type of engineer."

"Nevertheless, Brother Leonard, you have a greater appreciation of electronics than anyone else since Sister Tracey left us."

"You still don't have an antenna!"

"Ah, but we do. The Good Lord has provided."

Just two miles northwest of town, but nearly a thousand feet up on the Blue Ridge, was Fisher's Peak, one of the many peaks and ridges comprising the Blue Ridge and the scenic Blue Ridge Parkway National Park. Parks and community facilities along the ridge received power from a grid that included hydroelectric, solar, nuclear and fossil fuel power plants throughout North Carolina, Virginia, and Tennessee. Lowgap residents could look up the mountain and see that the navigation lights were still lit at the four television and radio broadcast antennas on Fisher's Peak. Occasionally a car would slowly make its way down the switchbacks on NC 89 and tell of mountain farms and communities that remained relatively free of Zees.

Pete Long prepared a group of residents to raid Witness Hill, while Pastor Garber and Len planned for a smaller group to attempt a more difficult sortie up Fisher's Peak. Ordinarily, repair crews serviced the antennas via a long access road originating on the north side of the Blue Ridge. Even though Lowgap and the transmission antennas of Fisher's peak were both south of the Blue Ridge Parkway, there was no direct road to the facility.

There was, however, a steep, narrow trail running from the top of Witness Hill to the end of Fisher's Peak Road about three-quarters of a mile away and five hundred feet uphill. The trail was barely navigable by four-wheel all-terrain vehicles uphill to the gravel road, but would likely be too steep for the downhill return. Therefore Len, Don, and two other men would accompany the larger group to Witness Hill, then begin the climb to Fisher's Peak. Once their task was completed, they would decide whether to risk the downhill trail, abandon the ATVs and climb down on foot, or take the greater risk of following the access road through areas with uncertain conditions and suspicious residents.

"I still don't understand how the ham radio is supposed to connect to the transmitter."

Len was going over final plans with Don, Pete Long, and Pastor Garber. Pete was primarily in charge of the team that would inspect and salvage ammo and supplies from the fortified homes on Witness Hill, but he was in overall charge until Len, Don, and the rest of their team started up the trail. For once, Pastor Garber had been overruled and would be staying behind; the elderly minister had developed a deep cough the past few weeks, and all of the residents feared for his health.

Garber tapped a dusty, leather bound book on the table in front of him.

"Sister Tracey found my son's radio log. In it he talks of the Ham Club repeater installed at the Channel 12 antenna. With our tall aerial broken, the radio will only reach a few miles and is affected by the mountains. The club installed the relay to assist members with limited funds and low power. Once you make certain that the repeater is on and powered, set the frequency, and we will be able to broadcast and listen from here."

The minister began to cough again, and Len excused himself to assist the pastor back to the parsonage. After seeing him to bed, Len returned to the planning session.

Pete had changed the plan to one pickup truck and one ATV. Many of the vehicles that had been occupied by refugees remained parked at the camp due to the fuel shortages and missing ignition keys when the owners became Infected. However, there was a small pickup that had been configured as an off-road monster truck with high clearance, four-wheel drive, and oversized off-road tires. While the chromed crash bars, lights, and winch were intended for show, they were fully functional. The new plan was to carry one ATV in the bed of the truck and make good use of the 4WD and winch to navigate the steep trail as much as possible. The good news was that the truck would allow them to carry more tools, supplies and arms.

The day of the raid dawned clear, but with a hint of Autumn chill. Len's team would support the larger team as they quickly checked houses lower on the hill, clearing the path to the trailhead near the highest and largest house in the gated community. There was no movement, nor survivors at the first house they encountered. Pete had divided the townsfolk into smaller teams tasked with defense, clearance or salvage. One of the salvage teams would return to check for salvage on their way back down, but they were not hopeful, as a quick survey suggested that the house already had been stripped of useful items.

Shots rang out as a minivan carrying one of the clearance teams approached the second home. The van ran off the driveway into a ditch. The riders bailed out and took cover as the shooter continued to target the van. Len heard Pete on the radio advising the other teams to bypass the house until they knew what else they would encounter in this neighborhood. The van had to be temporarily abandoned, and Len ended up with two additional riders in the bed of the pickup along with the ATV. There were no further incidents by the time they reached the trailhead near the furthest end of the development. There was one more house just past the next bend, but Len's party would part ways and head up to the transmitters from here.

They were between the first and second switchback on the trail, a quarter mile from the trailhead, and still a half mile from Fisher's Peak Road, when the truck began to slip. Clay Davis was driving the truck and Don was on the ATV; everyone else was on foot. Don had unreeled the steel cable from the winch and was headed uphill to tie it off to stabilize the truck. The grade was about thirty degrees, and without the line, the truck was in real danger of tipping.

Len called out, "Don! Stop!" but the ATV was too far away. He keyed the radio that they had borrowed from the Scout camp. "Don! The truck is slipping, release the cable!"

There was slack in the winch line, so Don had it looped it over the tie-down rack on the back of the ATV and was holding the end in his hand. The truck began to slide, and Len could see the slack rapidly disappearing. If Don didn't release it, it could flip the ATV over—or worse.

Clay was working the steering back and forth to try to get traction for the truck without turning sideways to the slope. It didn't seem to be working, though, and the truck continued sliding toward the drop-off at the edge of the first switchback. Don felt a sharp pain from his hand and tension in the cable, so he turned to look over his shoulder but didn't release his hold on the steel cable. The continued motion of the ATV caused three things to happen in rapid succession: First the steel cable dug into the flesh of Don's hand, drawing blood. Second, the tension on the ATV caused the front wheels to lift from the ground. Third, the combination of forces on Don caused him to be pulled off the ATV as that vehicle flipped end-for-end.

The sliding truck came to a stop partially against a large rock at the edge of the switchback. One tire was hanging out in midair and the rear axle was firmly wedged against the rock. A trickle of dark liquid started to leak out onto the rock.

Clay got out to check the truck while Len and the others hurried uphill as fast as they could. Don was lying unconscious in the trail, bleeding from hand and head with one leg caught under the overturned ATV. Frances Matthewes, the fourth member of the team, righted the ATV while Len tended to Don.

"Rear differential's cracked," said Clay as he approached. "We could disconnect the driveshaft and just use the front wheels to drive it, but that requires tools we don't have here."

"Doesn't matter, now." Len said, pointing at Don's lacerations and the purple coloration of his leg. "We need to get Don back to the doc. Can you two get him down the hill?"

Clay was a big man, the caricature of a mountain man now that his beard had grown out, but Frances was the slim runner type. Her looks were deceptive, though, since she used to help her husband install home air-conditioning units before he became Infected. She nodded, as did Clay. "We'll rig a sling. I can carry him on my back, and Frances can belay me with the ropes in the truck. What are you thinking?"

"Pastor's right, we need the radio. It looks like the ATV's not too bad. I'll lash the tools to the rack and head on up myself. If the worst comes, I'll walk." Putting actions to words, Len checked the ATV to make sure it would function.

"Pete's not going to be too happy—you off on your own." Frances pointed out. "Besides, I'm not sure we should move Don."

"Yeah, well, I'll deal with Pete when I get back." Len stopped, and considered his friend's injury. "You're probably right. Someone will have to stay here, and the other one can go get help."

"I'll go," said Frances. "I can run faster than Clay and I'm used to cross-country."

"Good. Clay, watch Don, but don't move him unless you absolutely have to."

"Got it. Good Luck."

Len strapped some tools, a shotgun, and spare ammo to the ATV while Frances headed back down the trail. Soon he was past the switchback and climbing the mountain with the roar of the engine in his ears. He never heard the sounds of disturbance coming from the trail behind him.

*He slept fitfully on the bare concrete floor. In his dream he was back on the pickup running from the crowd. He saw too many familiar faces behind him, twisted by disease and hatred. Sally, Sean, Garrett, Pete, Don, Frances, Clay, his parents. They were reaching for him and they were gaining. The truck was just not fast enough.*

*"You must give them Grace," said Pastor Garber, suddenly looking up at him from beside the pickup. "Cleanse them, they are impure."*

*Now Len was standing at the door to the transmitter, he was looking in the direction of the town, but all he could see was columns of smoke rising from somewhere in that direction. He looked down at his hands, there was a flame-thrower, but he didn't recall picking it up or where it came from. He heard Garber's voice. "It is the only way."*

Len had seen no one since the roadblock at the switchback of NC 89 coming down off the Blue Ridge. The semi-tractor trailer truck loaded with granite blocks and gravel had been overturned right at the point where vehicles descending the road would have to slow down for the tight turn. Don had told him that they didn't want to risk anyone picking up speed on the downhill and ramming the roadblock on the north end of town.

He had expected more than just a single guard, and a barely past teenage boy at that. It wasn't someone that Len recognized, and the young man wasn't too talkative, just waved him on after he showed identification. It was still two miles into town, and Len had been gone for five days. It was only ten miles by road from the transmitters, but he'd only been on the road for the last mile. The Parkway was a dangerous place these days.

The town was quiet. There were a few people out, but they avoided him. Considering his torn clothes, dried blood and limp, he was surprised he wasn't greeted with gunfire. He limped on, carrying only a long branch that he'd had to use as both cane and club.

With approaching dusk, he saw no movement or light in the parsonage, with pale candlelight coming from the lower level of the church. As he opened the door, he was assaulted by the smell—blood, vomit, feces and antiseptics. He stopped and stared at the row of cots filled with broken and bandaged bodies. A woman he barely knew from town meetings came up and guided him to a chair next to Pete Long's cot.

"Len. You made it."

Pete's head, chest, and arms were bandaged, one eye was also covered.

"Well, you may be figuring out now that it was a trap. We lost ..." Pete coughed. He raised a bandaged hand to wipe his mouth. The bandages were red with blood, whether from his wound or coughing, Len couldn't tell. Pete coughed several more times, and the familiar-looking woman sat him up to give him water from a hard plastic cup.

"The houses were booby-trapped. There was still someone living in one—you saw that one—but the others had mines. We tripped them when we started to search."

"What about Don? Frances? Clay?" Len started looking around the room for other familiar faces.

Pete was grimacing with pain. Len was getting a stern look from the woman. She was Pete's wife, he remembered, now. He'd only been introduced to her when he first bought the property. She and Sally hadn't gotten along—not that that meant anything now.

"We never saw her. Frances. Clay came back into town the next day, carrying Don." More coughing. There were tears coming from the unbandaged eye. "He was too far gone, he never woke up. Clay stayed all night, and when Frances didn't return, he carried Don back down the mountain. It was too late, though."

His eye closed and he lay back down. Pete's wife started to make her patient comfortable, then turned and gave Len a look that told him it was time to leave.

Clay met him on his way across to the parsonage. "They told me you were back. Please tell me you were successful." He sat down on the steps to the back door of the building, effectively blocking Len's entrance to the residence.

"I did it. I have the access frequency to the transponder, and it's powered... for now." Len sat on the step beside Clay. "But the Blue Ridge is dangerous. There's gangs up there on the Parkway. It took me days to work my way around them." He paused a moment. "And you? Tell me what happened."

Clay sighed. "Don didn't make it. I waited all day and all night. I didn't move him, I kept him warm, but he never woke up. When Frances didn't come back I knew something was wrong. I saw what looked like a brush fire, so I knew I had to move. I put Don in a fireman's carry and headed down the mountain, right into the aftermath of Pete's raid. Apparently Frances ran right into it as it was happening. We didn't find her body for another two days." He put his head in his hands. "It's been bad. We lost too many people. I don't know whether we'll make it."

Len hung his head. Don had been a good friend and neighbor. Len had never quite come to terms with the fact that he still hated Don for Sally even once he understood the necessity. They had worked together these last months, but it was never the same. Still, now that he was gone, Len felt an empty place inside.

He stood and moved toward the door. "Pastor will know what to do. I need to tell him about the transmitter."

Clay put a hand on Len's arm to restrain him. "Len, wait." Clay's face showed more pain and emotion. "He's... not well. This has been hard on him, and his age is catching up. He should be happy to see you though; he was very worried when you didn't return."

Len entered the parsonage. The back door led into the kitchen. It had gotten completely dark, so he navigated to a drawer by memory, pulled out a candle and matches, lit the candle and placed it in a disk on the counter. He moved over to the radio further down the counter, lifted the box controlling the relay and set the transponder code to match the one he had seen in the small concrete room at the transmitter tower. He switched on the radio, and got the usual static, then turned the tuning dial. More static, but then music and a voice: "This is the voice of Free Texas..."

It worked. He hoped it was worth it.

Taking the candle, he made his way through the darkened main level to the stairway. He could see the dim flicker of candlelight coming from the pastor's room. Garber was propped up in the bed, reading. He put down the book, looked up and smiled at Len's approach. "These are dark days, my son. It is a blessing to see you again. Does the radio work?"

"Yes, Pastor. At least it receives. I checked it a few minutes ago." Len sat down in the chair by the bed. It would break the pastor's heart to hear the rest of his story. "The transmitter still has power, so as long as that lasts, it will work. There is a generator, but someone had stolen the fuel."

"It lifts this old heart to hear your news, Brother Leonard, but you seem troubled. Surely as long as the power is on, we can send messages...and with your return, we know that it is possible to go up and back. We should be able to take fuel to the generator if needed."

"No, Pastor, I am afraid it is not that simple." Len had trouble meeting the elderly minister's gaze, and when he did look up, it was to see a worried look in his eyes. "There are bandits, Pastor Garber. When I found that the generator tank was empty, I went out on the Parkway to see if I could siphon fuel from some of the abandoned cars. I had to hide from armed men several times. I saw them do...bad things, and I fear that if we draw their attention, especially after what happened..."

Garber's expression faded, and with it most of the color in his face. It was clear that the confidence and energy he had held in reserve was failing. The pastor looked old...showing his age and then some. He leaned back into the pillows and whispered. "Brother Leonard, you must! People need to know that God has a plan, they need to know that they can come here and be safe."

His voice grew faint.

"You are our blessing." His eyes closed and his breathing stilled.

People at the church heard the anguished screams and the sound of breakage. Clay had briefly gone inside the parsonage, then come back out to keep the others away.

As Len's rage was spent, he fell to the kitchen floor and wept. "WHY GOD? Why? How can I fulfill the pastor's wishes and still keep the town safe?" He stared at the radio with its red power LED and yellow-lit indicators, but all he could see were images from his own dreams.

*Cleansing fire.*

"THESE ARE THE END TIMES! IT IS GOD'S JUDGEMENT! THE WRATH OF GOD UPON THE WORLD FOR ITS SINS! THOSE WHO HAVE BEEN TAKEN ARE THE SINNERS OF THE WORLD AND THE RIGHTEOUS HAVE BEEN SPARED..."

# 200 Miles to Huntsville

CHRISTOPHER SMITH

"Can you please turn that shit off, man?" Taylor could tolerate talk radio for a while, but this fire and brimstone preacher was just too much. "I mean, c'mon guys, ain't you got satellite in this heap?"

"This bother you, scumbag?" John Leyva turned to look at him from the passenger seat. "Too bad. All we get out here in the sticks." He dialed up the volume a few notches. Being an officer in the Department of Criminal Justice had its moments.

"Brothers and Sisters, the time has come to shun the unworthy, the unclean, the unrepentant. The countless evils of modern man have brought down the Wrath of the Holiest of Holies. 'Know Me, sayeth the Lord, for I have made Thee!' Those that use the Lord's gift of knowledge to make themselves into gods among men, have forsaken the Lord's loving hand, and brought the rest of mankind into the void of Hell!"

"Jesus," Taylor said, "You'd think this guy was gonna hole up with a shit ton of food and ammo, and blast anyone that came near." He shook his head. "God bless Texas."

"You know, a little churchin' up might be good for you." Leyva gave another smirk, one that Taylor desperately wanted to smear all over the windshield.

"Oh, me and God are on good terms." Taylor turned to look out the window of the van. "He don't talk my ear off, and I don't bother him by whining."

He tried to make himself comfortable—not an easy thing to do after Leyva short coupled his restraints—closing his eyes and ignoring the other man. Maybe faking sleep would keep the asshole from bothering him.

"They're gonna love you up at Huntsville." No such luck. "Them boys'll think you're real cute. You're just dark enough for the Bloods, and not too dark for the Aryans. And that pretty shaved head of yours?" He gave a sadistic chuckle. "You'll get more turns than a doorknob."

Taylor didn't move. "What's the matter, boss? Pissed you can't have a go? Didn't figure you for that type." He opened one eye. "Not that I give a damn, I just don't swing that way." Leyva's face clouded over, as Taylor continued, "Don't worry, though, I'm sure there's plenty of boys back home that would be happy to take you up on it."

Leyva glared at him through the divider. "You're lucky I can't get back there, jailbait." He turned around.

Taylor couldn't resist throwing a parting shot. "Yeah, I'm tired, and don't want to have to keep one eye open to preserve my virginity."

He found out how difficult it is to smile with your lips smashed into a metal grate.

"Brake check, sorry." David Pascoe smiled in the rearview before turning back to the road. Being in the TDCJ definitely had its moments. "Keep the flirting to a minimum. I've got enough to worry about."

"Like what?" Leyva gestured at the countryside. "There ain't shit out here but the occasional tumbleweed."

Taylor silently agreed. They'd been on the road for a few hours and the scenery hadn't changed much. Low scrub, a few trees, farmland, and cows. Lots of cows. Typical southeast Texas.

"Been reports of heavy cartel activity lately, expanding their territory up from Corpus," Pascoe said. "And with our guest here on their short list, I'd rather not take any chances."

Leyva chuckled. "You're still stuck in the sandbox, New Boots. Looking for IEDs behind every bush. Lighten up."

Taylor studied the younger man in the mirror. Early thirties, medium height but muscular build, dark red hair growing out from a high and tight. His eyes seemed to be everywhere—scanning the road ahead, flicking to the side mirrors—until they met his again. Taylor recognized what he saw in them—he'd not only seen shit, he'd been in it pretty deep. At his slight nod, Pascoe blinked in surprise, then looked away quickly. The kid had seen it in him, too.

Pascoe turned to Leyva. "I made it back, with all my parts. I'm comfortable with my paranoia, thank you." He jerked a thumb towards his partner. "If you'd been just a bit more careful this morning, you wouldn't have lost a chunk of your hand."

"And if you hadn't gotten froggy with the fresh meat, you wouldn't be here today," Leyva said. "Whatever. No one would'a seen that comin'. Lousy nutjob gang banger." He fell silent. Taylor wondered how long it would last.

About thirty seconds.

Leyva squirmed in his seat. "Hey," he said, "how far till the next town? I gotta piss like a racehorse."

"Louise is a few miles up. We can stop there."

"Step on it, will ya?" He grabbed the radio and keyed the mike. "Unit five-four to base, come in."

"Base here, five-four. What's up?"

"Gotta make a pit stop, shouldn't be long."

"That super-sized soda finally catch up with you, Leyva? What's the location?"

Leyva glanced at the GPS. "Looks like there's a place on the south side of Louise. A 'Stop and Sip,' just off Highway 59 and FM 271."

"Roger, fifty-four. Out."

Taylor spoke up. "I could use a break too."

Leyva sneered. "No one gives a shit what you want, scumbag."

"New policy is you have to let me relieve myself on trips longer than three hours, boss." He looked around the back of the van. "I don't see a honey pot back here."

"He's right, and the last thing we need is a complaint. Besides, we're in the middle of nowhere." Pascoe said, "We'll make sure he drains the vein before we get stuck in Houston traffic."

"Fucking Robocop." Leyva grumbled. "Guy takes down two border guards and you're worried about complaints."

Taylor kept his voice low, "Shouldn't have called me 'nigger.'"

"What was that?" Leyva turned as far as the seat belt would let him. "You say something, shit heel?"

"Yeah, said your homeboys at the border should'a kept their mouth shut." His grin was feral. "Don't have a choice now. Jaws are all wired up, aren't they?"

Pascoe eased off the highway and into a parking lot. "We're here," he said. Leyva stayed quiet, focused on disengaging himself from the seatbelt. Watching him struggle against his paunch and gun belt, Taylor ignored the pain from his split lip and grinned. Leyva caught it in the rearview.

"Keep it up, scumbag." The belt released and he bolted for the store.

"Don't antagonize him." Pascoe looked pained. "I know you don't owe me anything, but I'm trying to do my job here. I'm responsible for your safety during transit. Whether or not I think you're a dick is meaningless. Leyva has seniority—he beats the shit out of you, and the report says 'you fell,' got it?"

"All right," Taylor said, "Thanks for being straight with me. Just be aware—Dunkin' Donuts tries shit, I'll make him regret it."

"And I won't regret tasing you." Pascoe got out and moved to Taylor's door. "All right, by the numbers. We'll go in, hit the head, grab some grub, and move out."

The blast of hot air was a shock after the air conditioned van. Taylor kept his movements slow and careful, holding his legs out for Pascoe to inspect.

"I think you're taking this a bit too far, Pascoe." He jerked his chin at the landscape. "I mean, really, where am I going to go? There's nothing out here but that trailer park, and that ugly-ass church, and more nothing. Both of them are far enough away that you'd be able to catch me or shoot me before I got anywhere near 'em."

"Procedure. Get sloppy and things go to Hell." He jerked his chin towards the store. "Inside, nice and easy so we don't freak anyone out."

Taylor grunted as they made their way, slowly, to the door.

The guy behind the counter turned as they walked in. Taylor smiled and waved, making sure to clank the chains connecting his cuffs.

Pascoe muttered, "Knock that off."

The store was empty, aside from the cashier. Good thing, since the chest-high shelves were so close together, Taylor had to turn sideways to squeeze between them. They made their way toward the reach-in cooler running along the back wall.

"So, boss, tell me—any of this seem odd to you?"

Pascoe shook his head. "Not really, just another offender going to a new joint." He scanned the selection of sodas.

"I'm getting the fast-track. What makes me so special?"

"You put two in the morgue, and two in the infirmary. Brass decided to flush you." He shrugged. "Nothing strange there."

"If they hadn't tried to shiv me in the shower, I wouldn't have had to." He looked at Pascoe. "It ever cross your mind why that group of assholes decided to come after me?"

"Nope. Not my problem, offender. Yours."

"You know why I'm in the joint in the first place?"

"I read your travel card."

"Humor me, and I'll stay quiet no matter what Leyva says."

"Hmmph." Pascoe glanced at him, "All right. You hit a bank, and your buddy got popped. Rolled on you for a better deal."

"Yeah. Next question: you and Leyva usually on transport?" Uncertainty flicked across Pascoe's face; Taylor pressed his advantage. "A rookie cop, and a guy that just got off sick leave, escorting a solo prisoner. It's a setup, and you're the lamb, boyo."

Pascoe shook his head. "No way. Shut the fuck up."

"All this open area, out in the middle of nowhere." He swept his cuffed hands in a small circle. "Be real easy to say I got the jump on you—took you hostage, whatever—while the Dirty Boss calls some friends. You end up on the side of the road, I end up in Piedras Negras minus a few extremities."

"And what, you want me to help you escape? Is that it?"

"Nah. Nowhere to run. Just keep your eyes open."

Pascoe grinned. "What if I'm in on it, too?"

"You ain't."

"You sure?"

"Yeah." Taylor said, nodding, "You saw some shit in the sandbox, and it's stayin' with you, like you gotta do something to prove to yourself you can make the world better." He gave him a sad smile. "Trust me, I seen that thousand-yard stare on a bunch of vets. Some give up on the world and themselves. Others—like you—get harder, but try to get the world right again."

"Hmmph."

"Yeah, 'hmmph.' I see how you watch that pink fluffy motherfucker. He's got the pull to make your life hell again, or at least he thinks he can. He ain't seen but what? A few small brawls in the joint, maybe some street time twenty years ago?" Taylor jerked his chin towards the restroom. "He hates you for trying to do something right. Wants to bring you down or make you like him."

"You talk a lot."

"Yeah, well, ain't like there's nothin' else right now, is there. Just think on what I said." Taylor pointed toward the handwritten sign in the back of the store. "Gotta use the head, boss."

Pascoe nodded, grabbed a soda, and walked towards the wooden door. "Leyva," he said, knocking. "We're coming in."

The reply was muffled. "Yeah, give me just a sec." Clothing rustled, followed by a faint zipper sound. "Clear."

"Hey, boss," Taylor raised his hands as far as the short-coupled chain would let him. "A little help? I'll be good, I promise."

"The cuffs stay on," Pascoe said, disconnecting the belly chain. Taylor rolled his shoulders and sighed in relief as they walked through the door.

Taylor was surprised; the bathroom was larger than he expected for such a small store. Two stalls and a urinal were opposite the sinks and mirror. Clean, too, he noticed, the air carrying a strong odor of pine disinfectant. The porcelain tiles on the wall were slightly yellowed with age, but lacked the usual phone numbers, obscenity, or crude attempts at art.

"All right," Pascoe said, "Get done and let's get out of here."

"I got this, rook," Leyva said, his jaw set.

For a split second, Pascoe looked like he might protest. Leyva narrowed his eyes. "Why don't you get me some chips?" His tone made it an order, not a suggestion. Pascoe nodded, shoulders slumping slightly as he walked out.

Leyva turned to Taylor. "Use the pisser, so I don't have to worry about you trying anything." He moved to the sink. "You know, punk," he said, turning on the faucet, "you don't have a lot of friends, inside or out. You should watch that smart mouth."

Ignoring Taylor's grunt, Leyva continued, "Now, me? I have lots of friends. Some who would love to find out exactly where you are right now." He scrubbed harder, muttering to himself. "Damn meth head convict. Hand's infected or something. Itches like crazy." To Taylor he said, "Now, a smart man would think about being my friend, too. Maybe giving him some information, like exactly where something is hidden."

"Someone like me could maybe," Taylor heard the water pressure increase as Leyva continued, "I don't know, tell his other friends a little white lie about where you are, maybe help you get somewhere else besides Huntsville."

"Uh huh. All I have to do is tell you where everything is, and you'll help me get away. Pull the other one."

"All I'm sayin' is that you have very few options." His voice became edgier as he dug his nails into his hand. "What the fuck did that bastard do?"

Taylor finished and turned to the TDCJ officer. Leyva looked like he was trying to take his skin off.

"Let me put it this way, scumbag. You can take your chances with me, you can hope that my friends will let you live if you come clean, or you can take your chances in the pokey." He gave Taylor a toothy smile. "Option C is unlikely. The guys I texted an hour ago are waiting for us." He scratched harder.

"Tempting. How do I know you won't kill me as soon as I talk?" Taylor watched as the long gashes on Leyva's arms began bleeding.

"You think I'm stupid?"

"Yes."

"Fuck you. I know how this works. I kill you, and my friends don't get what they want. That puts me in a bad spot." He continued scratching, moving up to his chest. "You and I take a ride, I keep Pascoe quiet, and we split the money ninety-ten."

"You only want ten percent? Mighty reasonable, boss."

"You stupid fuck, I get the ninety. Besides, my friends only really want the financial stuff. If it was just the money, they'd kill you quick, as a lesson. The other... well, that's gonna make you hurt." The smarmy little smirk was back. "I imagine they'll start with your testicles, then take out an eye, then..."

"Go fuck yourself."

Leyva's face grew red. "Listen, you little pissant! I'm trying to help you out here, give you a chance to get out of a bad situation!"

"Bullshit, you're trying to help yourself get in with your 'friends.'" Taylor snorted. "Ten seconds after I give you what you want, you put a bullet in my head, or call them." He nodded towards the officer. "You should probably get some cortisone or something before you take the skin off."

"Shut the fuck up!" Leyva tore open his shirt, exposing his chest. "Give me the money, goddammit!" He launched himself at Taylor.

Taylor's reflexes saved him, bringing his cuffed hands up to block as the other man fumbled at his clothes, trying to get a hold of his neck.

"What the fuck, you crazy bastard!" Leyva only howled in reply, lunging again. Taylor leaned back, jamming the chain of the cuffs into the officer's throat. Leyva turned his head, biting at the air.

Taylor had the reach and muscles, but Leyva wasn't restrained with cuffs, and massed about the same. He might have been doughy, but the shorter man was surprisingly strong. Taylor backed up and set his feet. "Pascoe!"

The bathroom door burst open as Pascoe charged in, taser drawn. "What the..."

"Just shoot him!" Taylor was struggling, the restraints keeping him from using his full strength against the smaller man. Leyva turned with a snarl, dropping Taylor in lieu of the other officer.

"Leyva—shit!" Pascoe hesitated, giving Leyva the opening he needed. He grabbed Pascoe's arm, and bit down on his sleeve.

"Stun him, dammit! He's gone nuts!" Taylor threw his cuffed hands over Leyva's head, hooked the chain under his nose, and jerked back hard.

Pascoe shook loose, stepped back, and fired. Leyva continued struggling, jerking his head in an attempt to dislodge the chain. His movements pulled the darts free, scraps of cloth and meat coming with them.

Taylor jammed the chain in Leyva's mouth, keeping his hands clear of the teeth. Pascoe fired again. Leyva dropped to the floor spasming.

"Keep it on him." Taylor kicked the now unconscious officer. Or tried to. The leg chains made the strike ineffective.

"Knock that shit off." Pascoe said, holstering the taser. "What the hell was that?"

"I don't know, man, dude just went nuts." Taylor looked at Pascoe's arm. "You okay?"

"Yeah," Pascoe rolled up his sleeve. "Didn't break the skin." Dark tooth marks were visible. "Gonna have a hell of a bruise, though." He looked lost. "Shit, what am I supposed to do now?" he muttered.

The rookie was way out of his depth, and Taylor felt for the kid. A little. His situation was infinitely worse, all things considered. Bad enough getting popped in the first place, but this had just gone off the rails into "What the fuck?" territory.

Huntsville. He had contacts in Huntsville. If he could get there in one piece, he had a better chance. Problem was getting there.

All righty then, a little nudge was in order. "Hey, boss, I know you're in a bad spot here..."

Pascoe looked at him like a lost butterbar. "Yeah, a bit."

"All right, so what's procedure?"

"Secure the prisoner. Never let the prisoner have the upper hand. Maintain discipline and control of the situation."

"So, what's the play?"

Pascoe seemed to find comfort in the routine. "First thing is to secure the prisoner, so I'll be cuffing you to the stall." He drew his cuffs from his belt. "Please extend your hands, slowly."

Taylor complied. Pascoe closed one of the cuffs around Taylor's wrist, the other to the upright of the stall.

"Okay, I'll take Leyva to the car, you stay on good behavior." Pascoe took Leyva's cuffs from the unconscious man's belt, and moved his hands into the "hogtie" position. The cuffs ratcheted shut.

Pascoe, in better shape but smaller than Leyva, had trouble with the heavier man. "Shit." After several good tries he couldn't get the other officer to move. Leyva began to stir.

"Okay, new plan," Pascoe said. "He's coming to. Give me your leg."

Taylor extended his foot. Pascoe unlocked one of the leg irons, and secured it to the frame of the stall. The second cuff clicked closed on Leyva's ankle.

"Well," Pascoe said, "when he comes to, he won't be able to get far."

"May want to gag him," Taylor said.

"Good point." Pascoe pulled a handkerchief from his pocket, tying it around Leyva's mouth.

Leyva snapped fully awake, struggling against his bonds. The red checked cloth barely contained his inhuman howls.

"You hang tight here, I'll go call it in. We'll have to sit on him for a little while until I can get an ambulance or something, get him checked into the local quack shack."

Time to tip my hand a bit, Taylor thought. "Pascoe, I think we should move, call it from the road."

"No," Pascoe said, shaking his head. "Can't leave him here like this. He could hurt himself or someone else." For emphasis, Leyva began pounding his head against the floor, moaning and howling. A strong smell came from his direction.

"Jesus, he just shit himself." Taylor made a face. "At least take me out there with you. Guy is creeping me out."

Pascoe nodded, unfastening Taylor's hands, and recuffing them behind his back. "You're a very thorough man, boss."

"Live by the procedure and everything tends to work out."

They started out of the restroom, and into the shop proper. Taylor spoke, "Boss, Leyva said something about some 'friends' of his waiting for us. We may want to take a different route."

"Unh, huh. Right."

"Dead serious. What I took is real important to certain people. They want it back. I don't want to be anywhere near them, you dig?"

"Right, like I'm taking the word of some scumbag."

Taylor was cut off by the store's clerk. "You boys just stay right there." The black Mossberg he held didn't waver.

"You've got to be fucking kidding me," Taylor said. He stared at the clerk. "I swear to God," he glanced at the other man's shirt, "Buford, if you say 'Bring out the Gimp,' I'll kill you."

Buford jerked the shotgun towards the back room. "Move."

"I think there's been a misunderstanding . . ." Pascoe started.

Buford's finger caressed the trigger. "I said, move."

They moved, keeping their motions slow and steady. Taylor had no desire to test the limits of his luck. The small back room was filled with mops, a rack for the fountain sodas, and cleaning supplies. A cheap braided cloth rug covered most of the concrete floor.

"Pull it back," the clerk said, nodding at Pascoe, "nice and easy."

Taylor rolled his eyes as the trapdoor was exposed. "Seriously, I've seen this movie. It doesn't end well for you. Don't let the skin tone fool you, I'm more of a Bruce Willis than a Ving Rames."

"Shut up." Buford nudged Pascoe with the barrel of the Mossberg. "Open it. Get down there." Pascoe made his way down the ladder attached to the wall.

"Hey, man," Taylor said, rattling his cuffs, "how do you expect me to climb with these?"

Buford shrugged, then snapped the stock of the shotgun forward. Taylor's vision exploded into color as the wood connected with his chin. He staggered back involuntarily, realizing his mistake just as his foot dropped into the trap. He plunged into the hole, striking the back of his head on the frame.

Taylor came to in a small room. He squinted against the harsh light of an incandescent bulb as he took in his surroundings. The walls were wooden panels, seemingly slapped in place over two-by-four frames. Hard packed dirt peeked out between the pieces of scrap plywood that made up the floor. The rich, musty smell meant they were still underground.

"Welcome back to the land of the living," Pascoe said. "Was worried you'd miss all the fun."

"You have a very fucked up sense of fun."

"Yeah, well, I'm still trying to figure out what the hell's going on."

Taylor sat up and took stock. He had a blinding headache. His hands were still cuffed behind him. Pascoe was on the opposite wall, hands and feet zip-tied, stripped of anything useful.

"Okay," Taylor said, "we know we're underground, somewhere near the gas station. Small room, only one door, no windows. What else?"

"As far as I could tell, we walked about three hundred yards, give or take. That should put us under the church we saw."

"How'd I get here?"

"Two other guys dragged you over. They came from the other end of the tunnel and met us at the ladder. Clerk probably called them before he drew down on us." A piercing howl came from somewhere outside. "Oh, and Buford had them go back for Leyva."

"Shit. So I was out for a while." Taylor's head felt like a hippo was using his ear as a birth canal. That, coupled with the time he was down, pointed towards a concussion. Not good. "Any idea what these guys want?"

Pascoe snorted and shook his head. "Hell if I know. They seem to be pulling from Koresh's old playbook, though. Militia? Cult? Some combination of the two? Don't know."

Taylor pressed. "C'mon, boss, what did you see? I know you didn't leave your situational awareness in the sandbox."

"Cut me some slack, I was a little freaked out by the whole thing. Preoccupied with staying upright and breathing."

Taylor stared at him, trying to ignore the pain in his skull. Pascoe sighed.

"There's not much," he said. "Just a shored-up tunnel, with a couple of doors here and there." He nodded at theirs. "Wood, so's the frame. Seems to be set into the dirt, but it didn't wiggle too much when they closed it, so probably reinforced as well."

Taylor began working the cuffs behind his back, twisting the metal links around each other and applying careful pressure. He could bring them around to the front of his body, but didn't want to take the chance of someone walking in while he worked. "Can you get out of those?"

Pascoe's hands were in front of him, bound at the wrist. He wiggled them a bit. "No, they're pretty tight."

"Hold your arms out in front of you, and snap them into your chest." Taylor had the chain on his cuffs tight. A quick twist of his wrists and the weld broke. He held his arms out in front of him. "Like this." He demonstrated.

Pascoe followed suit, the flex cuff popping off with the motion. "Whoa."

"Yeah, you pick things up."

"All right," Pascoe said. "Now what? We still have to get through the door."

Taylor looked around the room, searching for something useful. Nothing jumped out; the room was devoid of any furnishings, supplies, or tools. He moved to the door and examined the frame.

"Don't suppose you have a knife or something hidden on you we can use to jimmy this door with, do you?"

Pascoe shook his head. "No, they patted me down before they cuffed me. Oh, wait!" He reached under his uniform shirt and pulled out a wallet. "I do have this." He removed what looked like a thin metal card. "This folds out into a knife. Cheap quality, but may do the trick." He did what looked like origami and held out a small blade, roughly four inches long.

"Well, if it doesn't work," Taylor said, taking the knife, "we could always use that pink credit card next to it. What was that, Victoria's Secret?"

Pascoe turned about three shades of red in two seconds. "I like their cologne."

"Uh huh." Taylor gave him a grin. "Hey, boss, I'm not judging. What you do in the privacy of your own home is up to you."

"Shut up and get the door open."

~~~
~~~

Some work with the knife and a few solid kicks had gotten them into the tunnel. No guards, just a hundred yards of reinforced dirt walls and bare bulbs strung to light the way. Taylor led the way up the stairs at the end.

Again, no sentries, as they came out of what looked like another storage room. The sound of singing greeted them, hundreds of voices joining into something resembling harmony.

"Let's get to high ground, see what we may be dealing with," Taylor said. Pascoe followed him towards the stairs marked "Balcony."

Crouching, they moved softly up the stairs and around the corner, carefully making their way towards a low wall that separated the upper deck from the congregation area below. The singing stopped.

People were packed into the pews, the silence broken by random sniffles, coughs, and sneezes. All looked like they had just gotten over a bad case of the flu, or were in the process of going through it. Several were wrapped in blankets, huddling against a chill he didn't feel. All eyes were on the man behind the pulpit.

The preacher wore blue jeans, boots and a faded green chambray work shirt. His tanned face had deep creases, evidence of long hours in the sun. This wasn't your everyday sip-tea-and-study-scripture type of parson. This man worked outside when he wasn't sermonizing. Earthy, personable, close to his flock. One that had experienced the hardships of rural life, not just heard about them from the others. He appeared to be in his mid-fifties, but his fine white hair hinted that he was older.

To his left a large cross lay horizontally, a few feet behind a marble altar. Heavy cable, attached to the cross by a large eyebolt, ran up to the ceiling, disappearing just out of Taylor's line of sight somewhere above and behind him.

"Brothers and sisters, rejoice!" The preacher raised his hands and inclined his head, eyes closing in rapturous delight. "For the Lord has given us our salvation. The wicked will be struck from the Earth, as they were in the time of Noah, with a mighty hand of Judgement." He paused for effect, allowing the words to hang in the relative silence before continuing. "The evils of Man and the science of Satan have brought the world low, and God Himself has chosen to start anew with His Chosen!"

The whispered, "Amen," of the congregation was loud enough to carry to the balcony. Taylor and Pascoe shared a glance.

"The temptation to play God, the arrogance of Man to believe himself equal to the Lord, and the turning away from the Almighty have forced His will upon us. You have heard of the sickness spreading in the sunken pits of depravity—New York, Los Angeles, even Houston," The audience gave a low murmur, punctuated with coughing, only silenced by the preacher making a patting gesture. "I say let them fall! We, my flock, my family, are the meek, and we shall inherit a brave new world! Disease is pestilence, sent by Satan, germs and virus are his minions. These cannot touch the Faithful, those that have accepted God's love and salvation!"

Taylor whispered, "Right. These folks are batshit. Let's go."

"Yeah," Pascoe said, nodding. "I think I've seen just about everything I need to see. Think can we get out of here without getting caught again?"

Taylor's reply was cut off as the preacher began speaking again.

"Behold, brothers and sisters, the Lord has delivered to us one of the wicked!" Taylor recognized Buford as he and another man dragged a violently thrashing and shirtless form up on the dais.

"Holy shit, that's Leyva."

The pudgy corrections officer appeared to have resisted heavily—both of his captors had bloody gashes on their face, and Buford was sporting a fresh bandage on his arm. By the way Leyva's legs were flopping behind him, it appeared that Buford and company had taken out some of their aggression on him. With tire irons.

"Damn," Taylor said with a wince, "that looks painful."

"Yeah," Pasco replied, "but he doesn't seem to notice. Probably has multiple compound fractures at this point." Sure enough, Leyva was still trying to get his feet under him, only to have them collapse.

Buford and his friend wrestled Leyva to the cross, forcing him onto it. After he was secure, the preacher reached under his pulpit. A mechanism above him hummed as the cross rose.

"What the hell are they doing?"

"They're crucifying him." Taylor swallowed hard, lips forming a snarl. His voice was harsh. "The sons of bitches are crucifying him."

"What the fuck is wrong with these people?"

"Cult of personality. Strong leader with a Messiah Complex. Trusting, somewhat isolated group of faithful, but no other teacher. Makes me sick."

"Really? Wouldn't have figured this would bother you that much."

"Look man, I'm probably going to hell for things I've done." He watched as Leyva thrashed ineffectively against his bonds. "But I also believe in forgiveness. Way I see it, that's between me and the Lord to figure out when the time comes. At least I've never perverted the teachings, and I've never claimed the evil I've done has been in His name."

"You're a very complex man."

Taylor snorted.

The preacher reached under the podium and withdrew a clay chalice. "The wicked must suffer, brothers and sisters, before they can repent. This man has been found lacking in God's eyes, and has been afflicted. His faith has been discarded, he has given himself over to Satan." He approached the base of the cross, eyes level with Leyva's knees, and nodded to Buford.

The bearded redneck crossed the stage and entered a small alcove. He returned shortly, carrying a wooden pole topped with an iron blade.

"Jesus, Mary, and Joseph," Pascoe breathed, turning pale.

The preacher raised the chalice, stretching his arms until it was next to Leyva's ribcage. At his nod, Buford stepped forward, extended the spear, and carefully inserted the tip between the second and third rib, piercing the skin slightly. A stream of blood flowed down the bound man's side, into the waiting cup.

After a minute, the preacher lowered his arms, placing the chalice gently on the altar in front of him. He raised his hands in benediction, once again inclining his head and closing his eyes.

"O mighty God, bless this, the blood of your fallen child, so that the penitent and faithful may live."

Taylor tore his eyes away from the scene below and studied his companion.

Pascoe sat quiet, eyes wide, the shudder running through him a sign of either abject terror or barely suppressed rage. Taylor hoped for fear. Rage was all well and good, but could be an issue if Pascoe got the idea to wade into the crowd and fight his way to the podium. No, in this case the fear could be channeled into will to live. Or at least to get the hell out of here. As long as it didn't paralyze him.

"Come, my children, let us partake of God's blessing. The possessed can only be cured with Faith! By taking of his body into ourselves, we can cast the demon out!" He raised the cup, took a small sip, and set it down again. "God has given us a test, we would be less than worthy in His eyes if we did not accept it." He smiled, lips stained deep red. "Come forward and receive God's blessing."

The parishioners slowly approached the altar single file. The preacher blessed each person as they took a small sip from the chalice, in a surreal perversion of Communion. "What Man hath wrought, God may tear asunder."

Taylor leaned forward, risking a look further into the gallery below. The balcony's drywall, cracked and stained from years of neglect, gave way as he shifted his weight, landing on the row of pews in the back of the room with a loud thud.

The canvas of his shirt cut into his neck as Pascoe pulled him back, saving him from falling into the crowd below. The preacher snapped his head up at the noise, his initial surprise disappearing as his face clouded over.

Taylor landed on his butt just as the congregation looked in his direction.

"Hey folks, don't mind us, just enjoying the cannibalistic ritual." He made a "get on with it" gesture. "Please, carry on. I'm sure God has been missing the human sacrifice aspect of worship."

Taylor pointed at Buford, slowly drew his middle finger across his neck, and finished the gesture by extending it.

The preacher's frown deepened as he shot a glance at Buford and the other goon. The two lugs nodded, turned abruptly, and left the way they came.

"Looks like it's time to go," Taylor said. "And this time I mean it."

The preacher turned back to his flock. "Friends, we can see here that Satan is ever vigilant in corrupting the faithful. The Criminal and the Oppressor working hand in hand to infiltrate our congregation. They are the ones that brought this evil into our midst." He gestured at Leyva, howling through the gag and thrashing against his bonds. "This is their vessel of demonic influence! They are trying to keep us from healing the wretch, undermining our efforts to purify the Fallen!"

The crowd's vibe turned, going from quietly reverential to a murmuring hostility. Several parishioners had turned to glare at the pair on the balcony, pushing and shoving those around them in an effort to make their way forward.

A heavy tread on the stairs behind them alerted them to the approaching goons.

"Shit. We're trapped." Pascoe looked at the busted drywall. "'Bout fifteen-foot drop. Think we can jump?"

"Psh. Doubtful we'd make it five feet after we landed, if we don't break both legs in the fall." Taylor moved towards the stairs. "We gotta hit 'em head on. Let's go." He picked up speed as he approached the stairwell.

Rounding the corner, he paused briefly at the top step, just long enough to shift into a crouch. Buford, leading his partner as they climbed the stairs, clearly hadn't expected a confrontation so soon—his eyes widened as he saw Taylor.

Capitalizing on their hesitation, Taylor sprang. His shoulder slammed into Buford's chest, taking both men down the stairs in a heap. He regained his feet, snapping a vicious kick at the second goon's temple. The man's eyes rolled back as he slumped, unconscious.

Buford recovered somewhat faster, attempting to bring a shotgun around. Taylor slammed one foot down on the bearded man's hand, holding it and the gun, immobile.

"Taylor!" The inmate looked up at Pascoe's voice.

Taylor caught Buford's movement just as the man's pistol cleared the holster. He drew back his free leg, bringing it down hard on Buford's throat.

Buford dropped the gun to clutch at his crushed windpipe. His lips moved, but produced only wet, gurgling sounds.

Pascoe reached the bottom of the stairs and stepped over the unconscious man, approaching Buford as Taylor lifted his foot. "Don't do it, inmate."

Taylor shifted, lowering his foot to the hardwood floor. "Wasn't. Piece of shit can die slow." He bent down and retrieved the pistol and shotgun, handing them to Pascoe. He took them, eyes questioning.

Taylor shrugged. "I figure you'd feel more comfortable with 'em." He turned back to the dying man, staring him in the eyes. "I was wrong, you redneck piece of shit. Looks like I am more Marcellus than Butch. Tell Saint Peter I sent you." He searched Buford's pockets and belt, coming up with a folding knife and spare magazines. He passed these over as well.

"I get this guy's stuff." After another kick, he stripped the unconscious man of his gear. "Ready when you are, boss."

Taylor busted through the door, stopping short to squint in the evening sun.

The church sat slightly forward of the trailer park he had seen from the Stop 'n' Sip, the various single and double wides forming a rough circle around a central parking area about fifty yards away. Trucks, cars, and other vehicles were arranged in neat groups all facing the road.

It seemed that the parishioners had learned a lesson from the events in Waco—keep the units separate, don't group everything together in an easy to assault fire trap, and allow for a quick dispersal of many people in an evacuation situation.

"What's the plan?" Pascoe was leaning against the door, doing what little he could to secure the rear.

"We need to find a vehicle. I'm guessing they got rid of your van as soon as they got us underground, just in case." He started for the trailers. "I really don't want to be standing in the open when they decide to come find us, though." He stopped, turning to look at the church. "Wonder why they haven't—"

The sound of the crowd came suddenly, cutting off the rest of his question. What had been almost reverential silence erupted into a cacophony of voices—shouting punctuated with screams.

Not screams. Howls, like Leyva's.

"Oh, shit." Taylor glanced at Pascoe, and as one they ran for the nearest trailer. Their meager luck held—it was unlocked. He and Pascoe ducked in, slamming the door behind them.

The stench was overpowering, like the aftermath of an IED without the reek of burning plastic and metal. Out of the corner of his eye, he saw Pascoe shift into high alert, bringing Buford's Mossberg into ready position. Taylor drew his pistol, looked at the other man, and nodded.

The trailer was a standard doublewide, kitchen and dining area in the front, separated from the living area by a short bar. Beyond that, a hallway led back into what he assumed were the bedrooms.

The immediate vicinity was clear, and fairly clean. No signs of forced entry or that anyone had put up a fight. Pascoe, motioning with the shotgun, indicated that he'd take the right. They moved forward.

Taylor's first door was closer to the front, he carefully turned the knob and opened it inwards. Inside, a workbench covered in reloading equipment monopolized the space in the center of the small room. Surrounding it, boxes of ammo shared the floor space with rifles, shotguns and large crates.

Taylor gave a low whistle. "This guy was ready for everything short of secession."

Pascoe nodded and turned to his door. He opened it, revealing a bathroom decorated in a baseball motif. Neatly folded towels, sheets and other items occupied the closet just inside. The empty shower's curtain hung bunched against the back wall.

The smell grew steadily stronger as they approached the end of the hallway. Taylor choked back a gag as they approached his next door.

The scene inside could have been direct from any slasher flick. Blood, collected in black pools, lay everywhere, with what looked like strips of muscle tissue and skin floating in the blood.

"Jesus." Taylor forced himself to distance the horror in his mind, compartmentalizing it so he could observe the scene objectively. Boy's room, approximately eight to twelve years old, as indicated by the robot toys and dinosaur posters. Fresh kill, no more than a few hours old. The sickly sweet odor of rotting carcass hadn't had time to set in. He shook his head, closing the door and turning to the one across the hall.

This seemed to be a girl's room, late teens. Posters of boy bands and pop groups decorated the walls, some torn to shreds. The smell of excrement and urine assaulted them, coming from the bed. No blood in here, just filth. They closed the door on the empty room and moved to the last one.

The stench hit them like a ton of bricks. Blood, open intestines, urine and shit mixed into an unholy miasma. What was left of the mother lay on her bed, eyes wide, throat torn out. The remains of the boy were there as well, most of the torso poking out from under the frame. At least one arm was conspicuously absent, while the other had been stripped to the bone.

Taylor heard Pascoe retch behind him, the sour vomit adding to the overall stench. He turned to see the cop bent at the waist, voiding what little had been in his stomach.

Taylor moved towards him, stopping as the other man raised his hand.

"I'm fine," Pascoe said. "Just give me—"

A howl from the bedroom cut him off. Taylor spun in time to see the girl charge, clawed hands caked in her family's blood. His pistol struck the doorjamb as he snapped it up, the unexpected shock causing it to drop from his hand. He backpedaled into the hallway, catching a heel on the ruined carpet in his haste. He hit the floor.

The Mossberg's roar in close quarters was deafening—the girl's chest blossomed into a bloody mess as the pellets tore into her. She dropped, showing Taylor the destruction to her back. The buckshot had blown open her ribs, bloody bones poking through in several places. She twitched weakly for a few more seconds, finally becoming still.

"Holy shit, that was close." Taylor stood up. "Thanks, boss, I owe you another one." He looked at Pascoe. "Boss?"

The TDCJ officer stared at the body of the girl, eyes wide and jaw slack. He dropped the shotgun as he sank to his knees. "I just killed a kid."

"You had to." Tayor hunkered down next to him. "You gotta block it out. You didn't have a choice. You had to do it."

"No, no. She was just a kid, man. God, I killed a kid!" Pascoe was shaking as the realization hit him full force. "I'm supposed to be the good guy. This is so fucked. I'm so fucked."

"C'mon, boss, I need you with me here. We ain't out of this mess yet. Get your game face on."

"I can't . . . it's too much . . ." Pasco sat back, wrapping his arms around himself and rocking slightly. "Fucked. So fucked."

Taylor took a step back and considered his options. Not good. Solo in unknown hostile territory doesn't end well most of the time. Fuck.

Pascoe was sliding further into himself, muttering quietly. "A kid. Probably just had her first prom."

*No time to look for clothing that fits, and these are going to peg me for an escapee. And until we get out of here, I'm going to need someone to watch my back. Dammit.* Taylor approached the other man.

"Boss." No reaction. "PASCOE!" That got his attention. "You were infantry, right?" Pascoe nodded, eyes vacant, before dropping his head again. Taylor pulled out his best Drill Sergeant imitation. "Soldier! I'm talking to you! You don't turn away from me!" Pascoe's head snapped back, old instincts taking over. "That's right, grunt. You look at me when I'm talking to you. What is your mission?"

Pascoe's voice was soft, hard to hear even in the relative silence of the farmhouse. "To deliver the prisoner."

"I can't hear you."

Stronger this time, "To deliver the prisoner."

"I SAID I CAN'T HEAR YOU, ASSHOLE!"

"TO DELIVER THE PRISONER, SIR!" Taylor watched the change in Pascoe's face, the officer's eyes flashing in sudden anger. "To deliver you, inmate."

Taylor smiled. "Good to have you back, Pascoe."

Pascoe's anger drained from his face as the exchange sank in. He laughed in spite of himself. "You know, I think something like that could get you tossed from the Fraternal Order of Bank Robbing Scumbags."

Taylor shrugged. "Eh, let my membership lapse a while back. I'm not a lodge kinda guy. And I don't look good in a fez." He helped the other man to his feet. "We need to get moving. Things are going to get real nasty around here soon."

"Right. Let's get as much ammo and weapons as we can carry. I saw a truck through the bathroom window, it's right outside. With any luck, it's unlocked with the keys in it." He looked Taylor in the eyes. "And thanks, Taylor."

"I need you as much as you need me right now. Don't read into it too much."

"Right. Let's move."

In the gun room, they found two backpacks and stuffed them full of ammo and empty magazines. "All these guns, and no Tavor. Lame." Taylor grabbed an AR and loaded it.

"Beggars, choosers, crazy rednecks with a death cult," Pascoe said. "You takes what you can." He rummaged in the closet, pulling out two tactical vests. He filled the pockets.

Both men turned to the window at the sound of more howling. As if on cue, the church's doors burst open as several congregation members ran out into the fading daylight. Taylor winced as a larger man was tackled by several howling, naked others. His screams as they bit into him trailed off suddenly. More naked parishioners followed, chasing after anyone still clothed.

"They're distracted, but I don't think it would be a good idea to use the front door," Pascoe said.

"Girl's room window?"

"Sounds good."

They scrambled through. Even though it was a tight fit with the weapons and gear, they made it into the parking area. Taylor scanned the vehicles.

"That one." He pointed to a silver and white Chevy with a camper top, the two-toned paint job succumbing to rust and age. "Those older models have a backup gas tank and don't have fancy electronics like the newer ones." They ran for the truck. "Looks like it's full of gear, too."

Fortunately, the crazies were still occupied with the runners, and hadn't noticed them yet. Pascoe reached the door and pulled the handle.

"Thank God, it's open," Then, "Shit. No keys." He looked at Taylor. "Gonna have to hotwire it, cover me."

"You know how to do that?"

"You don't?" Pascoe pulled his knife and pried the cover from the steering column. "Shouldn't that come with the 'Bank Robbing Scumbag' territory?"

"I missed that meeting."

A chill ran through him as a chorus of howls split the air.

"Pascoe!"

"On it!"

Taylor kept his head on a swivel, trying to cover all avenues. A howling, naked man appeared between two trailers, fifty feet away. Taylor fired, catching him in the chest, then watched in shock as the crazy continued forward, ignoring the wound.

"You fucking kidding me?" Taylor shot again, and again, the bullets ripping into the man's ribcage. He finally dropped, blood loss and tissue damage catching up to him.

Another freak appeared, accelerating towards him, howling at the top of his lungs. Taylor squeezed off three more rounds.

"They're on to us!" Taylor backed towards the truck. "These guys aren't slowing down!"

"Moving as fast as I can!"

"Unbunch those frilly little panties and move faster!"

"I buy the cologne!"

Taylor spun, aiming quickly at the closest approaching whacko, firing, then moving to the next. Click. "Damn." He slapped in a new mag before the empty one hit the ground.

The fucking NATO round did little to nothing against the crazies. Granted, it did allow him to service targets at range, but dammit, it would be nice to drop the fuckers with only one shot. He worked the growing number of targets as fast as he could.

"Aaand . . . got it," Pascoe said. The truck's motor tried to turn over. "C'mon girl, you can do it." The engine grumbled again, failing to catch.

Taylor spun, taking aim at a middle-aged woman. The rifle clicked as he pulled the trigger. "Fuck." He let it fall onto the sling and drew his pistol, two quick shots dropping her. He tracked the next closest target.

This one had clothes, causing him to do a quick double take. It was the preacher. Taylor's finger tightened on the trigger.

A pursuer appeared just as the preacher started in his direction. Taylor adjusted aim and put three into the naked man before turning back to the now kneeling preacher.

"Please, have mercy! Take me with you!"

"You've got a lot of nerve," Taylor said, approaching. "A lot. Of. Fucking. Nerve." He placed the barrel against the man's forehead, taking satisfaction in the dark stain spreading across the front of the other man's jeans.

"My name is Merwick, I can help you." Tears rolled down his face. "I know of safe places, other compounds where we can hide."

Taylor hesitated. He wouldn't get far in prison garb in a *sane* world, and if this place was any indication, sane just took a long vacation.

"Taylor!" Pascoe's shout brought him back. "Behind you!" One of the crazies, quieter than the others, had managed to get into bad breath range. Taylor spun, just in time to duck under the lunging grasp, jamming his .45 into the man's ribs and firing.

The guy ignored the new holes in his chest and lunged again, getting a lucky swipe on Taylor's gun hand. "Shit." Taylor narrowly avoided a bite, responding with a quick pistol-whip to the temple as he swept the crazy's leg, dropping him to the ground. A bullet to the forehead kept him there.

As quick as he had been, the extra time had allowed more rabid parishioners to close in. A sudden movement caught his eye—Merwick ran forward, tackling another crazy in Taylor's blind spot.

The preacher shoved the crazy's chin upward as Taylor approached, gnashing teeth narrowly missing his fingers. Taylor stomped, holding the crazy man's head still as he pulled the trigger. Brain and bone painted the gravel.

More naked people, their faces covered in blood, appeared between the trailers. Taylor swung the pistol, firing quickly as he hauled Merwick to his feet.

"Son of a bitch," he muttered, shoving the older man towards the truck. "Go! Before I change my mind."

The engine caught, the big V-8 roaring to life. Taylor dropped two more attackers as he made his way to the passenger's side door, taking the last one as the slide locked back. He wrenched the door open and got in, slamming it shut just as another crazy hit the window.

Pascoe glanced over at him. "It's eighty-five miles to Houston, we've got full tanks of gas, a shit ton of ammo, it's getting dark, and we're wearing tac gear."

"Just shut the fuck up and drive."

Pascoe floored it, gravel and dust flying from the rear tires. He jerked the wheel to avoid the small mass of remaining people, fishtailing before he got it under control.

"Jesus, boss, don't get us killed before we leave the driveway!"

"Backseat driver."

Taylor turned, sliding the glass partition open between himself and the preacher. "You and I have a reckoning coming, but it'll wait until we get some distance between us and your clusterfuck back there. You feel me, old man?" He felt the bump and the change in road surface as Pascoe turned onto 271.

"O, God! Why hast thou forsaken me?"

"Maybe because you perverted His Word to levels no one has seen before?"

"I was proud, thinking that I could see into God's mind. This is my fall from Grace." The older man's shoulders slumped as he spoke. "My flock followed me, yet I led them down the wicked path. My weakness and blindness led them astray!"

He leaned forward, taking Taylor's shoulder. The old man's grip was fierce. "No! You don't understand! You can't see what I can see!" His head snapped up, red-rimmed eyes wild and overflowing with tears. "You are blind to the truth as I was!" He began squeezing harder.

"You need to move that hand before you lose it."

"His entire world just came crashing down, Taylor," Pascoe said. "Cut him some slack."

"This crazy piece of shit crucified a man, drank his blood, and had us lined up for the next course." Taylor raised the empty pistol. "I should end him right now."

"He deserves it, sure." Pascoe said. "But remember, 'Vengeance is mine, sayeth the Lord.'"

"I'd just be arranging the meeting."

"Leave him for the courts, Taylor. It's the right—"

He was cut off by the preacher. "I will show you the light! You must let me cleanse your soul! Aaargh, God has sent the serpents to torment me until I fulfill my penance!" He began tearing at his shirt. "THE SERPENTS ARE HERE!"

Taylor dropped the mag, slammed home a new one, and brought the gun up. The preacher lunged forward just as Taylor slammed the window, bisecting the barrel as he pulled the trigger. Blood and brains covered the bed and boxes of supplies with red and gray lumps. There was a thump as the former holy man's corpse fell back into the seat.

"Say hello to God for me." Taylor said. He pulled the pistol back and shut the window. "Okay, now that we have some breathing room, what's the plan?"

Pascoe shook his head slightly. "I don't know. We're out of touch with base, as well as anyone else that could tell us anything. We need info, first and foremost."

"Yeah. Problem is, you saw how fast that went downhill back there. Chances are that whatever this is, it's spreading. Hell, most of those people back there looked like they were getting over the flu, before they went through with the communion."

"Best I can come up with now is to find a remote location, small, out of the way gas station or something, and make some phone calls." Pascoe glanced down at the truck's radio, and clicked the power knob. "Surf through the airwaves and see what you can find. We've got some time before we hit another town."

Static crackled as Taylor spun the dial. The occasional burst of music was punctuated with voices.

"...And the Texas Department of Health confirmed another attack was caused by the 'Human Rabies Virus,' H7..."

"...Local health officials remind the citizens to stay indoors as much as possible, avoid contact with anyone that may be infected, and to use common safety precautions. Wash your hands, use antiviral sanitizer..."

"...The CDC announced today that the H7 virus is a major concern, and that a vaccine is still in the development stage..."

"...No word as of yet as to where the strain has come from, only that it is not a naturally occurring form of the flu. State and Federal officials are requesting that anyone with any information..."

Taylor clicked off the radio. "Think we've heard all we need to hear for right now. Looks like this shit is spreading fast."

Pascoe nodded. "Yeah, if that little speck on the map had it, I can only imagine how the bigger cities are getting screwed."

"Zombies. The word no one is using." Taylor laughed. "And with all the media in the last several years. Hell, I can't believe I'm saying it." His chuckle became louder, growing into a full-throated guffaw.

Pascoe held out a little longer, but a smile crept across his face. "Heh. All those times I've gone home worried about getting shanked in the lockup, and I really should've been worried about some prom queen feeling peckish."

"Starved herself for months to get in that dress, what did you expect?"

"It's the Om-nomnomageddon!" Pascoe was able to contain himself long enough to get the truck to the side of the road, then doubled over.

They both laughed, on the edge of hysteria, purging the strain and tension of the last several hours.

Taylor recovered first, wiping his eyes. "Oh man, talk about your totally fucked up situations. Zombie apocalypse, and I'm stuck with a cop as my battle buddy."

"Hey, look at it from my side—I have to deal with a murderous scumbag, and he's the best choice I have."

"Speaking of murderous scumbags," Taylor said, "I can contact the guys that hired me. Tell them to forget the lawyers, but bring guns and money. They have safehouses all over, maybe we can hole up until this blows over."

"Better than anything I got." Pascoe shrugged, adding, "I don't think this is blowing over, Taylor."

"Yeah, me neither."

The other man nodded, his face set in determination. Without another word, he eased back onto the asphalt, guiding the truck towards the next town, and an uncertain future.

# Best Laid Plans

JASON CORDOVA & ERIC S. BROWN

The best laid plans of mice and men often go awry.

Or at least, that's what he grew up hearing. *Strange how a Scottish saying could infiltrate a strict Bavarian family,* he thought as he noticed a strange smell in the apartment. It took him a few moments to realize that the smell was Paris itself, no longer being crowded out by the familiar scents of Chinese cooking. The family downstairs must have contracted the same disease that had been talked about in the news that day, he figured. That did bring him back to the discussion at hand, though.

"There is a strange illness rampaging across Europe," Günter Schneider said to the men assembled around the dining room table. He jabbed a finger at the detailed, hand-drawn blueprints that were spread out across the top of it. The form of the Louvre was obvious to all involved. It had been their life for the past six months, and they knew it better than they knew their own apartment. Many hours had been spent within the museum taking notes, as well as infiltrating the security personnel with one of their own, to achieve such a perfect floor plan.

"The Avian Flu, perhaps? Nobody is sick yet, *ja*, so we do not have to worry about this. Many staff called in sick, or have acted rather strangely during their shifts. This has left a hole in the perimeter of the security. We had agreed to wait a month more before we strike, but this opportunity is too good to pass up. I say we push the time frame forward and strike tonight."

"You think it will work on short notice?" Hans Flick asked, his tone filled with skepticism.

"Nothing can stop us from succeeding," Günter declared.

"Except for the zombies..." Hans muttered in a low tone. The others around the table nodded in agreement.

"There are no such things as zombies," Günter said. He was growing tired of this argument with his men.

"No zombies? Then we shall call them dead people who walk around eating the faces of others," Hans threw his hands into the air in exasperation. "Günter, *mein Freund*, rational people do not act like this. It is a sign, one that is telling us to not attempt this. Not now. Not while the world seems to be at a tipping point." His face suddenly brightened. "Perhaps they are within the confines of the Bundestag, *ja*?"

"We do not know that they are undead," Günter reminded him, though the mental image of certain Bundestag members being eaten alive warmed the darkest cockles of his heart. "They could have ingested... what is it, bath salts?"

"*Oui*, he has a point." The team's inside person and lone Frenchman, Chetan Neghiz, spoke in a soft voice. The security guard shrugged his shoulders as Hans glared at his apparent betrayal. "We do not know that they are dead. What we do know is that the Louvre is practically unguarded right now. Monsignor Lajoinie has asked me to come in tonight to help secure jewelry and smaller items in the unlikely event that the Louvre must close for the duration of this... crisis. So Günter is correct—this must happen tonight."

"Sooner or later someone is going to find that USB drive Chetan hooked up to their servers," Folsom Duncan said around his cigar. The American nodded thoughtfully. "To be honest, I'm surprised nobody's found it already. Any old cell phone could have tried to access it and been denied. That would have gotten me curious, that's for damn sure. Sorry, babbling again. That WiFi is only good for up to one hundred yards, and the signal's gonna be faint as is. The fewer people with their cell phones inside, the better it will be for me. We need to go tonight."

"So it is settled, yes?" Günter looked around and saw affirmative nods. Only Hans seemed uncertain. He glared but decided to let it go for now. "It is settled then. Tonight we shall burgle the Louvre as we have planned. In two weeks time we shall be in the Cayman Islands, drinking champagne. Once our fence moves the goods to his Russian friend, we shall live the rest of our lives as billionaires."

"Besides, we've had six good dry runs so far," Folsom added. He looked at each of them and smiled. "What could possibly go wrong?"

"This," Chetan said through tightly clenched teeth, "is why one does not tempt fate, Folsom Duncan. May there be a pox upon your house."

En route to the Louvre that night they learned three very important, earth-shattering truths about themselves as they drove through the dark streets of Paris.

The first truth: the reports of the Avian Flu and bath salts turned out to be grossly incorrect. There were people fleeing across Champs-Elysee, and naked men and women in hot pursuit. The first few had been amusing to the four men, but as they drew closer to the Louvre it became obvious that the naked people were no longer living. Indeed, it appeared that Hans had been correct and Paris—perhaps all of France, perhaps all of Europe—had been invaded by zombies.

Oddly enough, the zombies milled aimlessly around the Peugeot, ignoring the electric SUV while pursuing other cars roaring down the road. It got to the point that Folsom quit trying to dodge the fallen zombies that were struck by other vehicles. This, however, was far more disturbing than watching the zombies chase down and eat unaffected human beings.

The second truth was a harsher one. High-end jewelry thieves, as they styled themselves, were typically not murderers. The mangled corpses of the zombies they left lying in the road behind them affected each of them differently, with Hans growing more disturbed with each passing bump. To Günter, it seemed as though Folsom had the least trouble with the uneven drive. He would normally have chalked it up to typical American brashness except that he had known Folsom since they had met at Cambridge ten years before. The so-called "American cowboy" was anything but.

The third and final truth was one which they would never openly admit. Each and every one of them was greedy. A zombie apocalypse could not contain their greed. If Günter or any of the others had felt differently, the heist would not ever have been executed while the world burned. Especially after seeing the pyre that the Montmartre district had become.

Their planned entry point was less congested than anticipated, all things considered. Even so, there were a few zombies wandering around the loading dock. Their heads swiveled almost as one when the bright, LED headlights flashed across them. Chetan pulled the SUV as close to the loading dock as he dared and parked. Two zombies fell on top of the hood from the raised landing dock, their piteous moans muffled through the windshield. Chetan yelped and turned on the window wipers. The arms began to glide across the window and a spurt of cleaner helped clear some of the collected dirt from its face.

The zombies remained on the hood, growling.

"Window wipers? Really?" Folsom asked with a frightened giggle. Chetan chuckled nervously. He turned the wipers off.

"We have no other choice," Günter decided. "Chetan, you close the door to the dock as planned. Try to hurry before any other zombies make it down here. Hans, you and I will get rid of the zombies. Folsom, you may proceed."

"*Allons-y*," Chetan muttered and swung open the driver's door. The zombies turned as one and focused on the Frenchman. He slammed the SUV door shut and sprinted to the automatic rolling doors of the loading dock, the two zombies hot in pursuit. Their howls echoed loudly. Answering howls responded from outside the loading area.

Folsom produced an ancient-looking .38 from the pocket of his jacket. "Did anyone else think to bring a gun?"

Günter glowered at the American. "I said no guns! We are thieves, not killers!"

"As long as you don't count our completely organic road bumps out there in the street," Folsom muttered as he shoved the pistol back into his pocket. The motion had far too much reluctance in it for Günter to remain happy. The American grabbed his laptop from the floor and booted it up. Moments later he smiled. "I'm in. Amazing reception down here. The dry runs up top only gave me two bars, max. I'm getting four down here. Sweet."

"Hans, there is a prybar on the floor," Günter said. "Hand it to me."

"Why?" Hans asked as he picked up the metal rod from the plush, carpeted floor of the vehicle. He passed it forward.

"Because I must clear the dock so Chetan can get back," Günter said as he grabbed the crowbar. He took a deep breath before he swung open his door. "*Gott mit uns.*"

The first zombie to reach him appeared to be a young one, about to start university. Günter swung the crowbar with all his might and cracked the skull of the undead. It staggered under the blow but came right back at him, unfeeling and uncaring about the pain. Günter took a step back and jabbed the pointed end of the rod into the zombie's face. Through a combination of skill and blind luck the point drove straight into the eye socket of the zombie. It jerked violently as Günter twisted the crowbar and yanked it back out. The zombie managed to remain on its feet, though it was obvious that the crowbar had done significant damage. Günter gabbed the rod with two hands and swung again, putting all his weight and strength into the swing. The bar opened the zombie's head like a ripe melon, blood and brain matter spraying all over him. The undead collapsed to the concrete floor, finished.

Günter stood still for a moment, hands shaking as he clutched the gore-covered crowbar. He looked at his hands, which were coated in blood, then down at the zombie, which was clearly dead. A thought suddenly came to him and he bit down a manic giggle.

*Is an undead dead when it dies?*

Günter heard the doors of the loading dock slam shut as Chetan managed to close the bar. He screamed something in French and barely managed to escape from the clutches of the two zombies pursuing him. Another zombie appeared from around the corner, drawn to the SUV by the howls of the others. It appeared to have been a little old lady once, though the gaping maw and blood-curdling shrieks put to rest any doubts of what Günter should do. He swung the crowbar and struck her in the neck. The frail neck combined with the German's strength decapitated the zombie. Her head went flying through the air and struck the SUV's rear passenger door while her body rolled on the ground.

He shook himself and turned around. Chetan was trying

to make it to the SUV but was cut off. Günter looked around quickly but saw no other zombies. Without a second thought he charged the undead by Chetan, his crowbar high over his head, a war cry in his throat.

The undead howled in reply but Günter was having none of it. Ensuring that he had a solid grip on the blood-covered crowbar, he drove the point right into the face of the first zombie. The force of the blow jerked the crowbar from his grasp, leaving him unarmed. The zombie dropped like a sack of potatoes, but the second was near. It howled and grabbed him. They tumbled to the ground, the teeth of the undead coming within inches of his neck. He screamed in fear and rage as he tried to push it off of him, but the zombie was strong.

"Still no gun?" Folsom called out from the SUV, his window rolled partly down.

"No! Gun!" Günter screamed back. He turned his face away from the snapping teeth of the undead and put his forearm into its throat. "Help!"

Brain matter suddenly coated his face as the zombie's head exploded above him. The dead weight of the undead fell fully on top of him. Günter struggled with the corpse for a moment before someone helped pull it off of him. He found himself looking at the pale face of Hans. He was holding a long metal pipe.

*"Ich fand ein Rohr,"* Hans muttered, forgetting for a moment that neither Chetan nor Folsom spoke his language. "Sorry... it is a good pipe. I shall keep this pipe."

*"Gut."* Günter nodded, panting slightly as he tried to stand up. He slipped in blood and brain matter but managed to climb to his feet. He patted his friend on the shoulder. *"Gut germacht."*

"Any more of them?" Chetan asked from the far side of the car. His face was sweaty despite the cooler air of the loading bay.

"No, it appears that they are all dead," Günter said as he switched back to English. He wiped his bloody hands on his pants before he knelt down and picked up his messy crowbar. He grabbed his Bluetooth and slipped it into his ear. "Comms check."

"The app is up and running... now," Folsom said. "Get your ears in, people."

Chetan and Hans both managed to get their Bluetooth in without too much hassle, though Hans left a bloody streak on his cheek. They each checked in with Folsom, who gave them a thumbs up. They looked back at their leader, who was trying not to look at the zombies on the ground.

"*Schnell,*" Günter said. "It probably is worse inside, and I do not want to get caught in the Mall if the power goes out. That would be . . . bad."

Chetan was wearing his security outfit just in case, but if there were any guards still inside, the group did not encounter them. The lights had remained on throughout their trip through the Mall, just as Günter had predicted back at the apartment. Even the Starbucks had been deserted, which came as a surprise to them, Folsom most of all.

"I mean, I expected maybe some hipster yuppie zombie demanding his half-caff skinny latte or something," the American had marveled over the comms as the team moved deeper into the Louvre. He was safely ensconced in the SUV still, armed with a laptop and locked doors. Günter was mildly jealous, though the original plan had not involved zombies of any kind. "I'm kinda disappointed, truth be told. Not even one."

Günter, who had never fully understood his American friend's sense of humor, ignored the jibe. He led them up the stairs and to the first floor slowly. He scanned the area but saw no sign of guards or zombies.

"Let's go," he said. A howl from down the hall sent shivers up his spine. Something was approaching them, and fast. "Hans!" Günter shouted in warning as a zombie came out of the shadows near the display where Hans stood.

Hans grabbed a small marble head that looked vaguely Roman and swung it with all his strength. The solid sculpture brained the zombie, dropping it to the ground. Hans leaned over and smashed the sculpture against the zombie's head a few more times just to make sure before he stood back up. His face, chest and arms were covered in gore. He was grinning.

"You just used a second century Roman statue to kill a zombie!" Chetan howled, the cry filled with pain and anger. Hans looked at the bust in his hand and shrugged, his grin disappearing. Chetan snatched the sculpture out of the Berliner's hand and began to wipe the bits of skull and brain matter from the marble as best as he could. "Now it's covered in gore and . . . and . . . *merde!* This is a priceless artifact! Have you no shame?"

Günter shook his head. He had been worried about Hans losing his grip on his sanity, but this proved the man was at least willing to fight for his life when it was on the line.

"I'm robbing the Louvre during the end of civilization," Hans reminded the Frenchman as he saw Günter looking at him. "I have no shame."

Günter patted Hans on the back, a smile slowly forming on his face. "I might have done the same."

"*Je peux sentir ta chatte...*" Chetan muttered and looked away, angry.

"Quiet," Günter said, his focus settling on the job once more. "This area looks to be clear of them. We will move to the next floor and get all that we came for."

"Aw, c'mon guys," Folsom whined through the Bluetooth. "At least go back and steal the Mona Lisa for me."

"No, that was not part of the plan," Günter replied. "We stick to the plan."

"But... the *Mona Lisa?!*" Folsom continued to protest.

"No."

"You suck, dude."

Günter did not have time to reply. More zombies were waiting for them around the bend in the next corridor.

"Quick! Into that room!" Chetan called out. They ran into the antechamber and looked around. It was filled with paintings that Günter did not recognize. Chetan, however, was as comfortable as one could be with a horde of zombies pursuing them. "Down that hall, then turn right!"

"Where does that lead?" Günter asked as they ran, their breath starting to come in short gasps. A painful stitch in his side began to form.

"To the other stairwell," Chetan replied. The Frenchman, in spite of the copious amounts of wine and foul-smelling cigarettes he regularly partook of, seemed to be handling the run just fine. More howls erupted farther down the hall as more zombies took up pursuit. "*Merde!* Left up here!"

Günter slid a bit as they rounded the corner, Hans hot on his heels as they followed Chetan through what was rapidly becoming a maze to the Germans.

"How... much... further?" Günter asked between breaths.

"Left, then two rights, then up the stairs," Chetan replied. The bastard was not even short of breath, Günter saw.

"This would be hilarious if not for the zombies chasing you," Folsom commented over the Bluetooth. "You run in one room, the zombies chase you, you appear to run into another room, they chase you."

"How are you watching this?" Chetan asked. Günter was curious as well.

"That USB drive you hooked up to their servers for me also gave me access to the security cameras, as well as their sound system," Folsom replied. "In fact... hold up, I need to download something."

"*Ich werde verdammt töten*," Günter hissed. The stitch in his side was growing worse.

"What was that? That sounded kind of garbled over the comm," Folsom said. "Ah, found it! You're gonna love this."

Saxophone music suddenly blared over the intercom of the Louvre, drowning out the howls of the zombies and the thundering footsteps of the men who sought to rob the museum. It was a frantic saxophone, with accompanying music. It was familiar to Günter but he could not immediately place the song. He ran into another room and suddenly it clicked. His eyes widened.

"*Benny Hill?!*" Günter fairly screamed. "This is not funny!"

"I know, right? This shit is *hilarious!* I would put this up on YouTube... well, except for the fact that we're robbing the Louvre, I mean," Folsom laughed. "Who doesn't love a good Yackety Sax scene?"

"*I will mount your balls on the wall of my mega yacht!*" Günter promised.

"Somebody's testy... get it? Testy?" The music stopped. Folsom gave a long-suffering sigh. "Germans have no sense of humor..."

"We lost them," Chetan said and slowed to a jog. He looked around. "We're close. There, the stairwell. This will lead us directly to the room we want." Gathering their breath, they pressed onwards up to the second floor.

The group ducked into the smaller room near the stairwell and found their target—the crown jewels of Louis XV. The display room appeared to be empty of zombies, though Günter was quickly learning that even the slightest bit of darkness could hide one of the creatures. He pulled out a small aerosol can and began to spray the edges of the glass. The glass began to sizzle as the acid chewed through it. The other two men carefully removed the glass to expose the jewels within.

There were dozens of necklaces, earrings and pearls on display. Prominently featured was a crown covered in gems and diamonds. A scepter similarly decorated lay next to it.

Another howl echoed from somewhere in the Louvre. Günter nervously looked around but spotted nothing. He motioned at the other two.

"Quickly," he said, his breathing finally back to normal. "We do not have much time."

"The crown looks very expensive," Hans said, his voice filled with awe and wonder. Chetan snorted in disgust.

"Covered in fake jewels," he said. "Louis XV was a cheap bastard. He was forced to wear this cheap imitation because he used the real jewels to pay off his debts."

"What a shame," Hans shook his head. Günter knew from past experience that his friend was trying to focus on the task at hand. It helped block out the carnage that they had wrought on the zombies in the loading dock.

Hans picked up a gorgeous necklace decorated with green gemstones. "What about this one? Is it a fake?"

"Those are real," Chetan confirmed. "They weren't on the list because they were supposed to be cleaned this week and taken off display. Since *le fin du monde* has decided to occur . . ." He shrugged. "We would be fools to leave these behind."

"Good," Hans smiled and tossed the necklace into the silk bag.

"Not like that!" Chetan fairly howled. "Do you know how long it will take to untangle that now? You are a savage! Günter, why did we bring this *débile* along?"

Günter felt a headache replace the pain in his ribs. Perhaps he could get away with one murder in his lifetime? Other than a zombie, in any case.

They cleared out the rest of the jewels, including the ones that were not originally on their list. Günter knew that they would make them wealthier, even if the end of the world might interrupt their flow of cash from their Russian benefactor. Still, they were almost priceless, and they could be used as barter should there be more zombies blocking their way to the Caymans.

"Chetan, we need to find a different way out," Günter suggested. "Folsom, is there any way you can pick us up somewhere other than the loading dock?"

"Maybe," the American answered in a hesitant voice. "I might have an idea..."

"If we continue down this corridor we will see more display rooms," Chetan replied immediately. "The only exit that way is the north stairwell. That can take us to the first floor, and then further down into the Mall."

"I thought we were going to avoid the Mall?" Hans asked as they hurried down the hall, away from the zombies who might be pursuing them.

"That was before I was reminded of the Starbucks," Chetan answered in an anxious tone. "Somebody thought it was a good idea to put that in. I wish to burn it down."

The Frenchman was a purist, Hans knew. He would always find something to be unhappy about, whether it be the differing brush strokes between eighteenth-century Dutch painting masters or if the Louvre allowed a Starbucks. It would never be a mystery to Hans why Chetan was perpetually single.

The trio encountered a few more of the scattered dead as they raced through the building but no actual zombies. The dead appeared to be half-eaten, which Günter knew would give him nightmares for years to come. Their last bit of trouble met them at the door to the Mall—or rather, outside of it. The street outside was packed with the undead.

"Where are you, Folsom?" Günter growled as the zombies outside began to howl in earnest. They could not see any sign of regular people.

Headlights appeared in the midst of the crowd of zombies. Günter blinked for a moment, trying to get his eyes to adjust at the increasing brightness before he realized that the SUV was headed right for him. He dove to the side as the SUV came plowing through the glass doors like a metal juggernaut. Folsom slammed on the brakes as he reached their position, causing the vehicle to slide around perfectly in front of them. Günter picked himself up off the floor and along with the others, hastily climbed inside.

The zombies swarmed the SUV. Chetan kicked one in the face just before it could get inside.

"See?" Folsom said as Chetan fell onto the back seat, gasping for breath. Günter slammed the door on one of the zombie's hands, breaking it. Hans climbed over the front seat to get into the back where the others were. The American accelerated and the SUV began rolling out of the Louvre and down the packed streets, dragging the zombie alongside. More crashed into the grill and fender but they did not stop the determined driver. Another bump and the zombie that had been stuck fell away, leaving its hand as a parting gift. "And you guys made fun of me for playing so much Grand Theft Auto."

"Get us out of here!" Hans demanded loudly.

"I'm trying!" Folsom shouted back at him. "Zombies! I can't go too fast or they'll bust the car up more. It's barely hanging on as it is! I think I broke something important when I crashed through those doors."

"I thought you said you could drive?" Günter snapped, his temper finally at a boiling point. He began to quote the American, heavy Southern accent and all. "'I roll dirty on GTA and I drive the same.'"

"Screw you," Folsom grunted but shifted into another gear. He flipped the four-wheel drive button and the SUV lurched as it activated. He floored it, plowing through the sea of zombies. Disgusting bits flew up and got stuck on the windshield wipers. Their dark blue SUV began to look decidedly reddish. "Next time, I'll just leave you in the middle of the damn zombie apocalypse, you ungrateful Kraut!"

"Just get us to the Le Havre," Günter ordered, his voice back to normal. "You have the route mapped?"

"As best as I could," Folsom nodded, the momentary anger gone as quickly as it came. He turned the SUV down another crowded street. "Haussman gets us to the Normandy route fastest, I think. It's the most direct route."

"The boat will wait for us until noon tomorrow." Günter consulted his phone. Service was still up and running, though his reception bars were low. "We have nine hours to make the two hundred kilometer drive."

"Piece of cake," Folsom said as he plowed through another zombie. "What's the worst—"

"Shut up! Don't you say it!" Chetan cried out.

Günter sighed. It was the end of the world and this was the

best that he could come up with. He rubbed his forehead. Sand. Women. Warm weather. The fact that everyone in the SUV was now a billionaire. He could handle this. He could deal with their peculiarities. He had done it for the past nine months, since the plan took shape. He could live with this for just a little while longer.

"The Bahamas will be nice," he predicted, trying to cheer himself up. For a newly minted billionaire, he was very unhappy. "Good food. Swimming. Warm waters. Naked women. None of this zombie nonsense, no doubt."

"No doubt," Hans agreed.

They drove on, uninterrupted save for the occasional bump in the road from where a zombie fell beneath their tires, and a wave of zombies behind in hot pursuit.

# The Meaning of Freedom

JOHN RINGO

"Hmmm . . . that's odd."

Dr. Rizwana Shelley had never been entirely comfortable with running the main vaccine production facility in the post-Fall world. While she had, reluctantly, come to the conclusion that making vaccine from human spinal cords was a necessity, it was always an *unpleasant* necessity.

As others had been found who could manage the production, she had segued smoothly back to research. As much as could be done under the current circumstances. Which was why she had been handed this particular conundrum.

One of the Gurkhas tasked with acquiring "materials" had turned up something odd. The primary infected threat were the alphas, the insane, violent, sub-sentients that the H7D3 virus had left of humanity. As such, they were the main primates "collected" for the attenuated vaccine. The Gurkhas collected their spinal cords as they cleared portions of the suburbs surrounding London. Metro London itself was still too rife.

One of the spinal cords, however, had been found to be uninfected. Normal spinal cords were white or yellowish. The H7D3 virus infesting the spinal cord and brains of infected was a distinct crimson.

"I hate to ask this," Dr. Shelley said, holding up the spine in a ziplock bag. "But are you sure that all you collected were from *infected*?"

The words were in fluent Ghorkali. Dr. Shelley had not spoken Ghorkali prior to the Fall so it was her twenty-eighth language. She agreed in general with other linguists that after about the eighth most of the rest got easier.

"They were all naked," Captain Surigar replied. "All acting as if they were infected. None called out to us in any way, Doctor. We are Gurkhas. We would not clear a human."

The Gurkhas made it a point of pride to never kill a noncombatant. Infected were combatants even if they used teeth and hands to do the fighting.

"Let me do some work on it," Dr. Shelley said. "And if you find any more that are clear, try to recover the bodies as well, please."

"Yes, Doctor," Captain Surigar said. "Is it . . . fading?"

"That is the interesting question."

"We have found another, Doctor."

Rizwana had managed to set up something of a complete laboratory from the wreckage of civilization. The king had been insistent on the subject. Britain was barely in the beginnings of recovering from a devastating plague. Having their top microbiologist fully equipped was right up there with ammunition for the Gurkhas.

Examination of the first spine had yielded little in the way of information. The person it came from was a slight woman of Middle Eastern descent. Which could have described Dr. Shelley. One point she'd determined was that it was not from her own missing, presumably dead or infected, daughter. No close genetic link. Based on mitochondrial DNA markers she was probably from the Syrian region but that was at best a guess. She'd been pregnant at some time. She was malnourished. That was about it. There wasn't much you could really tell about the woman's life from a spinal cord. There were markers for H7D3 antibodies, which meant the collected had been exposed but no trace of the virus.

"And where did this come from?" Dr. Shelley asked, looking at another spine in a bag. "Do we know?"

"Private Bahadur was clearing a house and shot him," Captain

Surigar said. "He did not attack. The private believes he was hiding and may be what the Americans term a 'beta.'"

"Hmmm..."

That posed a conundrum. There were only two ways to find out if someone was actually infected with H7D3. Symptoms, notably the violent insanity and nakedness characteristic of alphas and a brain autopsy. You could test for antibodies but as proven with Subject A that was no proof of presence of the virus. She hated what she was about to say, but the world was a very unpleasant place.

"Discuss this with your higher command first," she said. "But I need you to collect some betas for... analysis. Two dead, two live will do. You'll need to refrigerate the dead ones. I'll find someone to do the autopsy. Don't strip the spines. I'll need them whole. And we'll need to set up a confinement facility for the live ones...."

Steven John Smith, Secretary of War of the United States (SecWar), rubbed his face and wondered if he was *ever* going to get a break from zammies.

"They're clean?" President Rebecca Staba said.

"Entirely," Dr. Dobson said over the video conference.

They were barely starting to get East Coast cities reduced to about orange using a variety of Subedey systems. Their initial plan to use mostly radiological killers wasn't a bust but it was only part of the program. In places, they'd found stored toxic chemicals in partially cleared areas and moved those forward to supplement. A recent trend had been to pack containers with ammonium nitrate fuel oil explosives, put lights and speakers on top, drop by helicopter well away from potential survival shelters, let sit for a few days then blow the IED. That usually took out a few thousand at a time, especially if the chopper got a feeding frenzy going by machine gunning a few infected.

Approximately thirty million to go and Atlanta and the CDC were sort of, well, *inland*. They were getting there. Slowly. In the meantime, video was the way to go.

"We, well, *Emory*, managed to get a few individuals clear of the virus before the Fall," Dobson said. "Massive doses of rare and difficult to manufacture antivirals did it in a couple of cases. Not all. And what you got back for your trouble were... vegetables. No higher brain activity. Just..."

"So that's what happened with betas?" Steve said. "They got the disease then . . . threw it off?"

"It's the most likely scenario," Dobson said. "The human immune system is a complex engine. Just because you've got a disease doesn't mean you keep it. And the H7 virus was never really structurally robust. Could have just . . . fallen apart. The main thing to keep in mind is that from the point of view of H7 they're a non-threat. Now, they tend to carry other diseases, but . . . not H7."

"What about the lack of clothing?" Steve said then shook his head. "Stupid question. They would have gotten the formication at the beginning, thrown off their clothes then later thrown off the H7. So still *en nue*."

"Yes," Dr. Dobson said. "But not a threat."

"That's good to hear," Steve said.

"And it creates a real issue," President Staba said.

"Why?" Dobson said.

"What you just pointed out, Doctor, is that there are approximately two million additional *human* survivors who are a non-threat but also incapable of caring for themselves," the POTUS said in exasperation.

"Killing all the alphas is a horrible and bloody necessity. We can't get anything done, rescue the remaining sentient survivors, with them in the way. I am not my predecessor but, by the same token, some human charity toward the *betas* now seems . . . more or less a moral *requirement*. They are American citizens who truly are simply victims of a horrible plague. And we don't have unlimited resources."

"Please don't ask the Army to help," Steve said. "We've got enough on our plate."

"I foresee a Cabinet meeting," the President said, shaking her head. "What fun."

"There's not much we can do," Steve said. "There are two problems, tactical, sociological if you prefer—and logistical."

The Cabinet of the United States Federal Government was a far more informal group than it had been before the Fall. Among other things it was significantly reduced; most of the positions were gone. All that remained, currently, were State, War, Interior and Treasury. Most of the other positions were either unfilled or had been regrouped. Transportation, Housing and Agriculture, for example, were all filed under "Interior."

The President's mansion, still called the "White House," was a "McMansion" in Alexandria, Florida, across the river from Jacksonville proper and near the Mayport Naval Air Station. They were meeting in the "Florida Room" which looked out over the pool and the St. John's River. It wasn't the largest room in the house but they were a small group.

"The tactical problem is that betas look upon sentients as just a different kind of alpha," Steve continued. "Thus they avoid us. They even tend to avoid each other. Even if we *want* to help them, we'd have to literally hunt them down. The logistical problem is that we'd have to feed, house and clothe up to three million crazy people. Betas might even run as high as our sentient surviving population. I don't think it's *doable* Madame President."

"We haven't really determined what 'it' is, yet," President Staba said. "I'm not even saying something must be done. Just that it is worth discussing."

"Are they trainable?" Carlton Ryan asked. The Secretary of the Treasury was a former VP of Goldman Sachs who'd been picked up rather early in Wolf Squadron's history. He'd spent most of his time as a civilian boat captain until the reestablishment of the U.S. government. "To at least mostly take care of themselves? Get dressed, use the bathroom instead of shrubbery?"

"Unknown," Steve said, shrugging. "I know from Faith's reports that they tend to collect stuff and use shelter. But that's about it."

"Who do we have that can set up a research facility?" President Staba asked. "It seems that what we need first is information. Then we can start to look at the problem. As if we haven't enough."

"I'm not sure if it's in my bailiwick or not," Steve said, temporizing. "I don't really see it as a military 'thing.'"

"Wasn't pointing at you, Steve," President Staba said, smiling. "Sounds like a job for... Interior?"

"Gah," Olivia Alvarado said. She'd gotten the job courtesy of being a former bureaucrat in the Florida Department of Agriculture. Since Interior was mostly concerned with getting roads and agriculture back up and running, she had sufficient credentials and knowledge for the job. The "Congress," which mostly met in Texas given it was the only state officially back up and running, had approved her at long distance. "I was afraid it would fall on my department. Sorry to point it out, but I need budget for it. And don't ask me how much. No clue as yet."

"Try to keep it down," President Staba said.

"I'll take the job of capture," Steve said. "Just tell me when you need them. Plenty to be found."

"And the answer is: betas are trainable," Secretary Alvarado said, happily, as the subject came up at the next Cabinet meeting. "I'd like to introduce Mr. Abraham Powers. He worked in a home for the mentally challenged before the Plague and runs the Beta Analysis Program. Mr. Powers?"

"Betas are trainable," Powers said. He was a big man with a rumbly voice, bushy beard and bright blue eyes. "Compared to my previous experience with the mentally challenged, they're fairly similar to Down's Syndrome. They even tend to be docile once they become assured they are not in a threatening situation. That may, however, be selection. From the reports we got from the Marine teams detailed to capture them some were more hostile and were simply left to their own devices. So we tended to get the most docile.

"After fairly minor training they respond to most verbal commands and may even retain some memory of language. They'll frequently respond to *untrained* verbal commands and even . . . normal social niceties. One of our earliest subjects retained understanding of some dressing rituals, she only needed to be shown how to put on a dress once and when faced with buttons figured them out on her own. Others will tend to sit on a chair rather than on the floor. We've trained a few of the more advanced to use forks and spoons, although they tend to be clumsy with them. At this point we have a total of ten subjects and of those, six have learned basic social rituals including how to bathe themselves, make beds, et cetera.

"They don't tend to interact badly socially but there are issues. Males tend to react . . . very much as males in the presence of females. When there is a point of contention they don't have linguistic skills to work them out so they tend to get physical fairly quickly. That being said, they do . . . communicate. But it is mostly at the grunt and body language level. In terms of IQ, they run from around sixty to eighty. Which puts them in the severe to profound intellectual disability categories. I would like to give a practical demonstration. I brought along one of our more advanced subjects if you'd like to meet her."

"Is there any threat?" Steve asked. "No offense. I've been around betas before, but we're talking about the Cabinet and a plague."

"Katherine is not a threat," Powers said. "Epidemiologically or physically. She is extremely beta but still comparatively bright. And has no trace of H7. If we weren't in this environment you'd assume she was just... normally mentally challenged."

"Service?" President Staba said.

"We already have analyzed the threat, Madame President," Agent Phillips said. "I agree with Mr. Powers that she does not represent a significant threat. And if she presents a threat she can be taken down fast enough."

"I'm fine with it," the President said. "How does she respond to new people?"

"Well," Powers said. "Or I wouldn't have brought her, ma'am. But probably best not to get too... aggressive if you don't mind. She tends to try to run and hide if people get aggressive."

"Bring her in."

Subject Katherine was probably in her twenties, about five six, had red hair, blue eyes and...

"Okay," President Staba said softly. "For some reason I hadn't expected her to be *pretty*."

"And pregnant," Steve noted.

The beta was distinctly round in the tummy.

"She arrived that way, Captain," Powers said in a soft, rumbling tone. "Katherine, these are friends. Friends?"

Katherine hooted and ducked her head, avoiding eye contact, as he led her to one of the open chairs.

"Can you sit, Katherine?" Powers said.

The beta carefully took her chair, continuing to avoid eye contact.

"Okay," the President said. "This really brings my point about the human catastrophe home. Steve, we can't just let these people die. They're people."

"Tactical and logistic difficulties continue to exist, Madame President," Steve said. "But my pragmatic bloodymindness just kicked in, damnit."

"Having long experience of your pragmatism, that makes me uncomfortable immediately," Ryan said. "What is Captain Carrion thinking, now?"

"Nothing anyone is going to want to hear," Steve said. "Mr.

Powers and Secretary Alvarado are especially going to get it right up their noses. I am thinking what I submit Secretary Alvarado *should* be thinking. That we have a significant shortfall in labor in the agricultural industry, mostly because people don't want to do the admittedly hard work of planting and harvesting. Better to just scrounge for salvage food rather than pick beans. Or to put the point in more focus: cotton. As in, my first thought was 'they'd be *great* at picking cotton.'"

"We don't have a crying need for cotton at the moment," President Staba said, frowning.

"I take it you're referring to groups who *used* to pick cotton, Mr. Secretary," Secretary Alvarado said, frowning. She was frequently mistaken for black.

"And putting the spotlight on the issue," Steve said, clearly thinking. "We have two separate and serious problems, among so many, facing America at the moment.

"First the humanitarian issue. These are nonthreatening humans who through no fault of their own are now surviving on the barest margins. They have no decent access to the bare minimums of food, clothing and shelter. Well, skip shelter because they find that from all reports. Clean water? Hardly. Medical care? Definitely not. There are, always have been whatever people might think, constitutional issues about the Federal government becoming involved in charity. But these, yes, people *need* our help. Unquestionably.

"The second, apparently separate, problem is a lack of labor in industries where people really don't care for the work, often because it is boring, repetitive, mind-numbing or frequently physically hard. Not just farming. We have some groups who are doing assembly work that might possibly be taught. And, face it, we just have a massive and acute labor shortage, period.

"Sometimes when you have two problems..."

"They take care of themselves," President Staba said, looking at the beta thoughtfully. "Which brings up *enormous* moral issues..."

"Which was why I said it was going to get up people's noses," Steve said.

"They have no ability to express free will," Powers said uncomfortably. "Are you talking about putting them to work on farms?"

"I'll continue your statement with where I started, which is 'Isn't that a lot like slavery?'" Steve said. "And if you think there wouldn't be abuses, you don't know human beings. I didn't express it except in the implication, but your quick response of 'she was pregnant when we found her' was clearly even to *you* an answer to the implied 'have anything to do with her pregnancy?' On the other hand, being the pragmatically minded SOB I am, that, again, is an answer to a burning issue."

"Which one now?" Alvarado asked.

"The point of Wolf Squadron was not to save *the human race*," Steve said. "Save individuals? Certainly. But the human race was going to survive. We're like weeds; we're very hard to kill."

"Tell me about it," Staba said, chuckling.

"What was going to fail, might *still* fail, is *civilization*," Steve said. "At least civilization enshrining the rights of man and all that stuff. We had a massive baby boom. We still have a major generation gap and after the boom there is no indication of a similar following. Based on anecdotal evidence, pregnancy rates have fallen to something around pre-Fall levels."

"And that's a problem why?" Alvarado said. "Or do you think all us women should get knocked up and spend all our time barefoot and pregnant."

"I'll remind the Secretary about not getting hostile around the visitor," Staba said. "On the other hand..."

"Western birth rates have always been below those of Eastern cultures," Steve said. "History matters, Madame Secretary. And pre-Fall birth rates were below replenishment in the United States and Western Europe. We made up for it in immigration. There is now still immigration but it is fragmentary and comparatively small. And we have how many estimated survivors?

"If we continue to reproduce at a bare two-point-one births per female or below, we *cannot* create and sustain a population capable of returning to anything like pre-Fall conditions in the foreseeable future. Far more likely to devolve into tribalism.

"On your direct question I haven't encouraged my daughters to drop their careers in favor of making babies, Madame Secretary. But being honest, Faith could probably do more good for the long-term good of the world if she dropped being a Marine and started dropping babies. And, yes, even at her age."

"That is..." Alvarado said, her face working.

"I frequently engage in 'wrong-think,' Madame Secretary," Steve said, shrugging.

"Which is why we've made it as far as we have as quickly as we have," Staba pointed out. "You're saying that even if we free all the trapped survivors here and elsewhere . . . ? What? We'll eventually devolve societally?"

"Virtually guaranteed," Steve said, shrugging. "Civilization always wins over barbarism in the *long-term* but barbarism is much easier to sustain in these sorts of conditions. Especially with a society based entirely around salvage. Failed states at the very least. Mad Max or equivalent at the worst. That is our future absent sufficient population growth and education of that population. Not guaranteed, but virtually so. The baby boom of the post World War Two period over at least two to three generations would be a very good thing for us societally. If Secretary Alvarado cares to characterize that as being kept 'barefoot and pregnant' she may feel free to do so. As with the issue of using betas for labor, the moral and political issues are fraught. But, again, ignoring the moral and political issues, Miss Katherine also shines a light on one potential solution."

"That's simply . . ." Powers said, his face suffusing. "You're suggesting . . ."

"I'm not *suggesting* either using betas as labor or as baby factories," Steve said. "I am pragmatically and cold-mindedly pointing out their *utility* in both cases. Because I am pragmatic and can be very cold-minded when the survival of civilization is at stake, Mr. Powers. Please note, for the sake of your love of betas, that in both cases they suddenly turn from liabilities—mentally deficient humans who are a huge logistical drain—to assets, mentally deficient humans who can provide types of labor that mentally proficient humans, including those Madame Secretary and Madame President and for that matter Madame Vice President, choose to avoid at present. Stacey used to have a vegetable garden. She hasn't been doing a lot of gardening lately. Because all three women have things that are *more important* to do than have and rear babies. Because they have brains and can use them. Even though, long term, making good babies is equally or *more* important than, say, this meeting."

"Jesus, Steve," Staba said, laughing. "Do you go around *looking* for worm cans?"

"From the first boat I cleared my experience has been that if you do *anything* in this fallen world, you kick over a worm can," Steve said, shrugging. "The only way to avoid it is to do nothing. Any idea how many of my early boats legally fall into the category of 'piracy' not 'salvage'? Worm cans have been my daily lot, Madame President. If I stopped to think about whether it was a worm can or not, I'd have gotten nowhere.

"But, no, Madame Secretary, I don't think that all the women of this nation should spend the rest of their lives barefoot and pregnant," Steve said, looking at the Secretary. "Again, even if I *were* so misogynistic, we need the *intelligent* labor far too much. Making a baby requires little to none. Caring for them, at least at the feed, clean and clothe level, requires not much more. Again, it all comes down to labor. But I've said my piece. Other thoughts?"

"Skip the whole 'baby factories' question," Staba said. "Toss around the labor issue."

"There will be abuses," Daryl Hughes said. The Secretary of State had thus far had no input on the meeting. He was a long-term State bureaucrat who'd been found in one of the shelters in D.C. So far he seemed to be working out. Not that there were many other governments to interact with. But there were a few. "I suspect the Scandinavians will get their noses in a joint. British as well."

"The Norwegians and Swedes have essentially no beta population," Steve said. "They all died off with the alphas or before from the cold. Ditto, we have essentially none in our northern belt. Betas, since they can't compete physically, tend to find the ecological niches outside the best where the alphas reside. At least that's how it appears from what little study we've given it. So they were going to die off faster in the sub-arctic than alphas. As to the British . . . They face the same issues and will face the same moral dilemmas.

"As to abuses . . . we're still not at the point of making a decision. If you mean abuses in the proposed labor market . . . yes, there will be. Policing it, especially given how fractured we are, will be very difficult. And probably a job of the States as opposed to the Federal government."

"Human Rights is a *Federal* issue, Mr. Secretary," Alvarado said tartly.

"I said *policing* it, Madame Secretary," Steve said. "Not the basis under which it is policed. But that is what legislation is for. There is no way in hell that the reduced Federal government can police a labor force scattered over three million miles, much of it still hostile. As to increasing the size of the Federal government to do so, we have rather severe budget constraints compared to our previous condition: State's duty."

"And if the abuse is sexual in nature?" Powers asked, still clearly unhappy. "That *is* going to happen. It was hard enough to police pre-Fall in my industry."

"That actually goes to the question of their legal status," Steve said. "It's not rape if they're owned. Are they humans with all rights? Can they vote? I would hope that we can come to a reasonable answer on that one: No. But are they 'human' for purposes of rights, or chattel? Even chattel can have restricted rights. No beatings, can't be put to death, minimum standards of care, et cetera."

"If they are chattel, they are slaves," Alvarado said angrily.

"Calm, Madame Secretary," Steve said. "My position on this is at best as disruptor—he who asks the tough questions. The reason that slaves were imported to the New World was . . . ?"

"Labor," Secretary Ryan said. "As in lack thereof in the Americas. I just realized that . . . oh, that is *so* wrong."

"Missing something," Staba said.

"If we go that route," Ryan said. "Not suggesting it but if we did. Most of the betas who survived are in *southern* states. Like you said, they mostly die out up north."

"Ouch," Steve said. "Yeah, hadn't gotten that far. Gah. I've *never* been a supporter of those *particular* state's rights. Simply bringing up reinstituting slavery is making my skin crawl, trust me."

"Slavery is *wrong*," Alvarado replied. "Period. It's wrong."

"Agreed," Steve said. "One hundred percent and absolutely. So is sex with a person who cannot give knowledgeable and intelligent consent. The term there is rape.

"So is leaving fragile, helpless human beings to die lost and alone in a howling wilderness. So is famine from lack of agricultural workers. So is the rights you are fighting for dying out for lack of an educated supporting population, being replaced by a tide of barbarism, Madame Secretary. Which, since women will have *no* rights, will at least eventually solve the population problem.

"Last but not least, whether we like it or not slavery *will* occur. History matters. Slavery has *always* been, back to prehistory, a reaction to labor limitations. See also: human trafficking in the pre-Fall world.

"We need labor. Once it gets out that betas can be trained they *will* be rounded up and used for labor. Once that happens, abuses will occur and young ladies like Miss Katherine *are* going to end up barefoot and pregnant. Probably in brothels. And if one of them has AIDS or retains the H7 virus in its blood form despite the lack of symptoms? *Wow*, do we get problems.

"We can make laws against it. It will still occur, as will the abuses, and being *already* illegal that much harder to police.

"There are *no* good choices left in this world, Madame Secretary. Only less bad ones.

*"Which do you choose?"*

# Afterword

## JOHN RINGO

> There is something about the destruction of civilization that connects with the modern reader.
>
> —Gary Poole

Humanity has become a mass of ciphers gathered together in huge lumps called cities and countries. No individual human, from a person working in a mall to the President of the United States has any real control over his or her existence and even presidents have little long-term effect on history.

People go through life affecting little or nothing save, if they so choose, by having children who may or may not have more effect. By the same token they live lives of quiet ineffect in relative security and generally free from violence. This is the nature of a truly "good" civilization. That it is boring and humdrum. When it ceases to be so it is by definition "bad things happening."

But humans are not designed for "boring." We evolved in small tribes, constantly on the ragged edge of destruction and scrabbling for survival against both the environment and other humans. In World War Two, the height of human misery and violence since the Age of Agriculture, approximately five percent of the planet's population died due to violence. The current rate, despite how it might seem, is below one percent.

Early human hunter-gatherers on the other hand died from violence twenty percent of the time, *four* times the rate during the years 1937–1945, and for *hundreds of thousands* of years. The history of the Paleolithic is a history of constant warfare to make Mad Max pale in comparison.

It is also a history of small groups gathering together to defeat well-nigh impossible odds. It is that, in my opinion, that is the resonance to every "post-apocalyptic" story, a harkening to an age when things were simply do or die and everyone in the group knew each other and had the choice of cooperate to survive or die.

There is no "every man a cipher" aspect to post-apocalyptic fiction as there was none to those early tribes. Good guys or bad guys, every character knows every other character, their good side and bad, their strengths and weaknesses. Every individual of the tribe must strive with their last ounce of everything to ensure the tribe's survival. Every character is important to the survival, for or against, of every other.

Apocalyptic is pre-medieval.

Apocalyptic is . . . primal.

Thus as long as humans maintain boring, humdrum civilization, post-apocalyptic or apocalyptic fiction will remain popular. Because it is who we are in our hearts.

At our core, we are all savages.

# About the Authors

**John Ringo** brings fighting to life. He is the creator of the Posleen Wars series, which has become a *New York Times* best-selling series with over one million copies in print. The series contains *A Hymn Before Battle, Gust Front, When the Devil Dances, Hell's Faire,* and *Eye of the Storm*. In addition, Ringo has penned the Council War series. Adding another dimension to his skills, Ringo created nationally best-selling techno-thriller novels about Mike Harmon (*Ghost, Kildar, Choosers of the Slain, Unto the Breach, A Deeper Blue,* and, with Ryan Sear, *Tiger by the Tail*).

His techno-thriller *The Last Centurion* was also a national best seller. A more playful twist on the future is found in novels of the Looking Glass series: *Into the Looking Glass, Vorpal Blade, Manxome Foe,* and *Claws That Catch*, the last three in collaboration with Travis S. Taylor. His audience was further enhanced with four collaborations with fellow *New York Times* best-selling author David Weber: *March Upcountry, March to the Sea, March to the Stars* and *We Few.*

There are an additional seven collaborations from the Posleen series: *The Hero*, written with Michael Z. Williamson, *Watch on the Rhine, Yellow Eyes* and *The Tuloriad*, all written with Tom Kratman, and the *New York Times* best seller *Cally's War* and its sequels *Sister Time* and *Honor of the Clan*, all with Julie

Cochrane. His science-based zombie apocalypse Black Tide Rising series includes *Under a Graveyard Sky, To Sail a Darkling Sea, Islands of Rage and Hope* and *Strands of Sorrow.* A veteran of the 82nd Airborne, Ringo brings first-hand knowledge of military operations to his fiction.

**Eric Flint** was the creator of the *New York Times* best-selling Ring of Fire series, the best-selling alternate history series of all time. Beginning with *1632*, Flint—along with dozens of cowriters—chronicled what happened when the twentieth-century town of Grantville, West Virginia, was transported through time and space to seventeenth-century Europe. In addition, Flint was the author of the Crown of Slaves Saga, with *New York Times* best seller David Weber, and of the Belisarius series, with best-selling author David Drake. Eric Flint passed away in 2022.

**Jody Lynn Nye** is a writer of fantasy and science fiction books and short stories. Since 1987 she has published over 45 books and more than 140 short stories, including epic fantasies, contemporary humorous fantasy, humorous military science fiction, and edited three anthologies. She collaborated with Anne McCaffrey on a number of books, including the *New York Times* best seller, *Crisis on Doona*. She also wrote eight books with Robert Asprin, and continues both of Asprin's Myth-Adventures series and Dragons series. Her newest books are the third Lord Thomas Kinago adventure, *Rhythm of the Imperium* (Baen Books), a humorous military SF novel, and *Wishing on a Star* (Arc Manor Press), a contemporary fantasy. Jody runs the two-day intensive writers' workshop at DragonCon. She and her husband are the book reviewers for *Galaxy's Edge Magazine*.

**John Scalzi** is the author of *Old Man's War* and other novels.

**Dave Klecha** has been making up stories since he can remember, and once he learned to make them up about fictional people instead of what happened to the cookie jar, things really took off. His fiction, unrelated to cookies, has appeared in *Subterranean*

*Magazine*, *Clarkesworld*, and the Baen anthologies *Armored* and *Operation Arcana*. Dave is a veteran of Iraq and father of three children, living with PTSD from one or both of those experiences. He resides in the Detroit area with his lovely wife and three adorable but dastardly adversaries.

**Sarah A. Hoyt** writes everything except men's adventure and children's books. Her short stories have been published in *Analog*, *Asimov*, *Weird Tales*, numerous DAW anthologies and even more respectable venues such as this one. Her novel, *Darkship Thieves*, won the Prometheus award in 2011. She was born in Portugal and lives in Colorado with her husband, two sons and an ever-increasing number of cats. Everything else about her is unimportant.

**Kacey Ezell** is an active duty USAF helicopter pilot. When not beating the air into submission, she writes military SF, SF, fantasy, and horror fiction. She lives with her husband, two daughters, and an ever-growing number of cats.

**Michael Z. Williamson** is a best-selling and award-winning SF and fantasy author, best known for the Freehold universe. He has consulted on disaster preparedness for various theatrical productions, private clients and the DoD. The latter are woefully unaware of the impending zombie threat. A veteran of the U.S. Army and USAF, his hobbies include fine Scotch, antique swords, and firearms. Having successfully outgunned the nations of Iceland and Barbados, he is currently in an arms race with Bermuda. He lives in central Indiana, where the post-glacial terrain offers a good, clear field of fire. He can be found online at MichaelZWilliamson.com

**Mike Massa** has lived a diverse and adventurous life, including stints as Navy SEAL officer, an international investment banker and an Internet technologist. His greatest adventures, though, have been in marriage and parenthood. Mike is a university cyber security researcher, consulted by governments, Fortune 500 companies, and high net worth families on issues of privacy, resilience, and disaster recovery. He lived outside the U.S. for several years (plus military deployments!) and has traveled to over eighty countries. Mike is pleased to call Virginia home, where he passionately follows the ongoing commercial space race, looks forward to family holidays and enjoys reading the latest new books by his favorite SF&F authors.

**Tedd Roberts** is a research scientist who writes both science fact and science fiction. His research as a neuroscientist is on the cutting edge of human memory, prosthetics, and brain-to-computer interfaces. Tedd also advises SF writers, game developers, and TV/movie writers on incorporating accurate science in science fiction. His Hugo-award-nominated nonfiction appears multiple times per year on the Baen Books website, and has been archived in the Baen Free Library nonfiction collections since 2012. His short fiction often incorporates near-future themes from medical research or from his background as an Eagle Scout, Boy Scout leader, teacher, professor, and musician.

A native Texan by birth (if not geography), **Christopher L. Smith** moved home as soon as he could. Attending Texas A&M for two of the four years he lived in College Station, he learned quickly that there was more to college than drinking beer and going to football games. Deciding that a change of venue might be more beneficial, he moved to San Antonio, attending SAC and UTSA, graduating in late 2000 with a BA in Lit. While there, he also met a wonderful lady that somehow found him to be funny, charming, and worth marrying. (She has since changed her mind on the funny and charming, but figures he's still a keeper.) After the birth of his first child, and while waiting on the second, Chris decided that he should start his own business, and has been running it since 2001. In a fit of creative inspiration, Chris began writing flash fiction in 2012, and has moved on to short stories. His first, "Bad Blood and Old Silver," appears in the *Luna's Children: Stranger Worlds* anthology, from Dark Oak Press. His two cats allow him, his wife, their three kids, and two dogs to reside outside of San Antonio.

A 2015 John W. Campbell Award finalist for Best New Author, **Jason Cordova** was born in California and promptly moved out as soon as he legally could. He has sold fiction in horror, fantasy, steampunk, and science fiction. A former teacher and military veteran, he has circled the globe at least once (and never got arrested or hospitalized, something of a record for him). He currently resides in Virginia and is the "International Ambassador of the Kaiju Awareness Foundation."

**Eric S. Brown** is the author of numerous series including the *Bigfoot War* series, the *Crypto-Squad* series (with Jason Brannon), and the *Megalodon* series to name only a few. His short fiction has been published hundreds of times in markets like the *Onward, Drake!* anthology from Baen Books and the *Grantville Gazette*. He has also done the novelization of movies like *Boggy Creek: The Legend is True* and *The Bloody Rage of Bigfoot*. The first book of his *Bigfoot War* series was adapted into a feature film in 2014 and his book *The Witch of Devil's Woods* was adapted into a feature film in 2015.

**Gary Poole** has been in the entertainment and publishing industry for nearly thirty years. He's worked directly with John Ringo on over a dozen novels, and has adapted several of them into screenplays (all of which remain in development). When not working with Ringo, he is the managing editor of a successful alternative newsweekly in Tennessee and spent years on the radio as a talk show host and award-winning broadcast journalist.